CHOICES

A Story About Adultery,
Greed,
Police Corruption,
and Murder

C. Ed Traylor

A novel by
C. Ed Traylor

Choices
A Story About Adultery, Greed, Police Corruption, and Murder
C. Ed Traylor
Twin Oaks Publishing

Published by Twin Oaks Publishing
Copyright ©2020 C. Ed Traylor
All rights reserved.

No part of this publication may be reproduced, stored in a retrieval system, or transmitted in any form or by any means, electronic, mechanical, photocopying, recording, scanning, or otherwise, except as permitted under Section 107 or 108 of the 1976 United States Copyright Act, without the prior written permission of the Publisher. Requests to the Publisher for signed copies, purchases of bulk quantities, or permission to use excerpts, should be emailed to ed@royell.org.

Limit of Liability/Disclaimer of Warranty: While the publisher and author have used their best efforts in preparing this book, they make no representations or warranties with respect to the accuracy or completeness of the contents of this book and specifically disclaim any implied warranties of merchantability or fitness for a particular purpose. No warranty may be created or extended by sales representatives or written sales materials. The advice and strategies contained herein may not be suitable for your situation. You should consult with a professional where appropriate. Neither the publisher nor author shall be liable for any loss of profit or any other commercial damages, including but not limited to special, incidental, consequential, or other damages.

Names, characters, businesses, places, events and incidents are either the products of the author's imagination or used in a fictitious manner. Any resemblance to actual persons, living or dead, or actual events is purely coincidental.

Cover Design and Illustration: Mike Paulis

Editor: Laurel Shea

Project Management and Interior Design: Davis Creative, DavisCreative.com

Publisher's Cataloging-In-Publication Data
(Prepared by The Donohue Group, Inc.)

Names: Traylor, C. Ed, author.

Title: Choices : a story about adultery, greed, police corruption, and murder : a novel / by C. Ed Traylor.

Description: [Waggoner, Illinois] : Twin Oaks Publishing, [2020]

Identifiers: ISBN 9781736188019 (paperback) | ISBN 9781736188033 (ebook)

Subjects: LCSH: Police corruption--Illinois--Fiction. | Theft--Illinois--Fiction. | Murder--Illinois--Fiction. | Adultery--Illinois--Fiction. | Avarice--Fiction. | LCGFT: Thrillers (Fiction) | BISAC: FICTION / Thrillers / Psychological. | FICTION / Thrillers / Suspense. | FICTION / Thrillers / Crime.

Classification: LCC PS3620.R388 C46 2020 (print) | LCC PS3620.R388 (ebook) | DDC 813/.6--dc23

ACKNOWLEDGMENTS

The author wishes to extend his grateful appreciation for help in the creation of this work to Taylor Pensoneau, Jane Primrose, and his wife, Pat.

Also, the author wants to thank his friends who allowed their names and/or businesses to be used in the writing of this novel.

CHAPTER 1

That shift had begun as any other for Trooper James Kincaid as he rolled along on routine patrol on the starlit early morning of Friday, November 27, 2015. For the last fifteen years, he had zigzagged along these lonely highways on the 11-to-7 shift every night, five days a week. He glanced at the rearview mirror and saw his receding hairline, a shock of brown hair that encircled a spreading patch of baldness.

He looked considerably older than his forty-nine years, and his ruddy complexion reflected his pack-a-day habit and increasing reliance on alcohol. As a result, the 190 pounds he carried on his five-foot-nine frame were paunch rather than muscle. The look was further diminished by an unkempt persona, his tan shirt and khaki pants usually rumpled, his shoes rarely shined.

Though many officers despise the night shift, Kincaid actually welcomed it. He was a mediocre trooper, constantly receiving reprimands from supervisors for his low activity. While many of his counterparts held the citizenry to the letter of the law, Kincaid didn't particularly care if someone was going twelve miles over the limit, or why someone was parked on the shoulder. As a result, a twenty-two-mile stretch of Interstate 55 on Kincaid's patrol had earned the nickname "Indy after Dark," a nod to the famous auto race, since motorists could fly down the road at practically any speed they wanted without fear of reprisal from him.

It was a departure from the heady days of his time at the academy. He was a lad of twenty-two when he enrolled to become a state trooper, and he could still recite the date of his entry, February 1, 1989, a freezing cold day in the state capital of Springfield. After twenty-six weeks of intensive training, he graduated that August, and the following month married his high school sweetheart, Judy, a medical receptionist who was studying to land a better job in the field.

Judy retained her good looks well into the marriage, and Kincaid proudly carried photos that displayed her flowing dark locks, soft curves, and stately carriage. Within a year, they became the parents of a daughter, Sally, and Kincaid joked that he was grateful the lovely little girl looked like her mother rather than him. Two years later, Sally was joined by a sister, Mary Ann, who, fortunately for all involved, also resembled Judy.

Kincaid's first assignment with the Illinois State Police was in District 15, which was the Illinois Tollway system in the Chicago area. Traffic is seemingly endless on these highways that stretch five lanes wide or more, and rush hours packed in vehicles like sardines, barely able to move, crushed to a standstill at the tiniest fender benders. These rivers of traffic sometimes wind around Chicago's toughest neighborhoods, and gunfire pierced the darkness like the moonlight above.

Within months, the youthful enthusiasm that Kincaid brought to the job had dissipated and by age twenty-four, he was seriously doubting his career choice. Though he had bought a comfortable split-level ranch house in the suburbs, he disdained the impersonal surroundings, where each home on his cul-de-sac looked the same and shopping was one sterile strip mall after the next. Few of his neighbors, with their upper-middle-class yuppie careers and snooty attitudes, appealed to him, and he came to resent practically every motorist who charged past him in their imported sedans, on the way to their white-collar, rat-race professions.

By July 1991, he decided he had enough. He requested a transfer and was sent to District 18, which was headquartered near Litchfield, a town of 7,000 people twelve miles from Raymond, that was fast becoming a stopover on Interstate 55, with fast-food joints and chain motels springing up around the highway. Its world-famous predecessor, Route 66, also rolled through the area.

Another appeal was that the transfer brought Kincaid closer to home. He had grown up in nearby Girard, a town of 2,200 some twenty-five miles south of Springfield, and still had family in the area. He came from the stereotypical family of four, or so it seemed. His father, Alfred, worked at the nearby mine in Virden, four miles north, and had a reputation as one of the hardest-working guys underground. Standing five-foot-eleven with a barrel chest and 185 pounds of pure muscle, he clearly had the physique and strength for a demanding job like coal mining.

His work ethic and union membership earned a good salary, but much of it never made it home. For all of his good points, Al was an alcoholic, blowing good chunks of his earnings in the local bars, where he never failed to buy the house a round, particularly when he'd had a few too many himself. As a result, Kincaid's mother, Bettie, took on odd jobs, trying to make ends meet while raising two young children, often on her own.

Bettie was a petite lady, only five-foot-three and 118 pounds, with naturally curly frosted hair that Kincaid loved to wrap around his fingers as a baby. An immaculate housekeeper, she looked like June Cleaver in her cotton dresses and faux pearls, though she had a bawdy side that the kids rarely saw, cracking an occasional dirty joke late at night to Al or her friends as she knocked back a cold one or two herself, straight from the bottle. But she was the rock of the family, always there for the kids and propping up the household for whenever Al stumbled back in.

One night in the spring of Kincaid's fourteenth year, the phone rang, and he watched as his mother picked up, listened for a few seconds, then dropped the receiver, breaking into wrenched sobs. It was the bartender at Al's favorite nightspot with devastating news. Al had been laughing with his buddies when he suddenly clutched his left arm, falling backward off his barstool. He never regained consciousness, even as the paramedics scrambled to save him from a massive, fatal heart attack.

As Al lay in the local graveyard, the latest victim of the vice of alcohol, Bettie took a job outside, finding work as a bookkeeper in a local insurance office while holding on to all of her odd jobs on the side. With his mother gone for most of the day, Kincaid had more time to himself, which was not always a good thing. Like his father, he loved to partake, but he stayed dry when he was with Judy, who loved him despite his bad-boy behavior. As he escorted her on the rounds of the beauty pageant circuit each summer, Kincaid made sure he was well-dressed and attentive, knowing that Judy could have any one of the legion of guys that she always attracted.

If Kincaid strayed from time to time, his little sister, Maureen, made a habit of it. Six years younger, "Mo," as she was known, was always the rebel, bucking Bettie at every step and constantly exerting her independence against teachers, babysitters, and neighbors. Mo had worn the shortest skirts in class since she was thirteen and found her way into the beds of most boyfriends as well as her sophomore social studies teacher, Mr. Pencros, whose employment was terminated later that year.

At seventeen and against the pleas of her parents, she had run off with her latest boyfriend, who found work as a mechanic when he wasn't high on marijuana, which was often. That union lasted little more than a year but by then, Mo was already on the move, finally settling down with an ex-con who worked as a used car salesman. Despite his checkered background, she married him and raised two children in a dilapidated ranch home in Standard City, Illinois, just a few miles from Girard. Eventually, she threw him out when his philandering became too much to tolerate, and she stayed with the kids in Standard City while periodically finding male comfort when the kids weren't home.

Thanks to Mo's errant ways, Kincaid looked better in comparison, with his promising career, good salary, and loads of benefits. Bettie, embarrassed by Mo's open defiance, never failed to sing her son's praises, especially in her new residence, the Sunshine Acres nursing home in Virden, where she moved four years ago from now. There, she frequently regaled her bingo buddies and the staffers with stories about her "Jimmy," her pet name for Kincaid since he was three, and how he was "working hard to keep all of us safe."

*****

District 18 offered few of the nerve-wracking traffic jams, incessant crime, and hell-bent drivers of Chicagoland, and Kincaid found a way to relax and find some pleasure in the tedious daily patrols. The respite, however, was not to last. He soon tired of his choice of transfer, but Judy, longing for a quiet, white-picket sort of life, relished it. The couple had settled into a fifties-style bungalow on a dead-end street in Raymond, and Judy found ample time to devote to her growing daughters while decorating the home to her eclectic artistic tastes.

Her husband, meanwhile, could not get along with the supervisors on the day shift, who repeatedly needled him for his low activity and job performance that lagged behind his peers. Finally, in the summer of 2001, Kincaid saw a better choice. He successfully requested a transfer to the straight 11 p.m. to 7 a.m. shift, knowing he would basically be free of supervision. In his new time slot, he could report to work, do what he had to, and go home.

Many in law enforcement wear the badge proudly, while some wear it with arrogance. Kincaid was among the latter and was known for his high-handed treatment of the few arrests he made. Despite his history of mediocrity, Kincaid loved to regale his friends at the local taverns with stories of how he chased down speeders, busted the dealers, and hauled in the hitchhikers.

After his shift, Kincaid would arrive home around the same time that Judy was heading for her new job as a physician's assistant at the Litchfield Medical Plaza. That meant less time together, and as his marriage ended its second decade, it suited him just fine. Eventually, he began going to bed later in the day, so he could wake up just in time to head to work. The switch gave him less of the evening to spend with Judy, who filled the void with as much "domestic bliss" as possible, with or without her husband.

It also helped him avoid the never-ending cycle of his daughters' activities. Off hours became a cavalcade of soccer and basketball games, recitals, and tumbling exhibitions that quickly wore on his nerves. Judy, though, reveled in it, and cheered the loudest of any parent when her girls knocked in a goal or stuck a tumbling pass. Her husband, meanwhile, stared off into space, stifling sighs of boredom.

As Kincaid dropped his weary frame on the snow-white sectional on weekends to watch the Cardinals or pro wrestling, Judy raced from store to store, in search of the best bargains to stretch the budget. When she returned, she headed for the cordless phone, lining up her next volunteer opportunity at the Methodist Church or figuring out who was driving the carpool to the soccer tournament in whatever town was next on the schedule.

Every weekend, it seemed a new vase, curtain, end table, or towel set made its way into the house, the result of Judy's compulsive shopping, yet another something to show off to girlfriends who dropped by from time to time. In her few spare moments, she settled into her swivel chair across from the flat screen in the parlor, reached for her laptop, and logged on to Facebook to keep in touch with her 807 friends, mostly high school chums and buddies from work, church, and sporting events.

Like most small towns, everyone knew each other in Raymond, and small talk abounded. In the Kincaid house, the husband caught most of it. Neighbors openly wondered why Judy, a working mom, attended so many games and productions herself, while Kincaid never found the time. *Dumb asses*, he thought. *I'm a state trooper, and my job's tougher than yours. And don't tell me what the hell I should do with my time.*

Chatter on youth sports, especially those infernal soccer games, dominated his encounters with the townsfolk. Kincaid found himself thinking the same thought each time another father approached him at the gas station or across the fence. *If I hear one more word about soccer goals, who we're playing this weekend, and why so-and-so's on the field and my kid isn't, I'm going to punch someone's lights out.* After a while, Kincaid elected to sleep in on most weekends, telling his girls that "Daddy works hard and needs the rest."

In time, Kincaid began to feel that he was just working for his wife and kids, and not himself. Life in the squad car was drudgery, but at least he was on his own. At home, he petulantly saw Judy and the kids sucking the life out of him, and his clock-in at eleven each night could not come fast enough.

By now, he was forty-two, and as he traversed the highways of the Illinois flatlands each night, he looked back on his choices with plenty of doubt. *This job is killing me*, he thought. *I should have done something else. Something with better hours and more money. Something less demanding. It's different than when I was in training. Too many assholes on the streets, and I'm expected to get rid of them all*, he thought, even though he actually got rid of relatively few of them.

Life inside the walls of the bungalow was a daily chore, and outside those walls it was little better. Raymond, which had so appealed to Kincaid after his escape from Chicago, now seemed so stifling that it almost made him long for the ten-lane traffic headaches of the Windy City.

He frequently complained to his cohorts on the state police. "Sounds like a mid-life crisis, Jim. Poor old man who thinks life is passing him by," they scoffed as they hopped in their squad cars and contently headed home to their wives and kids' activities. Kincaid, though, refused to believe them, and usually drowned his sorrows with coffee at the Busy Bee Truck Stop, one of several nostalgic venues along Route 66 in Litchfield that attracted passersby from around the globe.

From the outside, the Busy Bee was a dingy, white-block fifty-square-feet edifice that looked less like a restaurant and more like an auto shop, a point accentuated by the cars and trucks that filled its gray gravel parking lot. The lot was rarely empty, and with good reason. Though the burgers and fries came with plenty of grease, the diner had the best steaks and seafood around, with a heaping all-day breakfast menu and coffee that, customers joked, "could wake the dead."

The coffee was not the only thing that made Kincaid a regular in his usual spot, a dark red vinyl booth with a worn black-and-white checkered tablecloth in a back corner. That seat was the station of waitress Sharon Kennedy, who provided plenty of eye candy to a tired soul.

*****

Male patrons at the Busy Bee liked to joke that Sharon had a smile that was even bigger than her breasts. Indeed, she was unusually voluptuous at five-foot-three, and envious female diners claimed Sharon was surgically enhanced. Their husbands and boyfriends, however, couldn't have cared less. They were drawn to Sharon's hair, blonde and thick, slightly curled and stretching down her shoulders, though her dark roots belied a sloppy dye job.

That was reflective of Sharon's tumultuous life. Though just twenty-seven, she was already a divorcee, the result of a broken marriage to a concrete hauler two years before. Their four-year union was marked by rumors of her infidelity, and judging by her decorum with the male customers, it was easy to fathom. She frequently batted her green eyes and fake eyelashes at many of the men in the Busy Bee, and the salmon-colored dress she wore as a uniform was always slightly unbuttoned, to display some cleavage.

Sharon always found a way to lean just far enough over her tables to lay her attributes out even further, and usually took home the biggest tips of any of the other girls working the room. That helped alleviate the minimum wage she earned on the 10 p.m. to 6 a.m. shift and, most days, she returned home to her 12x60, off-white mobile home off I-55 north of Litchfield just after sunrise.

Kincaid was only too happy to tip like the rest, but he preferred the conversation that Sharon unfailingly offered. She always found a way to tell him how good he looked, regardless of the truth in the statement, and repeatedly told him how much she liked his brown and tan uniform. In turn, he'd pepper her with clichés, like ordering "coffee and a big helping of you." Kincaid pulled in to the Busy Bee on breaks once or twice a week for Sharon's flattery. Then he became a nightly fixture.

One morning, Kincaid was drinking his usual black coffee with a pinch of sugar while Sharon was engaging in her usual flirtations, playing up to the trooper as she made one unnecessary stop after another at his table. As she slipped the check onto the table, she mentioned that she was off the next night, and invited him to drop by her trailer for a "good" cup of coffee.

Kincaid responded with a toothy smile that showed the yellowing of his pack-a-day habit and his fondness for the Busy Bee java. He replied that he was working the 11-to-7 shift the next night, as usual, and that he could not stop by until 1 or 2 in the morning. Sharon chuckled, said that would be no problem, and grabbed a white napkin. On it, she jotted down her cell phone number.

She handed him the napkin with a come-on look on her face. Kincaid stuffed the cloth inside his shirt pocket, careful not to leave it lying around when he returned home a few hours later, just in time to see Judy leave.

He had never been unfaithful to Judy before, but now the choice to cheat seemed an easy one. Though the hours dragged agonizingly on during most nights on patrol, this time they could not fly by fast enough. The excitement, however, was tempered by a fear of potential embarrassment.

While many of his cohorts on the state police kept in reasonable shape, Kincaid was careless with his body and blew off his doctor's repeated directives to drop fifteen pounds and knock off the nicotine. Coupled with his fondness for the bottle, Kincaid had developed high-blood pressure, and that caused a problem that most forty-something men dread.

His sex life with Judy was practically nonexistent, so it really wasn't that much of an issue–until now. Expecting that Sharon had other things on her mind than "good" coffee, he took proactive measures after showering for work. He opened the faux-wood medicine cabinet over the sink, reached for his months-old prescription of Viagra, and shook a couple of pills into his shirt pocket for use that night.

Around 2 a.m., Kincaid pulled out his personal cell phone and dialed Sharon's number. She answered with a sensuous "hello," and Kincaid informed her that he was on his way but could only stay for a few minutes. Sharon told him she would have the coffee on and to hurry up.

Sharon's trailer was parked at the end of a one-lane dirt road off I-55 and was not visible from the highway, as it was completely shrouded by a thick grove of pines. Kincaid turned into the driveway and slowly rolled down its length. Even though the trailer could not be seen, he was distrustful by nature, and parked in the rear of the mobile home, for added protection. He left the car running in case he received a call on the small portable radio that he carried with him.

He did not have to knock. Sharon heard him pull in, and she opened the door with a cup of coffee in her left hand. That was not what attracted Kincaid's attention. She was dressed in a sheer, see-through white nightgown that left little to the imagination. With Sharon having nothing on underneath, Kincaid had a full view of her curving figure as she stood with her back to the glowing overhead lights of her kitchen.

Kincaid took the cup from her hand and followed her inside, fixated on her fleshy buttocks that were barely covered in the lacy fabric of her gown. No words were spoken as he set both the cup and his radio on the kitchen counter and pulled Sharon into his arms with a long, passionate kiss. After several seconds, Sharon broke free, slid her hands up his chest, and began unbuttoning his uniform shirt. She then slipped her hands underneath his gun belt, loosening it until it slid to the floor.

He picked up his portable radio and trailed Sharon down the narrow hallway to her bedroom. She dramatically pulled her gown back across her shoulders until it bared her body, and she tossed the gown to the floor as she pulled back the cream-colored sheets on the double bed that consumed most of the space in the cramped bedroom. Kincaid, in turn, removed the rest of his clothing, first his tank-style T-shirt, then his black work shoes, socks, and his khaki pants. Sharon finished the job by sliding both hands to his backside and gently tugging his briefs until they started down his legs to the floor.

She ran her lips down his chest to places below, then dropped onto the bed and patted the mattress as an invitation to join her. He readily accepted, and a heated interlude followed, bodies sweaty, hips pulsating, legs tangled, moans louder and louder. As his arousal skyrocketed, Kincaid relaxed, knowing that his manly performance was no concern. Their climax was powerful, breathtaking, and prolonged, leaving both of them trembling in the afterglow.

Despite the intensity of the encounter, Kincaid was hardly the romantic, and he lay on his back for several minutes as Sharon lay beside him, not touching. Some murmurs of conversation finally opened before he suddenly rolled out of bed and reached around the floor for his scattered clothing, knowing that he was still on the clock and had to return to patrol.

Sharon remained in bed, completely naked, throwing back the sheets to entice Kincaid once again as he yanked on his briefs and pants. As he pulled on his socks and shoes, Kincaid turned to Sharon and asked when he could see her again. She coyly smiled, ran her right hand over her breasts and down to her thighs, and told him she was off again the next day–and he could stop by for more coffee.

That jolt of caffeine was nothing compared to the fire racing through Kincaid's body, and he was again driving down the lonely dirt road to the beat-up trailer and Sharon's kisses on his next shift. Those kisses were placed on many other parts of his body than his mouth in their second encounter, and Kincaid laid back, letting Sharon's lips go where they may.

It was the beginning of a searing affair that lasted for months, and Kincaid routinely visited the trailer for more servings of Sharon's "coffee" on her days off. He also began stopping in on his own off-days, making up excuses to Judy about playing golf when, in fact, his clubs would never leave the bed of his cherry-red Silverado that he bought new the previous year. He also readily offered to drive to Litchfield on weekends for shopping at Wal-Mart, adding that he might stop for coffee on the way but neglecting to mention the exact "cup of joe" he was referring to.

*****

With both of their daughters now in college, Judy was experiencing empty-nest syndrome, and began to concentrate on her new career as a physician's assistant. That lifted her to a position of some authority at the medical plaza, and the doctors began including her on trips to conferences and seminars that sometimes lasted a day or more. Once, Judy's boss, Dr. Karen Canadeo, took her along on a weekend seminar to Milwaukee. Her absences freed Kincaid to spend more time with Sharon, and not just down her lonely dirt road.

Knowing that small towns like Litchfield and Raymond offered zero privacy, Kincaid would sometimes take Sharon to dinner in St. Louis or Effingham, another interstate stopover an hour and a half away. They would also take in an occasional movie, usually choosing to sit in the back row, where Sharon's hand invariably made its way across his lap as her kisses blocked his view of the screen. Twice, they stayed over in Effingham at the Slumber Inn.

Less than a year later, Kincaid had decided he was in love, choosing to ignore the age-old question, "Is it love or lust?" He also elected to ignore how Sharon kept on flirting with practically all of her male customers, and that she hired one or two of the younger ones for menial tasks around the trailer that Kincaid had offered to do himself. Still, she pressured him to leave Judy and his daughters and move in with her.

The thought of living in Sharon's dilapidated mobile home offered little appeal, since it was a drop from Judy's beloved bungalow in Raymond. But the bungalow felt more like a dungeon, and its master bedroom offered none of the manly pleasures of Sharon's tiny sleeping area. He also thought of his paycheck, how Judy would get a chunk of it in a breakup, and he wondered if Sharon simply saw him as a passing fancy, another notch on the bedpost that surely had many others.

He pleaded with Sharon that he had to think of his daughters, his wife, his reputation with other troopers. But his words were as empty as his loyalty to home, and he couldn't stop thinking about how Sharon's lips reached parts of his body that Judy's hadn't in years.

Finally, he promised Sharon that he would seek a divorce and contacted Clarke McNally, a family lawyer in Litchfield who, despite being in his mid-thirties, was already an elder in the local Presbyterian Church. McNally seemed only too happy to help until Kincaid mentioned that he had a girlfriend, news that was met with a wince and a change in tone.

Judy's reaction was far more emotional. One of her coworkers, who openly longed for a physician's assistant job of her own, claimed that she was only concerned for Judy's feelings with the tip that she had seen Kincaid particularly enjoying his coffee with a blonde waitress named Sharon at the Busy Bee. She also casually mentioned where Sharon lived. As a result, when Kincaid told Judy he was heading for Wal-Mart one Sunday morning, she followed him in her black Chrysler Pacifica from a careful distance.

Her stomach churned as she watched his Silverado turn off the highway and down the dirt road to Sharon's trailer. Judy could barely keep her Pacifica between the lines on the way back to Raymond, and hardly maintained her composure as she threw back the doors of the medicine cabinet to find her husband's now half-empty bottle of Viagra.

Still, Judy thought of her daughters, now away at college, and urged her husband to seek marriage counseling together. But Kincaid had made too many promises to Sharon to turn back now. Though he felt his attorney was sympathetic to Judy, based on the seemingly unusual amounts of marital assets and alimony negotiated along with half of his pension, he wanted out.

He drove the twelve miles from Raymond to Litchfield on the day he was to sign off on the divorce, but for once, his mind wasn't in Sharon's bed. This time, he thought of Judy, how they met, their first years together, and the pride he once felt–and perhaps, still did–in her dog-eared pictures in his billfold. He also thought of the many things she did right, how well she kept herself, how she kept moving up at work, how thoughtful she was. Though he tried to push it out of his mind, he knew that he was still in love with her. He turned up the country station on the truck's satellite radio as the Jerry Lee Lewis classic "Middle Age Crazy" told a story that seemed all too familiar.

As he neared Litchfield on Interstate 55, he dreaded the terrible mistake he was about to make, but the choice had been decided. He signed the papers, returned to the bungalow to pack his belongings in the bed of his Silverado, left his house key on the breakfast bar, and headed for the dirt road to Sharon's trailer.

*****

Others on the state police shook their heads when Kincaid told them where he lived, wondering why a trooper, with the good salary that came with years of service, wasn't in better surroundings. Then, as Kincaid turned away, they muttered in hushed tones.

"What the hell was he thinking? He had a nice house in Raymond, and such a nice wife," said one trooper.

"You're telling me? His wife was a looker. Wish my wife were that hot," chuckled another. "Now he's living off a trailer hitch with a bleach-blonde bimbo?"

"Yeah, wonder how long that will last. I've been in the Busy Bee, and she'll hit on anything in pants. Can't imagine her staying faithful for long."

"No kidding. I used to go to the Busy Bee sometimes, but it's been a while. I never thought the coffee was worth a damn."

Unbeknownst to Kincaid, Sharon had tossed away her birth control pills and, within five weeks of moving in, announced she was pregnant. A month later, Kincaid and Sharon were married at the Montgomery County courthouse, surrounded only by two of his buddies from the state police and her sister. The honeymoon was a night at the Budget Haven Motel in Collinsville, an Illinois suburb of St. Louis. Nine months and three days after Kincaid moved in, a daughter, MacKenna, was born.

Shell-shocked by the quick turn of events, Kincaid recognized the magnitude of his choice. Now he rarely saw his daughters from Raymond, away at college and loyal to Judy, mortified by what they called "Daddy's trailer trash." With their one-word answers and rolls of the eyes, the girls made it clear that they were very loyal to their mother, and they never saw their father except on holidays. Not wanting more children, Kincaid ordered Sharon back on the pill but, she claimed, she forgot one night. The result was a son, Alex, born two years after MacKenna.

In Kincaid's previous life, Judy maintained a lovely home and raised the girls well in his absence. As a result, all the neighbors marveled at how well-behaved the children were. Sharon was far less of a disciplinarian, and two screaming youngsters in a cramped trailer left little room for relaxation.

In time, Sharon wanted to change her shift to days, so Kincaid could watch the kids as she worked. Begrudgingly, he accepted, filling his off-hours with filthy diapers, sloppy feedings, and television cartoons with the sound turned up. Then when Sharon returned home, the kids were nearly ready for bed, and she had a few hours to relax in relative peace as Kincaid collected himself for his own shift.

In the past, the bungalow in Raymond may as well have had iron bars. Now, it seemed calm, clean, and serene compared to the screaming, jam-packed trailer that Sharon seemed so reluctant to leave. Kincaid begged to move the family to a better place, closer to town, nearer to shopping and schools. But Sharon was as wed to the trailer as she was to Kincaid. While the trailer was a constant, their flirty exchanges evaporated, replaced by shouting matches that left him sulking and her in tears.

Her relentless sex drive was also on the way down–or so it seemed. In his top dresser drawer, Kincaid kept the white napkin on which Sharon had written her cell number, setting up their first encounter. Now, nearly five years into the marriage, Kincaid found another white napkin, carelessly hanging out of Sharon's leopard-print handbag, with a telephone number in her handwriting with the name "Tim."

Tim turned out to be a twenty-six-year-old flatbed driver on the St. Louis-to-Chicago run who also liked the coffee at the Busy Bee. Using the interrogation tactics he was trained in, Kincaid grilled Sharon, but like the guilty often do, she denied any wrongdoing. Kincaid, though, was not satisfied. Once again, he made an appointment with Clarke McNally, the same attorney who handled his first divorce. After listening to Kincaid's story for a couple of minutes, he smirked, tapped his fingers together, and said, "Didn't work out like you thought, huh?"

After ignoring three messages from Kincaid on his voice mail, McNally quickly negotiated $800 in child support payments for MacKenna and Alex and moved on to his next case. Though Kincaid secretly hoped Sharon would contest the divorce–implying that she still wanted him–she offered little resistance. Once again, Kincaid signed papers ending his marriage. This time, his choice came with few of the regrets that he harbored on that day five years before, when he signed off on Judy.

*****

Though he reveled in Sharon's lack of inhibitions in the cramped bedroom, he had come to loathe the trailer, for more reasons than its sardine-can lifestyle. Now, as Kincaid packed up what was left of his life and rolled back up the dirt road to the highway, he was heading for something similar.

He had rented another mobile home, this time a brown 12x50 model parked a quarter-mile off Illinois Route 138 on the edge of White City, a village of some 250 that was in the heart of the coal-mining region of the area. One of the few amenities of the trailer was an attached two-car metal garage, which afforded enough room for his truck and extra storage space. Just a few hundred yards away was Interstate 55, though Kincaid was such a sound sleeper that the incessant whirring of passing traffic went unnoticed.

His paycheck, the envy of the neighbors back in Raymond, did not go as far as it used to. Now there was alimony and child support to two former wives, and he settled into a pattern of living week-to-week.

After some anguish, he made the choice to sell his beloved Silverado and use some of the money for something cheaper. A dealer at the Litchfield Auto Mart liked the truck's high resale value and made a fair cash offer. He also had something on the lot Kincaid could use, a forest-green 1996 Chevrolet S-10 pickup for $3,495 with a pair of dents near the rust on the passenger-side running board and several more dings on the front bumper.

Though the transmission was balky and the air-conditioning worked when it wanted to, it was good enough to get around in, and Kincaid left the lot with some cash in his pocket and less of a truck than before.

He seemed to have fewer friends on the force now, and it was harder finding golf and fishing buddies than it used to be. His only friends now seemed to be the regulars that hung out at Martin's Tavern, a one-story grayish sheet metal building at the intersection of Old Route 66 and Illinois Route 138 at the edge of nearby Mount Olive, that was the watering hole of the area.

Now the father of four, he saw his children less and less. His first two daughters now found ways to blow off their rare visits, always claiming they were busy with college. He once learned of their dean's list grades by reading about them in the newspaper, weeks after the fact.

After several years as a single mom, Judy was dating one of her old friends from college, Roger Daniels, a dark-haired strapping sort who played first base in the minor leagues years before, and had come to the area to accept the vice presidency of a local bank. Any of Kincaid's contacts with Judy now required a wait time until she got around to returning his messages, if ever.

He still saw Sharon sometimes, on the occasions when he visited his children from that marriage. But those kids were too small to remember much of him, and he still cringed at their bratty behavior. He also remembered once when he went for a visit at Sharon's trailer and Tim answered the door, dripping bath towel wrapped around his 32-inch waist, telling Kincaid that "we, uh, she's in the shower."

As a result, Kincaid spent his nights alone in his squad car, most of his days alone in the trailer, and most weekends alone as well, save for his jaunts to Martin's. However, as the months passed, he picked up a new friend down at the tavern. Her name was Debbie Marks, one of the bartenders, who never failed to greet each patron with a smile and a sympathetic ear.

*****

For the last fourteen years, Debbie had manned the bar at Martin's, the latest stop in a career that had included jobs at virtually every tavern or restaurant in the area. Finally, she had settled on Martin's, where her wages were supplemented by tips in a clear glass mug at the end of the bar. At fifty, she knew this was probably her lot in life, but she rarely complained, ruefully laughing about the hard knocks that she knew plenty about.

She bragged that she was a natural blonde, but the grays were more abundant than before, and her shoulder-length, curling-iron hair now had an off-white look. Her eyes were as blue as ever, though her brownish-yellow skin was feeling the effects of someone who was never without a cigarette in her hand. Boisterous and sometimes profane, she was a spitfire at five-foot-seven and 125 pounds, full of energy and rarely requiring seven hours of sleep a night, a trait that made her long evenings behind the bar that much easier.

Mount Olive had been a mining town, and most of the current population of 1,700 either was related to one another or at least knew each other. They also knew all the secrets, though Debbie's life had been an open book. Debbie's first marriage to an over-the-road trucker had crashed amid her husband's violent ways, which left her with a skull fracture and him with a ten-month sentence in a medium-security prison.

Her second marriage, to a brawny construction worker with a shaved head, seemed to be going along much better until she discovered his numerous cell phone calls to a nineteen-year-old wild child, who had slept her way through high school and now wanted to try out an older guy.

Her unions had produced two children, beginning with a son, Dylan, who himself had done plenty of time in the county jail for a cocaine habit that he couldn't seem to break. Finally, he did, and now he worked part-time for a landscaper in a nearby town. Next came a daughter, Shannon, who earned her GED after a pregnancy cut her senior year short. She ultimately married the baby's father, choosing to overlook the one-nighter he had with an ex on the weekend that she delivered. The couple now lived in St. Louis, where she answered the phone for a wholesale florist as he continually looked for a job to his liking.

But as she reached middle age, things finally seemed to be stabilizing for Debbie. Though she admittedly drank too much, she found some other methods of relaxation in her three-room basement apartment in an aging, two-story white-brick house, just off Main Street near the railroad tracks that bisected Mount Olive. At home, her kids called every couple of days and dropped by from time to time, particularly on weekends. At work, her customers were friendly, and she was a favorite of her boss, Russell Martin, who had owned the place since buying it from his brother-in-law twenty-three years ago.

Customers laughed that Martin had entered the tavern business solely to sample the product, and judging by the two hundred pot-bellied pounds he carried on his slumping five-foot-eight frame, it looked like he had done plenty of that. A fifty-nine-year-old confirmed bachelor, he rarely combed his scraggly, dark gray hair or worried if his tag-sale shirts and pants were stained or wrinkled.

Known to light one convenience-store cigar off another, Martin was gruff and sometimes rude to patrons he didn't know, but to his regulars, he was everyone's best friend and a soft touch for anyone who stopped in needing a donation for new school equipment or a sick child. He lived in back of the tavern in a 20x40, prefabricated add-on that was accessible through the storeroom. His living quarters, dominated by tossed-about clothing, dirty dishes, and beer cans, were decorated with a handful of pictures of his three years of Army service and his long-ago high school football days as a linebacker who helped the team to back-to-back second-place finishes at state.

Customers whispered that Martin was sweet on Debbie, since he always flew off at the slightest little criticism of his favorite bartender. Martin had also taken a liking to James Kincaid and was only too happy to have a state cop around, in case some liquored-up jerk decided to start a bar fight or some drugged-out punk thought he could knock over the place for crack money. Kincaid, in turn, liked to shoot the breeze with Martin and the regulars, who loved to hear the behind-the-scenes stories of his daily routine and the small-time criminals he had cuffed.

Debbie seemed to enjoy the stories most of all and had no problem with Kincaid's endless craving for draft beer and shots of Jack Daniels. She was only too happy to set him up, and her smile was a little bigger whenever he came in for the night on his weekends off. Eventually, they exchanged cell numbers and talked on the phone several times before he finally asked her out.

Their first date was at another bar, in nearby Gillespie. Over the next two weeks, they took in bars in four other towns, laughingly calling it their "Beer-Drinkin' Tour" before they finally had a date somewhere else, at McDonald's in Litchfield.

Kincaid had not been with another woman since Sharon, and Debbie had not enjoyed male company in more years than she cared to admit. Their first sexual encounter was apprehensive, as both were fortified with plenty of drink, and neither really knew what to expect. But each noticed how strong the climax was, and that they couldn't wait to do it again, especially when sober.

Two months after their first date, Kincaid asked Debbie to move in with him. She had been on her own for nearly nine years and was hesitant to say goodbye to her freedom and once again deal with a man's demands, dirty laundry, and dirtier smells. Still, she liked Kincaid more than any man since her second husband, and the thought of growing old alone terrified her. So she piled all of her belongings in the bed of his tattered Chevy pickup and moved her life into the trailer in White City.

In his first marriage, Kincaid and Judy seldom conversed, and in his second, the conversations usually broke down into screaming matches. Debbie, though, brought her relaxed persona home with her, and their exchanges were equally relaxed, though often bawdy and R-rated.

It has been written that alcoholics look for like-minded people, and in the case of James Kincaid and Debbie Marks, that seemed to ring true. They each showed little restraint when it came to the bottle, and as a twosome, the need only grew. Rare was the day when Jack Daniels was not the choice, and Kincaid would often have liquor on his breath as he reported for duty each night at 11, ready to serve the public good.

CHAPTER 2

For James Kincaid, the night of November 26 began with an explosion. Debbie had the night off, and they spent the evening in bed, where she gave him a special surprise. By 10:15, they were still lying naked under the blankets, smoking cigarettes and shooting the breeze. Finally, he glanced at the clock, and his feet lurched for the floor as he threw back the covers.

"Damn. I've gotta get going," he muttered, shaking his head. "The time really got away from me."

Debbie stretched out, arched her back to lift her pelvis off the bed, dropped back into place, and threw her left hand over her forehead in mock anguish. "Men. They always leave in the afterglow," she teased.

"You bet we do," Kincaid shot back, grinning. "You know how it is. Slam, bam, thank you, ma'am. And some of us have to work, after all."

"Like I don't?" she replied, tongue in cheek. "Hell, it's just nice to be off my feet for a while. Standing on Martin's filthy concrete floors for eight hours a night can take it out of a girl."

"No shit," said Kincaid as he headed for the bathroom to shower. He clapped both hands on his bulging stomach. "Sitting on my ass for eight hours a night doesn't do much for me either." He glanced at Debbie's slender nude body as she pushed back the covers to rise. "You've aged a lot better than I have, babe."

"Thanks. I try." Debbie slid her hands up and down her sides before running them over her ample breasts. "These melons can still turn some heads."

Kincaid laughed as he stepped into the bathroom, but not before another gaze at Debbie. Finally, I got it right, he thought. She's what I need. Warm thoughts of Judy raced through his head, only to be suppressed by the pain of his poor choices that wrecked the marriage. He took a passing glance at himself in the mirror, seeing a need to shave, noticing the bags under his eyes, the growing double chin, the ever-retreating hairline. A fleeting memory of the happiness of the home in Raymond, once viewed by him as a prison, whizzed by in his mind, knowing that he still held some love for Judy and that he would never be important in his first daughters' lives.

He reached for the hot-water valve and turned as jets of water shot from the spigot. Memories of Sharon came next, the five-year mistake that he cared not to remember. How stupid could I have been, he thought. Gave it all up to live in a trailer. What the hell was I, seventeen years old or something? He remembered his fiftieth birthday that had come and gone a few weeks before. Couldn't those brats have at least drawn me a picture, or wrote "Happy Birthday, Daddy" in crayon? Pissed away that $800 a month in child support, didn't I? At least my oldest girls went to Wal-Mart for a forty-seven cent card, even if they didn't sign it "Love" and it came two days late.

The water tepid, he stepped into the shower, let the water wash over him, and reached for a bar of Irish Spring. He heard Debbie's voice over the pounding of the water, "Want some company?" "Better not. No time," he replied, knowing that if she came in, he'd never be able to leave. He also knew that, for him, experiencing manly pleasure once a night was no sure bet, and twice was practically impossible.

But he smiled as his fingers worked some Head and Shoulders through his thinning hair, knowing that she wanted him. He had relaxed more the last few months than he had in years, ever since she had moved in. He needed to tell her more often that he loved her, whether he did or not, and whether or not she really loved him. Still, Debbie smiled and listened, and she liked to do the same things that he did—watch baseball, hit the fishing hole, go out drinking. His mid-life crisis fading, he felt a comfort level with a woman that he appreciated at the dawn of his fifties.

His body free of soap and shampoo, he stepped from the shower, wiping dry with a worn white terry towel as he quickly shaved and slapped on a dollar-store knockoff of Brut. Briskly, he walked back to the bedroom, winking at Debbie as she sat on the side of the bed, still naked with her legs crossed, playing with her cell phone.

Stepping to the closet, he pulled out several hangers, tugged on his uniform, pushed a comb across his scalp, buttoned all the necessary places, and reached for his gun. He then sauntered to the refrigerator, pulled out a bottle of Budweiser, and gulped it down before heading out the door, ready for his final shift of the week.

Debbie, now dressed only in an oversized, smoke-gray T-shirt, gave him a quick peck on the cheek as he walked out the door to his squad car in the driveway. She then poured herself a glass of Southern Comfort and reached for the remote to see what was on Lifetime.

*****

That shift had begun as any other for Kincaid as he rolled along on routine patrol. It was Thanksgiving night, and the traffic was even lighter than normal. An hour into it, Thursday became Friday as the broken center lines passed as if one and the telephone poles shot by amid the endless prairies. For Kincaid, the minutes could not fly by fast enough.

When he was fresh out of the academy, Kincaid loved everything about being a cop, from the drives up and down the highways to the radio calls, not to mention the respect that the uniform and badge sparked with the public, particularly wide-eyed little boys. He even found a way to enjoy the paperwork that most of his cohorts dreaded. The job was invigorating, exhilarating, everything he thought it would be–for a while. Now, nights on the two-lane highways and Interstate 55 in central Illinois were as dull as the concrete mazes of Chicago were draining.

Kincaid glanced at his dashboard and saw the square digital lights that read 2:30 a.m., now Friday morning. That meant four and a half more hours on the road before he finally could head home. As he maneuvered his fully marked squad car along the occasional gentle curves on Illinois Route 48, he approached his former hometown of Raymond, a sleepy village of 700 an hour south of Springfield that sat perched among the flatlands of this largely agricultural area. Because his old home with Judy was built on a seldom-used side street, he rarely had to endure the discomfort of driving by where his ex-wife slept, sometimes with her new lover if the children were elsewhere.

The soil of central Illinois is among the richest in the world and serves as the breadbasket for the rest of the nation. Land prices had reached record heights in the last decade, and the farm economy is paramount in an area where manufacturing and white-collar jobs are scarce.

Just weeks before, the farmers reaped a sizable harvest, stripping the lands of their valued crops of corn and soybeans. Now, the view could be measured in miles across the prairies, as only empty fields lay in front of the occasional house, barn, or machine sheds that housed high-priced farm implements needed to tear open the land for planting in spring, then gently collect the rewards of nature in the fall.

Kincaid couldn't have cared less about the view, or lack thereof. His trained eyes scanned the countryside, glancing for anything out of the ordinary. But on this night, like most others, no wrongdoing was found. Crime rates in District 18 were much lower than in locales like Chicago, especially in Raymond and the surrounding towns, and with winter fast approaching, most people chose to stay indoors at this time of the morning.

As Kincaid rolled down Route 48 and through the tiny burg of Harvel, a few miles east of Raymond, a voice emerged from his radio. It was the blunt, raspy tones of radio dispatcher John Edwards, a veteran of thirty-one years with the Illinois State Police, a man affectionately referred to by troopers as "the voice of District 18." Troopers liked to joke that no one knew what Edwards looked like, only what he sounded like.

"District 18. This is 18-39, go ahead," was Kincaid's reply.

"District 18. Report of a serious 10-50 on west I-55 frontage road." Edward's words referred to a vehicle accident. "Approximately one-half mile south of Route 48. One vehicle off the road, struck a tree."

Kincaid answered. "10-4 District 18. 18-39 en route. Estimated time of arrival ten minutes." He hung up the receiver, activated his flashing red lights, and pushed hard on the gas. With the clear weather and the dry pavement, Kincaid could drive as fast as he wanted, and the white needle on his speedometer quickly jerked hard to the right, settling at just over 100 miles per hour.

He slowed slightly as Route 48 fed into Raymond, where the state route is also the main street. As he cleared the outskirts of the village on the west side, his right black shoe pressed the accelerator once more, and his speed topped out at three digits as he flew the three miles from Raymond to Interstate 55. He crossed the overpass of Exit 63 and reduced speed just enough to safely make a left turn onto the frontage road, heading south.

Since many frontage roads are in poor condition, Kincaid was forced to drop back off the gas, and he felt like his car might launch off the ground as he bounced off a couple of deep potholes. Within seconds, his halogen headlights picked up the accident scene, a car that had plowed into an enormous oak tree just off the right shoulder.

*****

His red lights now reflecting off the mangled wreckage of the accident, Kincaid pulled his squad car onto the gravel shoulder and radioed Edwards with a 10-23, that he had arrived on the scene. As he looked through his passenger-side window, Kincaid, like most officers, could easily detect the make and model of the car in distress. It was a gray, two-door, Chevrolet Camaro, and turning his head left, Kincaid observed that the vehicle had apparently been traveling south on Interstate 55 and had left the roadway.

He noticed the interstate fence, flat and tangled on the ground, indicating that the Camaro had blasted through the barrier after it left the pavement. Tire tracks pockmarked the partially frozen surface from the remnants of the fence to the virgin oak that had finally halted the vehicle's errant path.

The car had crumpled, and its front end was now virtually nonexistent. Knowing that survival of the driver or any passengers was unlikely, Kincaid radioed Edwards and requested an ambulance.

"District 18, 18-39 requesting ambulance. West frontage road of Interstate 55, one-half mile south of Exit 63. Serious injuries likely."

Edwards instantly responded. "10-4, 18-39." Kincaid again hung up his receiver and shined his spot light on the accident vehicle, illuminating the scene with a piercing, sweeping white light. He then reached for his flashlight and squeezed open his door handle, swung the door outward, and stepped out.

Expecting more mud, he stepped gingerly, only to find the ground hard enough that he could walk as normal. Kincaid deliberately approached the Camaro, which was partially enveloped by steam wafting from the impact in the crisp late fall air.

He fully expected to find a morbid outcome, an instinct which proved correct as he spied a lifeless body in the driver's seat, doubled over forward, dead from severe head trauma. Kincaid swept his flashlight across the front seat and saw damp, grayish clumps of material on the twisted steering wheel and the crushed windshield, as the corpse's brain had exploded when the body was hurled forward against the engine of the car, which had been violently thrust back into the passenger compartment and now pinned the torso of the corpse against the seat. Based on the driver's caramel-colored skin, now torn by numerous lesions, and coal-black shock of hair, he appeared to be foreign-born, likely a Hispanic.

Though he had seen this sort of thing many times before, Kincaid could never quite get used to the gruesome sight, and his stomach churned slightly as he glanced away. The horror was fleeting, though, as he was distracted by the many other tasks at hand. With the headlights of his squad car illuminating the scene, his eyes swept the area, looking for any passengers who may have been thrown from the vehicle. But the ground was empty, save for scattered pieces of the vehicle. He then walked around to the passenger side, shining his flashlight on the front seat and then the back seat in a check for more occupants. But no one was found, for the driver was the only soul lost on this night.

His blood pressure now heightened and his head beginning to throb, Kincaid took a couple of deep breaths to force his body back to normal. He stepped toward his squad car, opened the door to reach for his radio, and called Edwards.

"District 18, 18-39. Accident scene contains one person, who is deceased."

The familiar, businesslike tone of Edwards was heard in mere seconds. "18-39, do you need backup?"

"District 18, no backup is needed. Accident vehicle is well off the road, and no traffic hazard."

"10-4, 18-39. Lance Ambulance Service from Litchfield is en route. Estimated time of arrival twenty minutes."

Kincaid was in no hurry to return to such a horrific scene, though he knew there was plenty left to do, and quickly signed off. "10-4, District 18."

He settled into his driver's seat to wait for the ambulance to arrive. Officers are trained to be efficient in every situation like this and to use their time wisely. In Kincaid's case, he used the extra time to start the necessary accident report.

"18-39. District 18."

Edwards quickly replied. "Go ahead 18-39."

Kincaid responded, requesting a registration check, "District 18, requesting 10-28 on Illinois registration AR 212."

"Plates are clear on 2014 Chevrolet Camaro. Registered to Avis Rent-A-Car, O'Hare Airport, Chicago, Illinois."

Kincaid was writing this information down and took a few seconds to respond. "10-4, District 18." As he continued his paperwork, he was distracted by a red light that was barely visible down the frontage road in front of him. Within seconds, he realized the light was moving closer and the harrowing scream of a siren pierced the quiet darkness, indicating that the ambulance was responding to the scene.

*****

As the lights neared and the siren wailed louder, Kincaid radioed District 18 headquarters that the ambulance was 10-23, or had arrived. He stepped out of his squad car and waved his hand, directing the ambulance driver, Randy Anderson, where to park. The orange-and-white vehicle slowed, veered to the left, and found a small patch off the road with enough pea gravel for a makeshift parking space.

The front doors to the ambulance swung open nearly in unison, and from the driver's side stepped Anderson, dressed in his usual navy blue uniform with white lettering "EMT." Anderson had been on the job for twelve years and, like

Kincaid, was used to these type of scenes. A tall, wiry, athletically fit thirty-five-year-old with blond hair and a ruddy complexion, Anderson, like most skilled paramedics, knew there was no time to lose in situations like this, though on this night, there was no hurry, since Kincaid had radioed that the driver was deceased.

His partner, Billie North, emerged from the passenger side, dressed in the same navy-and-white garb as Anderson. North was nearly as tall as Anderson, approaching six feet, though she was actually more muscular and larger than her male counterpart. A thin, black tattoo poked out of her long-sleeved shirt, and an eyebrow piercing dominated her large, circular face more than her dyed-black, cropped hair. Though she had earned accolades in her seven years on the job, many wondered why she was never connected to any men in her personal life.

As North removed a gurney with a dark gray mattress and orange straps from the rear door of the ambulance, Anderson quickly moved toward Kincaid and offered no greetings. "What's the story here?"

Kincaid had little to add. "Kind of obvious. Looks like the guy went off the road, plowed through the fence, and ended up here. I looked, and he's dead from head trauma."

Anderson pulled out a black flashlight, approached the accident vehicle, and shined the light inside as North followed, two steps behind. "Yeah. No doubt about it. He's dead," muttered Anderson.

"I haven't called the coroner yet," said Kincaid. "I guess I should."

"He's gone anyway," replied Anderson, referring to the county coroner, Melvin McGinnis. "He took an extra few days off to run his vacation into Thanksgiving. Went to Louisiana, where it's a hell of a lot warmer than it is here."

"Yeah, no kidding," said Kincaid, watching his breath drift away in the chilly air. He remembered the many hats that Anderson wore. "You still the deputy coroner?"

"Yep. Good thing that McGinnis got re-elected a few days ago," chuckled Anderson. "Tough campaign for him. But he wanted it, and he got it, so I'm still around."

Kincaid was not in the mood for Anderson's small talk. "Then you can make the pronouncement?"

"Sure. He's dead at the scene," replied Anderson. In response, Kincaid contacted District 18. "Deputy coroner on scene."

Anderson then snapped back into a professional vein, reaching for a digital camera to take photographs of the body before it was pulled from the vehicle. That task required plenty of effort, as Kincaid, Anderson, and North joined forces to try and yank open the driver's door, which, like the rest of the vehicle, was crushed. North, a former basketball player, grabbed the remnants of the door handle and pulled, grunting as she found little success.

Finally, the door opened just enough for Kincaid to slide his hands in, and together they pulled and grunted until the door finally gave way. They grasped the corpse by the shoulders and slid it out of the vehicle.

North shifted her hands underneath the shoulders while Kincaid took the ankles, and together they placed the body face up on the gurney. "Wait," said Kincaid. "I need to check his pockets." North gently rolled the body side to side while Kincaid stuck his fingers into every pocket of the driver's dark leather jacket that now had perilous tears, his tan button-down dress shirt soaked with blood, and his designer Lee jeans.

In the rear pants pocket, Kincaid felt a wallet, a sorely needed piece that may help solve the puzzle of this accident. The billfold contained the driver's license of the deceased, showing his name as Pascal Ramirez. There were also seven $100 bills in the wallet, all nearly new and slick to the touch. Kincaid kept the driver's license and handed the money to Anderson for distribution to the next of kin by the coroner's office. Anderson, in turn, provided a receipt to Kincaid for the billfold and money.

The body on the gurney was then loaded into the back of the ambulance, and Anderson nonchalantly yelled, "See ya," as North offered a brief wave. Kincaid watched as the ambulance backed out onto the highway and then turned south to Litchfield to deliver the body to the local hospital and file a report.

*****

Kincaid walked back to his car and sat down, reaching once more for the radio. "District 18, 18-39."

Though it was now nearing 4 a.m., Edwards' familiar tone showed no sign of wear. "Go ahead, 18-39."

"District 18, ambulance 10-24 from scene en route to Litchfield Memorial Hospital. Requesting tow."

Moments later, Edwards replied that Joe's Towing was en route from Farmersville. For Kincaid, this meant more time, and he began filling out the tow-in report, another part of the standard procedure that involved Kincaid taking an inventory of the vehicle.

Once more, Kincaid returned to the crushed vehicle and shined his powerful flashlight onto the seats. The sweep of the light found little that raised alarm. The first object that Kincaid spied was a white iPhone, lying on the seat next to one of the ghoulish clumps of gray matter that had blown from the driver's brain.

The inventory of the passenger compartment revealed one pair of brown, discount-store sunglasses and a pair of ordinary brown jersey gloves on the passenger seat. A half-empty bottle of Evian was lying on the floor of the passenger seat, sprinkled with some of the driver's blood. Next to the bottle was a pack of cigarettes, wrapped in the familiar red-and-white coloring of the Marlboro brand. Inside the glove box was paperwork related to the leasing of the vehicle.

Kincaid dutifully recorded each object in his report, along with the vehicle description, license plate, and the vehicle identification number. He then reached to the ignition and saw the keys, still dangling in place, and attempted to pull them out. Like everything else in the mangled wreckage, it was no easy task, and some effort and twisting was required to wrest the keys from the ignition.

The key was slightly bent from the impact of the crash. Kincaid, though, paid little heed to the damage as he walked around to the rear of the Camaro to inspect the trunk. Kincaid slipped the key into the lock, turned it, and heard the click. The lid of the trunk rose slightly, and with some help from Kincaid, it jerked upward to reveal its contents.

The trunk was empty, save for two oversized, military-style black duffel bags,, stuffed so full that the fabric bulged on both sides. Kincaid shined his flashlight on one of the bags and reached for the zipper, but the bag was so full that the zipper balked at any movement. After some gentle yanks, the zipper finally surrendered, and Kincaid shined his light once more, directly on the bag.

His body trembled at the sight. The bag was overflowing with cash—tens, twenties, fifties, and hundreds—bound in rubber bands and jammed into the bag as tightly as space would allow. Kincaid's blood pressure, already too high, spiked, and his head felt woozy before he took a deep breath to snap his system back into place.

He blinked to refocus, then blinked once more before plunging his hand into the bag, expecting to find the rest of the bag stuffed with clothing, or even drugs, and that there was money only at the top. But as his hand wiggled through to the bottom, he could feel the crinkled paper and hear the sound of crackling bills. With his flashlight, he confirmed the sight, that the bag contained only money–and lots of it.

As his hand slid through to the bottom, some of the bills, forced out of the bag for lack of space, spilled over onto the gray carpet of the trunk floor. He haphazardly grabbed the wayward bills and pushed them back into the bag. His body shifted as he reached for the zipper of the second bag, toyed with the zipper, and opened it.

It, too, was packed with cold hard cash, just as much as the first bag. In his twenty-six years on the ISP, Kincaid had been involved in several drug busts where money had been recovered, but never had he seen anything like this. In an instant, he estimated that he was looking at over two million dollars, likely money from a drug dealer or cartel.

Dazed, he practically stumbled back to his squad car, fumbled to open the door, and sank slowly into the driver's seat. His mind was a hurricane, thoughts racing and fragmented, as he struggled to mentally process the events of the last couple of minutes. He stared straight through the windshield, nervously tapping his hand on the dash, almost in musical rhythm.

CHAPTER 3

Men like James Kincaid normally think only of themselves, and as the warmth of his squad car wore the chill from the crisp night of his body, this was no exception. It has been said that in certain events, one's life flashes before their eyes. In Kincaid's case, the last ten years of his existence were flowing like a raging torrent through his head.

Damn, Kincaid thought. I can't get over how much money is there. I mean, hundreds of thousands. Couldn't even reach the bottom of those bags, there was so much. Son of a bitch! All that money. All that money, just sitting there…

Then fantasy began to take the place of the reality he was facing. God, what I could do if I had that, he mused. Hundreds of thousands of dollars right there, right in my hand. Some sumbitch somewhere gets that money to live in a mansion and drive a Lexus, and gets all the sex he wants. I'm up and down these highways night after night, and here's some asshole, flipping the finger at the law and making more money in a day than I see in years… Hell, the pusher in Chicago has more money than I do… He's probably got one of those black

Cadillacs with those stupid-ass chrome hubs and a dozen whores, just ready to put out…

Kincaid leaned back on the head rest and stared wistfully out the side window. The stars were shining brightly and the moon had a dusty shroud of cloud cover, a peaceful contrast to the alternating reflection of the red emergency lights that continued to illuminate the mangled accident scene.

As his bitterness trickled into his mind, his brow furrowed, and he pressed his tongue forward in his mouth, as if disgusted. I kept this frickin' job so I'd have a good retirement, he remembered. That's not going to happen… Working for everyone else, night in and night out.

He shook his head, rolled his eyes, and chuckled to himself. Didn't think I'd be living in a trailer when I was forty-eight. Hell, at this rate, I'll be living in one when I'm sixty, seventy, eighty…

Work my ass off for the paycheck I get, and everyone else gets a piece of it. Gonna retire next year, and Judy's in line for half the pension. Doesn't even return my messages, but she's probably sitting around, counting up my money. Never hear from her unless the alimony's late…

He paused, feeling a pang of guilt for what he had just thought, knowing deep down that Judy was not to blame for any of his lousy choices. He winced as remembrances of Judy, first in her white wedding gown, then in the teddy of white lace of years before that never failed to turn him on, shot through his mind. He also felt a twinge in his underwear at the image of the voluptuous, shapely Judy in that teddy, eyes piercing, ready to please him.

He then couldn't begrudge her alimony and half of the pension, even as he thought of her lying naked in bed with her dark-haired banker, perhaps in that same white teddy. She had kept her figure and could have certainly worn it well, even after all this time. His moment of bliss in Judy's sensuality was accompanied by a couple of other tender thoughts, of how Judy maintained such a nice home and was such a good mother to his girls.

He also couldn't resent those kids, though he rarely had contact with either of them. Those girls, he thought proudly as a hint of a smile drew across his ruddy face. Beautiful just like their mother. God, can't believe Sally's as old as she is. The most popular girl in her senior year of high school, soccer star, third in class rank… Too busy for the old man… Now she's a junior in college, gonna be a fashion designer. As much money as I've helped her spend on clothes, she ought to be good at it...

Then he thought of his second girl. Mary Ann, Mary Ann, he laughed to himself. Can't get a quiet evening in the dorm without phone calls from the boys. Wonder how she gets the grades she does, with that social life. Freshman year, going to the same college as Sally. It's nice to have them together...

As always, though, Kincaid's thoughts snapped back to himself. Couldn't just go to a state school, like I'd asked them to. Been a hell of a lot easier to afford that, but no. They want to go the liberal arts route. Oldest one can't get fashion design at cheaper schools, and the youngest wants to major in poetry... Both pick the most expensive school in the state, and I'm on the hook for some of it... They're starting to call Judy's banker man "Dad," too...

While his life flashed before his eyes, he also remembered his other choices. Damn Sharon to hell. Sucked me in and gave me nothing in the end, except two monsters who act like I don't exist. At least Sally and Mary Ann pick up their phones and call every once in a while.

His contempt for Sharon kept racing through his brain, and he shifted uncomfortably in his seat. He reached his right hand and gently beat on the fabric to relieve frustration. Sharon's too busy with her boy-toy trucker and every other man she's screwing to give me the time of day, but she sure knows the time that my $800 a month's supposed to be there. I mean, God, $800 a month down the crapper for kids who don't even talk to me. Money down the drain...

Kincaid's flood of emotions gave way to a stream of practicality. As he ticked off his expenses in his mind, his impending retirement seemed worse and worse. All right... I make this much, and I'll get this much in pension... money goes to Sharon, money goes to Judy, tuition to my first kids...power bill, trailer rent, weekends at Martin's, phone bill, doctor, insurance, all that stuff.

His mind became a calculator, adding and subtracting, dividing among ex-wives with their hands out, kids who didn't care, daily expenses, future comfort. Though he had done it all before and knew exactly where his finances stood, the numbers kept crunching as he reached for the heat switch on the console, since the chill of the night had finally spread to the car.

Sure got a nice retirement coming, don't I? Drive up and down every night for how many years, put up with all the bullshit I do, and I can't even afford to go to a Cardinals game! I can barely pay my satellite bill so I can watch them on TV! I can barely pay my bar tab to Martin! For the first time, he thought of his current lady. Thank God Debbie works and pays her share. Otherwise, where the hell would I be?

All the while, Kincaid kept thinking about the bags of money in the crushed Camaro. God, there was so much of it. He wiped his hands on his pants. Can still feel the grit from the paper. Had to be over two million dollars there, easy. Going to some drug lord who wouldn't even feel it… Kincaid's thoughts, skipping around only moments before, came into laser focus, and his back stiffened as his head raised to attention. All that money… all that money… right there… all right there…

Eyes now wide, breathing now heavy, sitting straight up, Kincaid recognized the choice before him. I could just take that money, he realized. It's all right there for me. All my problems solved. No more worries. No more busting my butt. Good, easy retirement. Get out of that trailer, get me a nice place, live well. No more paycheck to paycheck…

The flip side of the choice, though, was obvious to a seasoned state trooper. God, though, what if I get caught? There'd be a criminal investigation, and they'd stick a microscope up my butt faster than… I've seen cops get nailed for a hell of a lot less. I remember this one guy I knew, all he did was take about a hundred bucks off a dead guy, thought no one would ever know. Someone figured it out, and they just hammered that poor S.O.B., found every last detail… Fired him for official misconduct and theft, and he did time over it… Made all the papers, and everyone knew it. His own family cut him loose! Last I heard, he's working at a 7-Eleven in Denver or somewhere…

The thought of being caught was enough to make droplets of sweat trickle down Kincaid's face. He reached over and switched off the heater in the car, though his mind kept turning over the situation. But who would ever know? I could just take one bag. Yeah, that's it. I could just take one bag. Then, there would still be some evidence left, and everyone would think that was all that was in the trunk…

No one could ever accuse James Kincaid of being a textbook trooper. Still, twenty-six years on the force did have some effect on his ethics. No way could I do this. No way… I've nailed a lot of people for a hell of a lot less. I've spent my life doing this. I mean, God. That day when my mother saw me graduate from the academy. She was so proud... worked her butt off to raise us kids, selling Amway, taking in ironing, whatever she could. Never told a lie in her life... Sitting in the nursing home now, still bragging that her son's a state cop... And all those guys I worked with, the guys I liked when I first started out, guys who showed me how it's done... not one of 'em did anything wrong... never...

The back-and-forth then continued. But who the hell would ever know? That guy who they pulled out of that Camaro, brains blown out, deader than anything. He sure as hell isn't going to say anything... And this is all drug money. What else could it be? What drug lord's going to blow the whistle on this? If they do, we'd have their ass and they know it... No way are they coming forward. Kincaid opened his palm, as to blow off a thought. His slid his mouth to the right and curled his lips. They'd have no choice but to let it slide, and the people at headquarters won't have a way to find out about it. They can't investigate what they don't know...

Just then, Kincaid saw faint amber lights rolling toward him down the southbound lane of the frontage road. He realized that the tow truck was on its way, just a mile off, the amber lights brightening as the truck came closer. He shifted in his seat, and the flab of his rear end rolled over on his billfold. In a flash, he remembered that he had a grand sum of eleven dollars in his wallet as he was waiting for another payday, and was living off credit cards once again.

In that instant, the choice was made. As the amber lights drew nearer, Kincaid threw open his door, rose from the squad car, and walked briskly to the still-steaming accident scene. He fumbled for the trunk key in his shirt pocket, pulled it out, and massaged it into the hole. The trunk slid open, and he grasped one of the bags of money, closing the trunk almost before his hand was fully clear.

Clutching the bag in both hands, he peered over his right shoulder to locate the tow truck, which was still a half mile away. At that distance, Kincaid knew there was little chance that he could be seen by the driver. He returned to the squad car at a run-walk, opened the trunk, and dropped the bag in.

Heart racing and his breathing rapid, he slammed the lid and strolled to the side of the road, deeply inhaling and exhaling several times to calm himself as he prepared to greet the tow truck driver as if nothing was amiss.

CHAPTER 4

Though his heart rate had hardly slowed, Kincaid nonchalantly threw a hand up as the brakes of the tow truck ground the vehicle to a stop. The metal of the maroon-and-white body creaked ominously as the truck swung a sharp right turn into the gravel at the side of the frontage road.

The white block printing on the side of the door told the world that the truck belonged to Joe's 24-Hour Towing. Seconds later, the driver's side door groaned as it swung wide, allowing the exit of Joe Murphy, the man who owned the business.

Such calls in the middle of the night were old hat for Murphy, who had endured plenty of them in his fifty-plus years on the job. He had begun working for his grandfather when he was only fourteen and tolerated high school long enough simply to earn his diploma and get in the shop full time.

He was a lifelong resident of Farmersville, a village of 500 just ten miles north of the accident scene that was, like the others in the area, a sleepy bedroom community for full-time jobholders in Springfield and farmers who chose not to live in the country. There, he operated the towing service and the

Mobil gas station that his grandpa had opened along Route 66 near the start of World War II.

The old man had worked there until his two-pack-a-day cigarette habit led to terminal lung cancer thirty-seven years ago, and he tapped Joe, rather than his own kids, to take over when he was gone. By then, the Mobil station was gone, the victim of progress when Interstate 55 was constructed to replace Old 66. But the towing business remained, and since it was the only one in Farmersville, Joe had the monopoly.

Grandpa Murphy was respected by everyone in town for his hard work, honesty, and willingness to do the right thing. The American flag flew proudly in front of the business, despite occasional complaints from the few area liberals and the infrequent hippie whose car needed to be dragged in.

Joe inherited those traits well. People laughed that Joe was never seen in anything but his blue coveralls with the white stitched nametag on the left breast, but Joe really didn't know anything else. He owned one suit that he hadn't worn in fifteen years, and by now, the 200 pounds spread across his six-foot frame were more upper-body muscle than soft belly. That pleased his wife of forty-eight years, a retired school secretary who never seemed to look at a man other than her hard-working husband, despite his square jaw and the shock of tousled gray hair on top of his unusually large head.

Mechanics rely on heavy-duty, gritty industrial soap to wash the grease off their hands, and Joe used plenty of that over the years. As a result, his burly hands were roughed up not only by an array of callouses, but by the harsh liquid required to power them clean.

As Joe approached Kincaid, he ran his left hand, covered in a dingy brown work glove, across the top of his brow, leaving a slight smudge. "What's the story here?" he inquired.

"Pretty cut-and-dried," replied Kincaid, whose nerves were finally starting to calm. Still, he fidgeted slightly, though Murphy paid little attention in the darkness. "Guy was heading southbound, left the roadway, plowed through the fence, hit the tree. Dead when I got here."

"Huh." Murphy had handled several of these fatals in his many years in the truck, so it was nothing unusual for him. "Where's he from?"

"Not sure yet," said Kincaid, who loved being in authority and liked to act as if he had all the answers. "He's a Mexican guy, that much is obvious. Car was registered to Avis at O'Hare in Chicago." He paused. "Let me do something real quick here." He walked back to the squad car, grabbed the tow-in report, and finished a couple of entries.

"All right," said Murphy. "I'll get it out of here." He turned back to the truck, since he needed to turn it around, back it in, and pull it close to the wrecked car.

"Wait a minute," said Kincaid, excitedly. "There's something you need to see first."

"What?"

"In the trunk. You aren't going to believe this, in a million years."

Murphy was always all business in his job and had little patience for this charade. "Yeah, what is it?" he barked.

"There's a bag in the trunk that's full of cash. Probably has over a million dollars in it." Kincaid spit the words out with such a straight face that he surprised even himself.

"No shit!" Murphy's gray eyes lit up, and his mouth fell open. "No kidding! What was it, drug money or something?"

"Probably. I don't know where else it would have come from. But there it is, a black military bag, with so much money you can't stick your hand in without losing some of it." Again, the words flowed from Kincaid's mouth with relative ease, though he shifted from one foot to the other more than normal.

Murphy was still in state of amazement and paid scant attention. "I gotta see this."

"Sure." Kincaid and Murphy started walking toward the trunk, almost in unison. Once again, Kincaid popped the trunk, and revealed the now single bag, still in place. He gently yanked the zipper, and bundles of bills again overflowed onto the floor of the trunk.

"Son of a bitch! Never seen that much money!" Murphy said before his own fantasies took over. "Hell and damnation! What I could do with all of that!"

"Yeah, but you know we can't. Gotta take it in." Kincaid managed a holier-than-thou persona to mask the obvious hypocrisy. Still, he wanted to play around a little and turned to face Murphy, though his eyes were pointed slightly to the side. "How much do you think is there?"

"Over a million, easy. Probably several million." Murphy snickered nervously. "Never seen that much money, so I'm probably a poor bastard to ask."

"You and me both. This is such a big deal that I'm going to call a supervisor out here. I really don't know how to handle this." Kincaid was only partially right on that score. "I'm not really comfortable with staying with all that cash. It's bigger than anything I've ever dealt with…"

His voice trailed, and Murphy saw something extra coming. "Would you stay here with me, until my supervisor gets here?"

The Illinois State Police were one of Murphy's best customers, and he felt obligated to respond affirmatively. Besides, the thought of so much money piqued his interest, and he wanted to see what would happen next. "Sure. I got nothing better to do. Besides, you guys woke me up, and there's no way I'm getting back to sleep now."

"Thanks. I'll call here in a little bit. Shouldn't be too long." With that, Joe climbed back into the truck, turned it around, and slipped it into reverse, to get close enough to the mangled car to hook up. Kincaid, meanwhile, removed the lone bag of money from the trunk before Murphy approached the vehicle. He then set the bag on the hood of his squad car, stepped back to his open window, and radioed for his supervisor to come to the scene.

The supervisor was Master Sergeant Jim Peal, who had been Kincaid's superior for the last four years. Though he frequently rode Kincaid for his low activity, Kincaid could not argue with the fairness that Peal brought to the job. A twenty-year veteran of the ISP, Peal joined the force after four years of service in the Marines and brought that same military-style mentality to his job every day.

Though he was forty-five, he looked a full fifteen years younger, largely because his five-foot-nine, 180-pound physique was packed with muscle from his countless hours on his home gym, often with his wife, an ex-cross country runner, and their two sons, both high school football stars. He had used his stout build to bring down many an angry criminal in his early days on the job, and now used his equally potent brains in a supervisory role. He was known to run his fingers through his thick, sandy-brown hair, clench his lips, and rip off any order that was needed. And, usually, they were the right ones.

Peal was at District 18 headquarters, which was eleven miles away from the accident scene. Never one to waste a moment, he left immediately and was standing next to Kincaid in twelve minutes. Kincaid deliberately recited the particulars of the accident scene to Peal, whose glare never wavered as he listened to every word. Unlike Kincaid and Murphy, his facial expression changed little as he heard of the bag stuffed with money in the trunk.

"That's a lot of money. We could be looking at something big here." Peal was known for sizing up the situation in the shortest way possible. He also was well aware of Kincaid's performance record, and was little inclined to have Kincaid handle much of the situation himself. "We need to deal with this one a little differently."

"What do you have in mind?" Kincaid had played it cool until now, but his voice took on a slightly higher pitch as he awaited Peal's response, knowing it could affect his own bag of money.

"I'll take the bag of money back to headquarters myself." Peal waved his left hand in the general direction of the duffel bag still on Kincaid's hood. "Then we need to tag it as evidence and put it in the vault. We may need it for an investigation, since there's so much of it. I mean, what are we looking at here? How big of a drug operation is this, and is there more where this came from? Anyone around here involved? We don't know any of this right now."

From James Kincaid's perspective, the less that Peal was involved, the better. But with his experience, he knew all of this would happen and saw no reason to buck his superior. "You're right. I've still got some things to tie up here, and Joe's got to sign the tow-in report. Can you wait a little bit?"

"Yeah," said Peal, answering the obvious. "We aren't going to rush something like this." As he spoke, Murphy was finishing his hookup. He then jumped out of the truck, knowing that he had to sign the report. He quickly brushed the pen across the clipboard, obtained his copy, said his goodbyes, and returned to the truck to drive away.

The money and the driver's cell phone were among the information listed on the tow-in report, along with the fact that both had been removed by Kincaid. After Murphy departed, mangled vehicle dragging perilously in tow,

Peal strode to Kincaid's hood, picked up the lone bag of money, and placed it in his squad car. He then dropped into the driver's seat for the drive back to headquarters, with Kincaid following.

*****

Most people on the street have no idea of the amount of regulations and paperwork that is required of law enforcement officers, and this situation was certainly no exception. Even though both men had been up all night, there was still plenty of work to do and a long day lay ahead.

After both arrived at headquarters, Peal filled out an evidence report, describing the bag of money, its contents, where and how it was found, and related details. Kincaid then signed the report before the money was tagged into the vault.

Kincaid, meanwhile, completed his accident report and then filled out a field report, which also described how the money was found in substantial detail. All the while, he kept thinking of his own bag of money, still in the trunk of his squad car. As his career progressed, Kincaid cared less for the paperwork. On this day, he hated it even more, because it prevented him from going home and having the excitement of seeing his money in private.

Next came a task that was both obvious and tedious. No one knew exactly how much money was in the bag in the vault, and Peal and Kincaid had to find out. They both headed for the vault to count it.

Only a banker or a government rep would have any idea how long it takes to count over a million dollars by hand, and Peal and Kincaid were about to find out. There is no room for imprecision in law enforcement today, so both men had to take each bundle of bills, remove the rubber band, and count each bill. Since the bag was so large and was stuffed so full, it was a heady endeavor.

By the time the men were through, their shifts had officially ended, and it was past breakfast time for most people. But they got the job done, and in the end, they discovered that the bag contained a total of $1,263,000.

Peal, as usual, was so consumed with the task at hand that he barely noticed the wry smile that kept popping up on Kincaid's face. Holy shit, Kincaid thought in the seconds in between setting one bundle of bills down and grabbing another. Wonder how much is in my bag. Probably as much, if not more. God, will the clock speed up and get me out of here… Got some counting of my own to do! Hell yeah!

*****

As Kincaid reveled in his silent euphoria, the small hand on the round black clock in the lobby pointed at eight when Captain Kent Small and Lieutenant Jim Mason arrived at District 18 headquarters. Small had walked through these doors five days a week for the last twelve years, never failing to glance at that clock to ensure he was on time, and he always was.

Small had earned a track scholarship to Illinois State University and still looked the part. Standing six-foot-two and carrying 220 pounds with an erect carriage topped by neatly combed chocolate-brown hair, he chose to spend two years in the Marines after college before entering the academy. After fifteen years on patrol, he earned a promotion to supervisor, though he subjected himself to more criticism than he did in the car.

But he was a mediocre supervisor and liked to leave a lot of his duties to other people. Some grumbled that Small couldn't make any decision without checking with his own supervisors in Springfield to gain their opinion. But the others liked the fact that Small would ask subordinates for any input that may be deemed valuable.

One of those subordinates was Mason, who was never without a cup of coffee in his hand. Friends laughed if that was the problem, since Mason routinely a had wide-eyed look that was accentuated by his drawn, angular face. Prone to fidgeting and known to talk too loudly, he was even thinner than Small, weighing barely 170 pounds while standing six-foot-one. Though he was barely forty-eight, he wore the hairline of a man twenty years older, so rather than watch it gradually recede, he simply shaved it off.

Small ran into Peal in the hallway. "Got something for you," said Peal succinctly. He led Small and Mason into a conference room where Kincaid was relaxing, finally getting a few minutes of peace after a jam-packed night.

Kincaid and Peal then briefed the supervisors on the events of the last few hours. Predictably, Small said that he needed to talk to his own supervisors in

Springfield. He practically sprang from his chair and strode down the hallway to another office.

The other three didn't say much while Small was gone. While the minds of the other two were turning with what needed to be done on this case next, Kincaid checked the clock once more, still hoping to leave as soon as possible. While he knew there was little chance that his trunk would be checked that morning, the thought of a million hot dollars in his car made him squirm in his seat.

"Stiff as a board," laughed Kincaid, trying to brush it off. "Sit on your ass in a car for hours in weather like this, it's hard on a guy." Mason and Peal simply chuckled, though neither had ever complained like Kincaid always seemed to.

Twenty-one minutes elapsed on the clock before Small returned. "Okay," he began. "Here's what he said. We need to take pictures of the money, because we'll need a press release on this. It's too big to blow off, and the papers and radio are gonna find out about this sooner or later." He turned to Kincaid. "You'll be in the pictures, since you were on the scene."

"Hell fire," said Kincaid, brushing his fingers through what hair he had left. "I'll look like crap in that picture."

"Yeah, whatever." Small didn't care for small talk at the particular moment. "Let's just get it done." A photographer was summoned from another room, and he walked with the four officers to the vault.

The five men determined the best angle and setting to snap the photos, and Kincaid was positioned in a chair, staring up at the camera while the bag and some of the piles of money were set on a conference table in front of him.

As the photo shoot concluded, Small reached for the nearest phone on the wall. He contacted the Farmers Security Bank in nearby Litchfield and inquired if the state police could use the bank's money counter to confirm the amount of money that Kincaid and Peal had determined.

The bank president advised Small that the bank had the capacity to handle the money count, and could use the money counter. Once again, Kincaid and Peal took possession of the bag and they loaded it into Peal's squad car and drove the bag of money to the bank in Litchfield.

By now, it was approaching eleven in the morning, and the clear of the previous night had given way to a partly cloudy cover and increasing wind.

Kincaid, though, jocularly blew off the deteriorating weather and did most of the talking on the drive to the bank, located in a new stand-alone brick building just off downtown. Peal said little and simply stared ahead at the spike in lunchtime traffic that was swerving into the row of fast-food joints along the main drag.

At the bank, the counter came up with exactly the same amount as the hand count from earlier that day. The president was a man in his mid-sixties, and he peered over his spectacles with a trace of a smile as Kincaid and Peal banded the bills together and then stuffed them back into the bag.

"Whole lot of money there," the president chirped. "Like to see those kind of deposits." He then caught himself. "The real kind—not as evidence."

Peal shot the president a blank look, while Kincaid snickered. The task at the bank done, the two officers then returned to headquarters with the money. Small greeted them as they walked past the entryway, asking if there had been any issues at the bank. Peal assured him that everything had went according to plan, and the money was signed back into the vault.

Kincaid asked if there was anything that he needed to do. "Not today at least," said Small. "You working tomorrow?"

"Nope. Saturday. Not scheduled."

"You are now," smirked Small. "We'll need you in here. You've got more paperwork to do, and the newspaper's going to be here. Once we send out the press release, they'll be all over it. Not too often that a million dollars is picked up in Montgomery County."

Kincaid nodded slightly, showing no emotion. "What time you want me here?"

"You're on day shift. Seven o'clock." Small brusquely dismissed his subordinate. "See ya."

That told Kincaid that he was finally done for the day, and after a basic "bye," he turned and headed out the door. Though he could have sprinted toward his squad car like an Olympic runner, he held himself back and stepped toward the car as if any other shift had ended.

Once in the vehicle, he turned on the ignition, pulled onto the highway as usual, and drove far enough away from headquarters not to be seen before he stepped on the gas. His future was resting in the bag in his trunk, and he had plenty of counting to do.

CHAPTER 5

Kincaid's trailer in White City was only nine miles down Interstate 55 from District 18 headquarters, at most a ten-minute drive on a normal day, but this was hardly a normal day. Kincaid passed car after car in the fast lane and practically shot up Exit 44 before turning to the right and entering White City.

He glanced at his dashboard and saw that it was now 2:09 in the afternoon. After maneuvering the squad car through the narrow streets of White City, he approached his trailer, which sat some fifty yards off the road and was surrounded by a stand of pines. Passersby could barely see the squad car that signified a state trooper lived there, and that was just the way Kincaid liked it. Rarely did anyone but Kincaid or Debbie come down that driveway, and that proved of great benefit on this early Friday afternoon.

Though Debbie had been off the night before and was supposed to be off today as well, she was scheduled to fill in this afternoon, since the girl that Martin originally lined up had a doctor's appointment. Knowing that he couldn't ask Debbie to work a double shift, Martin had lined up his nephew to step in for Debbie's normal evening slot, meaning that she would not return home until 7 p.m. or so. As a result, Kincaid knew he would be all alone for the afternoon.

For the last several years, James Kincaid had simply walked through life, bored with his job, living a spartan existence in the trailer, simply putting in his time with family or friends. Debbie had brought a spark of excitement at times, particularly when she was nude in bed, or soaping him up when they showered together.

But at this moment, he experienced an adrenaline rush that he had never experienced in his forty-eight years. He was like a child on Christmas morning, bursting to race down the stairs and open presents. In this case, his gift was a big bag stuffed with cash.

As he gently turned the car into the drive, he was at the same time terrified and ecstatic. He knew he had committed a serious crime and shuddered at the punishment that would be dished out if he was caught. That terror, though, was trumped by sheer joy. Holy shit! he thought. I'm on easy street. Played the lottery for all these years, never won a damn thing. Always wondered what it would be like to win… Damn, damn, damn! Never thought it would feel this good…

As his mind skipped around, he reeled off the obligations that were no longer a worry to him. No more worrying about money for Judy… can pay off Sharon-the-bitch whenever I need to… kids in college, done… Get out of this frickin' trailer… Gonna buy me a cabin on a lake… brand-new Silverado, better than my red one before… season tickets for the Cardinals… all the beer I can drink… money in my pocket for a change… whatever the hell I want, I get.

But Kincaid was a veteran cop, and he knew to expect the unexpected. Despite his racing emotions, he still had the presence of mind to examine the setting and see if anyone was watching. His head turned as he drove down the rest of the driveway and pushed the button to open the garage door. Once inside, he slid out of the seat and quickly pushed the opener again to close the garage.

He slipped out the side door and walked around the property, scanning his eyes to see if anyone was around. He then trudged up the open-wood steps to the front door of the trailer, inserted his key into the lock, and deliberately opened the front door, like he was on duty and fearing a bad guy was waiting.

Suspiciously, Kincaid peered into each room of the trailer—first the tiny kitchen, then the bathroom, piled-high storage room, and finally the cramped bedroom—to ensure that no one was inside. And no one was to be found. Debbie's kids never had a key to let themselves in, and none of Kincaid's own children cared enough to ask for one.

The closest neighbor, a steelworker whose job was thirty miles away, lived a half-mile down the road and never came over, since he and his wife did not approve of Kincaid and Debbie's drinking habits and living arrangements. No one else ever came by either, for that matter.

Satisfied, Kincaid then walked through the side garage door and put both hands on the trunk as if claiming his prize. He exhaled deeply, then popped open the trunk. The bag was sitting in place, where he had left it hours before, and the overhead utility light of the garage reflected on the bag, creating a sort of glow. Still looking around, Kincaid carefully lifted the bag from the trunk and carried it through the connecting door to the kitchen. As he passed into the trailer, he felt a pang of relief, knowing that he had made it that far, and another hurdle had been cleared.

He stumbled onto one of the secondhand ladderback chairs that surrounded the brownish, discount-store square table, unzipped the bag, and turned it upside-down, dumping its contents onto the table. The slick money slid around, some bundles piling in the middle, others slipping off the table onto the off-white linoleum floor. Kincaid instinctively scooped up the loose bundles and dropped them in with the others. He then threw himself back in his chair, gawking at the massive stack of money before him.

A lengthy, quiet pause enveloped the room as Kincaid simply stared, eyes wide, mouth turned upward, reveling in the serenity that now swept over his body. He had never attended church and rarely spoke to any of the police chaplains he came in contact with. But in this moment, Kincaid felt cleansed, as if all of his burdens were evaporating in front of him. His body went limp, all muscles relaxed, the tension of the previous few hours–and years—lifting away.

Most who experience a spiritual transformation will say it lasts for years, if not a lifetime. For Kincaid, it lasted exactly nine minutes. As if a hypnotist had snapped his fingers, Kincaid jerked upward in his seat, ready to address the task at hand. His future was sitting right in front of him, piled on the scratched-up table, and he had some counting to do. He started arranging the bundles of bills in small stacks on the table to help organize for the task at hand.

Kincaid counted the bills in each bundle individually, which added immensely to the length of the job. His smile never wore off as he excitedly saw the amount of money go higher, then higher, finally surpassing the contents of the other bag at headquarters. The final total was $1,383,000.

Normally sullen, Kincaid could not contain his excitement, and he stamped his right foot on the linoleum, in celebration of his choice. As he did, he felt his backside come down hard on the wallet in his back pocket, containing the eleven dollars that was his pocket cash for the next few days. With the gold mine in front of him, that was no longer a problem. He counted out $500 in tens and twenties and shoved them inside his pocket.

It was now approaching 6 p.m., and the November afternoon was quickly fading. Though there was the overhead light in the garage, it was hardly enough to brighten the garage in the dark of night, and Kincaid knew he needed a place to stash the bag. The tiny trailer was not an option, since Debbie was sure to find it somewhere, and if she didn't, then her kids, who were never inclined to stay out of her business, would discover it during their occasional visits.

As he had learned earlier with the bag in the vault, stuffing that much cash back inside took several minutes of effort. Once full, he lifted the bag off the table and stepped back through the adjoining door into the garage. He knew that Debbie was sure to find it if the bag was not hidden properly, and she routinely parked her banged-up red Toyota Celica in the garage. But he had a better idea.

Like many garages, there were open rafters above, providing an ample amount of wasted space. The previous tenant had left a 4x8 piece of plywood across the rafters, which Kincaid had always noticed but never removed. Today, it proved perfect for his needs. He reached for the eight-foot A-frame ladder that he had bought while still living with Judy in Raymond, pulled it apart to brace it, clutched the money bag in one hand, and climbed within reach of the plywood. He then slid the bag into the center of the plywood, where it proved an easy fit, with no fear of it sliding off onto the concrete floor below.

He climbed back down the ladder and walked around the garage floor, looking upward at the plywood from every angle. The dark bag was barely visible against the gray and brown ceiling of the garage, but that was not enough for Kincaid. In one corner lay a three-square-foot piece of black tarp, another remnant from his workshop back in Raymond. He quickly seized the tarp, climbed back up the ladder, and covered the bag.

That removed any chance of an easy view from below, as the tarp called even less suspicion. As Kincaid walked around the garage again, he spied a mouse that jumped from behind a five-gallon gasoline can, saw Kincaid, and raced for safety behind a portable generator along the wall. Mobile home owners often complain of mice, and since the trailer was only a few hundred feet from a cornfield, the unwelcome guests were frequent.

Mice also have a penchant for climbing things like rafters. Kincaid was still considering all external threats, and while there were plenty of unknowns, he could handle this one. He walked back into the kitchen, opened the door beneath the chrome sink, and pulled out the box of D-Con that had reduced the mouse presence throughout the trailer. A handful of metal beer bottle caps were lying carelessly on the countertop, the byproduct of last night's drinking binge before Debbie had propositioned him.

Kincaid grabbed a few caps, shook some D-Con into each, and returned to the ladder. Carefully holding the caps in his closed palm so they would not lose the poison pellets, he shimmied up the ladder again and spread the caps on each side of the bag to nail mice from any direction who had any ideas of penetrating the bag and its fragile contents. He climbed down the ladder, folded and replaced it along the wall, and exhaled deeply.

With dusk now approaching, Kincaid physically and emotionally began to hit the wall. He had been up for nearly twenty-four hours, and his hypertension and overweight physique could not stand the strain any longer. Suddenly weary, he went back to the kitchen, opened the refrigerator, and grabbed one of Debbie's bottles of Michelob Ultra.

He downed the beer in several swallows, sat the empty bottle down on the counter, and then pulled a second out of the fridge and downed it, too. Once done, he mindlessly tossed the second bottle aside on the counter. It tapped the first bottle with a loud clink that rattled him, and he jerked to attention, head once again swiveling.

Satisfied that the noise meant nothing, Kincaid strolled down the narrow hallway to the bedroom at the end, tugging off his uniform as he went. Finally, he was down to his white Hanes briefs. His walk was more upright and confident, because his triumph of the last few hours had given him a manly rush. He wished Debbie were there, naked and ready for a quickie, but his body was crying for rest. Awkwardly, he dropped onto the bed, pulling up the worn brown blanket around him.

Though he was exhausted, sleep would not come; his mind was still a whirlwind. Minutes before, he was reveling in the glory of his newfound riches. Now the other side of his choice haunted him. Damn, what have I done? he pondered. Stole more money than any bank robber I ever heard of… I better not get caught for this… I can't get caught… just can't…

The fear now pulsated through Kincaid's tired body. God, what if they found out, he thought. We got some of the best investigators there is, guys who never quit… just keep on going 'til they get what they need… they'll stick it up your butt before you know it… if they get wind of this, I'm up shit creek. I've seen guys get tossed for a lot less, and here I am, big Jim, big-ass Jim, holding over a million dollars of evidence…

In short order, his ego took over. Dammit to hell, James! he barked at himself as a parent to a wayward teenager. Who is ever going to find out? No drug dealer in his right mind is going to say a frickin' word about that money! What the hell are they going to say, "Oh, by the way, we lost a bag of money somewhere out of Chicago. Could you please give it back?" I mean, dammit. They do that, and they're signing up for prison.

Emboldened, he began to rationalize. And if some supervisor ever does find out, who the hell are they going to believe? Me, with twenty-six years with the badge, or some slimy drug dealer? I'm the only one that knows about this, and no one else saw me take the money… Murphy wasn't even there yet when I put it in the trunk, and no cars were going by when I got the money, and if they were, they wouldn't have any reason to suspect anything… after all, I'm the boy with the badge…

The only other guy who knew anything was the poor bastard whose brains were bashed in the front seat, and he's dead. He isn't going to say anything, don't have to worry about that. Kincaid basked in his self-perceived intelligence. After all, I left one bag alone. Could have taken both, but I didn't… I turned in over a million dollars, for God's sake… if that doesn't make me look honest, I don't know what does.

Though reassured, Kincaid still lay awake for a while before his body finally gave out. As he dozed off, a smug smile swept across his face as the newest richest guy in White City caught a few winks.

CHAPTER 6

Kincaid's blissful sleep lasted barely an hour. At 7:16, Debbie, done with her shift, came through the door and, as usual, never shied from making a big entrance.

"Hey, baby!" she yelled at the top of her lungs. Hearing no response, she tried again. "Baby! Where you at?"

Her shrill shouting rousted Kincaid from his slumber. "Here, in here," he mumbled, struggling to awaken.

Debbie flounced down the hall, plopped down on the bed, and playfully slapped her man's backside. She did it a little too hard for his liking, and he jerked slightly. "Oh, I'm sorry. Did I wake you?" she asked as she lit up one of her Virginia Slims.

The obvious question was not lost on Kincaid, who rubbed his eyes with one hand and massaged his stiff neck with the other. But he let the issue go. "Nah, not really. Just laid down for a while."

In that instant, his mind immediately switched back to the money in the garage. Is it still there? he wondered. Right where I left it? Was anyone else in there? Did she see it when she pulled in?

"Did you park in the garage?" he blurted out.

"Yeah. Why?" said Debbie, startled at the question. "I mean, where else... why do you ask?"

"No reason," Kincaid caught himself. "I just couldn't remember if I had parked the truck in there, too."

"Oh," Debbie brushed it off to her man's sleepiness. "Yeah, I'm in the garage. You parked the truck outside, remember?"

The tone of her voice seemed normal, so he had no reason to suspect that she knew anything was out of the ordinary. "Sorry. It's just been a really long day. I didn't get back here until past two."

"Too bad," she replied. "It was quiet down at the bar. Not too many in today." She stood up from the bed. "Want something to eat?"

"Yeah." Kincaid had been running on adrenaline, and had not eaten since he had gulped a Slim Jim in the car at one thirty that morning.

"I'll get supper," Debbie offered, turning to the hallway in the direction of the kitchen. "Franks and beans all right with you?"

"Sure, anything," responded Kincaid offhandedly as he rolled off the mattress and dropped his feet onto the floor. He also hadn't showered since last night and could tell by his own smell that he needed one. He strode toward the bathroom to do the job.

He barely noticed the steaming hot water trickling down on him, for thoughts of the bag of money consumed him, and he finally realized that he had soaped himself much more than usual. He quickly rinsed off, reached for a towel and his imitation Brut, and walked back to the bedroom to the closet.

After flipping through the rack, he pulled out an old pair of Wranglers and a double-breasted, black-checked Western shirt that was a personal favorite. He dressed and looked at himself in the floor-length mirror that hung on the back of the closet door. Ignoring his middle-aged paunch, rubbery skin, and balding pate, he turned in front of the mirror, looking at himself from side to side as the rush of the money still had its hold.

"Damn," Kincaid said out loud. "Looking good tonight." He glanced again at the back of his jeans, which were a size too small for his bulging waistline, though he didn't care. "Nice ass," he admired.

Just then, Debbie called from the kitchen. "Supper's ready." Apparently, Debbie thought he looked good, too, because she gave him a peck on the left cheek as he entered the kitchen. It was the second straight night that Debbie had kissed him like that, unusual in that she was rarely that tender. Normally, she was sort of "grabby" and liked to slide her hand across or into his crotch, or slap or squeeze his buttocks.

As they ate, they made small talk in the usual way, until Debbie asked the question. "You said you had a hell of a day. What happened?"

"Humph," Kincaid snickered. "I don't think you'd believe me if I told you."

"Try me. What was it?"

Kincaid was somewhat nervous at the thought of reciting the details, fearful that he may let a word or a look slip to Debbie. But he knew she would hear of the accident at some point, since it was about to hit the papers. "I had a fatal on I-55, just off the Raymond exit," he began. "Guy was southbound and he lost control, slid off the highway and through the guard fence. Wrapped it around a tree."

"Shit." Debbie winced at the thought. "Bet that was a nice one to see."

"Yeah, well, I've seen worse," replied Kincaid. "But that wasn't the half of it." He put down his fork and leaned in to the middle of the table, as if he was about to whisper a secret. "The guy was some Mexican, and he was driving a rental, this nice-looking smoke-gray Camaro that went back to Avis at O'Hare in Chicago. Looks like he was a drug runner."

"Oh, really?" Debbie was more concerned with her cigarette and plate than her reply. "Why, did he have drugs in the car, or money, or something?"

"Oh, yeah," Kincaid ignored the irony of her statement as he picked up his fork again. "He had plenty of money, all right. I opened the trunk, and there was this big duffel bag inside. We took it in, counted it up, and it came out to $1.2 million."

Debbie turned her neck hard to look straight at Kincaid. "Shut the hell up!" Her voice rose to a shout as she dropped her fork on the plate with a rattle. "You're frickin' kidding me! You were standing there, looking at a million bucks?"

Kincaid neglected to tell her that he was actually standing there looking at two million bucks, not just one. "Sure was. And this could be a big deal. We've called in extra people on it, and they took my picture. It's going to be in the papers."

"Son of a bitch." Debbie began to come back down from her excitement, and she rolled her eyes. "My boyfriend, the celebrity."

Kincaid saw her next question coming. "What went through your mind when you saw the money?"

"I was surprised, sure." Just a few hours into the heist, Kincaid was becoming quite the actor. "But it was evidence. That was how I had to treat it." No mention was made of the other bag, sitting in the rafters in the garage.

"Wow. I'd have wanted to keep it," mused Debbie before a sip of 7 Up and vodka from the black plastic glass by her plate. "But I know better. Evidence, and all."

"Yeah. Evidence." Kincaid looked down the table, paused, and cleaned up his own plate.

*****

Though Kincaid had barely slept and had to report to work tomorrow, energy was raging through his veins, and he wanted to unwind. He also wanted to see if he would ever be able to leave the money on the property alone, and now was as good a time as any.

"Want to go down to Martin's?" he asked Debbie.

Debbie had just spent the better part of the day there, and since she and Kincaid also hung out there, it seemed like she lived there. "Yeah, sure. Why not?"

They never passed through the garage, as Kincaid's green S-10 was parked on the side of the driveway. Debbie walked ahead, which allowed Kincaid the opportunity to scan the property and glance around the garage to see if any threats to the money existed. Seeing none, he followed Debbie into the truck.

Debbie liked trucks, and since Kincaid spent hours a day in the squad car, he was only too happy to let her take the wheel. A few minutes later, they were at Martin's, where the Friday night crowd was as full as usual. Martin greeted

Debbie with "Back again, babe?" and Kincaid with a welcoming "Get your ass in here!" as they ordered off the bar.

Fellow troopers whispered that Kincaid had a drinking problem, which was easy to spot by the smell of liquor that he often had on his breath when he checked in for his shift. Debbie shared the same affinity for drink and had no issue with her boyfriend's habits, since she drank about as much. She ordered her usual, a draft, while he picked his own brand of beer.

As he parked himself in a chipped-up wooden chair, Kincaid still thought of the bag on the rafters and wondered if he should have left it there. But a couple of beers later, he began to loosen up and socialize with some of the other patrons, who were now some of the few friends he could number.

They included Larry Adams, a well-weathered, retired ironworker with greasy black hair from nearby Gillespie, and his brother Del, four years his junior but dangerously overweight, a foreman on Mount Olive's street crew whose wife had left him for a thinner guy two years before. Also there was Ned Ullman, who at thirty-six was younger than the others, but complained like he was much older. Based on his haggard build, thin-rimmed glasses and prematurely gray hair tucked under an always-stained ballcap, he looked like it, too. Ullman was a school janitor, and never missed a chance to moan about how hard his job was, how horrible the schoolkids were, or how ugly his last girlfriend was.

The three of them were rarely apart when they were at Martin's, and they called Kincaid over to join them at a nearby table. Debbie, meanwhile, found a buddy of her own, Shelley Tipson, a retired grade school teacher with dyed-red hair who was spending most of her golden years and much of her pension in the bar.

The men paid little attention and shot the breeze about local politics, football, and the weather. Ned managed to stick in a few comments on how filthy the boys' bathroom was at the middle school that day. Finally, Larry asked, "Whatcha been doing, Jim?"

Kincaid was now on his first shot of Jack Daniels after three beers, and his inhibitions on the bags of money were evaporating. Still, he was with it enough to keep a mention of the second bag to himself. He regaled the other three with the events of the hours before, the fatal, the accident scene, and, most important of all, the one bag of money.

"Son of a bitch!" yelled Del, who was now on his sixth vodka tonic and was even louder than normal. "Son of a bitch! A million bucks!" The volume of the jukebox was turned up, and the strains of George Jones's country classic "He Stopped Loving Her Today" drowned out his shouts. The bar was so dimly lit that anyone who did hear something could have barely seen who said it anyway.

"Damn," said Ned the janitor, shaking his head wistfully as he stared at the longneck in front of him. "I'm cleaning up after every brat in town, and some drug dealer's livin' like a king."

"No kidding," said Larry, whose bleeding ulcer kept him from having more than two beers a night. The restrictions had made him a bitter man, though his long-suffering wife loved the change. "You ever handle something like that before, Jim?"

"Oh, yeah, sure." Kincaid loved being the coolest guy in the room and moments like this showed why, though his speech was starting to slur. He lit up a Camel to go with his drink. "I mean, I hadn't seen that much money at once, but it happens. You'd be surprised how much money is going up and down the road. Those drug cartels in Mexico, they're worth hundreds of millions of dollars. They aren't some small-time operation."

By now, Merle Haggard's "Okie from Muskogee" was blaring from the jukebox. Kincaid finished his shot of Jack and ordered another. "They send millions of dollars in drugs into Chicago, St. Louis, all over. I know it, because that's what you deal with when you're a cop. You know, I, er, we see it all the time. But most people, they have no idea how much money's out there. Shit, you drive down to St. Louis, you might pass twenty million bucks in drug money and not even know it."

"And you found over a million dollars," said Ned, in between sips off the longneck. "Hell, I found a twenty floating in a toilet stall in the girls' room on Monday morning and thought I was the big—"

"I got to ask, I got to ask," interrupted Del, who was sliding around in his =chair, having difficulty keeping his posture. He was also repeating himself. "I got to know. Were you… were you tempted to keep any of it?"

Even in his impending stupor, Kincaid knew this would not be the last time he would be asked this question. He also knew what to say. "Oh, hell no," as he chugged his second shot of Jack. He wiped his mouth. "I mean, I couldn't. That was evidence, and I had to turn it in. I never even thought about it."

"You dumbass!" bellowed Del, yelling even louder than before. "I mean, what the…? All that money, sitting right there, and you didn't even think about it?" Boastful by nature, Del was even more so when the liquor flowed through his veins, and he waved his arms in the air. "Son of a bitch, I would have grabbed me a couple handfuls at least! Maybe ten or twelve!"

He roared with laughter. Ned agreed with Del, adding that his job was killing him, and that he would have used the money to go to Florida or someplace warm.

"No." Kincaid was firm in his denial. "You guys got to understand. I'm a cop, and we've got rules. That money's evidence, and that's all there is to it. I had no choice."

"Good man!" said Larry, nodding his head in approval. "Good man! That's why we've got guys like you keeping us safe!"

"Damn straight," seconded Martin, who just happened by and heard the end of the story. He leaned down and mockingly cradled Kincaid's head in his arms, slapping him on the cheek with an open palm as a mother to her son. "That's why we love this guy!"

By then, Del had thrown his head back and dozed off, while Ned kept muttering about "my horseshit job and my horseshit life." Kincaid ordered three more shots, downed each one, and then staggered up from his chair and said his goodbyes. The red digital clock above the bar, adorned with a beer label logo, read 12:29 a.m.

Along with her pal Shelley, Debbie had knocked off at least six beers, or so she said before she lost count, and was in much the same state as her boyfriend. Both had to make an emergency stop in the bathroom on the way out the door, and since the girls' room was full, Debbie joined Kincaid in the men's, claiming a stall while he threw himself against a urinal.

State policemen devote too much of their time to drunken drivers, who are one of the biggest threats on any highway. On this night, as countless times before, Kincaid himself was one of them. Kincaid and Debbie zigzagged their way across the parking lot, arms wrapped around each other to steady their balance, and, after some deliberation, found their way to the truck.

They managed to return to the trailer despite weaving all over the empty highways at that time of night, somehow avoiding the city cops and Kincaid's fellow troopers who were on patrol. Kincaid was so inebriated that, for the first time all day, he forgot about the bag sitting on the rafters as he stumbled through the garage and into the kitchen.

CHAPTER 7

Kincaid was a sound sleeper, and, fortified with alcohol, he was oblivious to the world. He was also oblivious to where he was, as once in the trailer, he turned right toward the living room, instead of left toward the bedroom. He crashed onto the brown leather sofa and was asleep in seconds. Debbie, meanwhile, pulled off every bit of clothing she wore in the kitchen, threw it on the linoleum, and successfully found her way to the bed, where she lay backward, her head at the foot and her feet on the pillow.

Both had neglected to set the alarm, and as Kincaid was expected on the day shift and based on his spotty work record, he could not afford to be late for work. However, he managed to stir himself at 6:31, when he raised his head, opened his eyes, and felt the torment of a hangover-induced migraine.

His pounding head, though, harbored thoughts of the bag of money, and he trampled out of the kitchen and into the garage to make sure it was still there. He could see a corner of the covering tarp in place and knew it was undisturbed.

Back inside, Kincaid made his way down the hallway to the shower. Debbie, now awake and still naked, yelled something at him, greeted by a reply of "Oh God, keep it down!" from her boyfriend. After a fast shower, Kincaid gargled a generous quantity of Lavoris to try and kill the scent of alcohol that remained on his breath. He quickly dressed and gulped down three Excedrins as he walked the door. Once in his squad car, he radioed District 18 and went 10-41 at 6:59 a.m.

The drive from White City to Litchfield helped soothe his head, as did thoughts of his now-fruitful retirement. He arrived at District 18 headquarters, and his first duty of the day was to complete the seemingly neverending paperwork requirements from the accident. Later that morning came the newspaper interview, and waiting in a white-block conference room was Greg Kramer, a reporter from the Litchfield Chronicle.

Kramer was a young guy, fresh out of the journalism program at Eastern Illinois University, and he had that idealistic, change-the-world mentality that many new writers share. Chicago-born and bred, he loved to ask hard-hitting questions and impress his interview subjects in this area he derisively called "Hee Haw Land." Kincaid, with his sense of self-importance, had little use for such drivel, but with the public relations specialists of the state police joining him in the room, he knew he should be on his best behavior. He answered each question courteously and directly.

Eventually came the inquiry that seemed to be on everyone's mind. "Did you ever think of keeping the money? Or at least part of it?"

"No," said Kincaid firmly, finding a way to look the reporter in the eye across the table. "Never even crossed my mind. That's evidence, part of an investigation. Taking even a dollar of that money goes against everything I stand for."

The reporter pressed further. "But didn't it even cross your mind, at least once?"

"Nope. Like I said, never even thought of it. When you're a cop, that just isn't something you think about."

Kramer shook his head, for once admiring one of his interview subjects. He also remembered the pile of student loans he was burdened with, and imagined what a million dollars could have done for that situation. Later, when the article appeared in print, Kincaid and his superiors smiled when the reporter praised both his recovery and honesty, particularly in one sentence reading, "Trooper Kincaid stared down temptation, and stayed true to his job. Wonder how many of us would have done the same."

*****

Kincaid shook hands with the cub reporter and left the room. He then headed for the next item on his list, a meeting with Illinois State Police Detective Mike Miller, who had been called to work on this Saturday to meet with Kincaid. Among other things, Kincaid supplied the driver's license and cell phone of the deceased Camaro driver to Miller to open that end of the investigation.

Sergeant Miller was about to celebrate the twentieth anniversary of his career with the ISP, twelve of those in the Narcotics Unit. The top man in his state police academy class, he was energetic and inquisitive, a mental and physical reflection of his six-foot, 180-pound build that screamed of athleticism. An all-state point guard and an all-conference third baseman in high school, he still was a regular in the old-man's leagues, though he certainly did not look the part, and didn't play like it either. He jogged at least three miles a day, rain or shine, and shied away from alcohol.

His coal-black hair complemented his dark eyebrows and piercing dark brown eyes that could fixate on any subject and sometimes make them uncomfortable. Now forty-six, Miller had interned with the Capitol Police in Washington, D.C., during his days at Southern Illinois Univer-sity, where he caught the law enforcement bug.

There, he also met his wife, Julie, who outweighed her husband by fifteen pounds, and her height of five-foot-five created an unusual contrast with her tall, fit husband. But they were never seen without holding hands, and their tender bond had created a sixteen-year-old son, Tyler, and thirteen-year-old daughter, Adrianna, whose school activities Miller never missed. Peers wondered where he found the time, since he rarely left headquarters before six on any evening.

Such was the life of the go-to guy for investigations in District 18, and while Miller would never say so himself, his coworkers knew he was the best. Kincaid knew it, too, so he was little surprised to see Miller, who took the information he needed and then was on his way.

First, Miller ran the name of the accident victim through the Illinois State Police computer system. He verified the man's name as Pascal Ramirez, with an address on the south side of Chicago, near Interstate 57. Miller then downloaded all of the numbers from Ramirez's cell phone and forwarded the information to the ISP Intelligence Unit in Springfield.

A trip to the Montgomery County morgue came next. Miller called ahead to make sure someone was on duty and then walked outside to his squad car. The morgue was in the Litchfield hospital, a ten-minute drive from the headquarters location just east of downtown Litchfield, and Miller, alone in the car, used the time to mentally process the information he had and what to do next.

No one relishes a visit to the morgue, but Miller, like most seasoned investigators, had done it plenty of times before, so the shock was minimal. The supervisor had the body ready for him, and he fingerprinted the corpse before taking an array of photographs. Back at headquarters, the prints confirmed Ramirez's identity.

In these early stages of the investigation, Miller learned some eye-opening facts on the newly deceased. Ramirez had an extensive criminal record in his twenty-six years on earth, mainly drug-related, and had spent several stints in the Cook County jail. Later that day, Miller received a call from the ISP Intelligence Unit with more information. Their efforts revealed that Ramirez was associated with the Gangster Disciples, one of the toughest gangs on Chicago's south side and well known to the Narcotics Unit. Other friends or contacts of Ramirez were also identified, and most were small-time criminals themselves.

It was also learned that Ramirez was an illegal immigrant who had been deported three times by the Department of Homeland Security, only to make his way back across the border each time. A number of Americans believe in free and open borders, wanting to welcome anyone and everyone who wants to enter the country. Those in law enforcement, such as Miller, often have a different view, since they are the ones who have to deal with cases like Ramirez.

But Miller knew well that this case, with one of the larger amounts of drug money that he had ever dealt with, had plenty of layers. Having spent the best part of this Saturday at headquarters, he sat back in his swivel chair, drummed his fingers on the table in front of him, and pondered what was to come.

CHAPTER 8

The sun was rising over the Hueco Mountains near El Paso, just across the Rio Grande from Ciudad Juarez, Mexico, as Diego Garcia gazed out on the courtyard of his sprawling stucco mansion. Admiring the sunshine, he clutched the cross necklace that had often given him strength.

The mansion was part of a secluded compound that few residents of Juarez knew about, and Garcia was glad of it. The compound was the nerve center of a sweeping drug cartel, one of the largest on the border, which netted hundreds of millions of dollars a year.

Garcia was the head of it, and he reaped the rewards of the drug addictions of millions of Americans. He felt little shame, though, as he had practically grown up in the cartel, and had worked his way up to reside in the compound that ran it all.

He leaned in the doorway to the courtyard, resting his back and slouching slightly to appear shorter than his six-foot-two figure that usually stood taller than others around him. At 180 pounds, he carried a slight belly, but less than other men his age, having turned forty-nine in October. A thick head of dark hair, styled by a male beautician that he periodically imported to the cartel, dominated his persona, along with a neatly trimmed mustache.

Though he relished the fantastic wealth that came with control of the cartel, he had not been born that way. He had grown up on the mean streets of Juarez, where survival simply meant getting to tomorrow. In that underworld, he met Juan Rodrequs, a fellow street urchin, one of the many who are ignored in the everyday life of third-world Mexico. When Rodrequs reached his teens, he found a home in the cartel and a place to stay in the hacienda of a mid-level leader. He earned money as a messenger, running notes back and forth to the power brokers in the dark of the night, and he saw many men die bloody deaths along the way. As he moved up the ranks, he caused many of those same violent deaths with little hint of regard for the victims or their families.

Garcia found a place in the cartel as well, helping to lift the heavy bags of drugs into transporters, covering for Rodrequs as he ran messages, serving as a janitor in the homes of the cartel power brokers. He was paid not only in money, but also in trysts with high-end prostitutes that were frequent visitors to the mansions of the bosses.

Eventually, Rodrequs became a trusted confidant of the cartel leader, who took him under his wing and made him a prodigal son. Eight years ago, however, Rodrequs saw his own opportunity and shot the leader point-blank, making sure the leader saw who was pulling the trigger. He then seized control of the cartel himself and oversaw its growth into a financial juggernaut that would make many corporate leaders cringe.

Garcia became the second-in-command and worked at his old friend's side as the money and drugs flowed across the border. That was the payment for a hefty drug demand that was carried through a sophisticated tunnel that Rodrequs had constructed underneath the Rio Grande. Garcia was put in charge of some of the biggest drug deliveries, including one to Chicago three years before that proved his unraveling.

He took along his wife, Rosa, under the guise that they were to pick up some furniture from a relative. Since Garcia had met Rosa in Chicago, where she waited tables, it seemed a logical alibi. They traveled in a shiny black Ford F-150 with a secret compartment, a false bed that contained nine hundred pounds of high-grade cocaine.

But Rosa let her foot slide too hard on the pedal one night in central Illinois, and the couple, with their illegal cargo, was pulled over by an Illinois State Police trooper near the university towns of Bloomington-Normal. A record check revealed that Garcia had been picked up before and had served four years in a federal pen for drug trafficking.

The previous rap meant that he was facing twenty-five years to life in prison, and Rosa would do time as well. That meant a hard choice had to be made, but Garcia, in his desperation, had a card to play. Rodrequs was in league with a Pakistani national who wanted to smuggle terrorists across the border through the tunnel, part of a plan to blow up several of America's most beloved monuments and tourist centers.

Thousands of American lives were at risk, and Diego Garcia knew it. It was also his only way out, so he cut a deal with the FBI and became an informant, guiding the FBI, CIA, DEA, and other agencies step-by-step instructions to help them nail the terrorists, at the expense of his old friend Rodrequs. Ultimately, the terrorist plot was averted, Rodrequs was gunned down in the mansion by Mexican Federalies working in conjunction with the Americans, and the cartel was left without its leader. Diego Garcia, the second-in-command whom no one suspected of treachery, was left to step in.

Though Garcia was no longer a confidant to American officials, he still received occasional calls on a secret line with questions about activities on the border. Sometimes his conscience took over and he provided bits of information he thought the Americans would find useful. His role not only protected himself from future arrest, but it also helped the business, since he helped American law enforcement shut down several of his top competitors.

He now lived a life of luxury that most poor Mexicans–and even a lot of Americans–could only dream of, though his marriage hung by a thread. Rosa, with her rail-thin build, scraggly hair, and angular face, would have attracted the affections of few men, though Garcia was one of them, and he maintained the love he had felt since she had taken his order in that dingy diner in Chicago so many years before. The tenderness, however, was not returned. Ever ambitious, never satisfied with the money and possessions she would have never enjoyed without Garcia's provision, Rosa seemingly tolerated the union. For years, she had held such a warm opinion of Juan Rodrequs that it made her husband nervous.

The marriage had become even more distant since Rodrequs's gruesome death in the grand parlor of the mansion that Rosa now occupied with her still-devoted husband. She refused to stand anywhere near the spot where Rodrequs had died or where his blood had splattered on the plush French carpet, though she declined every opportunity to replace the stained covering, choosing instead only to lovingly clean it herself every few weeks. She had also locked the door to Rodrequs's master bedroom and, three years after his death, had never reached for the key. Most discomforting was the photo of Rodrequs, standing next to Garcia, on the nightstand of Rosa's bedroom where she slept alone, down the long hallway from her husband's own suite.

On this morning, Rosa was busying herself in preparation for another day in Juarez's finest boutiques and was waiting for her favorite black Mercedes from the cartel's fleet, with the driver who would escort her. Garcia had left a pile of spending cash on a small table outside her room, knowing that she would not wish him good morning or come to say goodbye as she left.

But Garcia had plenty to do on his own. He was waiting for the arrival of Pascal Ramirez, the drug runner from Chicago whom he had entrusted with over $2.5 million in cash from a major cocaine drop on the city's south side. Garcia had expected Ramirez to return with the money yesterday and wondered why he was so late.

In Ramirez, Garcia saw himself at the same age, for their hard upbringings were remarkably similar. Ramirez had been on his own since he was fourteen years old. His father, an unwitting bystander, had died in one of the many gun battles between rival cartels that pierce the dark Mexican nights with the ripple of flying bullets. His mother had moved in with a cousin in Chicago but had left Pascal behind, unable to provide for him as well. She entrusted him to the care of an aunt, which proved an unwise choice, since the aunt was more concerned with her schedule of male lovers than the needs of a lonely teenage boy. As a result, she left him to his own devices and made it clear he was unwelcome in the house whenever she had overnight guests, which was often.

Garcia was running another errand for Juan at two in the morning a decade earlier when he found Pascal, huddled against the side of a derelict building on one of Juarez's back streets, struggling to keep warm. Remembering how he had done the same thing as a youth, he stopped and asked Pascal if there were anything he needed. The boy jumped at the chance, voice mixed with elation and desperation, pleading that he would do anything for something to eat and a place to stay.

Not unexpectedly, Garcia had plenty of odd jobs to offer the boy, who eagerly worked to repay that kindness. And, as Garcia had done years before, Pascal worked his way up to become a trusted employee, always able and willing to do what was needed. For the last three years, Pascal had split his time between Chicago and Ciudad Juarez as one of Diego's top drug couriers. In addition, he had made lucrative contacts through some of Chicago's toughest street gangs, who were loyal customers of the cartel's products, as well as the south side's top dealers and pushers.

Standing a chesty five-foot-nine with a manicured goatee, Pascal also used his good looks and smooth-talking ways to find more buyers in the many women whom he met in the bars and clubs of south Chicago. Though he was careless at times, which led to several arrests and some jail time in Cook County, Garcia knew he was one of his best men and trusted him implicitly.

Still, as the sun warmed the frost from this unseasonably cool morning in the compound, there was reason for concern as Pascal was hours late and had not called. Never known for a temper, Garcia began to simmer and anxiously waited for the chance to browbeat his friend when he arrived for causing so much alarm. Had Juan Rodrequs been in charge, he would have fired Pascal the moment he walked in and possibly had him executed, smiling with each shot and every drop of blood.

Though Garcia was less disposed toward violence, three years in charge of the cartel had hardened him, and he knew that control of the cartel meant pulling rank whenever needed, at the point of a gun or not. He decided to give Pascal until noon before making any further decisions.

Twelve o'clock came and went. Now Garcia knew that something was amiss. He picked up the phone and dialed the cell number of his associate in Chicago, Tyrone Williams, the man who was to have received the drugs, and who was supposed to provide the money to Pascal for delivery to Garcia.

As his prime supplier, Garcia was one of the few men who had Williams' phone number, and one of even fewer that he would answer for. That was mainly because Williams had so little regard for the rest of the human race. One of the kingpin drug dealers in Chicago, he was also one of the most ruthless and accounted for a fair share of the murders in the city in any given year. Whether his victims were black or white, men or women, parents or not, mattered little. Much like Rodrequs, he seemed to revel in pulling the trigger and watching lifeless bodies crumple to the ground. If he didn't do it himself, he had plenty of others to do it for him since, as a leader of the Gangster Disciples, he knew many members who would whack someone for drug money of their own.

In his youth, Williams was a pickup basketball legend, and he still looked like he had plenty of game at six feet tall and 160 pounds. Now, he could buy and sell his old buddies from the playground, since he was probably the wealthiest man in the city who never filed a tax return. The Chicago police knew exactly who Tyrone Williams was and had arrested him on several occasions. As a result, he had spent over half of his forty-three years in a state or federal pen. But each time, he came back, bigger and richer than ever.

He also liked to taunt his enemies and the cops, perennially waving a middle finger to society. Not one to live in the shadows, he wore plenty of bling to go along with his flashy clothes, and he tooled around in a black Cadillac with shiny chrome hubs that screamed for attention. Anyone who got too close to the car, though, was likely to have their outline drawn in chalk.

He saw Garcia's number on his caller ID and picked up. "Diego, my man! What up! Get the money?"

"No, my friend," said Garcia tersely. "And that's why I'm calling. Pascal should have been here yesterday. When did he leave?"

Williams muttered a filthy word involving mothers and thought for a second. "What is today, Sunday? Hell, I last saw his ass on Thursday, around 9 p.m. He was here on schedule, and I gave him over two million dollars that I owe ya. Two bags, stuffed with it. Told me he was gonna haul ass back home right then."

"Well, he's not here, my friend. Do you have any ideas of what went wrong?"

Naturally suspicious and distrusting of practically everyone, Williams got defensive. "You sayin' I had something to do with it? My ass! I saw the two bags of money put in the trunk of the vehicle just before he drove off, dammit!"

"No, no," replied Garcia, surprised at the insinuation. "We've never had problems, senor. But something is not right here, and I must know why."

"Yeah, yeah, man," Williams's ferocious temper had been soothed. "Tell you what, man. I know Pascal's mother. Sweet lady, friend of my mom, they hang together. I'll give her a call, and get back wit' ya."

"Okay," said Garcia. "But do it soon. I must know what has happened."

Williams was not one to take orders, but he was not about to threaten the supply chain either. He hung up and dialed the number of Pascal's mother, Esmerelda. The greeting was a tearful "Buenos dias," and immediately, even the unfeeling Williams knew something was wrong. Between gasps and whines, Esmerelda told Williams that she had received a call from the Montgomery County coroner as she was fixing lunch on Saturday. The man had said that Pascal had been killed in a car accident somewhere south of Springfield.

Ever coarse, Williams barked another dirty word and asked if she knew where the accident had happened. She replied that it was a little town like Litchfield, or something like that. Williams offered as much sympathy as he could muster, promised that he would send some money to help her along, and hung up. He then dialed Garcia, who was sitting in the throne-like brown revolving chair at his ornate mahogany desk, waiting for the phone to ring.

"Got some bad news," Williams opened. "Pascal's dead. He was in a car crash in some little town downstate. Some place called Litchfield, I think. The county coroner called his mother and told her."

Garcia was never as hard-shelled as Rodrequs or Williams, and he felt a pang of sorrow for his lost friend. "Oh, no," he moaned before practicality took over. "What happened to the money?"

"That's the real bad news. Guess the state police took it in and confiscated it." Williams shook his head in disgust.

"Yes, my friend." Garcia's nonchalant answer belied the doubt in his mind. "I know where Litchfield is. I have driven by it many times, on I-55. I'd say it's about five hours south of Chicago. But I must know for sure. Can you get some verification of this?"

"What you mean?"

"Things like newspaper articles, senor. Whenever someone is killed in a little town like that, it makes the papers. Also, the police reports are open to the public, and anyone can see them. This is a very big deal to us, senor. We must know as much as possible."

An astute businessman, Williams always knew the score. He also knew he needed Garcia's drugs to keep his cash flow going. "Yeah, you're right. Tell you what. I don't know anything about this Litchfield shit but I'll call my lawyer. He kisses my ass whenever I need him to. He can get those newspapers in Litchfield and whatever the hell else I tell him to."

That satisfied Garcia about as much as anything could at the moment. "Gracias." He again clutched his cross necklace. "Today is the holy day, and everything will be closed. But call me as soon as you can this week."

The thought of a Sabbath did not register to Williams. "My ass. I'll call my lawyer right now." He swung his arm and pointed to the floor for emphasis, as if Garcia could see it. "That bitch always does what I tell him to."

"Whatever you say," responded Garcia, with a hint of a shock at the reference to a holy day as he hung up the receiver.

*****

Williams had barely broken the connection and was already dialing his attorney, Brian Smart, one of the shadiest lawyers on the south side. Unlike others in his profession, who usually enjoyed the niceties of upscale offices, Smart operated from the first floor of a shabby three-story brick building on a cramped two-lane street. His inauspicious surroundings masked his income as he made almost as much money as Williams, bringing in most of it under the table, handed off by any drug dealer, drunk driver, and wife-beater who stumbled through his door. He loved to brag to his buddies that he had graduated second-to-last in law school and still made more money than 90 percent of his classmates.

Few had found a way to skirt the law as well as Smart, who dressed in brightly colored clothes more appropriate for a late teenager than the forty-something man he was. Williams also helped Smart feed his two addictions; heroin and sex.

Smart was sitting in his office, about ready to shoot up, when the phone rang. "Brian, my man, Tyrone here. Need your help on something, need it right now."

Williams filled Smart in about the accident and the missing money, as well as Garcia's concerns. He emphasized that he needed the necessary information "faster than shit, bro. Get your ass on it." Smart assured him that he could get everything he needed, and he asked if Williams could send a few ounces of his product over, and maybe a couple of girls, too. Williams roared with laughter and said, "I'll give ya the best fix you ever had, and two sweet pieces of ass for ya."

He hung up, and Smart reached for his needle once again. He then went to work on Williams's needs. First, he logged in to his computer to determine what ISP district Litchfield was in. Finding it was District 18, he obtained the telephone number and called.

On the call, Smart confirmed the accident and asked for a copy of the accident report to be sent to his office. However, he was told that he would have to contact the ISP record section in Springfield on Monday. He was also advised that it would take at least two weeks before the accident report and any related documents would be available.

After arriving at his office on Monday morning, he contacted the ISP record section in Springfield and requested both the accident report and any other paperwork relating to the accident. The record section employee agreed to send the documents, but indicated it would be around three weeks before they would be available, for a fee of ten dollars. Small paid the fee with his credit card.

Next, he went back to the Internet and found the name of a local researcher in Litchfield, a retired widow in her late seventies named Peg, who just happened to be arriving home from a shopping trip when Smart called. He played up to the lady, identifying himself and telling her that he needed articles about the accident. Peg's busybody ways took over, telling him she had not heard of this accident, and that if anyone knew about it, she would have.

Smart, though, continued to butter Peg up, and by the end of the conversation, she was practically flirting with him. He offered to send her fifty dollars for her troubles, but she declined, laughing that he was so nice that she'd do the work for free.

He gave Peg his office address and made a couple more playful comments before he heard a knock on his door, forcing him to hang up. Waiting were the prostitutes that Williams had sent over, two girls who were barely eighteen, but the kind Smart wanted to satisfy his animal lust for the rest of that Monday afternoon.

*****

As expected, the ISP accident and related reports were received during the third week. Peg got on Smart's request the next day and by Wednesday, Smart had received copies of every newspaper article she could find, along with a note that included her cell phone number, e-mail address, and a link to her Facebook page.

When all the information was in hand, Smart placed a call to Williams, who sent over one of his people, a seventeen-year-old junkie working for his next fix, to pick it up. Williams was sitting in the office of his brown-brick $2 million mansion when the boy arrived with the packet of papers, and Williams handed him a dime bag of crack for his time. Within an hour, Williams had determined the identity of the trooper who investigated the accident, the name of the towing firm that handled the call, the name of the ambulance company, and where the wrecked Camaro had been towed. The field report, filled out by Trooper James Kincaid, reported that only $1,263,000, stuffed in one black nylon duffel bag, had been recovered from the car.

Williams knew over $2.5 million had been in the vehicle, because he was present and had watched Ramirez place both bags in the trunk. Enraged, he seized a glass of beer that was sitting in front of him and hurled it against the wall, shattering it in a thousand pieces. The glass barely missed his favorite prostitute, a glassy-eyed, dreadlocked, lanky number named Shanni. "Those assholes!" he screamed. "Those son-of-a-bitchin' assholes!"

He dismissed Shanni from the room and called Garcia, shouting with fury into the phone. "I got the info you wanted on the thing with Ramirez. The field report from this asshole state trooper says that only $1.2 mil and change was recovered. They only mention one damn bag." Williams pointed angrily at the receiver, as if Garcia could see him. "I saw that little prick Ramirez of yours put two in the car with my own damn eyes."

Stunned, Garcia turned and stared directly at his own receiver. "There was only $1.2 million? That's less than half of what you owe me."

"You heard me, bro." Williams was starting to calm down, if only slightly. "They only turned in one bag of money. Not one bitchin' word about the other bag or what was in it."

Garcia did not share Williams' fiery temper, but he simmered, nonetheless. His voice cooled. "Then where the hell did it go?"

"I don't know, I don't know. Maybe it was that trooper. Those guys always want everyone to think they're the good guys, but they always got their hands out, like everyone else. Or the tow truck driver. Son of a bitch is probably scraping to make ends meet and thought he had easy money sitting in that car." Williams kept theorizing as his vengeance simmered. "Or the dickhead who drives the ambulance. Hell, maybe it was all of them. Never know with people. They'll do anything for a buck, and lie their asses off to do it."

The irony of that statement was not lost on Garcia, but sitting in the opulence of his mansion, he clearly did not care. He also had another suspect in mind. "What about you? Did you screw me out of this?"

"What the…." Williams had bristled at the insinuation the last time Garcia broached that subject, and based on Garcia's tone, he was serious this time. "What the… You really think I could have done this?"

"All I know is I lost over $2 million," said Garcia coldly. "We had a deal. I'm sorry that my friend Pascal got killed doing it, but at the end of the day, senor, I'm still out the money. Part of it is sitting with the state police, and part is gone. Meanwhile, you're sitting there with a pile of my drugs that you're making money on, and I never saw a cent off it."

Williams rarely cared how he spoke to others, but Garcia, his top supplier, was too important to offend. He squirmed in his chair and began to stammer. "Listen, listen, my man. I mean, I would never do that to you. You're my man. We been like brothers for years in this business. You got to know I would never do that to you."

Garcia was moved, but only slightly. He tilted his head and pursed his lips, in silent agreement. "So you say, my friend. But you would have as much to gain from this as the trooper, or that man in the tow truck."

That gave Williams the opportunity he needed. "Yeah, bro, but you're forgetting something. If I took that money, you could send your guys in here and blow me away. You'd have my ass in the morgue before I knew it."

Garcia knew Williams was right on that point. He also knew that it would be easy for him to find out if Williams was the guilty party since the cartel had so many connections in Chicago and could easily get any information they needed on Williams. "All right, all right. So you're not the guilty one, my friend." Garcia's tone became chillingly authoritative. "But I need to know who is."

Williams breathed a little deeper. "You and me both, bro. I mean, I got to know myself. I wanna help you catch the bastards who did this."

He could hear the drumming of Garcia's fingers on the desk through the receiver before the cartel king began to speak. "Very well. I have an idea that I've used before. My old friend Juan Rodrequs, rest his soul, taught it to me. Hire a private eye to go to this Litchfield place and ask questions. Tell him to pose as an insurance investigator and see what he can learn."

Williams cocked his head, trying to figure out what Garcia meant. "You mean, act like he's an insurance guy, doing a report?"

"Si, si. That is the best way to learn anything."

Still exhaling in relief that Garcia no longer suspected him, Williams sat back in his chair, letting the tension out of his body. His voice assumed an easier tone. "No problem, man. I got a guy who does that shit all the time. I'd trust that dude with my life."

"Very well. Get back to me as soon as you know something."

Seconds after hearing the click from Garcia's disconnect, Williams was on the phone with his guy, private investigator Jose Hernandez. Like many in his profession, Hernandez knew how to walk a fine line between lawful behavior and criminal activity, and he counted clients on both sides.

The son of a cop in Monterrey, Mexico, Hernandez was drawn to the excitement of investigative work at a young age. His father, though, knew the real money lay in America and, unlike many of his compatriots, applied for legal citizenship when Jose was seven. The family ended up in Chicago, where they lived in a modest six-room bungalow on the near south side, away from much of the drug dealing and gunfire that raged further on.

Hernandez had met Williams when they attended the same Chicago public high school, but Hernandez's life had taken a more peaceful turn. Unlike Williams, who hit the streets looking for his fortune any way he could find it, Hernandez had attended community college, borrowed the money to start his business, and now spent countless hours in the flat that housed his two-room office on the south side. The resulting lack of exercise and never-ending doughnuts and sandwiches at the desk led to the 230 sagging pounds that were far too many for a man of his five-foot-six height.

While his body was lacking, his mind made up the difference. He was innovative in thought, tenacious in getting the job done, and had no problem associating with dealers or pimps if it meant a bigger payday.

Williams was a periodic client of Hernandez, especially recently. Eighteen months ago, Williams hired him to tail his fourth wife, whom he suspected of infidelity with a rival dealer. Hernandez proved him right and looked the other way when he heard the news that Williams's goons beat her so badly that she ended up in an intensive care unit for two weeks. Needless to say, she received nothing in the quickie divorce that Brian Smart handled, and she quickly left town as soon as the hospital discharged her.

When Williams wanted to meet with someone, it was understood that they would come to him, rather than vice versa. Even with a friend like Hernandez, that was the case. As a result, Hernandez climbed in his dark gray Escalade and drove the two miles to Williams's mansion for a clandestine meeting. Since money was on the line, Williams was all business, having dismissed his whores until that evening.

Williams advised Hernandez of the particulars of the case and suggested that he leave immediately for the Litchfield area to track down and interview people who were at the scene. Though Hernandez was facing a heavy workload and had rearranged his schedule just to be at the meeting, Williams told him that he'd make plenty of money on this case and needed a resolution as soon as possible.

There was also another suggestion. Williams told Hernandez to take along Carlos Santiago, one of his most trusted soldiers, to assist in whatever way needed. Hernandez instantly knew what Williams meant. Santiago was some of the muscle behind the violence in the gang, and the mere sight of him was enough to scare anyone to death.

Like Hernandez, the thirty-year-old Santiago was Mexican-born, a product of Baja California who made his way across the border at age fourteen to land a string of menial jobs in the American Southwest. He eventually made his way eastward to Texas, where he acquired his lifelong fancy for cowboy boots and attire, which paired well with his straight black hair and handlebar-style mustache.

That was the best you could say about Santiago, who stood five-foot-ten with hulking shoulders and forearms that hid the paunch where many of his 260 pounds sat. He wore a lengthy scar on his right cheek, the result of being struck with a beer bottle in a bar fight in his favorite watering hole on the south side. He also strode with a slight limp, created by a bullet from a rival gang member. While Santiago walked away from the altercation, the rival was carried out under a white sheet.

While in southern Texas, Santiago figured out that he could triple his income by helping some of his old friends move drugs across the border and, if that didn't work, then using his fearsome persona to frighten others into doing what he wanted. Now in Chicago, he had secured a job with Williams, and for the last nine years was one of the most hated, and best-paid, henchmen on the south side. He did whatever Williams asked of him, keeping the other gang members in line, handling drug sales for his boss on his good days, and murders or hijackings on his worst.

Santiago, as expected, was ready to go whenever Williams asked, and he was quickly summoned from the same bar where he had received the scar. Hernandez, meanwhile, made the arrangements and secured a reservation for a double room at the Prairie View Inn & Suites in Litchfield for the following evening, December 30.

The two men left at daybreak for the five-hour drive down Interstate 55 from Chicago to Litchfield. Riding in the back seat of the Escalade was a brown, genuine-leather carrying case that held copies of the newspaper articles relating to the crash, the accident report submitted by the trooper on the scene, the field report, and the tow-in report. The reports not only revealed the identity of Trooper James Kincaid, but also the name and location of the towing company,

Joe's 24-Hour Towing in Farmersville, also located on I-55, twenty miles north of Litchfield.

The tow-in report was signed by both Joe Murphy and Kincaid. It indicated that one duffel bag, containing an unspecified amount of money, was found in the trunk of the accident vehicle and had been removed as evidence along with a cell phone belonging to the accident victim. Murphy's towing business was just off the interstate on the eastern edge of Farmersville, and as fate would have it, the Escalade would pass within clear view of the business on the way to Litchfield.

"Right there," Hernandez took his right hand off the wheel and extended his index finger. "That's the towing business that handled the crash."

"Yep," grumbled Santiago. He instinctively balled his right hand and jammed it into his left hand, as if punching. "Looking forward to meeting that guy."

Hernandez knew that Santiago could be a loose cannon, so he reacted immediately. "Not now. We need to get information first. If we hurt the guy, that's not going to give us what we need."

"Right, right," Santiago reluctantly agreed. "I'll let you do the talking."

Twenty minutes down the road, the men pulled into Litchfield and made their way to the Prairie View Inn & Suites. Despite the normal 3 p.m. check-in time, the desk clerk, a slightly-built millennial named Austin, kept peering anxiously at Santiago before letting the men have the room early. Hernandez and Santiago dropped their bags in Room 273 and then grabbed some take-out at one of the fast-food restaurants that line the west side of Litchfield. They gulped their lunch in the Escalade before backtracking their way back up I-55 to Farmersville to visit the towing business.

As they pulled in, Hernandez turned and looked Santiago squarely in the eye. He was one of the rare men who did not fear Santiago, knowing if the henchman pulled anything, his school chum Tyrone Williams had his back. Santiago, then, would be the next homicide victim in Chicago.

"All right," Hernandez said firmly. "I'm going to do the talking"—a reasonable directive since Hernandez spoke perfect English, while Santiago had a heavy accent.

"Fine," sighed Santiago, knowing who was in charge. "I'll do whatever you say."

Joe Murphy was sitting at his grease-stained desk finishing his own lunch, a ham and Swiss on wheat with a little bag of barbecue chips and a coffee, when Hernandez and Santiago walked in. Hernandez clutched a clipboard, as if to take notes during the interview.

"Hello," said Hernandez in a businesslike manner, extending his hand. "My name is Jose Hernandez. I'm an insurance investigator for American Mutual." He slipped his fingers into the breast pocket of his brown, long-sleeved dress shirt and pulled out a fake business card, handing it to Murphy. Hernandez then turned to Santiago, who nodded in greeting. "This is my associate. We're here to ask you a few questions about an accident that happened around here on the morning of November 27. It was a car crash just south of here, a Camaro that left the roadway and smashed into a tree, killing the driver."

"Yeah, I remember." Murphy had a textbook memory for tow jobs and could recall the slightest detail in his business from years before. He glanced at the business card, set it on the desk, and took off his cap, rubbing his forehead with the back of his palm. "What can I do for you?"

Hernandez and Santiago each plopped down in a white plastic chair, bought at a discount store and more suited for porch use than for an office. "We see from the accident report that it happened just south of Route 48. That was the next exit down from here, right?" Hernandez knew full well where it was, but feigned ignorance and let Murphy nod in confirmation. "It was on the west frontage road. Were you at the scene?"

"Sure was." Murphy reclined in his chair and clasped his hands behind his head. His chair creaked and groaned under the strain of his shifting weight. "I remember it well. Car was crashed beyond recognition. One of the worst I've seen in a while."

Hernandez also knew to pretend to have compassion for the driver, like most other big-company insurance workers. "Yes, it was too bad. The driver was so young." He shook his head in mock sadness. "I've done this for a long time, and you never really get used to it."

"Tell me about it," said Murphy, shaking his own head. "I've been in that truck for over fifty years and seen it all."

"Bet you have," replied Hernandez, returning to the matter at hand. His eyes swung back to the clipboard. "Was there anything unusual about the scene that night?"

"The crash itself? No. I mean, that happens all the time," said Murphy, shrugging to indicate nonchalance. "Driver loses control, flies off the roadway, wraps it around a tree. Probably fell asleep at the wheel. I handle that several times a year." He rolled his eyes. "But what was unusual about this one was what was in the trunk."

"Oh? What was that?"

"There was a really large amount of money that was in the trunk of that car. It was more than anything I'd ever seen on this job."

"Money?" Hernandez scribbled with a black ink pen on his clipboard. "How much money?"

"Had to be over a million dollars, easy. It was in this black duffel bag, stuffed to the top." Murphy pulled his hands apart, to indicate the size of the bag. "Money was just bursting out of it."

Hernandez raised an eyebrow. "Did you actually see this bag, or did someone just tell you about it?"

"Nope. Saw it with my own eyes. The trooper on the scene showed it to me." Murphy lifted the white Styrofoam cup that held his coffee and took a sip.

"Uh-huh. And that trooper was…James Kincaid?" Hernandez shuffled through the sheaf of papers, pretending to verify the information.

"Yep. I've known him for a long time. We've worked a lot of accident scenes together."

"Go back to this money in the trunk. You said there was a duffel bag?"

"Yeah, kind of like what you see people holding when they're going for a workout. Or, like baseball players carry their bats back and forth in."

Hernandez still wondered how many bags there were. "You say you saw just one?"

"Yeah, just the one bag. That was the only thing in the trunk."

"Nothing else?"

"Nope," replied Murphy, shaking his head in affirmation. "That was it."

Hernandez kept writing on his clipboard. Periodically, he would peer into Murphy's face to see if he seemed to be hiding anything. Murphy, though, looked straight back at him, so Hernandez continued on.

"What happened to this bag of money?"

"Well, like I said, I first saw it when it was in the trunk. Kincaid then took it out and set it on the hood of his squad car."

"And what happened then?"

"It stayed there until Jim Peal arrived. He's Kincaid's supervisor, and Kincaid asked him to come in and assess the scene with him. Kincaid asked me to stay around until Peal got there."

Hernandez's pen gave out, and he reached into his breast pocket for another one. "I see. And where did the money go from there?"

Murphy hesitated, wondering why there were so many questions about the money. Almost nothing had been asked of the car, driver, or surroundings. Still, he answered the question directly. "Into Peal's squad car. Peal drove up, talked to Kincaid for a while, and then they put the bag into Peal's car. Took it to headquarters from there."

Doggedly, Hernandez kept pushing for answers. "What did you do then?"

"They signed the towing report, handed me my copy, and took off. I finished hooking up the car and dragged it back here." Murphy reached for a snack cake to finish off his lunch but continued looking directly at Hernandez the entire time, increasingly wary of what was going on.

As Hernandez politely grilled Murphy, Santiago walked outside to inspect the mangled car. In the daylight, the remnants of the car were even more gruesome than they were the night of the accident, and metal was sticking everywhere. The horrid sight of Ramirez' brain matter still remained on the wheel and the seat. Santiago grinned slightly, barely flinching at the sight.

Glancing back inside to see if Murphy was watching, Santiago saw that the tow driver was occupied with Hernandez's interview, and he took the chance to visually inspect the inside of the car from all sides. He then checked the trunk, which was ajar and could be readily opened. Satisfied, he returned to the office inside the garage, where Hernandez was not missing a step.

"Was anyone else around the car at the time? You know, passersby, someone walking or biking, anyone who wanted to see what was going on?"

"Nope. It was just me, Kincaid, and Peal. I don't even remember any cars who drove by us. That's just a frontage road, you know, and it doesn't get traveled too often, especially not at that hour."

"Yes, yes. Was the body still in the car?"

"No, thank God." Murphy rolled his eyes and tilted his head to the left to indicate relief. "It was gone by the time I got there. The ambulance had already been there and gone. I wasn't called until later."

"Hmm." Hernandez was still doing the best acting job he could muster. "What's next… oh, yeah. We'd like to interview the trooper as well. What's his name again?." Hernandez again flipped through the papers, as if to find out. "There it is, James Kincaid. Was he a night-shift cop, or when does he work?"

"He's on the 11-to-7 shift, every night. Has been for years."

"I see. And, do you know where that guy lives?"

In his half-century in the garage, Murphy had dealt with all sorts of insurance adjustors with a myriad of questions. Never before, though, had he been asked that one. "Well," he began, unsure if he should answer. "He lives in a trailer in White City, just south of here."

"White City, you say? Hmm, never heard of that. You said it's just south of here?"

"Yeah. It's a little place, near Mount Olive." Murphy cocked his head quizzically. "Why do you want to know?"

"We would like to interview him while we're here," said Hernandez, pressing his lips together and waving his hand to blow off the question. "Just trying to save myself a little time. This trailer you spoke of. Do you know the address, or where it is?"

"Off Route 138, back in some trees…." Shocked, Murphy spoke deliberately, dragging out every word.

"And, you said there was only one bag of money?"

"Yeah, like I said." Murphy's ire was starting to rise. "I already told you. There was only one bag—"

Santiago then chimed in, unable to restrain himself. He stepped toward Murphy, flashing his trademark fearsome glare. "Only one bag, you say?"

Murphy's doubts were now confirmed, and he rose from his chair, pointing his finger at the two phonies in front of him. "Hey, what the hell is going on? Who are you guys? You sure as hell aren't insurance investigators!"

Hernandez and Santiago simply looked at each other with blank stares, knowing their ruse was over. They turned on their heels, almost in unison, and walked out the door as Murphy looked on in amazement. He kept watching as both men climbed into the gray Escalade and peeled off, heading for the overpass and exit to get back to the interstate.

*****

Few words were exchanged as Hernandez and Santiago drove back to Litchfield and Room 273 of the Prairie View. Any conversation was unnecessary, because enough information had been gleaned from the interview that a back-and-forth debate was pointless.

Once in the room, Hernandez pulled out his cell phone and called Tyrone Williams, who was sitting up in his king-sized bed, dressed in a black silk robe. He was as blunt as usual. "Whatcha got for me?"

"We talked to the tow truck driver, the guy named Joe Murphy. Older guy, seemed credible. He told us that the trooper found one bag of money and transported it back to headquarters. Said he had seen only one bag with his own eyes."

"What the hell… So you're telling me this old guy saw only one bag?" Williams was naturally distrustful. "How you know that he's telling the truth? How the hell do we know if he's got the other bag stuck somewhere, thinking he's gonna retire on it?"

Countless people had lied to Hernandez in his many investigations over the years, but he did not think Murphy was one of them. "I don't see it, Ty. I think he's telling the truth. He seemed to have it all together and kept looking straight at us. Never gave any hint he was lying."

"Son of a bitch. Anyone else there that night? Anyone else who could have screwed us?"

"Nope. He didn't mention anyone at all."

"Well, I'll be… Hell, maybe this Murphy asshole wasn't involved after all. That brings us around to that trooper, Kincaid, or whoever the hell he is. Whatcha got on him?"

"Quite a bit. The tow truck guy told us where the trooper lives and when he works. I gotta tell you, I think he's our guy. When the tow driver acted the way he did, it confirmed it in my mind. The trooper's the one who took the bag."

"Yeah, me, too. Sumbitch probably thought he could get away with it." Williams saw nothing wrong with that statement. He rolled out of bed, sat on the edge, and crouched like a tiger about to strike, waving his finger at nothing in particular. "Where'd you say this dickhead lives?"

Hernandez was used to Williams' coarseness and could tolerate it, since he was one of his most frequent, and highest-paying, clients. "In a trailer in this little town called White City. It's about ten miles south of here. He works nights, 11-to-7, all the time." Hernandez added the words that Williams wanted to hear. "Time to pay this guy a little visit. We'll find out exactly where he lives, what he drives, when he comes and goes."

"Damn right you will," barked Williams. "And if he's our guy, I'll put his ass in the graveyard." He punched the "end" button on his smartphone, slammed it into his pocket, and threw himself back on the bed, staring at the ceiling and simmering in thought.

*****

The next morning, December 31, dawned cool and clear, a beautiful early winter day in the Illinois prairies. Juan Hernandez did not notice, and Carlos Santiago could not have cared less. Their only concern was finding the exact location of James Kincaid's trailer. It was now 9:36 a.m. and they knew that, by that time, Kincaid should be home from his shift, assuming he had worked the previous night.

Eleven minutes later, the Escalade was pulling off the Interstate 55 exit ramp and into White City. After slowly driving up and down the several streets that made up the town, they made their way to the edge of the village, where they saw a mobile home sitting at the end of a lengthy driveway, partially obscured by a stand of trees. Suspecting this might be the place, Hernandez slowed the Escalade to provide a better view of the property. There, they saw a marked Illinois State Police car, parked in the driveway next to the mobile home.

The presence of the squad car was proof in their minds that they had found the right place, and they returned to Litchfield and the motel. Once inside Room 273, Hernandez again dialed Williams,

"We got it," said Hernandez. "We saw where the trooper lives. It's a trailer in the location that Murphy gave us, and there's a squad car in front. White City is so damn small, it has to be him. Can't be anyone else."

"Get your ass back here then," commanded Williams. "I gotta get a plan together. Leave as soon as I hang up."

Hernandez and Williams had never unpacked and only had to collect their toiletries and dirty laundry bags. They proceeded to the front desk, where it was four minutes past check-out time of 11 a.m. But the same millennial, Austin, was working and happily told them that was no problem, not to worry about it. Using the word "sir" several times, Austin readily accepted the key cards and smiled a shaky grin as he bid the travelers goodbye.

Hernandez and Santiago walked outside to the Escalade for the trip back to Chicago. Once there, they met Williams at his residence, where they spent New Year's Eve partying with numerous friends and fellow gang members.

CHAPTER 9

The next morning found Hernandez and Santiago, both with hangovers, in the great room of Williams' mansion, surrounded by piles of bags of drugs and a small arsenal of weaponry. Santiago strolled around the room, smiling at the power of the guns in front of him, particularly the assault rifles that could kill a crowd of people in seconds. Hernandez, meanwhile, studied his notes in preparation for the meeting.

Finally, Williams strode in and snapped his fingers for his houseboy, a nineteen-year-old named Lamar who had been orphaned seven years ago, when both parents overdosed, and now worked for room, board, and all the hookers he could handle. Lamar asked each if they wanted anything, and the two visitors said no. Williams, though, asked for his favorite cereal and a bottle of vodka.

"All right, then," said Williams, calling the meeting to order. He plopped down in an oversized black leather recliner. "Anyone here not think this asshole cop stole the money?"

Hernandez spoke for Santiago, who lovingly rubbed the barrel of an AR-15 before crouching down in a mock shooting position. "Nope. He's our guy. No one else had the opportunity to steal the money. He's got to be the one."

"Yeah." Williams lightly tapped his fingers together before reaching for his shot glass. "That sumbitch. Thought he could get away with it, didn't he? Well, we'll show his ass." He turned back to face Hernandez. "Do a complete background check on him. I want to know everything that piece of shit is doing. How much he makes, how much he's got in the bank, who he's sleeping with, how often he plays with himself, anything you can find."

"No problem," said Hernandez, the words that Williams always expected. "I'll get on it."

Williams sprang from his recliner and paced like a caged animal, waving his right hand in anger. "I'll get his ass. I'll get his ass if it's the last thing I do. He ain't gonna get away with screwing me."

Santiago interrupted. He was mesmerized by a ten-inch machete that he found lying on an end table and made several stabbing motions with it. "I'll do it. Just say the word."

"All right, bro. He's yours. And when you do, make sure that asshole knows damn well who we are and that he dies as bad a death as possible. I want to send that bastard to hell in style."

That ended the conversation, and Hernandez and Santiago left the room. Williams sat back down in the recliner. He had done his usual thing with guys who worked for him. Now, he had to change gears and deal with someone who had the real power. He took a slight breath and pressed the numbers into his phone.

"Garcia here," said the voice on the other end. Diego Garcia had been waiting for word, and as he sat alone at the head of his palatial dining room table on this late morning, he was in no mood for small talk.

"Got the news you wanted, man," said Williams, smiling weakly on the other end. "I sent my people out, and they got some information. Looks like our guy is the state cop who investigated the accident."

Three years in charge of the cartel made Garcia as distrustful as Williams. "Are you sure about that? How do you know?"

"I did what you told me to do, bro. Sent my best guys down to Litchfield, posing as insurance investigators. The old shit who's the tow truck driver seemed clean and checked out. We think it's Kincaid, the shithead cop, and he's acting alone."

"All right, then." Garcia needed more, since plenty was riding on it. His voice retained its coolness. "What are you doing about it?"

"Got it covered, man." Williams waved his hand in the air, for reassurance that Garcia could not see. "I got my PI doing a financial check. He's gonna turn up anything on any money that Kincaid has. If that bastard is in financial trouble, we're gonna know it. And it'll prove, once and for all, that he's the asshole we need."

Garcia then pressed Williams for detailed descriptions of Hernandez and Santiago, both of whom he was familiar with, since he made a point of knowing all the major players in the many cities in which he did business. But he wanted to know more and fired a barrage of questions at Williams about their trustworthiness, professional qualities, background, toughness, and willingness to do whatever was asked. Satisfied with the answers, Garcia was through for the time being.

"Very well. Get this all done as soon as possible, and keep me informed." Garcia broke the connection and slapped his open palm on the cherry wood table in front of him. He then summoned his butler to bring him his usual lunch, a healthy choice of vegetable soup with wheat bread on the side and bottled water to drink.

*****

In January in Chicago, it's not unusual to have several inches of snow on the ground. It makes life that much more unpleasant in the south side ghettos, where violence and poverty battle for supremacy.

Driving to his office, Hernandez had other things to think about on this morning than the snow. First on the agenda was the financial background check on James Kincaid, ordered by Tyrone Williams, who had zero patience for waiting.

Hernandez arrived at the flat that was home to his office, unlocked the door, and strode over the newly installed navy carpeting to his desk, in the second of the two rooms. On the way, he stopped at a small side table, fired up the Keurig machine for his morning coffee, and rifled through a sheaf of messages on small pink sheets left by his answering service. Once the Keurig was done, he settled into his white leather office chair and turned on the computer.

Several screens, a password, and a few clicks later, Hernandez was staring at a cache of personal and financial information on Kincaid. First, he learned that Kincaid had been married and divorced twice, and that between the marriages, he had four children, two from the first and two from the second. The oldest, both girls, were college-age, while the others were five and seven.

The salaries of state employees are public record, and through that, Hernandez determined that Kincaid earned $82,000 per year. Divorce documents are also public record, and they revealed that Kincaid was shelling out $800 a month to his second wife for child support. He was also on the hook for $6,000 a year for college expenses for the other two daughters.

Hernandez kept scanning his eyes over the divorce documents and found that, once Kincaid retired, his first wife would receive half of his pension, which would be approximately $41,000 per year. As he read, Hernandez wrote all of this information down on a yellow legal pad, adding and subtracting as he went along.

After considering all the figures, Hernandez determined that Kincaid was left with about $25,400 a year. That, more than anything, convinced him that Kincaid was their man.

CHAPTER 10

On Monday, January 11, Hernandez was back at the mansion for a conference with Williams to report his findings. "He's the one, isn't he?" snapped Williams, eyeing the printouts that Hernandez handed him. "James Kincaid. James Kincaid… I'll pin that sumbitch to the wall if it's the last thing I do."

The meeting lasted barely an hour before Hernandez was on his way back to the office. He had barely started the Escalade outside when Williams was dialing Diego Garcia.

Garcia was listening to a CD of Mexican folk music in his dark-wood private study when the phone rang, and he turned down the volume on the enormous home entertainment system that looked like it belonged at a concert venue. No hellos were exchanged. "What do you have for me?"

"My guy verified all the information. It's definitely the trooper, this James Kincaid dude. He's hurtin' for money and has a shitload of obligations to his exes and his kids. He's heading off into a shitty retirement and probably took our money to help out."

"My money, senor," corrected Garcia. "What next?"

"I'm gonna take his ass out. He ain't gonna get away with doing this to you." Williams had caught Garcia's correction. "First, obviously, we're gonna go in and get the money, find it wherever it is, pull it out of his ass if we have to. I got guys that know how to do it and won't quit 'til they do. Either way, his ass is mine. I'll put him in the ground for what he did to you."

As the most powerful cartel leader in northern Mexico, Garcia expected loyalty and appreciated it even in someone like Tyrone Williams. But he still had reservations. "You must be very certain about this. It is a great risk to go after a police officer, as you describe. I mean, the repercussions, my friend. The consequences."

"Damn right, I'm certain. This sumbitch is our man. And he's got the money somewhere, sitting in a bank, buried in his frickin' backyard, in his shithole trailer, somewhere. And like I said, he's gonna pay for it."

"Well, my friend, my primary concern is not whether he lives or dies. If he has to die, then so be it." Garcia had seen plenty of men killed to protect the cartel and wasn't worried if one more had to. "My first concern is the money. I want the money before anything else."

Garcia's business sense was taking over and, since Rodrequs had been taken out, he had a need to do things himself, his own way. He liked the fact that Williams was willing to do the job for him, but that was not Garcia's style. He also knew that Williams was too rash, too impulsive, and could not be trusted alone.

As Garcia pondered the situation, an uncomfortable pause fell over the line, and Williams became antsy. "Hey, man, you still there?"

"Yes, I'm still here," Garcia replied absentmindedly as he formulated his plans.

"What do you want from me, man?"

"I will send one of my men up there from Mexico. He'll meet your guy, the Carlos Santiago that you've mentioned, in the Litchfield area. They'll take care of the problem as I tell them to."

Williams uttered words that rarely rolled off his tongue. "Whatever you say, man. I'll do whatever you tell me to."

"Very well, my friend. I'll be in touch when I'm ready to move. Have Santiago ready when I need him." Garcia hung up the phone, reached for the volume on his music, and sat back in his chair, relaxing to the strains of the rhythm.

*****

After several minutes of contemplation, Garcia picked up his phone once more and summoned his second-in-command. Twelve minutes later, Miguel Perez was walking through the door of the study.

Perez filled the role that Garcia himself had been to Juan Rodrequs, but was much more violent in doing so. Garcia dubbed him "the fixer" because he was the guy who could take care of any problem. Standing five-foot-ten and weighing a robust 200 pounds, Perez looked more like a gym instructor than a drug enforcer. He also spoke fluent English, so good that it was hard to believe he was not an American citizen.

He had grown up on the streets of El Paso, across the Rio Grande, the son of illegal immigrants who cashed in on the American welfare system. But Perez had bigger plans and learned that income from the drug trade could set him up for life. Garcia had met Perez when he was sixteen and had taken a liking to the industrious lad, whose ambition was matched only by his eagerness to please.

Unlike many members of powerful cartels, Perez was college-educated, a graduate of Ohio State University who had put himself through school by selling drugs from his dorm room. His business proved so lucrative that he not only covered all of his tuition, but he also cruised around campus in a late-model BMW, leased from a local dealer. He earned a degree in international business, which he used to assist Garcia with the day-to-day operations of the cartel.

Running a large drug cartel calls for all sorts of skills, and Perez had plenty. In the morning, he could be at Garcia's side, crunching numbers and making calls. In the afternoon, he could physically assist the loading of trucks of drugs that were smuggled under the noses of lax border patrol agents. In the evening, he could be holding a knife to an enemy's throat, smiling as he did it.

Unyielding in his loyalty to Garcia and the cartel, Perez stepped into the study and saluted, as if awaiting orders. In his other hand was a laptop for taking notes. "Diego, my friend," he cheerily greeted. "What may I do for you on this lovely day?"

"Sit down," Garcia directed him into a tan suede easy chair that sat across from his desk. He reached for a sifter. "Brandy, senor?"

"Ah, yes," said Perez, grinning in approval. "You always know what I like." Garcia poured a glass and handed it to Perez, who savored his first sip. "And you always have the best, my friend."

"Men of success should have nothing less," boasted Garcia, channeling the arrogance exhibited by his old boss, Rodrequs. The pleasantries ended there. "I have a job for you."

In his usual great detail, Garcia briefed Perez on the shipment from Chicago, the accident, the stolen money, and the likely suspect, James Kincaid. Perez carefully typed the information into his computer, frequently looking up from his keyboard to look his boss in the eye. He asked several pointed questions as Garcia spoke.

When Garcia finished, Perez hit "save" and shut the cover of his laptop. "All right. What do I need to do?"

"You will go to this Litchfield place and rent a hotel room. I am asking for Williams to send us Carlos Santiago. You may remember that name." Knowing all the associates of the cartel's trade, Perez nodded in agreement. He remembered having met Santiago once or twice on his trips to Chicago for Garcia.

Garcia leaned back in his office chair. "I know you are overseeing the drug transport to Chicago and Atlanta," he said, looking directly at Perez. "Once those transports are completed, I want you to meet Santiago in Litchfield." He paused for effect. "When do you think you will be able to leave?"

Perez thought for a moment before his response. "I believe I could meet Santiago on January 25. Then I will call our friend Williams and make those arrangements. I will also provide you with Santiago's phone number."

"Very good." Garcia nodded in approval. "The two of you will put the trooper under surveillance for several days to learn his routine, what he does every day, when he comes and goes. Then, when you know all of that, go back to his residence and confront him. Get the money back that way."

Perez looked at Garcia quizzically. "If I am not successful, shouldn't I kill him?"

"No," replied Garcia firmly. "I don't want to get into killing American police officers. There's too much risk, and what we're doing is risky enough already. But make sure he knows you are there. I want to scare him into doing what we tell him to." He tapped his fingers on the desk and picked up a gold-plated ink pen, which he held like a trophy. "We have the power, and he doesn't. He needs to realize that."

"Very well, senor. I will do as you say," said Perez, nodding reverently. "As always."

"I know you will, senor," Garcia returned the respect. "Now, if you will excuse me. I must call Williams to inform him of my plans."

Perez doffed his hand across his temple in another informal salute and turned to exit the study. Garcia then dialed Williams who, despite his own wish to annihilate Kincaid, readily agreed to his supplier's more methodical, less violent idea.

Garcia gave Williams the cell number of Miguel Perez and told him to share it with Carlos Santiago. He directed that their meeting was to take place Monday, January 18, and that Williams was to do nothing "until you have heard from me, my friend." Garcia hung up without a goodbye, leaving Williams staring at the receiver.

Business attended to, Garcia then reached for a homemade DVD of his favorite pornographic movies, as wife Rosa was on a shopping excursion, as usual, and had left without saying goodbye.

CHAPTER 11

The next morning was Tuesday, January 12, and James Kincaid was taking a late break before his shift ended. As the clock struck 6 a.m., he was drinking coffee at Art's Motel and Restaurant in Farmersville, a landmark for decades on Route 66 before Interstate 55 was built.

The waitress, a buxom redhead named Sherri with a large flowered tattoo on her upper thigh that was clearly visible beneath her short rust-colored dress, flashed a welcoming smile at Kincaid each time he ordered another cup. Now flush with a pocketful of cash, he had become her biggest tipper in recent weeks, a fact that made her even more attentive.

He was on his third cup, and Sherri was leaning forward across his table even more than before when Kincaid's portable radio went off. It was the throaty voice of John Edwards, the ever-present voice of District 18, who advised of a report of a disabled vehicle at mile post 75 of northbound I-55, three miles north of the Farmersville exit.

Kincaid rose, tossed a ten-dollar bill on the table to pay for his coffee and the tip, and winked at Sherri as he walked out the door. Once outside, he climbed into his squad car and drove at an unnecessarily high speed to the scene, where he found a green Volkswagen Jetta parked on the shoulder with its hazard lights blinking. Kincaid parked behind the Volkswagen and activated his red lights.

He then contacted headquarters. "District 18, 18-39. 10-23 at scene of disabled vehicle."

"18-39 District 18, 10-4." Kincaid advised Edwards of the registration plate number on the Volkswagen and walked up to the vehicle.

The female driver hit the button to roll down her window as Kincaid approached the car. A tall dishwater-blonde of thirty-five who was dressed in a dark red skirt outfit, she said that she was on her way to an early work day in an accounting office in Springfield when her car began making a strange noise and then just stopped running. She then imitated the noises, and Kincaid tried to stifle a smile at the odd utterances rising from her mouth. "Sounds like you need a tow truck," he said, and she agreed.

Kincaid strode back to his squad car and radioed Edwards at headquarters to request that a tow truck be sent to the scene. As he did, she stepped out of the car, and her stately, five-foot-ten carriage was revealed, striking in her appearance, as if she were a model. From his seat, Kincaid noticed that she was not wearing a ring.

As she walked to his squad car, he rolled his window down and asked her to have a seat in his car so she could wait for the tow truck. As the morning was very cool, she accepted his offer.

They spent the time chatting until he saw the familiar maroon-and-white tow truck of Joe Murphy a few hundred yards away. Murphy slowed to swerve in front of the disabled vehicle and pulled onto the shoulder, deliberately backing the rear of his truck to the car.

Murphy slid out of the cab, introduced himself, and smiled as Kincaid bragged about Joe's prowess as a mechanic, adding to the lady that "he knew who the best car guys were." Joe asked the woman to pop her hood and, after three minutes of inspection, determined that he could not repair the vehicle on the roadside and would have to tow it to his garage. The stranded driver rolled her eyes and threw her head back in frustration.

As Joe hooked up the vehicle, the woman pulled out her cell phone and called ahead, advising that she would be late to work, if she arrived at all. Once finished, Joe asked Kincaid to transport the lady back to the garage while he towed the car in. Kincaid was only too happy to accept, though the lady, her patience wearing thin from her troubles and tiring of Kincaid's bluster, was less enthused.

Meanwhile, Kincaid contacted Edwards and advised that he was transporting the female back to Farmersville, and provided his vehicle's mileage. He followed the tow truck to the county line crossover, where he turned around to the opposite lanes and drove to Murphy's Towing in Farmersville.

Though Kincaid tried to engage his passenger in conversation, she offered only half-smiles in response. When they arrived at Joe's, she offhandedly said, "Thanks for your help," and quickly exited the car, choosing to wait in the grimy seating area that provided three white plastic chairs like those in Murphy's office, a recycled end table, and a small stack of dog-eared automotive and entertainment magazines.

As she headed inside, Kincaid again contacted Edwards and provided his mileage, which is ISP procedure when transporting a female. Afterward, Murphy approached Kincaid from the truck. "Hey, Jim," he called. "Got something you may need to know."

"Yeah?" Kincaid's shift was now about to end, and he never liked to extend it any more than he had to.

"You know that fatal that we handled on the frontage road, the day after Thanksgiving? Well, just before New Year's, I had a visit from these two guys who said they were insurance investigators, from American Mutual or something like that. But I don't think they were."

"Whaddya mean?" Kincaid shifted around on one foot, hoping to end the conversation.

"Well, they were two Mexicans." Immediately, Kincaid came to attention. "One was tall, well-dressed, clean cut, not a bad-looking guy. The other one, though, made me very suspicious. Big, hulking son of a bitch, with a scar on his face and mean look in his eye. Looked like he'd rather kick my ass than give me the time of day."

Kincaid felt his heart begin to race, and underneath his uniform, the hairs on his arm began to quiver. "What did they want?"

Joe, in his habitual way, took off his cap and brushed the back of his glove over his forehead. "They asked me all sorts of questions about the accident. Only, they really didn't seem to care about the particulars of the car or the driver, like I usually get from insurance guys. They kept asking me questions about the money, had I actually seen it myself, how many bags there were, what happened to it. They also wanted to know about you."

Suddenly, Kincaid's stomach began to churn, and he felt like he was about to lose the three cups of coffee he had downed an hour ago. His heart was racing so fast that he felt he would pass out, and he hoped that Joe would not notice his anxiety. "Like what?"

"Oh, where you lived, what your shift was, things like that." Joe nonchalantly dropped the cap on top of his head, where it now sat cocked at a slight angle. "I've never had an insurance guy ask those kind of questions. And all they really cared about was the money. The mean-looking one started coming toward me, and I sat up and asked who they were and said that I didn't think they were insurance investigators."

A lump in Kincaid's throat had formed that felt like he had swallowed a golf ball, and he could barely speak. "What then?" he said weakly.

"Huh?" Murphy hadn't heard the response and leaned forward to get it the second time.

Kincaid mustered enough strength to make his voice sound normal. "What then, I said."

"Guys just turned around and left. Never said a word. Just got in this nice-looking car, a Cadillac Escalade. Drove off, and I haven't seen them since." He remembered that one had left a business card, unbeknownst to Murphy that it was fake. "I've still got the one guy's card somewhere on my desk. Give me a sec, and I'll get it."

"No, thanks anyway," interrupted Kincaid. "I'm late as it is. Gotta go." Murphy shrugged, said a quick, "Okay, bye," and turned back to the disabled vehicle, which was still on the truck.

Kincaid hurried back to his car, his mind a whirlpool of thoughts, emotions, and fears. He started the car, backed up, and turned onto the frontage road, rolling at a high rate of speed, anxious to get away from the bad news that he had just heard. But he knew there was no escape. The cartel had figured out that one bag of money was missing and was now looking for him.

CHAPTER 12

The White City exit was thirty miles from Farmersville, and it seemed an eternity to James Kincaid. He nervously looked in his rearview mirror, expecting to see someone following him. His head throbbed as his blood pressure spiked, his chest heaved slightly, and his stomach was knotted. The cartel knew what he had done and was after him.

How could they have found out? he wondered. What did I do wrong? I mean, God, they found out so quick. And that was how many weeks ago that they were at Murphy's. God only knows what they've done in the time since.

He began to imagine every scenario of revenge. Starting my truck, only to trigger a car bomb… Walking out the door and being gunned down by a hail of bullets… Rolling down the road and being shot in a drive-by… Jumped from behind by goons and beaten senseless… Stabbing… Shooting… and that was only for himself. Oh, shit, he thought. What about the family? Sally and Mary Ann, Judy, my mother, Debbie, Sharon and the kids? Those bastards take no prisoners. They may come after them just to get back at me.

It seemed like the drive would never end as he drove straight to his trailer, arriving at 7:12 a.m. Debbie's battered Celica was parked in the garage, which he could see because she had neglected to close the garage door. In terror for the money in the rafters, Kincaid sprang from his car and ran inside the garage to shut the door as quickly as possible. Dammit! he raged to himself. Door standing open just like that! Hope one of those frickin' Mexicans didn't see inside.

He knew that Debbie would be likely to suspect something if he didn't collect himself, so he drew a deep breath, strolled to the door leading inside, and tried to put a smile on his face. He walked into the kitchen to be greeted by Debbie, standing at the counter with a cigarette protruding from her mouth.

"Hi, babe!" she said in her usual upbeat way. He smiled and said, "Hey yourself," though with much less enthusiasm than normal. Kincaid barely broke his stride as he stepped through the kitchen and started down the hallway. As he did, she lunged forward and grabbed his right buttock.

Normally, he liked to be felt up by Debbie and would always produce a mischievous grin. Today, though, he simply flinched, as if her advance was unwelcome. His verbal greeting, coupled with his indifference to her wandering hands, alerted her that something was wrong with her man.

"Hey," she said, scrambling to catch up with him. "What's the matter?"

"Oh, ah, nothing," he feigned. "I'm just tired, that's all. Tough night."

"You're tired every time you get home from work. That's not all that's bothering you, and you know it. Now tell me. What's eatin' you?"

Kincaid knew he was busted, since he had been home for less than sixty seconds, and Debbie could already tell something was wrong. He also knew that he could never say that a powerful Mexican cartel was after him because he had taken a million dollars of their money. So the wheels in his tortured mind started turning, and as he concocted a story, he turned back to face her in the hallway.

"I had a threat on my life," said Kincaid quickly, practically spitting out the words. "Came in last night, while I was on shift. I think this could be serious."

Debbie shrank in her stance. "What... what do you mean? What happened? Is it serious, or is someone just bullshitting?"

Kincaid drew another deep breath. "It's serious enough that I'm gonna have a security system installed. I'm gonna call a guy I know, Bob England, who does that sort of thing. I know I'd feel a helluva lot better if we had one here."

Stunned, Debbie walked back up the hallway as Kincaid followed her back to the kitchen table. She sank into a chair, her body as limp as a dishrag, and dropped her elbows onto the table, as if she needed the support.

"Oh, baby… What kind of threat is this? What's gonna be done to you?"

Kincaid slipped into the chair across from her, choosing not to look her directly in the eye. Rather, he chose to stare up and down the wall. "I don't know, didn't say. Could get shot, could get stabbed. Don't really know what the specifics are."

"I'll be damned," said Debbie, throwing up her hands in frustration. "I guess I should have thought this could happen. After all, the people that you have to deal with…." She then pressed for details. "Who's the S.O.B. who did this?"

Kincaid knew that he couldn't stretch this lie much further, so downplaying was the next-best option. "It's a guy I arrested for burglary and DUI a few months ago. I got a call that a house had been burglarized, and I checked it out." The fibs kept flowing. "As I drove up, I saw a guy who ran out and hopped in a car. I took in after him, and pulled him over.

"When I got up to the car, I smelled the alcohol on him and saw that he had an open container on the seat next to him. He had the stolen goods in back, a TV, computer, some tools, things like that. Guy's ass was dead to rights. The homeowner came in and identified all of goods right away, so there was no doubt."

"Who told you about the threat?" inquired Debbie.

"A buddy of mine in Litchfield told me about it. He said he was talking to the guy in a bar, and the guy said he was going to put me away for good."

Debbie sat, fixated on her boyfriend as he recited the details. "So why isn't this sorry son of a bitch in jail? I mean, if he did all this stuff, why isn't his butt behind bars?"

Kincaid hadn't expected that response and kept making it up as he went along. Fears of the cartel and the conversation he had with Murphy circled his brain as he spoke. "You know how it is. The judge was a candy-ass and gave him a little piece of shit bail. He posted, and he's out on the streets to await a trial date."

"Dammit," Debbie lit up another cigarette and then threw the pack aside in disgust. "Guys like you bust their ass to keep the country safe, and then that happens."

"Yeah." Kincaid kept weaving a tale and wanted to make sure it didn't end up fraying. "Actually, the guy who made the threat is a real weird character. I've known him for years, have picked him up before. When he's sober, he's absolutely harmless, wouldn't hurt a flea. He's got a decent sense of humor and can keep you laughing. But get him drunk, and there's no telling what he might do. He's a mean drunk, the kind that gets a couple of drinks in him and thinks he can kick every ass in the room."

"I know the type," lamented Debbie, who saw her share of drunks on a daily basis at Martin's. "The kind that gets hammered, then goes home and beats the shit out of his wife."

"Exactly," agreed Kincaid. "Only this type may do worse. So I really want to get that security system. I'd sleep a hell of a lot better if we had one." He also thought of the money in the rafters, which would also be protected.

"Yeah, me too. So much for life with a cop," said Debbie, with a rueful chuckle. "But, how much do those things cost? Can we afford one?," she asked, unaware that her boyfriend could now afford anything he wanted.

"Oh sure, no problem. I can cover it, and if I can't, I can make payments. It'll come out of my money, not the household. It'll be worth every dime."

"I agree. Go ahead, and let me know what happens."

With that, Kincaid rose, patted Debbie on the left shoulder, and headed back down the hallway. As he did, she mentioned that she was going out to have breakfast with her son, and she would be leaving in a few minutes. She added that she was working the early shift today as well, since the regular girl "had to go back to her gynecologist. Guess her boyfriend never told her he had the crabs." He replied that he was going to take a shower and get a few winks before calling Bob England, the self-styled guru of home security in the area.

*****

Actually, Kincaid had no intention of a nap, as he wanted to contact England as soon as possible. But knowing that would raise Debbie's concern, he opted for the shower first, though it would not be a normal bathing. Oblivious to Debbie, Kincaid reached into his gun belt and removed his duty weapon, a 9-mm handgun. He then slipped into the bathroom, locked the door, and placed the 9-mm on the toilet tank, within easy reach of the shower if needed.

Debbie was the type of woman who did nothing quietly, and even as the running water pounded in the tub below, Kincaid could hear the front door slam, signifying that Debbie had gone. He cut his shower short, dried off, and threw on a faded blue sweatshirt with a pair of ripped pants. He slid the 9-mm into his belt and walked up the hallway to the phone on the wall by the table to call about the security system.

On the other end was Bob England, a familiar face to all the cops in the region, because many city, county, and state officers used his services in their own homes. Unlike the big companies that spend millions on television ads to peddle the same products, England cut out the middleman by handling everything himself, and only put an occasional display ad in the local papers to promote his products. He was also known to hang homemade fliers on telephone poles or in public bathrooms, for additional visibility.

England worked out of the basement of his home in Standard City, a sleepy settlement of some 250 residents some twenty miles northwest of White City that, in its glory days seventy years ago, was a mining town and the unquestioned haven of watering holes in the area. A reported ten to fifteen taverns lined the streets back then, and though only one or two were left, Saturday nights in Standard City were a little less quiet than the rest of the week.

He acquired his expertise in electronics in his job as a coal miner, which he did for twenty-nine years before his retirement eleven summers ago. When it wasn't deer season (which, for England, could have been year-round), he could always be found in his basement, tinkering with the latest gadgets, killing time until the next job came in. At six feet and 175 pounds, he was fit enough to climb the highest ladders to install his products, and if he couldn't figure something out at first, he would simply brush his hand through his salt-and-pepper hair or his beard until he thought up a solution.

Kincaid had drunk coffee with England a few times, most recently about six months before, and his voice was familiar when England answered on the sixth ring.

"Hey, Bob, this is Trooper Kincaid," he said in his normal, offhanded way. "Been a while."

"Yeah, Jim, it sure has. What can I do for ya?"

No words were wasted as Kincaid spoke tersely. "Bob, I've had a threat on my life, and I need a home security system. I'd like this done as soon as possible. What do you have today?"

Taken aback by the directive, England hesitated for a few moments. "No way could I do it today," he finally replied. "I've got an appointment, someone who's been waiting for a while. Today's not good at all."

Kincaid could hear a muffled rustling sound, as England shifted the white paper calendar that covered his desk. "I really couldn't get to you for several days."

"Come on, Bob," Kincaid said impatiently, jumping around on one foot, then the other. "This is serious. I've got a guy who's made it clear he wants to kill me, put my ass in a pine box. I can't wait that long. I gotta have something now."

"Well," England took a moment to scan his calendar again, "I guess I could move the appointment off today. That's the best I can do. Geez, I'm booked for days. It seems like everyone wants a system at the same time."

"So you can get here today?" Outside, a pickup pulling a wagon motored by and bounced over a pothole, emitting a loud rattle. Kincaid jerked his head around and reached for the 9-mm before he realized the origin of the noise.

"Yeah," agreed England. "Exactly what do you need? You still living in that mobile home?"

"Mm-hmm. Same place as always. I want protection for the trailer, the garage, and the yard. I want to nail anything that even sticks a toe across the property line. Anything and everything around here has got to be covered. And it's got to have a recording device."

"How big is the yard?"

"We sit on a 70x200 lot. It's irregular, not in a rectangle or anything. Got a little side yard to it, and some backyard." Kincaid pulled back the kitchen curtain slightly, enough to peer outside and see if any intruders were around.

England jotted the dimensions on a spiral notepad. "You want an alarm with that?" He was used to customers asking for an alarm to go along with their home security systems.

"Nope. Just want cameras. I want something I can do surveillance with."

"Huh." England was mildly startled at the response. He flipped his pen in thought, and spoke deliberately. "I think I've got the material you need. I can get it in today."

"What time?"

"I can be there by ten this morning. You live in White City. How do I get to where you're at?"

Kincaid gave him detailed directions and told him he could pay him on the spot, neglecting to ask the price. He nervously glanced at the clock on the microwave, which flashed 7:43. The next two hours were spent pacing up and down the hallway, in and out of each room of the trailer, hoping that no cartel goon had found his way in, or that goons in black leather jackets weren't prowling around outside.

At 9:01, the telephone rang, which set Kincaid's heart racing and dropped his stomach. After the four-ring default, the answering machine picked up, only to receive a message from Debbie's friend Shelley Tipson, the hard-drinking retired teacher, asking if Debbie wanted to hit this new bar and grill that had just opened in Carlinville, twenty miles to the north.

Exactly fifty-two minutes later, Kincaid was frightened by the rumbling of a vehicle pulling into the driveway. His police training kicked in, and he ran to the front door, standing just off to the left of the doorway, gun pointed upward in hand and out of sight to anyone who may enter. He leaned forward just enough to look out the window of the door and heaved a sigh of relief when he saw it was the rusted, light blue half-ton Ford truck of Bob England, now parking behind the squad car.

England stepped out, dressed in a thick green flannel jacket with a pair of tan Carhart work pants, and strode toward the door. Kincaid opened it just enough to let him through, and then slammed it behind him, sliding the deadbolt across and hooking the chain for good measure.

"God, Jim, you are nervous," exclaimed England, looking wide-eyed in startled amazement. "This must be one helluva threat."

"Sure is," said Kincaid, heart still racing from the shock of the sound of the truck. "Glad you're here." He put his gun back in his belt. "Take a look around, and do what you have to do."

England went to work and spent the next several hours on the scene, analyzing each corner and nook inside, every angle and vista outside, and nearly every external threat that he could think of. Small, wireless cameras were placed both inside and outside the home as well as in the garage, and a recording device was hidden in a secret compartment inside the bedroom closet. Kincaid left England alone for most of the work in the trailer, but he followed him into the garage, thinking of the duffel bag in the rafters.

He knew that cameras would need to be placed at high angles, so he watched intently as England stood on an A-frame ladder and installed video surveillance in all relevant places. Finally, England glanced up to notice the tarp that concealed the bag on the plywood.

"What's that?" he inquired, pointing. "That mean anything?"

"Nah," Kincaid said as he waved his hand, as if to dismiss the thought. "That's just a pile of hoses and cables. Last guy that lived here left them, I guess. I checked when I moved in, and it's nothing."

Satisfied, England finished his work in the garage, and then moved outside.

Daylight was fading as the work proceeded, and it was completely dark as the microwave read 5:37 when England knocked on the door. "Done," he told Kincaid. "That was a bigger job than I thought. Can't remember the last time someone wanted me to put this much of a system in a place this size."

"Sorry," offered Kincaid. "But this threat has really rocked my world. I don't want to take any chances."

"Understood. That's what I'm here for." England was holding a pad of job tickets, and he filled in some information to present the cost of the job to Kincaid. He then showed Kincaid how the system operated.

"How much you want for all this?" asked Kincaid, reaching for the billfold that he had placed in his back pocket a few minutes before.

"Oh, eight hundred should cover it. That takes care of labor, electronics, everything you need."

Kincaid withdrew the wallet, counted out eight $100 bills, and handed them to England, who blinked. "Don't get too many cash transactions," he said. "Hell, I won't have to report this one to the IRS."

"I won't tell if you don't," snickered Kincaid, the first time that he had laughed all day. "Thanks. Appreciate the fact you worked me in."

"Anytime." England turned on his heel and headed out. "Have a good one," he said as he stepped down the four front stairs that led to the driveway.

CHAPTER 13

England's cheerful wish was visionary, as Kincaid's life settled down considerably as the new year wore on. As a result, Kincaid found himself remarkably relaxed, serenely peaceful as he flipped on the television and lay down on the bed.

The Christmas season, weeks ago, had been a whirlwind, and he barely had time to celebrate with any of his family. Now, on a whim, he had asked all of his family to join him at the trailer for a huge dinner, a sort of late Christmas celebration, to make up for lost time. To his delight, everyone accepted. He had wondered how each of his exes would react to his invitation and to the fact they would all be in the same room for the first time. But everyone was coming, and Kincaid was as excited on this day as he had been since he was a kid.

Rather than the standard ugly sweater, showing a clunky ski scene or a green triangle that passed for a tree, Kincaid chose to wear his dress uniform, which had been a favorite of every woman in his life. Judy had always said how handsome he looked in it, while Sharon said it made her hot. Debbie liked to grab a piece of his buttocks every time he wore it. So, unorthodox as it was, it seemed the perfect choice on this special day.

Judy arrived first, wearing a flowing white winter dress trimmed in fur that she had worn many times on the Christmas Eves when they were married. He had always loved seeing her in that dress and appreciated the fact that she had chosen it today. Sally and Mary Ann arrived next, each wearing dark sweaters with white blouses underneath and dark tan, knee-length skirts that reflected their college age and their good taste in clothing that had always made Kincaid proud. The outfits accentuated their good looks acquired from their mother, and their long, dark hair sat neatly on their shoulders.

Next came Sharon, who said she had left the kids with a sitter. She was dressed in a dark red, skin-tight dress of thigh-high length, offering plenty of cleavage. This, too, had been a favorite of Kincaid, and she always wore it when, in her words, "she prettied up." Her platinum-blonde hair, newly dyed, made her look as eye-catching as she had on those nights when he had first seen her at the Busy Bee. As she sat down to slip off her platform heels, she crossed her bare legs, causing her dress to hike up enough to reveal she was not wearing panties.

Judy and the girls simply smiled at Sharon from their seats around the table, and she joined them, smiling in return. Debbie was not dressed up, electing to wear a black Harley Davidson tank top and a pair of dark blue skinny jeans with sparkles on the seat. She had not met either Judy or Sharon, and she exchanged the same smiles with everyone.

The next knock on the door was that of Kincaid's mother, who was coming through the garage, the easiest route for her to enter the kitchen in her wheelchair. Kincaid was amused to see that she was wearing the same attire, a tan housedress with pockets on either side of the skirt and a string of pearls, which he had enjoyed as a boy. Her short hair now white-gray and her thin-rimmed spectacles sitting on her wrinkled face, she beamed adoringly at him and smiled at each of the women sitting around the table.

Kincaid was doing the cooking on this day, and he waited anxiously for a succulent twenty-eight-pound turkey, complete with all the trimmings, to come out of the oven underneath the counter. In the meantime, he dished up the sides that he had always loved, such as mashed potatoes and gravy, three-bean salad, corn-on-the-cob, and the raspberry Jell-O that had been a favorite since he wore training pants. He also looked at the apple crumb pie that he had baked yesterday and had turned out much better than he expected. The women at the table still smiled at one another, and Sally hooked her arm into her grandmother's, leaning her head lovingly onto her shoulder.

Everyone turned and admired the Christmas decorations that were still up in the living room. Kincaid, who normally wanted the season to be over on December 26, did not have the heart to take them down this year. Even at this late date in January, they sparkled as much as ever, particularly the artificial tree that Kincaid had lovingly decorated. Seven elegant feet tall, it barely fit under the ceiling of the trailer and was adorned with many of the same ornaments that he had hung on trees since he was a boy. An artificial pine candle wafted through the air, and the lights of the tree blinked a warm glow. Debbie turned on the boom box and pulled out a CD of Christmas music, and a classic version of "Silent Night" purred softly from the speakers, to everyone's enjoyment.

As Kincaid reached for the oven to pull out the turkey, he could not help but glance back at the table and all of the important people in his life sitting around it. He knew he made poor choices, which had disappointed them all and, for long periods, kept them out of his life. But now he was richer than ever, with a bag full of money in the garage and good relations with everyone. A self-assured smile broke across his face as he turned toward the table, turkey pan clutched in hands covered by flowered oven mitts, ready for the feast.

As he set the turkey on the table and received the "oohs" and "aahs" of his appreciative guests, there was a heavy pounding at the front door. "POLICE! OPEN UP!" was the command shouted from outside.

In that instant, the serenity that had come over Kincaid evaporated. Before he could move, the door burst open as four officers poured into the kitchen from all angles, guns drawn. A collective gasp arose from the ladies, while a chill swept over Kincaid.

"You're under arrest," said one cop, "for official misconduct and stealing evidence."

Kincaid's first instinct was to run, and he lunged in an attempt to make it down the hallway, hoping to reach a window that he could open to shimmy out. All of a sudden, he felt a painful urge to go to the bathroom.

Two of the officers rushed forward and tackled him from behind before he was even out of the kitchen. They wrestled him to the floor, face down, as terror raced through his veins. He felt one officer pull his right arm back to place a handcuff, and he squirmed in an effort to free himself. His need for the bathroom was now agonizing, and he desperately hoped to hold himself in.

As one cuff was snapped onto his right wrist, he was finally overpowered, and his left wrist was secured with the other half of the cuff. As the officers held him down, his body shifted back and forth against the floor and his tortured bladder gave way, warm torrents streaming into his briefs and down his legs, soaking the front of his pants.

The officers pulled Kincaid to his feet, whimpering like a wayward child after a hard spanking, as he faced the table of his guests. Judy sat wide-eyed in stunned silence, and the girls screamed and cried in anguish. Debbie jumped from her place at the table and ran out the front door. Sharon pointed at the huge wet spot on his pants and began laughing hysterically. Tears of shame trickled down his mother's weathered face, and she placed her right hand over her eyes, too embarrassed to look at her son.

Kincaid himself was sobbing as he stood, humiliated with hands behind his back and pants stained, as the officers read the Miranda rights, informing him that he had the right to remain silent, and was entitled to an attorney. As they finished and were about to about to walk him to the open door, five burly Mexicans, dressed in black jackets and clutching assault rifles, burst inside.

Without a word, they opened fire, spraying the room with bullets which ripped through the women at the table, killing them instantly. Kincaid watched in horror as the blood spurted from their bodies, twisting in shock as one by one they fell away dead. The officers fell next, gunfire tearing through their bodies that shook grotesquely as they dropped, red pools of blood streaming across the floor.

Finally, he was the only one standing as the Mexicans turned to him, laughing at his helplessness. The piercing sound of the rapid-fire weapons and the flash of the discharges then raced through his mind as he felt the bullets tear through his body. As the life drained from him, he thought of his loved ones dying horribly before his eyes, the shame of knowing that they deserved better, and his damnable choice to take the money.

*****

"NOOOOOOOOOO!" Kincaid's scream was blood-curdling as he sat up in bed, pouring in sweat, muscles aching, head pounding, heart about to leap from his chest.

"My God!" Debbie yelled as she ran down the hallway, her cowgirl boots pounding the linoleum as she neared. "My God! Jim! What's the matter?"

Kincaid was beginning to realize he'd just had a nightmare, though the shock still pulsated through his body. He jerked his head from side to side, seeing that he was in his bed, that he was still here, that his family was still alive, that nothing had happened.

Still, he gasped desperately for breath as his chest heaved. Debbie had now reached the bedroom and threw herself on the bed beside him. "Jim, it's all right, it's all right! It was just a dream!" Not known for affection, she took his head in her arms and cradled it against her breasts.

"Oh God, oh God!" Still trying to catch his breath and the horror of the dream still fresh in his mind, Kincaid nonetheless could tell a story. "It was that guy. That one I told you about, the death threat. I dreamed that he came here and killed us."

"Oh, Jim, what's happened to you?" Debbie kept caressing his face, and he saw her fingers pass over him through widened, glassy eyes. "You're never like this. Oh, baby, baby, I'm so glad you got the home security system. It's worth every penny, if you're this scared."

Finally, he started to calm down and pulled away from Debbie. He wiped the sweat from his face with a still-shaking palm. "Yeah. Wow." He chuckled nervously. "Never had a nightmare like that. It was so real, so here and now, like it was really happening."

"Dreams can do that," said Debbie. "I remember one time a few years ago, I dreamed I was getting my ass beat by a little green man from Mars. Sounds crazy, but I thought it was really happening." She was settling down herself, and she pulled out her pack of Virginia Slims to light up. "Probably had a couple too many shots that night. Damn, was I glad when I woke up."

"Hmph," Kincaid stifled a laugh. "Wish mine had been that good." He collected himself and set his feet on the floor. "Let me take a couple of minutes here, and I'll be all right." Debbie nodded and walked back up the hallway to the kitchen. Kincaid slowly rose from the bed, stood at the foot, and put his hand on the back of his neck, still trembling from the glimpse of what was at stake from his choice.

CHAPTER 14

Miguel Perez and Carlos Santiago were hardly close friends, but they knew who each other was, and they exchanged a flurry of phone calls before their anticipated meeting on the Kincaid situation. On Monday morning, January 25, they finally met in Litchfield. Perez drove up from Ciudad Juarez in a rented black Honda Accord, which Diego Garcia had determined would be the most effective for a stakeout, since it would attract the least attention. Santiago came down from Chicago in a silver Chevrolet Monte Carlo with Texas plates, which he had maintained from his days along the border.

For lodging, Santiago had remembered the Prairie View Inn & Suites from his stay with Juan Hernandez weeks earlier. Since he had liked the adult films he could get on pay-per-view, Santiago recommended it to Perez. Austin, the nervous millennial at the front desk, became wide-eyed when he saw Santiago walk through the door once more and could not help the men get checked in fast enough. After taking great pains to make sure the two would have the best room possible, with plenty of "yes sir" utterances, Austin handed over the key cards to Room 267.

Santiago also remembered the exact location of Kincaid's trailer and knew the best spots for surveillance. As a result, Perez and Santiago spent hours in the black Accord, partially concealed behind a stand of shrub brush a few hundred yards from the trailer, watching intently.

Each had brought along their favorite illegal substance. Perez had traveled with a few grams of cocaine, while Santiago had some marijuana, since he liked to roll his own cigarettes, believing that smoking complemented his cowboy persona. They kept the drugs in the glove compartment but never indulged while on stakeout.

They already had the information that Jose Hernandez had gleaned in his fake insurance interview with tow driver Joe Murphy, including the time of Kincaid's shift, 11 to 7. After a few days of observation, they learned that Kincaid had a housemate, a girlfriend who worked as a bartender at Martin's Tavern in Mount Olive. This they learned firsthand, as they tailed Debbie's red Celica as she drove to the tavern at the same time on three straight days, an indication that she was working, not just hanging out.

They also noticed that Kincaid did not seem to work on Saturday or Sunday. On Friday nights, they watched as Kincaid drove his dark green S-10 to Martin's around 6:30 p.m. After carefully tailing him on two straight Fridays, they learned that he and his girlfriend drove home in their separate vehicles at around 11 p.m. Perez, never without his trusty laptop, typed in every bit of information as it became available.

Twelve days were spent on surveillance, as Perez and Santiago quietly sat in the Accord, staring at the trailer and its surroundings, living on cold sandwiches, doughnuts, and coffee. Their task was made more difficult by the central Illinois winter as the cold winds blew across the flatlands and buffeted the Accord, causing its occupants discomfort. But Diego Garcia had chosen his men well. Miguel Perez was a dedicated soldier, willing to do anything for his boss, while Santiago was either crazy or slow enough not to care.

When the twelve days were up, Perez and Santiago decided to confront the pair as they arrived home from Martin's on Friday night, February 5. Ever the dutiful lieutenant, Perez contacted Garcia to advise him of the plan. Garcia approved, and Perez hung up the phone.

"Got it," said Perez. "He says to do it." A toothy grin broke across Santiago's face at the thought of a bloody confrontation, while Perez was more practical.

"Diego still says no violence. Unless we have to," he said, watching Santiago's face fall. "He says the primary goal is to get the money back. That's what's most important to him. He wants the money, and we're gonna get it for him."

*****

Two nights before the planned confrontation, Perez and Santiago were back at the trailer in the Accord, ready for more surveillance. At 7:14 p.m., they watched Debbie's Celica slow down to turn into the driveway. Eleven minutes later, they watched as both Kincaid and Debbie left in his Silverado. Perez and Santiago allowed the Silverado to get just enough of a head start before pulling in behind, tailing them once again.

This time, they followed the Silverado into Litchfield to the Pull Up, a popular bar and grill, and watched as Kincaid and Debbie went inside. From their vantage point at the back of the large parking lot, they had a clear view of what was happening. Always calculating, Perez began to formulate a plan.

"Okay. This is an opportunity," he said. "We know their trailer is empty right now, and we need to know what's inside. If the money is in there, we can get it now and get out of here, like Garcia asked."

Santiago's mind could process far less than that of Perez, and merely followed along. "What do you want me to do?"

"I'll stay here and keep watching this place. While I'm doing that, I'm going to send you back to the trailer to get inside. We'll drive back to the motel and pick up your car, and you drive down to the trailer. I'll hustle back here and keep watching."

Quizzically, Santiago stared into Perez's face. "What happens if they leave the restaurant?"

"I'll call you immediately," assured Perez. "That way, you can get out of there before Kincaid comes home."

Satisfied, Santiago agreed. Perez drove Santiago back to the Prairie View Inn & Suites to pick up Santiago's silver Monte Carlo and then hurried back to the same spot in the parking lot of the Pull Up. Santiago drove at speeds approaching eighty down Interstate 55 to the White City exit and then his sly nature kicked in. He slowed considerably, deciding he should not attract attention, and deliberately motored down the lane to Kincaid's driveway.

Seeing no other headlights in the vicinity, Santiago slowly pulled up the driveway and parked behind the garage to conceal his vehicle. Since the ground was frozen by a recent cold snap, no tire tracks were left. Dressed in his usual black leather jacket with dark jeans and caramel-colored cowboy boots, Santiago did not attract attention in the darkness, and he left his trademark tan cowboy hat in the Monte Carlo to blend in even more.

Approaching the front door of the trailer, he found it locked, which was expected and of little concern. Reaching into an inside pocket of his jacket, Santiago removed a set of lock picks sophisticated enough to make a magician jealous. In less than a minute, he was standing in the kitchen.

He ventured from room to room, opening closets, drawers, cabinets, and anything else that could hold even part of the money. He dropped to all fours to look under beds and sofas, and he peered behind curtains, television stands, and easy chairs in search of what he was looking for. Though he was careful not to disturb or upset anything, alerting Kincaid that someone had been there, he diligently investigated the trailer for any sign of the money, to no avail.

Next, Santiago headed for the bedroom and, after peering under the bed and in a chest of drawers, approached the closet, where Kincaid had placed his surveillance monitor. Santiago opened the closet door and found no bag of money. He then stalked up the hallway to leave the trailer, heading for the kitchen and the door leading to the garage. As he started to open that door, his cell phone's ringtone, Freddy Fender's "Is Anybody Going to San Antone," went off. He answered to hear Perez's voice on the other end.

"They just left the restaurant," said Perez excitedly. "I just turned onto the interstate right behind them, and it looks like they're southbound, heading home. Meet me back at the motel, and fast."

Santiago then turned to the back of the garage where his Monte Carlo was parked, scanning the area as he went. He threw it into reverse and rolled down the driveway, onto the lane, and, in seconds, back to the main street of White City that doubled as Illinois Route 138. The interstate was just over the rise, and he flew down the exit of the northbound lane, joining the nighttime traffic flow that concealed him in the darkness.

Back at the Prairie View, Perez was waiting in Room 267 when Santiago did their agreed-upon secret knock on the door. Once inside, Santiago told Perez that he had discovered nothing in the trailer.

In frustration, Perez wadded up a loose piece of paper and threw it absent-mindedly at the trash can by the wall. But Perez was even more annoyed to learn that Santiago did not have time to search the garage, as he was forced to leave after receiving the phone call that Kincaid and Debbie were on their way home from the Pull Up.

*****

Kincaid saw that his discount-store wristwatch read 9:26 as he and Debbie arrived back at the trailer. He entered the front door and immediately reviewed the tape from the newly installed home security system, which was controlled from the bedroom. Debbie, meanwhile, sat down at the kitchen table, cigarette in one hand and cell phone in the other, after pouring herself a big red plastic cup of tequila.

Upon reviewing the tape, fear raced through Kincaid's veins once more as he saw a Chevrolet Monte Carlo roll up the driveway and park behind the garage. Slowing down the tape, he saw the vehicle had a Texas license plate of CF 6741. From the camera at another location, Kincaid observed a large male approach the trailer, unlock the door, and walk inside.

From the inside surveillance, Kincaid saw that the entrant appeared to be a mustached Mexican wearing a leather jacket, cowboy boots, and a Western-style shirt. Kincaid watched as the unwelcome guest prowled from room to room, rifling through drawers, opening doors, and peering under furniture and beds. In his terror, Kincaid felt a pang of relief that he had spent the $800 for the security system, for he would not otherwise have known of the intruder's presence.

Kincaid sat, riveted to the screen, watching the man browse the trailer before finally heading to the door. Just then, he stopped to answer his phone before hurriedly leaving the trailer, walking to his Monte Carlo, and leaving the property.

His heart racing and his breathing short, Kincaid knew his troubles were increasing. He quickly wrote down the license plate number of the Monte Carlo and erased the tape, concerned that Debbie might see it. Just then, he heard Debbie call for him from the kitchen, and, swallowing deeply, he tried to collect himself for the walk up the hallway.

Still, he could not hide his anxiety well enough. "Jim, you know my mother's hip is still bothering her—" She interrupted herself when she laid eyes on him. "My God, Jim, you're shaking, and you're positively white! What's the matter?"

"Oh, ah, nothing," Kincaid tried to cover. "I think I'm just getting sick or something. My stomach is rumbling like you can't believe." He chuckled weakly and pushed his right fist into his chest. "Must have been those onion rings at the Pull Up."

"Yeah, I wondered if you should have those," said Debbie. "Personally, I didn't think the food was that great tonight. My ribs weren't anything special. Usually it's better there."

"No kidding." Kincaid actually was not lying about his stomach, because he felt like he may throw up at any moment. "If you would, don't mention those ribs again. Or anything else we ate tonight, for that matter."

"Sure, sure." Debbie studied her boyfriend's face and demeanor. "You think you're able to go to work?"

"Yep," said Kincaid, drawing every bit of acting ability he could muster. "I'll be fine." He glanced at the clock on the microwave, which now flashed 10:29. "Shit, I better get going," he exclaimed as he went back down the hallway to put on his uniform.

He mumbled a goodbye to Debbie on his way out, but she only responded with a half-hearted wave, too engrossed in her cell phone and a second cup of tequila to notice. Kincaid barely cared either, since his mind was on the events of the last twenty-four hours, particularly the visitor in the cowboy gear from the security tape. As he climbed into his squad car, a fleeting thought of Debbie, alone in the trailer, came over him, only to be bumped out of his mind by his own anxiety.

The clock on Kincaid's dash read 10:50 as he headed down the driveway, ready to begin his shift. On this night, though, he took a slightly different route. He headed straight up the northbound lane of Interstate 55 back to Litchfield, wondering if the Monte Carlo from the security tape may be parked in a motel lot.

First, Kincaid cruised through the outside of the Best Rest Inn and the Welcome Lodge, finding nothing that resembled the Monte Carlo. Next, he came upon the Prairie View, where he immediately spied a silver Chevrolet, parked facing the building on the left of the lot. Deliberately approaching the car, Kincaid saw that it was a Monte Carlo with the same Texas plates from the security tape.

The stress-packed day had worn on Kincaid, and this latest development proved too much. Large beads of sweat rolled across his balding head as his stomach returned to the tempest of a few minutes before, at the trailer. Twenty-six years of experience had supposedly prepared Kincaid for any emergency, but this one was not in the manual, and he panicked, not knowing what to do. With few other options, he returned to his patrol duties, knowing that he could, at least, control that situation.

Inside the motel, Perez and Santiago decided to go to the Pull Up themselves for a late dinner and a few drinks. Since the place was open until 2 a.m., there was plenty of time, and after a hard night's work of snooping around, both had plenty of appetite. Since each had a large expense account, courtesy of Diego Garcia, they saw little reason to trim back, ordering steaks with loaded baked potatoes and beer and whiskey to wash it all down.

Midway through the feast, Perez leaned forward in his chair to lessen the chance of being heard by anyone nearby. He pointed his steak knife directly at Santiago for emphasis. "Today's Wednesday. We'll wait until Friday," he whispered to Santiago. "Two days from now will be the time for us to pay James Kincaid a little visit."

Santiago, mouth full of food, simply nodded in agreement. Perez then returned to his plate, using the knife to slice through the juicy medium-rare sirloin in front of him.

*****

That shift and the next one passed uneventfully, though Kincaid found little reason to relax, worrying about would happen next. But on Friday, two days after the intrusion of the mysterious Mexican, Kincaid ended his shift at 7 a.m.

and returned to the trailer. Once inside, he promptly checked the security camera, observing no activity since he had last viewed it the previous evening.

Debbie's mother, who had just turned eighty-three and lived in nearby Mount Olive, was struggling with a right hip that needed replacement but, in her usual cantankerous way, said that "no damn doctor's gonna touch me until I say so." A widow for the last sixteen years, she hardly looked the part of a frail old lady at five-foot eight and 240 pounds with jet-black hair straight from a bottle at the drugstore, but her mobility was fading fast. As a result, Debbie had spent the previous night there in an effort to share caretaking duties with her sister, a dispatcher for a local trucking firm.

Kincaid dialed Debbie's cell phone and heard the familiar greeting. "Hi, baby!" she said cheerily.

"Hi yourself. Are you all right there?"

"Sure, no problems at all. Mom's fine, tough as ever," she laughed. "Any problems on your shift?"

"No. The security tape was fine here, too." Kincaid had mentioned the same thing the last two days, neglecting to offer what he had witnessed on Wednesday night. "But this threat still has me rattled. I keep feeling like someone's about to stick a knife in my back."

"Oh, Jim," replied Debbie, somewhat dismissively. "I think everything's going to be okay. After all, the shithead who made the threat has had plenty of time to do something by now."

"I hope you're right," said Kincaid, knowing she wasn't. "Tell you what. I'm going to bed for a few hours. You're working the 3-to-11 shift today for Martin, right? Why don't I meet you down there after I get up?"

Debbie agreed, and a couple of offhanded pleasantries were exchanged before the conversation ended. Kincaid nervously lit a Camel and made sure that all doors to the trailer were locked. He peeled off his uniform down to the Duluth Trading Company underwear that helped massage his male ego and readied himself for bed. As he climbed under the blankets, he placed a loaded 9-mm Smith &Wesson under his pillow.

*****

Kincaid awoke to find himself covered in sweat, having slept fitfully. Still, he felt more rested than when he had laid down a few hours earlier. He reached for the alarm clock radio on the yard-sale dresser next to the bed to see that it was 2:39 in the afternoon.

Wiping the sleep from his eyes, he stumbled to the bathroom, taking along the 9-mm as he went. Kincaid then placed the gun carefully on the toilet tank, as before, as he hurried through a shower.

His time under the water was so quick that he barely got himself clean, but with so much on his mind, he didn't particularly care. He went back to the bedroom and threw on a red, faded St. Louis Cardinals sweatshirt with a pair of jeans. Never one for feminist views, Kincaid believed that housework was woman's work, but the kitchen was in need and he felt a twinge of guilt, knowing that Debbie's life was now in danger, too.

So he did some spot cleaning on the counter and around the sink, followed by a few passes with the vacuum across the midnight blue carpet remnant in the living room. As he worked, he knocked back a bottle of Michelob Ultra, then another. Finally, he returned to the bathroom for some mindless wipes of the toilet bowl with a blue-and-white swab brush. The 9-mm stayed in his belt the entire time.

It was 5:31 p.m. when Kincaid changed his clothes once again, tossing the sweatshirt aside for a brick-red shirt bought off the rack at a megastore and a pair of Wrangler jeans, before heading to his beat-up Silverado for the drive to Martin's. Though he normally did not carry a weapon when he was off duty, he jammed the 9-mm into his belt, just in case. His untucked shirt, coupled with the thermal Carhart jacket that he had purchased six years ago, concealed the weapon.

Once at the bar, he was greeted in the usual way by Russell Martin, who bellowed, "Jim, how the hell are ya? Get in here and get a beer, buddy!" Kincaid did just that, ordering a Coors to go along with a cheeseburger with everything on it and a basket of peanuts off the bar. With Valentine's Day approaching, a few red paper cutouts dangled from the walls in Martin's half-hearted attempt to make the place festive.

Debbie's shift did not end until 11 p.m., so Kincaid contented himself to hang out at the bar. Still, he downed his Coors before switching over to Jack Daniels, as was his custom. Several of his drinking buddies were sitting at tables around the room as usual, including Larry and Del Adams as well as Ned Ullmann, the perpetually dissatisfied school janitor, who nursed his beer bottle and groused about how dirty the elementary cafeteria had been after lunch today.

Months before, Kincaid had been jovial, boasting of his brilliance from the accident scene. But on this evening, he was much more subdued and kept looking around the room to see if anyone looked suspicious. The jukebox pumped out Alan Jackson's rendition of "Mercury Blues," which Kincaid found both loud and annoying.

As the beers added up, Del roared louder with laughter at the littlest things. Now with a pitcher under his belt, he was the life of the party. "I got to get me a piece of ass!" he shouted, out of the blue. "I got big needs! I'm a big man, if you know what I mean!" He cuffed Ned on the shoulder hard enough that Ned rocked in his chair.

"Yeah, well," Ned took a long swig off his beer, "My last girlfriend was three hundred and sixty-six pounds of pure evil. Never had a minute's peace with her. Never saw her comb her hair. Rode me all the time, night and day."

"Then why the hell did you move in with her?" barked Del.

"I thought she needed a real man," lamented Ned. "Course, that's the same thing she said on the day she threw me out."

Del bounced up and down with laughter as Ned stared down at the table, shaking his head. Finally, Del settled down and stared at Kincaid.

"Jim, you dumb son of a bitch!" he said, clearly slurring. "What the hell's your problem? You look like you just came from the funeral of the hottest babe you ever got naked with!"

Kincaid snapped back to attention with Del's shouting. He looked down at the partially eaten cheeseburger on the paper plate in front of him. "Oh, I'm just tired," he said. "I haven't slept worth a damn in days, and it's been a helluva week anyway."

"Tell me about it," said Ned, shaking his head.

"Oh, go to hell, Ned," rasped Del. "It's not like you've got anything better to do."

Ned wadded up a napkin and threw it at Del in disgust. "Don't remind me. My life sucks like a vacuum." He tossed a handful of Beer Nuts in his mouth and pulled his cap off to run his left hand through his scalp. "And damned if my vacuum didn't quit on me first thing this morning when I was in the principal's office." He mumbled something about "all the bullshit I put up with" before Larry chimed in.

"Hell, Jim, you work harder than the rest of us," said Larry, drawing a glare from Ned. "What's buggin' ya, boy?"

"Oh, the same stuff," said Kincaid, never failing to spin a tale. "You know, too many people driving like idiots, too many druggies, too many supervisors with their heads up their asses. The usual."

"Tell me about it," said Ned. "That principal I just mentioned is the biggest—"

"Too bad, Jim," interrupted Larry. "Geez, you guys work your butts off to keep those people off the streets. I mean, whatever you get, you're underpaid. You deserve a helluva lot more than whatever you make."

Kincaid's mind flashed back to the bag in the rafters for what seemed like the millionth time today. Regrets over taking the bag were not far behind. "Yeah. Underpaid." He finished off his second shot of Jack and ordered another.

By then, it was 11:03. Debbie had just finished her shift and was on her way over to Kincaid, who gladly left Larry, Del, and Ned behind to join her at a small table in the corner that offered an unobstructed view of the room as well as the front door. Debbie was carrying an oversized mug of draft beer, though for once, Kincaid didn't want anything else to drink. Again, Debbie asked if he was all right, only to be weakly reassured. She shrugged and took several big belts off her glass.

Meanwhile, back at the Prairie View Inn & Suites, Miguel Perez and Carlos Santiago were climbing into the black Accord in the parking lot for the drive from Litchfield to Martin's Tavern. Since they had carefully discussed their plans in the motel room earlier, few words were exchanged, and Santiago, as if he were an athlete, liked to be in the right frame of mind before any job. He simply took off his cowboy hat and, having seen Steve McQueen do so in a movie once, twirled it back and forth in his hand. Perez simply looked straight ahead through the windshield, finding his own focus.

They had arrived at Martin's at 8:16 p.m. to find business light and the parking lot mostly empty. The lot had no overhead lights, so Perez was able to park in a darkened location, barely discernible to anyone who passed through the front door. There the Accord sat, its occupants setting up surveillance, waiting for Kincaid and Debbie to leave.

Finally, at 1:19 a.m., they saw the couple exit the bar and head toward separate vehicles, Kincaid his Silverado, Debbie her Celica. Before they could leave the lot, Perez slipped the Accord back onto the street and drove toward the trailer, driving at a fast pace to ensure they would arrive first. Glancing in the rearview mirror, Perez could see that neither the Silverado nor the Celica were behind, so he knew that he had an extra minute or two.

Indeed, they got to the trailer well ahead of Kincaid and Debbie, and Perez pulled the Accord into an unimproved roadway leading to a wooded area just off the street, completely concealing the vehicle in the darkness. The two men exited the car and ran to a secluded area in the yard, near the trailer, that was equally tough to see in the black of night. Santiago clutched a Colt .45 semi-automatic pistol, while Perez held his own 9-mm semi-automatic. They stood in the darkness, watching and waiting.

Within moments, Kincaid arrived first, the rusted Silverado creaking up the drive before coming to a halt, the whine of the brakes echoing in the quiet of the night. He climbed out of the truck and waited for Debbie, whose Celica, in need of a new muffler, rumbled into the driveway, her headlights illuminating the area around the trailer.

She was about ready to flip off her headlights and open the door to step out of her vehicle when Santiago and Perez rushed out of the darkness, guns drawn. "All right! Both of you inside! Now, dammit!" Santiago yelled as terror filled Kincaid's body, knowing the moment he had dreaded had just arrived. Debbie screamed from shock and scurried behind Kincaid to get inside, leaving her car door wide open.

Kincaid still had his own 9-mm in his belt and instantly thought of pulling it, but he knew that he would have no chance, staring into the barrel of Santiago's pistol. He unlocked the trailer door, and as the gunmen and their victims walked through, Perez glanced toward a wall, found the light switch, and flipped it, illuminating the kitchen of the darkened trailer.

Though Debbie was petrified from the moment that she first heard Santiago's orders, she managed to hold it together until she entered the kitchen and then sat on the living room couch, where she lost all control. Huge tears now streaming down her face, she became hysterical, with screams of fear that ricocheted off the paneled walls of the trailer.

Santiago had no use for Debbie's histrionics. "Shut up, bitch!" he shouted as he drew his left hand back and slapped her with such force that she tumbled backward across the couch. Collecting herself, she sat on her knees, still sobbing and trembling, scared for her life, begging the gunmen not to kill them.

Though he was rocked by the specter in front of him, Kincaid maintained some presence of mind. "Who are you," he demanded, "and what do you want?"

"You know damn well who we are," replied Santiago in a loud, threatening shout. "Don't give me that shit! We want the money you stole from us, asshole, and we want it now!" Perez stood silently, gun pointed straight at Debbie.

"What money? I don't have any money," feigned Kincaid. "I don't know what you're talking about. I don't have any money."

"Bullshit!" screamed Santiago, even louder than before. "Don't lie to us, asshole! There were two bags of money in that car, and you only turned in one of them! That's over a million dollars, dickhead! Now where the hell is the other bag?"

Kincaid didn't need Santiago to go into any more detail, since he knew what he was talking about. Debbie, meanwhile, had climbed to her feet, tears flowing down her face, looking at Kincaid with wide, haunting eyes. Kincaid extended both of his open palms in front of him, as if to attempt to slow down and calm Santiago. He spoke in a cool monotone.

"Now listen to me. I only saw one bag of money in that car. That was all that was there. I turned it in, like I was supposed to do. That's all I found."

He continued before Santiago could cut in, and he tried to change the narrative. "There were never two bags of money in that trunk. I only saw one. I don't know, maybe one of your guys stole the money. I only saw the one bag. Maybe you ought to be asking your own people."

"LIAR!" Santiago was unmoved, and his anger was raging. "I was there when the car was loaded! There were two bags of money! Don't play me for a dumbass!" He slowly enhanced the pointing of his gun, to emphasize that it was aimed straight at Kincaid's head. "I'm tired of the bullshit! Give me that other bag!"

Debbie looked at Kincaid, who said nothing. "Oh, come on! Please, please let us go!" she pleaded. "We don't have any stolen money." She waved her arms, as if to entice the gunmen to look around. "I mean, look at this place. Does it look like we have a million dollars?"

She then waved toward Kincaid, drawing attention to him. "I live with this man. We're together all the time. If he had taken the money, I would have known about it!"

Outwardly, Kincaid appeared calm, his years of training on the force having prepared him for moments like this. Inside, his mind was a cesspool, as his fears swirled around a trifle of guilt that Debbie was now in this situation and didn't know the story. He hoped Debbie's plea would have some effect. Sadly, it had none.

"I'm losing my patience with these assholes!" barked Santiago as he looked over at Perez. In that instant, Perez threw his right arm back, still holding his weapon, and smashed Debbie across the face with the barrel of his 9-mm. She fell backward, crashing into an end table before falling face-first into a tall, brown-glass lamp, the fixture shattering into her eyes as she landed on the floor.

Her face now a mask of blood, she struggled to get up. As her body strained, Kincaid noticed that Santiago had turned his head to look over at Perez. At that instant, Kincaid drew his pistol from his belt and fired three shots directly at Santiago.

Each flash of the three shots caused a split-second white reflection like lightning, and the terrifying sound reverberated off the walls of the narrow metal trailer, producing a deafening report. Two of the bullets ripped through Santiago's clothing and into his chest, while the third pierced his forehead into his skull.

Santiago momentarily wavered on his feet, his body twisting as the shots rippled through him, blood spurting wildly in every direction. His life wasted away in a mere second as he tumbled to the floor with a thud, dead as he hit.

As Santiago met his gruesome end, Kincaid saw a flash and heard another shot from Perez that echoed off the walls. His head swung around to see Debbie's head explode from the bullet, blood gushing like a fountain from the remnants of her skull. Before he could react to the horrific sight, Perez whirled around and fired a wild shot at Kincaid, which slashed through his left hand, shooting off his little finger.

The burning sensation in the severed finger was only beginning as Kincaid and Perez fired at each other simultaneously. The ringing echo from the firefight reverberated inside the cramped trailer and became ear-shattering.

The shot from Perez ripped into Kincaid's right shoulder, knocking him backward from the velocity. In turn, Kincaid's bullet sliced into Perez's neck, severing his spinal cord and forcing his head to jerk violently in the opposite direction. His body convulsed grotesquely as he dropped to his knees and then the floor, dead.

An eerie silence fell over the room as the gunfire ended, a quiet of several seconds that seemed like an eternity. Now flat on his back, Kincaid was overcome with the intensity of the pain in both his shoulder and his hand, and his body was wrapped in the fresh shock of the wounds. After a couple of minutes, Kincaid recovered sufficiently, and he fumbled for the cell phone in the pocket of his now-tattered shirt. With a shaky right hand, he punched in the numbers 911.

As he held the phone to his ear, he used his left hand, blood pouring from his missing finger, to steady himself as he crawled over to Debbie. She was barely recognizable from the shot that had brutally taken her life, and Kincaid whimpered as he turned away from the sight. Just then, he heard the voice of the dispatcher at the Macoupin County E911 office, "What is your emergency?"

Though he was growing increasingly weak, Kincaid mustered enough strength to shout into the phone who he was, and that there had been a shooting at his residence. He also managed to give the correct address, pleading that an ambulance was needed as soon as possible. The dispatcher assured him that help would be arriving soon, but Kincaid did not hear the words. His phone slipped from his grasp and his body collapsed to the floor, gasping for breath and hoping that he could survive until the paramedics arrived.

CHAPTER 15

When the 911 message was broadcast, Illinois State Police Trooper John Smith reacted immediately. He was only three miles west of White City when he heard the call, and he activated his red lights as he raced toward Kincaid's residence.

Smith had been on the force for only three years, and this was the first shooting that he had responded to. That was not surprising, as his usual area, nicknamed the "south patrol" that extended southward from District 18 headquarters in Litchfield, was not a high-crime area, and gun violence was indeed rare. But Smith thought little of it as he rolled down the highway toward the scene.

A native of nearby Staunton, the energetic Smith was a cum laude graduate of the regional university, Southern Illinois University - Edwardsville, and immediately enrolled in the academy. Already he had impressed supervisors with his high activity. A fair-minded young man who still had an idealistic view of police work, he and his wife of two years, an elementary school teacher, were expecting their first child in July.

Unsure of what was waiting for him, he exhaled deeply to slow his racing heartbeat, rifled his hand through his sandy blond hair, and shifted his five-foot-ten, 185-pound body in his seat, anxious at what may happen next. He had never cared for James Kincaid, as he thought the veteran cop did not appreciate his job and was a poor family man, based on his multiple marriages and coarse banter. But Kincaid was another member of the force and was in trouble now. Smith eagerly accepted the challenge to help.

Smith pulled into the driveway and notified District 18 headquarters that he was 10-23, at Kincaid's residence. He noticed that the front door to the trailer was closed and only one light was on. He also saw that the Celica, belonging to Debbie, was standing with its door ajar. He parked, left his red lights flashing, and deliberately climbed out his car, gun drawn. Cautiously approaching the front door, he stood to one side and turned the knob, pulling the door open and peering inside with his body protected by the side of the trailer.

Lying on the living room floor was Kincaid, with Debbie lying next to him. His shirt was stained with blood from the gunshot wound in his right shoulder. But he was conscious and was able to see Smith's head looking in through the open doorway. "I'm alive," he called weakly to Smith. "They're gone. It's safe; come in."

From his prone position, Kincaid advised Smith that he had been shot in both the right shoulder and left hand and that Debbie was dead. As Smith's head swiveled around the room, he observed the body of one male, Santiago, with an obvious head wound, lying face up at the head of the living room. Smith then turned to see the body of a second male, Perez, lying face down with an exit wound to the neck.

Debbie was lying face up against the wall with what appeared to be a bullet wound to her forehead, which had shattered her skull and splattered blood in all directions. Smith knelt down to attend to Kincaid, who was crying and holding Debbie's cold hand.

Kincaid knew that Smith had questions to ask, and he headed him off. "These guys tried to rob us," he said through gasping sobs. "They said they'd kill us. I had no choice but to shoot them."

Smith tried to reassure Kincaid. "It's okay, it's okay," he said, mustering some soothe in his voice. Smith then rose to his feet, holstered his weapon and, using his portable radio, contacted District 18 headquarters to advise them that the scene was secure. He also informed them that Kincaid had been shot and three others had been killed.

He then turned back to Kincaid, reassuring him that an ambulance was on the way, and that everything would be all right. Still shaking in pain and tears, Kincaid slightly nodded in understanding. Smith returned to his kneeling position, withdrew his knife, and cut open Kincaid's shirt to examine his shoulder wound.

As he did, he could hear the whine of an ambulance siren just outside. Seconds later, Clark Helton and Larry Schiller, a pair of veteran EMTs who were familiar with every cop in District 18, looked inside the open front door before entering briskly. Helton, using his twenty-six years of experience, immediately attended to Kincaid's wounds, sterilizing them and applying pressure before wrapping Kincaid's shoulder and finger in heavy white bandages. He then measured Kincaid's blood pressure, heart rate, and respiratory rate. He reported those totals over the radio to the emergency room at Litchfield Memorial Hospital, where Kincaid would be transported.

Helton also described the nature of Kincaid's wound to the doctor at the emergency room and received instructions on further treatment, including hooking up IVs. As Helton worked, Schiller, who had fourteen years on the job, inspected the other victims, immediately determining that all three were dead.

Now stabilized, Kincaid was wrapped in a blanket, lifted onto a gurney, and placed in the ambulance for the trip to Litchfield Memorial. As Kincaid was being carried out, a smattering of people stood at the edge of the street, drawn to the flashing lights of Smith's squad car and ambulance. The voice of a male, barely visible in the darkness, inquired what had happened, but Wilson and Schiller, consumed in the moment, did not answer as they loaded the patient, climbed back in their seats, and raced for Litchfield.

CHAPTER 16

As part of the response, a detective was advised of the situation, and a request was made for a crime scene technician to be dispatched. The contact was sent to Sergeant Mike Miller, the highly regarded Illinois State Police detective whom Kincaid had worked with in the early stages of the crime investigation.

Miller was at his Litchfield home on early Saturday morning, finishing up two Redbox movies he had rented with his wife. The late-night movie binge on the living-room couch passed for a "date night," which the couple had not done in a while. When the call came in, the dispatcher briefed Miller on the situation.

The normal policy of the Illinois State Police calls for the Division of Internal Investigations, or DII, to be notified of any ISP-related shooting. Upon learning that an officer had been involved, Miller made the request to advise DII of the situation at White City.

A DII agent is the lead investigator on all shootings related to the state police and is on call twenty-four hours a day, seven days a week. Agents rotate duty calls on weekends, and on this frigid night, the duty officer was Lieutenant Roger J. McIntire, who was at his residence in Chatham, forty-five miles north of Litchfield.

Like Miller, McIntire (nicknamed R.J.) was a devoted family man and was asleep in bed at the time of the call. Earlier in the evening, he had taken his wife to dinner and a basketball game at Chatham Glenwood.

At six feet tall and 195 pounds, R.J. looked like he could have taken the court himself, but he preferred the bleachers, where he ran his hands through his reddish-brown hair and across his freckled cheeks with every home team basket.

McIntire was an eighteen-year veteran of the Illinois State Police, the last nine in DII, and his integrity and determination made him one of the most respected individuals in the division. It also made him a good husband, as he had married his wife of twenty-nine years, Darlene, during their senior year of college at Northern Illinois University and had remained faithful ever since. Darlene certainly didn't mind having her husband around, as his rugged physique was not only nice to look at but also could be of considerable help around the house since she had been a stay-at-home mom.

Their union had produced three kids, all of whom were grown and out of the home. The oldest, Sherri, was a nurse in Springfield, while the middle one, Becky, was a second-grade teacher at a private school in Effingham. The youngest was the boy, Travis, who had just graduated from the University of Illinois and now had a sales job in Florida.

Like Miller, McIntire somehow found time to spend at home amid the grueling hours that his position called for, exemplified by this call on this weekend after midnight. But McIntire was accustomed to it, and his seemingly endless supply of adrenaline left him well prepared.

Since Litchfield is closer to White City than Chatham is, Miller arrived first, just thirty minutes after receiving the call. He surveyed the crime scene as he waited for the DII agent and the crime scene tech. During the wait, he called District 18 headquarters in Litchfield, advising them to contact the district commander and inform him of the situation. In addition, he told headquarters to initiate a contact with the ISP Command Center in Springfield, so the area commander and the director of the state police would be notified.

Fifty minutes after Miller's arrival, R.J. McIntire was on the scene. Miller introduced himself and then updated McIntire on the latest activities and developments. Just then, the crime scene technician, Jason Webster, arrived from the Crime Scene Unit in Springfield.

At thirty-three, Webster was younger than the other two and was in his fifth year with CSU. He was considered the most articulate guy in the group, a conscientious professional who collected even the smallest details to provide the best overview of any case. Despite his relative age, he was seen as the go-to guy in CSU, even by guys who had been there longer.

Webster spoke briefly to McIntire and Miller before beginning his work of processing the scene. His work included a minute observation and description of the scene, with countless photos, to assist in the investigation of the shooting. In order for the crime scene to not be contaminated, Webster requested that the scene be secured and asked McIntire and Miller to allow no one inside the trailer until his work was finished.

It was old hat for Webster, one of the most detail-oriented staffers in CSU. The ISP also contacted the Macoupin County coroner, Chester Gage, since the bodies of the deceased remained at the scene.

As he processed the scene, Webster took numerous photos and measurements, made a sketch, and tagged and bagged pieces of evidence. As he worked, he noticed several small cameras on a wall and an overhead light in the living room of the trailer, and he wondered if a security monitor was somewhere inside.

Immediately, he yelled to McIntire and Miller, "Hey, we may have something here." Rather than wait a few seconds for them to get there, Webster strode down the hall, looking for the monitor. Just as McIntire and Miller were stepping into the kitchen, Webster opened the door to the bedroom closet, and found the secret compartment with the monitor. Switching on the video feed, he saw that the entire shooting had been captured in the recording.

"Damn!" he yelled in excitement. "It's all right here!" He walked up the hallway to the living room, met halfway by McIntire and Miller. "You're not gonna believe this, but the whole shooting is on tape. Kincaid had a home security system put in, and we've got it all."

McIntire and Miller stopped in their tracks, stunned by the development. "You're kidding," said McIntire after a few seconds. "He put a security system in here?" He looked around at the dingy walls of the trailer, wondering why anyone would install a system in a place like that.

"Guess so," said Webster. "Come back here and watch it."

They made their way to the bedroom, and Webster cued up the video. All three stood in silent amazement as they watched the shooting unfold on the tape, which revealed a remarkably clear view with favorable angles.

When it was over, McIntire stepped back and rolled his eyes in wonder. "God," he muttered. "I can't believe it's all here." Still in disbelief, he shook his head. "All the years I've been doing this, and I could count on one hand the times that we had any video at all, let alone something this good."

"Oh, geez, yes," said Miller, who was thinking the same thing. "What I wouldn't give to have had something like this every time out." He chuckled ruefully. "With luck like this, I ought to buy a lottery ticket today."

McIntire snickered along with him and then turned back to the task at hand. "That, right there, is invaluable," he said, pointing to the monitor as he turned to Webster. "Secure that tape, and keep it as part of the evidence from there. We're really gonna need that."

Though McIntire was eager to keep going, he was well aware of professional regulations. "But before we can take the tape, we've got to get permission from Kincaid to do it, or get a search warrant." He looked around the room. "I'll have someone keep the scene secure until we can speak to Kincaid, though I'm sure he'll consent to us taking it for evidence."

Webster nodded in agreement and went back to his work. After snapping numerous photos, he then bagged and tagged numerous pieces of evidence from the scene, including the three weapons used at the scene, belonging to Kincaid and the dead intruders. Next, he sketched and took measurements of the bodies and their locations, as further evidence. Webster also bagged the hands of each victim before the arrival of Gage, the coroner, who declared each person dead due to gunshot wounds. Gage advised Webster that he would contact Debbie's next of kin and would also attempt to make contact with the next of kin of the two Mexicans.

The bodies were then removed and transported to the morgue at Litchfield Memorial Hospital, the same medical center where James Kincaid was undergoing treatment.

*****

Major crime scenes such as that at the Kincaid trailer are visited by a host of police officers, and this was no exception. As the coroner examined the bodies, Deputy Mort Wood, a nine-year member of the Macoupin County Sheriff's Department, arrived to offer his assistance. Wood, a portly thirty-nine-year-old, stood and watched as the ISP went about their business, though he remained ready to act if needed.

Next came Captain Kent Small and Lieutenant Jim Mason of District 18 headquarters. Small, as expected, had already spoken to his superior in Springfield on what to do next. Both were briefed outside by McIntire and Miller, who discussed the situation, down to the last detail. McIntire told Small and Mason about the video and asked for the scene to be secured until receiving permission from Kincaid to obtain the tape. Small agreed to the request.

Once the scene was finally secured, the next order of business was to check on the condition of Kincaid. Miller and McIntire left from the driveway in their separate cars, followed by the squad car of Small and Mason, heading for Litchfield Memorial.

The cars parked side by side in the lot on the south side of the imposing brick complex and the men filed inside to the emergency room. At the desk was Julia Webb, the head ER nurse at the hospital for the last seven years, who looked up from her clipboard long enough to acknowledge the officers' presence. A subordinate called her from down the hall, but she spared enough seconds to tell the men that Kincaid was in surgery and could not be seen until sometime the next day. She then turned and walked briskly down the hallway.

While Small and Mason headed for the hospital cafeteria for coffee and breakfast, McIntire and Miller walked down the long hallways and past the various medical departments to the morgue to view the bodies of Debbie Marks and the two Mexican males. The pathologist on duty in the gray-walled, sterile-smelling facility was Dr. Richard Walker, a man in his mid-forties with thick black hair and a muscular build, and he informed the officers that he would perform autopsies on each body the following morning. McIntire and Miller then took possession of the personal property of the deceased males, including their billfolds, identification, and other effects.

The two men were nearly out the sliding front door to the hospital when Miller's cell phone rang. On the other end was Trooper Smith, the first on the scene at the Kincaid trailer hours before, advising that the police may have located the vehicle of the two Mexicans. The vehicle, a black Honda Accord, was parked on an unimproved roadway in a partially wooded area west of the Kincaid trailer.

Smith requested that McIntire and Miller return to the scene. McIntire asked if Webster, the crime scene tech, was still at the trailer, and Smith replied yes, asking if McIntire wished to speak to him. McIntire said no, that all he needed was for Smith to tell Webster to stand by to process the vehicle. As McIntire hung up, Miller looked directly at him, not needing an explanation since he could hear Smith's voice on the other end of the phone. They then proceeded back to their cars to drive to White City once again.

CHAPTER 17

By now, it was midday and the weather had turned raw, the sky a dark gray as a piercing breeze whipped the dry leaves that were the remnants of the previous fall. McIntire drove first, with Miller following, as they rolled back down the nine miles of Interstate 55 to the White City exit. Once at the trailer, the men were pointed to the car, and since it was just a few hundred feet away behind a stand of trees, they walked from the driveway to the abandoned Accord, instinctively looking down for any footprints, tire tracks, or bits of evidence that may have been left behind.

McIntire and Miller discussed the finding with Webster and asked him to take a photo of the vehicle before it was towed to the garage at District 18 headquarters so it could be processed and inventoried. Once Webster finished photographing the Accord, Miller then requested Smith to call Dale's Quick Tow in Litchfield, owned by Dale Wilson, whose son was a Litchfield city cop. Miller further instructed that Smith remain with the vehicle and follow the tow truck to headquarters for further processing by Webster.

Wilson, a rail-thin fifty-something man whose hair had turned prematurely gray twenty years before, couldn't sleep on this night, so he had went back to the garage and was on a slider underneath a butter-yellow 1988 Chevrolet Celebrity with the radio on his favorite country music station when the phone rang. He slid out from under the car, answered, and took the information from Webster before pulling on a grease-stained brown Carhart jacket and dirtied, insulated work gloves for his own trip down I-55 to White City.

Never one to waste a moment, Wilson was in White City in fifteen minutes, hooked up the Accord, and was on his way to District 18 headquarters, dropping the car off on his way back to the garage. By now, it was well past dark, and the temperatures continued to deteriorate as the winter wind gained in strength.

Webster, McIntire, and Miller made their way back to headquarters as well and completed their processing of the black Accord. A computer check revealed that the car was registered to Hertz Rent-A-Car in El Paso, Texas, and had been rented to an individual named Miguel Perez.

The vehicle was searched, and the contents were recorded. The items found included two cell phones, a pack of generic cigarettes, two lightweight coats, two boxes of 9-mm ammunition as well as a box of 45-mm ammunition, and three empty liquor bottles. There was also a small amount of cocaine and marijuana in the glove compartment.

McIntire, Webster, and Miller proceeded to the investigation office inside the headquarters, and each contacted their supervisors to update them on the status of the investigation. After they all hung up, the men talked over the case together, reviewing the evidence in hand and the events of a day that was excruciatingly long. Each sat back in their reclining office chairs, trying to relax their muscles.

Neither had eaten in hours, and Miller had some sandwiches brought in. As they discussed the case through mouthfuls, McIntire reached into his carrying case for a lead sheet and began to fill it out.

"What's that?" Miller always paid great attention to detail, and few things slipped by him.

"It's a lead sheet," said McIntire, peering up from the paper in front of him. "I always fill out one of these for every investigation I do." He turned the sheet around and slid it across the table for Miller to inspect. "I do this so no one that we need to interview is overlooked."

Satisfied, Miller pushed the paper back to McIntire and expected what was coming next. "Everyone present at the scene will be interviewed," remarked McIntire, turning his attention back to the paper. "We'll get everyone who was there."

McIntire worked for a few minutes, sometimes asking Miller for correct spellings or questions on someone whose face he knew but could not remember the name. When done, they continued discussing the case, and Miller, with local knowledge of the personnel of District 18, had some relevant facts.

"You know, Kincaid lived with the woman who was killed," started Miller.

"Yeah, that was kind of obvious," replied McIntire. "We found her effects all around the trailer. Stuff with her name on it, mail on the counter, whatever. Why?"

"She was a bartender at Martin's Tavern in Mount Olive and waited tables there, too. Little hole-in-the-wall place that's the favorite dive of the working crowd on weekends. I think she'd been married and divorced a couple of times before, and had worked at basically every bar and grill in the area." Miller shrugged his shoulders and used an open palm to emphasize points in his spiel.

McIntire raised his right eyebrow. "Oh, yeah?"

"Yeah. Kincaid and Debbie hung out there almost every Friday night. I guess when her shift was over, she'd stay on, or maybe she went back home and they drove back in together."

"How do you know all this?" Like the best investigators, McIntire wanted to confirm sources, no matter where they came from.

"Oh, hell, we all knew it," said Miller, waving his hand to blow off the insinuation. "It's common knowledge. I don't see a lot of Kincaid, since he works nights, but he likes to talk when you're around him. He'll tell you everything you want to know about himself, and more. He's mentioned Debbie to all of us, and he likes to tell you what happened when he's at the bar, who said what, what the scuttlebutt is." Miller chuckled. "Like we actually cared."

"Hmm," McIntire returned the chuckle.

"Kincaid kind of lives there on weekends, and his girlfriend damn sure lives there," continued Miller. "I guess working eight-hour shifts, then going back there to hang out, she must really like the place." Miller caught himself, since Debbie was no longer around. "Or, I should say, liked it."

McIntire didn't catch the slip. "You say this place is Martin's Tavern? Who owns it?"

"Some guy named Russell Martin," responded Miller. "Kincaid told us he's past middle age and kind of a slob. He lives in the back of the tavern, alone, never married. The bar is kind of his life."

"Hmmm…" McIntire's voice trailed off in thought. "We need to talk to that guy. What time is it?" he asked, turning his wrist to glance at his watch.

The watch read 3 p.m., for it was now deep into Saturday afternoon. "I'm sure Martin would still have to be at the bar," mused McIntire. "And if he isn't, he's at home right close by, like you said."

Miller was thinking the same thing as McIntire, and needed no prodding. "Let's go," he said. Briskly, the two men walked, almost in step, outside to the parking lot and McIntire's vehicle, for the drive back down the interstate to Mount Olive.

*****

The gray winter day had given way to sunshine, though McIntire and Miller were both so absorbed in thought that neither of them noticed or cared about the weather. When he saw the sign marking Exit 44 for Mount Olive, McIntire veered to the right, made the left turn at the top of the exit to head to town, and drove straight for Martin's Tavern.

The pair strode into the bar and quickly spied a dumpy-looking, older man behind the bar, dressed shabbily in a well-worn, checkered flannel shirt with a dingy towel thrown over his shoulder. Upon first glance, McIntire and Miller assumed the slovenly old man was Russell Martin. Together, they stepped toward the bar, to be greeted brusquely.

"Yeah, what can I get for ya?" barked Martin.

"Is Mr. Martin available?" inquired McIntire, in a crisp voice.

"You're lookin' at him." Martin yanked the towel off his shoulder, and tossed it on the countertop behind the bar. "What can I do for you guys?"

McIntire and Miller each identified themselves, and displayed their badges. Martin studied each, as if he were verifying their authenticity. Satisfied, he shifted his eyes upward to glare at each of the men in the face.

"We'd like to ask you some questions," said McIntire, looking around at the few patrons scattered about the room. "Is there some place we could talk in private?"

"Sure can." Martin pointed toward a secluded table in a dimly lit corner of the room, as far away as he could get from the other patrons. Though he was hardly a Rhodes Scholar, Martin was savvy enough to have an idea what this meeting was about. "Is this about the shooting at Kincaid's trailer?" he demanded.

"Yes, it is." McIntire and Miller waited as Martin rounded the bar and trudged toward the corner table. They followed, scanning the room as they went, in case there was something they needed to see for their investigation.

As he walked, Martin yelled over to a waitress, a bony, younger woman named Melody with dyed, jet-black hair, "Hey, watch the bar for a little bit, will ya?" Melody, engrossed in a flirtation with a portly, middle-aged male customer who was a big tipper, nodded.

As they sat down, McIntire opened his notebook, and looked directly at Martin. "So you are aware of the shooting?"

"Oh, hell, yeah," said Martin, waving his hand as he slouched in his chair. "News like that spreads like a wildfire in a small town like this. Everyone knows about it by now." He shifted uncomfortably, and reached for his knee, as if he were in pain. "I don't know much about it. All I know is that some shots were fired. Don't know anything else about it."

"Well, we'd like to ask you a few questions about last night," said McIntire.

"Sure. What can I do for you fellas?"

The awkward greeting aside, McIntire got down to business. "We'd like to ask you some questions about two people in your bar last night."

"Oh, yeah?" replied Martin, in his usual gruff tone. "Who?"

"James Kincaid and Debbie Marks. You know them? Were they here last night?

"Oh, sure. They're here every Friday night." Martin reached into his shirt pocket for a pack of discount-store cigars and offered each of his guests one.

They declined, causing Martin to shrug as he fired up a black Bic lighter with a flame so high that it nearby burned his eyebrows.

After a couple of puffs, Martin continued. "Debbie works for me, you know. Great gal, good-looking. She does the 11-to-7 shift normally. Has for what, fourteen or fifteen years now? Been a long time." He puffed again. "Course, tonight she was on the 3-to-11 shift. Not her usual slot."

"Mm-hmm," McIntire offhandedly replied as he hurriedly wrote in his legal pad. Miller had a stenographer's notebook and did the same. "Did she stay after her shift or just go on home?"

"Oh, no, she stayed," said Martin, puffing away as ashes fell onto his shirt. "Kincaid's her boyfriend. He comes down every Friday night, or at least, usually does."

"You know Kincaid well?"

"Damn right I do!" roared Martin. "Great guy, great guy. Love having him around. Lucky son of a bitch for having a chick like Debbie." He let out a loud belch and then pounded his fist into his chest as if to stop another. "I got a lot of respect for him, and guys like you."

With their years of experience in investigations, McIntire and Miller were used to filtering through the unimportant details in interviews like this. "So what time did he get here?"

"Around six or so. It was well before the end of Debbie's shift." Martin nodded his head back and forth, trying to recall the particulars. "Like I said, she got done at eleven, and they stayed down here, having a few drinks, shooting the bull with friends of theirs. I think they left around one. I mean, that's what they usually do on Fridays."

McIntire and Miller wrote away in their notebooks. "Did anyone else see them in the bar tonight?" quizzed McIntire. Martin nodded his head and provided the names of several regulars who were sure to have seen both Kincaid and Debbie, including the Debbie's friend Shelley Tipson, the Adams brothers, and Ned Ullmann, the perpetually annoyed school janitor.

"Thanks," said McIntire as he scribbled the names on his legal pad. "Did you see any young Mexican men in the bar tonight, or did anyone else mention anything about seeing young Mexican guys around?"

"No, I can't say that I did," said Martin, stretching out the words, trying to remember. He then recalled something that seemed insignificant at the time. "Now that you mention it, one of the guys in the bar did say something about seeing two people in a car in the parking lot."

Miller's eyes met McIntire's, and they knew they were on to something. "What was that about?"

"There was this one customer, Bill Adams, he's in here quite a bit, good guy. He came in around 8:30 tonight, and I was shooting the breeze with him. Around 10, he went outside to his pickup, to smoke a cigarette. When he came back in, he mentioned that there were two guys sitting in a car out in the lot."

Miller could feel another adrenaline rush in his veins as McIntire, his eyes slightly wider than before, kept on writing. "Did this Adams individual see anything on the make or model of the car, or if the occupants were Mexicans?"

"No, nothing. Never said anything about the type of car. All Bill said was that when he went out, he looked out the window of his pickup and saw two people sitting in a car." Martin shrugged slightly, indicating that he didn't think it was a big deal. "He didn't seem too concerned, never said anything else about it. He just thought they were waiting for someone."

McIntire and Miller had a good idea who they were waiting for. McIntire then moved on to the real purpose of the visit.

"Well, sir, we're investigating an incident from last night," said McIntire, looking up from his notebook to give Martin his undivided attention. "There was a fatality at the trailer where Trooper Kincaid lives. Two Mexican males broke into the trailer, and a shooting followed. Debbie Marks was killed in the incident, along with both of the Mexicans. Trooper Kincaid was wounded, but he's expected to survive."

"Son of a bitch!" In shock, Martin ran his fingers through his greasy hair and exhaled deeply. "Debbie was just here last evening. I said goodbye to her when she left." He shook his head in disbelief. "She was just like always—smiling, laughing, joking around. Best barkeeper I ever had, such a pretty little thing. And now, she's gone, just like that." He snapped his fingers for effect.

Martin dragged his tired body from the chair and wandered off a few feet before placing his hand on a wall to brace himself. "Pretty girl. Pretty girl.

Never gonna find another woman like that." Catching himself, he turned back to his visitors. "Another bartender like that, I mean."

"We're sorry to be the ones to tell you," said McIntire as Miller nodded in sympathy. "You mentioned this Bill Adams individual. What can you tell us about him? We'd like to talk to him, too."

"What? Oh. He's a mechanic for the Chevy dealer in Staunton, about four miles south of here," said Martin, still stunned by the news. "He lives in Staunton, but I can't remember where." He stumbled over to the bar and snapped at Melody to hand him a phone book. She shuffled some papers behind the bar, finding one and handing it to Martin, who stumbled back to the corner table.

"I can tell you, just a sec here," he mumbled as he flipped through the pages. "Right here. Bill Adams, 1962 Shiloh Lane, phone number…" McIntire quickly wrote down the address and phone number, and readied for the final question of the night.

"Thanks. One more thing. Did you notice anything different, or unusual, about the way that Kincaid or Debbie were acting last night? Anything different about their behavior?"

"No, can't say that I did. They seemed just like always. Everything just seemed normal, like any other night." Martin sniffed, seeing the irony of his statement.

McIntire and Miller raised themselves from the table and prepared to leave. "We'll probably contact you again with more questions."

"Sure, anything I can do," said Martin. "Anything for Debbie." He turned away and stared at the wall and ceiling. "Such a nice girl. Such a nice girl…"

*****

McIntire and Miller said their goodbyes, walked back to the parking lot, and climbed into the car for the drive back to headquarters. As the telephone poles flew past on I-55, they were the only ones on the highway at this time of the afternoon, as the clock on the dash flashed 5:30 p.m.

Few words were said as they turned left off the exit toward headquarters, a half-mile away. Their adrenaline fading, weariness now set in, as they had been up for almost twenty-four hours and had not slept since early the previous day. Both men knew it, but they were professionals and did not want to break it off.

Finally, McIntire bit. "That's really all we can do for now," he said. Though Miller only had to drive across town to get home, McIntire had nearly forty miles to go.

"Sure. Been a helluva day and night," laughed Miller. "What time do you want me here tomorrow?"

"9 a.m. Before I go, I'll call Webster, and tell him to meet us here then. I'll also call the dispatch center in Macoupin County to get the ID of the dispatcher who took the 911 call from Kincaid. I'll also see if I can get a copy of the 911 tape sometime tomorrow. We'll also drive down to Staunton, to see if we can get a hold of Bill Adams, and find out what he says."

"All right," said Miller, knowing the night would continue. "Let me use the bathroom, and I'll come back and help."

"Sure. I'll make the calls, and you come back and we'll update my lead sheet."

McIntire dialed the phone for the calls, and he was just hanging up as Miller returned. They then updated the lead sheet with several names on the interview list, including Bill Adams; Russell Martin; the dispatcher, and dispatch operator; and ambulance attendants from the 911 call; and the 911 tape itself. The list also included Trooper John Smith, who had initially responded to the 911 call at the trailer, as well as Kincaid himself.

With all of that finished, McIntire and Miller deliberately strode out of the building amid a snow shower that whitened the sidewalks and pavements. Undaunted, they brushed off their cars to head home for some much-needed sleep.

CHAPTER 18

With an eighty-mile round trip from home to Litchfield, R.J. McIntire's sleep time was greatly reduced, but for law enforcement professionals at his level, that is to be expected. He woke up with a start, showered and dressed, and went to the kitchen, to have coffee and chat with his wife, Darlene.

The conversation was light, just the way they both liked it, and they discussed the upcoming day, with the schedules for the kids and a quiet date night at some point, hopefully soon. R.J. admired Darlene's new maroon wool sweater and told her so, and she proudly swayed back and forth, flirtatiously showing it off. They hugged goodbye, holding on to each other for a few seconds, reveling in the warmth. At 8:50 a.m., he was breezing through the door at District 18, ready for more.

Mike Miller was only two minutes behind, having found time to spend a few minutes of pleasure in bed with wife Julie after he awoke from a deep slumber. Though she often fretted over her plump figure, Miller found no other woman that compared to her, and their intimate moments like those of this morning solidified an already strong bond.

His daughter had a junior high basketball game on this Sunday afternoon and he hated to miss it, but his job on this day left him no choice. As Julie and their daughter fixed breakfast, Miller was readying himself for the long day ahead back at headquarters.

While McIntire had a lengthy drive to Litchfield, he was not the only one. In Springfield, Jason Webster, the crime scene tech, was turning off Exit 52 from the fifty-minute drive, part of a grind that his own wife, Amelia, was just starting to understand. The couple had married four years ago, and she was learning on the fly about being a cop's wife. She owned a hair salon, and her regular hours clashed with the demands of Webster's frenetic schedule.

But they had plenty in common, even through the ups and downs of a new marriage. A couple of years ago, Amelia had carved a friendship online with an old flame during her many evenings alone, and she was tempted at the possibility of more. The scenario made her husband quite uncomfortable and, wracked with feelings of guilt, she broke off the friendship.

The experience had actually brought them closer together, and they now tried to talk more, and spend more time together. Even on this jam-packed morning, Jason and Amelia had enjoyed breakfast together, watching a few minutes of an old movie as they ate before he tenderly kissed her goodbye and headed back to Litchfield, not expecting to see her again until she was asleep that night.

Now, McIntire, Miller, and Webster were sitting around a metal conference table in an off-white, concrete block meeting room at headquarters. They had skillfully dodged some reporters in the lobby, who had gotten wind of the shooting and had plenty of questions that would be directed to the public information people at this point in the investigation.

McIntire opened the discussion as he turned to Miller. "What are your thoughts on this so far?"

"I've been turning this over in my mind," pondered Miller. "I know it's still early, but I don't see robbery as a motive. I think we've got to rule that one out."

McIntire sat up straighter in his chair and looked at Miller with quizzical eyes. "Why do you say that?"

"Because I just can't see robbers with that kind of weaponry breaking into a place like Kincaid's trailer," said Miller, shrugging his shoulders slightly. "They were sure well armed for a place like that. That trailer is run down, dingy, and there weren't nice cars or trucks or tractors parked around it. And those weren't just kids who broke in there. I'd have to wonder if they were professional criminals, to have weaponry like that and be so well prepared.

"Besides, Kincaid was always broke," continued Miller. "Everyone talked about that here. I mean, you saw that trailer. Guys who've been on the force that long don't usually live like that, and the robbers may well have known that."

Miller began to reel off points of discussion, counting each with his fingers. "For one, he's been married and divorced twice. He got soaked by his first wife, or at least that was the word around here. Second, he had two kids with his first wife who are college-age, and he's on the hook for some of the tuition. Then he had some high child support payments for the two kids he had with the second wife. It was something like $800 a month, I think. Pretty high, at any rate."

"So what's your conclusion on this?" McIntire saw where Miller was going but wanted to hear it in his own words.

"I'm saying that if Kincaid had anything worth stealing, I don't know what it would be. We both saw the inside of that trailer. There weren't any collections, or expensive furniture, or electronics sitting around. If he had any money in there, I don't know where it would have been. Nothing of any real value."

McIntire nodded his head and pushed his lips forward in thought. "That's all very interesting. I can't wait for Kincaid to be available to interview. We'll learn a lot more after we talk with him."

He then turned toward Webster. "What do you think about all of this?"

Webster drew a deep breath and then began speaking. "I've got to tell you, from the evidence at the scene, it looks like the shooting was justified. You look at where everyone was standing, and that's really the only thing you could think at this point. But we'll know more when all of the evidence is evaluated, when the ballistics tests on the bullets found at the scene are in, and when we obtain permission from Kincaid to get the tape."

The discussion was brief, and Miller and McIntire promptly left for the drive to Staunton to interview Bill Adams. It was nearing 11:30 p.m. when they pulled onto Shiloh Lane, a residential street on the edge of town that had as many farmhouses as ranch houses.

The Adams house was one of the farmhouses, a white two-story Victorian that badly needed a new paint job. The men knocked on the door and introduced themselves, with credentials displayed to Adams' wife, Martha, who was dressed in a tan smock top, a light choice for the cold weather. But both Miller and McIntire were nearly swept away by the blast of warm air emitting from the open door, a sign that the thermostat was turned way up.

Martha informed the investigators that her husband was at his job on this Sunday, trying to catch up on some work and get a little overtime pay, and would not be home until around noon. Rather than wait, McIntire and Miller told her that they would return when he was due back. With a newfound half hour to kill, they decided to drive back to the Kincaid trailer, less than five miles away, to observe and walk around the scene of the shooting in the daylight.

After a careful survey of the area from their vehicle, they both got out of the car and walked around the property once again. Having completed that, they drove back to the Adams house to find a battered red Chevrolet pickup in the driveway that had not been there before. Adams was waiting for them, and opened the door before they reached the steps.

At five-foot-eight and 160 pounds with a shaved bald head, Adams looked more like a linebacker than a mechanic and, based on the many tattoos that covered his arms, was more like a biker than a blue-collar worker in his early sixties. But few knew what made a car run better than Adams, which allowed him to remain in his current job for the last thirty-one years. His work on a Sunday reflected his work ethic, and both he and his bosses knew that he gave them plenty of time for the money.

Once inside, McIntire and Miller again displayed their credentials and introduced themselves. The heat was still turned up, and the house was stiflingly uncomfortable. Adams invited them to sit at the dining room table, which he had made himself in the workshop out back, while Martha offered the men some coffee. They politely declined as Adams accepted and then took the initiative to the meeting.

"I heard about the shooting at Jim Kincaid's place," he said in his usual brusque manner. "It was on the St. Louis news this morning. Horrible deal. Is that what you want to talk about?"

"Yes, sir, it is," said McIntire, setting up his legal pad on the table. Prior to the interview, he had obtained Adams' full name, date of birth, and address and phone numbers for both work and home. Miller, too, was laying out his own steno pad, readying himself for the interview. "Russell Martin, the owner of the tavern, told us you were there on Friday night. Do you recall anything unusual while you were there, or when you got there?"

"Well, yeah, there was something," responded Adams as he sipped from his dark brown china mug. "I got there around eight thirty, and pulled in like I always do." He laughed. "For whatever reason, I park in about the same spot every time, everywhere I go. My wife always rides my ass about that," he said, using his thumb to point to Martha, "but I just do that. Don't know why. At any rate, I went outside around 10 to have a smoke, and the only thing I recall is that there was this car in the parking lot with two guys sitting in it."

Writing away, McIntire asked, "Could you tell anything about these two guys? Anything that you saw?"

"Nah, it was too dark. I couldn't see their faces," Adams said, shaking his head. But his years as a mechanic had built up, since he knew the make and model of practically every car on the road. "I do know the car, though. It was a black Honda Accord, four-door, with Texas plates."

McIntire and Miller glanced at each other, knowing there was a witness to the Accord found near the scene of the shooting. "Go on," said McIntire.

"Not much else to tell," said Adams. "I didn't think much of it. I thought they were probably just waiting for someone." He took a big swig of coffee. "The strange thing, though, was that the two guys in the Accord were still sitting there when I left. It was around 11:15 or so. I looked over in that direction, and there they were, same spot, just as they had been when I walked in."

"Mm-hmm," McIntire was lost in thought of the news that the car was still there so late. "Is there anything you remember about the two men in the car? Anything at all?"

"Nope, I'm sorry," said Adams apologetically. "I couldn't see their faces. All I could see is that they were two guys. Neither one was a woman. I couldn't identify them, other than that." As Martha poured her husband a second cup of coffee, Bill looked McIntire directly in the eye. "Do you think those two guys were involved in the shooting?"

"Don't know," replied McIntire, looking over at Miller. "Do you remember anyone else who was at the bar? Any other patrons or people you knew?"

"Well, I don't know that many people there," said Adams. "I used to go down there and talk to a couple of old boys, but they both died about a year ago. I still go there and bullshit with some of the guys there. But I don't know their names."

"Anyone at all there that you do know their name?"

"Yeah, a couple. There's Rae Johnson, a lady that I went to high school with. Used to date her for a while. I see her every time I'm in there, with her husband Bob. He's part-owner of a hardware store in Mount Olive, and she used to work for him.

"Then there's Angie and Barb Morse. I saw them over in the corner, sitting off by themselves. They're sisters, never married. Each about seventy, or seventy-two, or something like that. Both of them were secretaries for this company in St. Louis, and they'd drive back and forth to work, each and every day. They still live together, in this tiny little house. They do everything together, never seen apart."

"All right," McIntire and Miller cared little for that sort of inference. "Anything else you remember?"

"No, that's really it. Nothing else comes to mind."

"Okay then." McIntire pushed his chair away, and Miller followed his lead. "Thank you for your time, Mr. Adams. If you think of anything else, be sure to give me a call." He handed Adams a card with his name, number, and e-mail.

"Sure will. Good luck to you boys," said Adams cheerily as he got up to hold the door for his guests.

McIntire and Miller stepped through the light snowfall from the early morning hours and headed back for their vehicle. Their next stop was back in Litchfield, as they hoped that James Kincaid had recovered sufficiently from surgery to be interviewed.

CHAPTER 19

Litchfield Memorial Hospital was a place that everyone in the town was proud of, but no one really wanted to visit–unless, of course, they were ill, at which time it was the first choice.

A complex of three buildings, each with five stories, the hospital was one of the largest employers in the area and had risen in prominence with its connection to the leading hospitals in Springfield and St. Louis. As a result, it was no longer just a band-aid stop on the way to treatment at a bigger facility. LMH was the largest hospital between those two cities and prided itself on the high ratings it received in popular magazines and online studies.

McIntire and Miller breezed through the front door once again and stopped in the tiny admission office, asking where James Kincaid's room was. They were advised that he was in Room 309, a private room, and rather than wait for the elevator, they chose the two flights of stairs.

The floor nurse at the station on 3 was Lee Baxter, a slim dark-haired woman in her late thirties, who was busy speaking to other nurses as McIntire and Miller walked up, and they had to wait for a couple of minutes. Finally, she was able to tell them that Kincaid's operation had been successful, and a full recovery was expected.

R.J. inquired if Kincaid was able to be interviewed, and Lee replied that he was being given his medications at the moment. She added that they should speak to his doctor before talking with him. The physician on the floor was Dr. Jonathan Jones and, following a brief wait, he gave them permission to talk to Kincaid, but only for a few minutes.

Hospitals are never quiet places, as there are always nurses running up and down the floor, patient beepers going off, and the rattle of gurneys, medical chests, and bedpans. R.J. and Mike entered Room 309 and immediately closed the door, to block out the background.

They found Kincaid lying on his back in bed, eyes closed, with an array of IV hookups and monitors across his body from the post-op. Though he had not noticed the door closing, he did hear their soft footsteps, and he opened his eyes as they approached the bed.

"Hey, Mike," he said in a weak voice, as he immediately recognized Miller from his previous encounters.

"Hello, Jim," replied Miller, some empathy in his voice. "How are you doing?"

"I've been better," said Kincaid, shifting his body slightly. "Got shot up pretty bad on this one. Feel like a freight train just ran over me."

"I bet," responded Miller, turning to McIntire, who introduced himself.

"Jim, my name is R.J. McIntire. I'm a lieutenant with the Illinois State Police Division of Internal Investigations. I was wondering if we may be able to speak to you about the shooting."

Kincaid cocked his head. "Why are internal affairs investigating this? What's going on?"

McIntire was unfazed. "It's the policy of the ISP that any time an officer is involved in a shooting incident, someone from DII is assigned as the lead investigator."

"Oh, yeah, right," said Kincaid. "I knew that. I just forgot."

"Not a problem. Well then, you feel well enough to answer some questions for us?"

"Sure." As Kincaid spoke, McIntire pulled up a straight-backed chair, the usual, uncomfortable provision of a hospital for visitors to sit in. He pulled out his trusty legal pad as Miller walked over to the windowsill, where he set up his own work space.

"We know this is hard for you, and we know this may not be the best time," said McIntire, whose training had encouraged him to connect with his subjects. "But we need to know what happened, and we want to hear your side of it. Do you think you could answer some questions for us?"

"Yeah, no problem. I'm all right." Kincaid never lost his jocular persona, even in his worst moments.

"Fine. Then, just tell us from the beginning. What time did you get off work on Friday?"

"At 7 a.m., just like usual. I wasn't overtime or anything. I was done at 7, like always."

"Uh-huh." McIntire was taking notes, in his normal way. "What did you do after that?"

"Oh, I stayed around the trailer. I went to bed, got up, did some housework. Nothing out of the ordinary." Nothing in Kincaid's life had been ordinary for weeks, but he played it down.

"All right. Did you leave the trailer at all that day?"

"Not until six or so. I went down to Martin's Tavern, where Debbie…" His voice trailed, remembering her gruesome death. "Where Debbie… worked."

"And what happened next?" The sound of McIntire's pen made a little scraping sound as it slid across the legal pad.

"Yeah, sure," said Kincaid, still finding his position in bed uncomfortable from his wounds and many hoses and lines inserted in him. He shifted his body awkwardly, seeking some respite. He spoke deliberately, still somewhat groggy from the surgical trauma of the last few hours.

"Well, I left home, and got to Martin's around six. Debbie…" Once more, his voice broke. "She finished her shift at eleven, and then she joined me. I was having dinner, and then we had drinks and talked with some of our buddies. Just like we always did."

"All right. When did you leave?"

"It was around one or so, I guess. Yeah, it was around that time. I remember looking at the beer clock on the wall, and that's about what time it was."

"Who else had been at the tavern when you were there? Anyone that you remember?"

"Oh, there were a bunch of people. There were these guys I talk to, Larry and Del Adams and Ned Ullmann. You know, just guys that you shoot the shit with. There were a couple of other people in the bar, but I don't really know their names. Wait"—something flashed into his mind— "there was this one guy, Bill Adams or Adamson or something like that, stocky guy, works on cars or something. Then there were these two sisters sitting off by themselves, almost like they wanted to be alone or something. Debbie was talking to this girlfriend of hers, Shelley, and she was there the whole time. I remember waving goodbye to her when we left."

"All right. When you went out into the parking lot, do you remember seeing anyone or anything out there?"

"Nope," said Kincaid, shaking his head weakly. "At least nothing that I noticed. I went straight to my truck. That's all that happened."

"Okay. Who was doing the driving?"

"We drove separate cars. I went home in my truck, and Debbie followed me in her car. She had driven it to work, like usual, so it was already there."

Law enforcement are trained to recognize the possibility of drunk driving, and to a seasoned professional like McIntire, the question begged to be asked. "You mentioned that you had been drinking. Were you intoxicated?"

On the flip side, alcoholics rarely admit to being drunk, saying that they only had "a couple" or "a few." Even from his prone position, Kincaid was no different. "Oh, no. I wouldn't say I was drunk." He shrugged his shoulders as much as the pain would allow and pursed his lips. "I mean, I'd had a couple drinks, and so had Debbie. But neither one of us was drunk. I'm a good driver, and I never do stuff like that."

Miller glanced at McIntire, as he had heard the rumors that Kincaid regularly had liquor on his breath when he reported for work. He said nothing, knowing this was not the time or place and they would discuss it later. McIntire, oblivious to the rumors, continued.

"All right. So you left the tavern and went home? Or did you stop off somewhere else?"

"No, we went straight home." His voice began to break, and his lip quivered. "And that's when it happened."

"What happened?"

"We got out of our cars and began walking up to the front door." Like many interview subjects, certain details are forgotten, and Kincaid did not remember that Debbie was not yet out of her car. "We were almost to the door, and all of a sudden, two guys with guns came up and ordered us inside."

"Uh-huh. And what happened next?"

"Well, we went inside. There was just enough light out there that I could see that each of them had a gun. One of them was yelling that if we did what we were told, no one would get hurt. I couldn't really make out their faces at that point. I just knew they were male." Kincaid turned his head, stared at the wall, and said the words that many victims say. "It all happened so fast."

"I'm sure it did." McIntire was used to hearing those words. "So, what happened when you got inside?"

"Once we got there, I could see that both gunmen were Mexicans. Debbie sat down on the couch, just sobbing and sobbing. We both asked them what they wanted."

"Had you ever seen either of these two individuals before?"

"Nope. Never saw them before in my life." Kincaid knew better, since he had seen one, Santiago, on the surveillance tape before.

"All right. What happened next?"

"One of the guys, the big one, pointed his gun at Debbie and told her to shut up. Then he called her a bitch and slapped her so hard that she fell off the couch. She pulled herself up on her knees after that…" Again, his voice and lips quivered. "Even though…even though that bastard hit her like that, she pulled herself together."

"Then what happened next?"

"The big one was pointing his gun at me and told me that they were there for the money. I told them I didn't know what they were talking about. I asked him over and over what he meant, and he just kept saying that I knew what he meant, and he was tired of the bullshit, and to give him the money right now.

Then…then he pointed his gun at Debbie again and told me that if I didn't give him the money…th-th-that…that he would kill her."

Kincaid's mind was a swirling blend of lies, guilt, and lingering recognition of professional duties. Though he wasn't telling the story exactly like it happened, he kept playing along. McIntire, in turn, kept writing on his notepad, knowing that his time in the room was limited and that Dr. Jones might come back any second.

"Keep going," McIntire prodded, trying to make the best of every minute.

"I kept telling the one that I didn't know what he was talking about. And he kept saying that he didn't believe me. Finally, he said that he was talking about the money that I had taken from that accident that I handled in November, the one that had the bag with over a million dollars in it.

"So, finally, I knew what he meant. I told him that I did recover a bag of money, and had turned it in. I also told him that I had pictures and the newspaper articles to prove it." Again, Kincaid was making up facts as he went along. "The gunman screams at me that I'm a liar, that I only turned in one bag of money, but that there had been two bags."

McIntire looked up from his legal pad with widened eyes. He turned his head and his eyes met Miller's, who had the same reaction. "You said two bags?"

"Yeah, that's what he said. I told him that he was wrong, that he was making a big mistake, that there were never two bags in the trunk, that I only saw one and had turned it in, like I was supposed to. He kept screaming that I was lying, and I tried to calm him down. I told him that maybe he was wrong, that maybe one of his own people had taken it."

"And what happened next?"

"They blew up even worse, screaming that I was lying, cussing us out, yelling at the top of their lungs. The big guy told me that if I didn't tell them where the money was, that they would kill both of us." Kincaid paused to collect himself and squirmed uncomfortably in his bed.

"And what happened next?" said McIntire, repeating the words familiar to anyone in a police investigation.

"Debbie was crying hysterically. She looked so bruised up from where that bastard had slapped her." A tear slowly rolled down Kincaid's right cheek. "She yelled at the guy that she didn't know anything about any money, and if I had taken it like they said, that she certainly would have known about."

"Uh-huh." McIntire and Miller wrote away. "Go on."

"She was just crying so hard, so scared." Another tear made its way down his face before he pulled himself together. "And then, the second guy, the smaller one, screamed at her to shut up and pistol-whipped her. Took his gun and smashed it across her face."

"Hmm. And what happened next?"

"I kept my eyes on the first guy, since he had the gun on me. When the second guy smacked Debbie like that, the first guy turned his head and looked at him. At that moment, I saw a chance. I had my duty weapon in my belt, and I pulled it out. I managed to get off three shots, bang-bang-bang. I hit him twice in the chest, and once in the head."

"Your duty weapon?" McIntire asked. "You were carrying your duty weapon?"

"Yeah." Kincaid knew that he had said too much. "Yeah, my duty weapon."

"Do you always carry your duty weapon?"

"No." Kincaid wiggled under the sheets, trying to keep cool. "I had it on me that night. I'd heard of a threat on my life from this guy I'd busted a year or two ago, and it spooked me. So I had it on me."

Normally, such threats are reported to headquarters, but since Kincaid had made the story up for Debbie, this was the first that McIntire and Miller knew of it. They glanced at each other and then continued.

"All right. And what happened next?"

"Well, after I shot the first guy, I heard a shot come from somewhere, and I turned my head to look at the other guy. I realized it was from the second guy, because I saw Debbie—Oh, God…" A long pause ensued as Kincaid worked his mouth, trying to maintain composure. "I saw Debbie fall backward against the wall, and saw the blood splatter on the wall, behind her head. That bastard"—Kincaid paused, as his voice trailed off—"had shot her…"

McIntire paused as well, knowing that the words were increasingly difficult. He spoke in a soft, but firm, monotone. "I know this is hard. Just tell us what happened next."

Kincaid swallowed a couple of times before speaking. "Just as I saw Debbie go down, the second guy fired a shot at me. It blew off my little finger." He pulled a bandaged left hand from under the sheet and held it up, indicating the wound. "I fired back at him, and he got one off at me at the same time. You know, simultaneously."

McIntire kept pressing. "And what happened next?"

"I hit the guy in the throat. Killed him instantly, he just dropped to the floor. He got me in the right shoulder." He used the left thumb sticking out of his bandaged hand to point to his injured shoulder. "I fell back on the floor but never went out. Never lost consciousness." Kincaid's machismo was still evident, and a tinge of pride came through in his words as he held his head up slightly to demonstrate his survival.

McIntire never responded to Kincaid's show of braggadocio. "And what happened next?"

"I crawled over to Debbie, and I knew she was dead. The top of her head was gone, just gone..." His voice drifted off again. "I knew I needed help, and I could reach my cell phone, in my pocket."

Kincaid then sat up slightly in bed as the cop in him ripped off the facts. "I called 911 and talked to the Macoupin County dispatcher. I told her who I was and that I had involved in a shooting at my residence. I told her I was wounded and that there were three deceased victims. The dispatcher responded that an ambulance and police were on the way." His burst of professionalism now ended, and he sank back, exhausted at the momentary display.

"And what else?"

"That's really it. That's what happened."

"Nothing else?"

Kincaid sighed and stared at the ceiling. "No. That's really all I can remember."

As Kincaid spoke, the emotions from the previous hours came to a head, and he began crying, tears streaming down his face. His acting ability, though, was still evident, at least in his mind. "I don't know why this happened. I mean, why the hell would those men think I had the money? I turned it all in." He turned to Miller. "God, Mike, you know what happened, you were there, you talked to me about it."

His tears turned to groveling, and he began to gasp for breath. "The worst part of it all…the worst of it all," he said through the gasps, "is that Debbie… died for nothing. Nothing at all. Not a damn thing…not a damn thing…"

Moments like this are difficult for investigators, but they have a job to do, nonetheless. "One last question," said McIntire. "While the crime scene technician was processing the scene, he found a security system, which included a monitor. The monitor we received shows the events as they happened. We would like your permission to have the tape as evidence, if that is all right with you."

Through his tears, Kincaid's mind snapped back to attention, and he kept playing along. "Oh, I forgot about that," he said. "You know, with everything that's happened and all. That should show everything that happened, both inside and outside of the trailer."

Kincaid had always managed to paint himself in the best light, and he was about to do so once again. "That will be my best evidence," he said. "Of course you can have it. Thank God I put that system in."

With that, McIntire had Kincaid sign a release for the tape. The signing was done with considerable difficulty, as Kincaid could barely rotate his injured right shoulder enough to move the pen across the paper.

McIntire knew this was the place to end, and he feared a scolding from the doctor if he saw Kincaid in such a teary condition. "I think that's all we need for now. You know that we may want to speak with you again about this."

Kincaid wiped away the tears with his good hand, wincing as his shoulder hurt while doing so. "I know. Anytime you need to."

"Thanks. Again, we're sorry for your loss. We both wish you a quick recovery and that you get out of here soon." McIntire and Miller both folded up their legal pads, said goodbye, and headed out the door into the hallway.

As before, they took the stairs from the third floor down to the first, saying nothing as they went. They were equally silent as they crossed over the parking lot to their vehicle, consumed with thoughts about what had just transpired and what was to come.

CHAPTER 20

The two-mile drive back to headquarters was as quiet as the previous few minutes until McIntire broke the silence. "What'd you think of the interview?" he said, turning briefly from the wheel to look at his passenger.

Miller tapped the back of his fingers against the dashboard in front of him, as if leading up to what he was about to say. "I was surprised at how much of that had to do with the money. Geez, how much time did he spend talking about that?"

"Quite a bit. I thought the same thing," replied McIntire. "And the part about the two bags. That was a new one."

"Oh yeah," said Miller, with a hint of laughter. "That one went through me. I looked over at you, and I knew you were thinking the same thing."

"Sure was. So what do you think of all of it? Do you think there was a second bag?"

"Well, the Mexicans sure thought so. I mean, why would they just make that up? You're telling me they came to a trailer in White City with some cock-and-bull story about a second bag of money to do all of this?"

"True." Like any seasoned investigator, McIntire was trained to consider all possibilities. "So let's say there was a second bag. Do you think the Mexicans were right and that Kincaid was their guy?"

"Hmm." Miller turned to the right and looked out his window for a second. He then turned back. "You know, that's the part that puzzles me. I don't think Kincaid took that money. I know the rumors, that he's living paycheck to paycheck. But I just can't see him taking that money, no matter how desperate he was. Assuming there was a second bag, of course."

"Well, like you said, the Mexicans were sure convinced that he did." McIntire slowed the car for an oncoming red light. As he waited for the green, he drummed his fingers on the steering wheel. "One other thing. You ever carry your weapon off duty?"

Miller looked at his partner. "You mean like Kincaid was doing? Did you pick up on that?"

"Yep. You ever do that?"

"Well, not usually. I don't normally have my duty weapon on my person when I'm not on duty. But I do carry it on me from time to time, depending on where I'm going. Or I might have it in the car when I'm traveling on vacation."

"Hmm." McIntire chuckled nervously. "I've been with the ISP for over twenty years and been in DII for what, nine years or so? Yeah, I know officers who carry their weapons off duty. But not many."

The lights were green for the rest of the way, and the conversation trailed off as the men approached headquarters. When they arrived, they found Jason Webster waiting for them in the meeting room. He had just returned from the autopsies of the deceased and had several files and small plastic bags on the table in front of him.

"What've you got?" inquired McIntire, foregoing any greetings.

"I've got the spent bullets that were extracted from the victims," replied Webster, flipping through his notes and pointing to one of the bags. "Obviously, we're going to check those out. I also took fingerprints and photographs of the victims. When I get back to Springfield, I'll run the prints through the AFAS and determine their true identity."

The AFAS is a national fingerprint database that helps law enforcement confirm identities. While people on the street think that the billfolds or identification, which were taken off the bodies by Miller the previous day, is sufficient, there is actually too much room for doubt. Law enforcement professionals, particularly in homicides, rely on the verification of the prints for the final determination.

"Good deal. What else do you have?" asked McIntire.

"The pathologist drew blood from each of the victims," said Webster. "I'll have the results on that later." He started to stand up to exit. "Do you need me for anything else?"

"Yes," said McIntire. "When we interviewed Kincaid, he gave us permission to take the security tape as evidence. So, you need to drive to the scene and get it, and take it with you to Springfield. While you're there, you can tell the officer at the scene that he can return to his regular duties. Be sure to lock the trailer when you leave, and take down the yellow crime-scene tape."

"Will do," said Webster.

"One more thing," added McIntire. "If you would, make several copies of the security tape. I know my boss and the director and the state's attorney will want to see it."

"Done," said Webster authoritatively. He gathered the evidence and files for the trip to the scene, and then back to the lab in Springfield. "I'll write my report and send you a copy."

"Thanks. We'll be seeing ya," McIntire waved his hand halfheartedly as a goodbye. Miller briefly smiled at Webster as he headed out the door.

Miller then led McIntire into his office to continue the discussion. They analyzed the case from every angle and considered what they had learned so far. The men also discussed at length the accident from November, when Kincaid had recovered the money.

After talking about the accident in depth, McIntire hesitated and looked at Miller. "Could you get the copies of the accident report, the tow-in report, and Kincaid's field report? Anything generated from that night that refers to the seizure of the money."

"Sure. Give me a couple of minutes." Miller pushed himself away from his desk and strode out of the room. While he was gone, McIntire reviewed his lead sheet.

Miller walked down the hallway to the record clerk and returned with the requested documents in a matter of minutes. R.J. read through them and wrote down every name that appeared on any of the reports onto his lead sheet.

"Why are you doing that?" asked Miller quizzically. "You want to interview those people, too?"

"Got to. Right now, we're going to have to rule out that Kincaid did or did not steal the money. Those Mexicans were sure that he had and were going to great lengths to get it back. I don't know if there's anything to it or not. But we've got to rule it out."

"What are you thinking?" Miller was unsure where McIntire's train of thought was going.

McIntire stopped writing, set his ballpoint pen down, and looked straight at Miller. He spoke in a calm, direct voice. "It's not unusual for troopers to have seizures of money like this. It happens more often than people think. I mean, yeah, this was a larger amount of money than usual. But it happens, and it's not that out of the ordinary."

Miller listened intently, eyes fixated on McIntire as he continued. "But I've never known a gang or cartel to retaliate like this. Geez, they sent two goons all the way up here from Texas, or down from Chicago or wherever, to get that money back. They cased the bar, they followed Kincaid and his girlfriend home, they were really committed. I've never seen anything like that, not since I've been in the state police."

He glanced at the tow-in report in front of him and pointed to a line on it. "Kincaid said here that a cell phone belonging to the accident victim was recovered," he said. "Do you know where that phone is now?"

"Yeah, sure," said Miller. "We downloaded all of the numbers on that cell phone and sent them to the ISP Intelligence Unit in Springfield."

"Well, we've also got cell phones off the two dead Mexicans," pondered McIntire. "Let's do the same with those. Download them, and cross-reference them on the ISP computer. Then send them to the Springfield office."

The numbers from those phones were downloaded and inserted into the computer. Then they were compared to the numbers taken from the driver who died at the scene. Many of the numbers matched.

"Damn," said McIntire, pursing his lips. "They all had to be connected in some way. The two guys in the trailer, the driver, all of them."

"Yep," said Miller, nervously scratching his forehead. "They were all in it together."

R.J. McIntire was never one to waste a moment in contemplation. When the evidence started piling up, he was already moving on, thinking ahead. "All right. Now we know something. We need more contacts to nail this down. You got anyone in the DEA?"

As expected, Miller had worked cases involving the Drug Enforcement Agency many times in his career, and one agent always stood out. "There's this guy who's a DEA agent named Tony Martinez," he said. "I've been on several cases with him. Really good guy to work with. Does whatever it takes to get it done."

"The kind of guy we need," seconded McIntire. "Set up a meeting with him here, at District 18. We need to give him the phone numbers from the cells we have to see if DEA has an informant, or if they can provide more information on these guys. We've got to know if there was a second bag of money in that trunk, and maybe Martinez could help us out."

Miller nodded as he rose from his chair. He knew that the seizure of the money likely involved one of the Mexican drug cartels, and there would be many leads throughout the country. He withdrew his cell phone from his shirt pocket and dialed the number of Tony Martinez.

CHAPTER 21

At 6:45 a.m. on Monday, Tony Martinez was rolling down Interstate 55 in his black Chrysler Sebring, covering the 110 miles from his home in Bloomington, Illinois to Litchfield and the headquarters of District 18. Heavy snow was predicted for later that day, and the approaching cold front brought a stiff wind that cut across the highway.

Most men would have blown off the mere notion of a meeting so far from home in such inclement weather. Martinez, though, never thought twice and did what the job called for.

Such was the life of one of the most respected DEA agents in central Illinois, though for Martinez, life did not start out that way. He was born in Texas to a Mexican-American family and was bilingual, an advantage in dealing with a drug trade that is dominated by Hispanics. He certainly looked the part, as his short, jet-black hair and dark complexion were complemented by piercing, black eyes that never seemed to lose focus. He stood so erectly that his height of five-foot-eleven seemed six inches taller, and his weight of 170 looked twenty pounds lighter.

He was a career DEA agent, with twenty-six years of experience that made him well versed in the illegal drug trade. Two decades of that service was spent in the Chicago suburbs, where he lived with his wife, Staci, and two sons in a quiet, split-level ranch home in the lovely residential suburb of Elmhurst. The serenity of the suburbs contrasted with the dealers, pushers, meth labs, crack houses, and pimps that he dealt with on a regular basis.

The neverending grind of Chicago finally wore on Martinez, and six years ago, he asked for a transfer to Bloomington. The fresh start and docile surroundings energized him, though Staci, who had grown up in the Dallas metroplex, was less enthused about leaving the big city. Still, she adjusted, and she appreciated that one factor in her husband's decision was to help their teenage boys attend Illinois State University in nearby Normal.

Though McIntire and Miller did not know it at the time, the seizure of the money involved Diego Garcia, the kingpin of the largest cartel on the Mexican-American border. It was a name that Martinez knew well. Three years ago, Martinez was involved in the infiltration of the terrorist plot in which Garcia was an informant, helping bring down Garcia's old boss, Juan Rodrequs.

Since Garcia had been nabbed while carrying nine hundred pounds of cocaine near Bloomington, Martinez was brought in to investigate and was the first to interview Garcia and his wife. The interview revealed the sweeping terrorist scheme, and, thanks in large part to Martinez, the plan was thwarted, saving thousands of American lives.

Martinez's role had earned him a promotion to a supervisory position, and he was now one of the ranking DEA agents in the state of Illinois. Though his position often took him back to the Chicago area that he had grown to hate, he sometimes was sent south, and this trip to Litchfield was one of those times. He drove with the radio off, lost in thought as snow flurries picked up, contemplating the basic details of the case that his friend Mike Miller had provided.

Martinez arrived at District 18 headquarters and walked inside as the harsh wind tousled his neatly combed hair. He ran his fingers through it to compensate as he passed through the doorway, greeted by Miller.

"Hey, Tony," welcomed Miller, extending his hand. "Thanks for coming down. How're you doin'?"

"Good, good," replied Martinez, engaging in a warm handshake. "Been a while, hasn't it? Looks like we're going to be at it again."

"Yep." The pleasantries then ended. "You've got the information I gave you. Let me take you inside. I want you to meet R.J. from DII."

Martinez followed Miller into his office, where McIntire was waiting. The men exchanged a cordial handshake before Martinez sank into a wooden, ladderback chair that was the other option for guests in Miller's office, as McIntire had already claimed the black swivel sitting across from the desk.

Miller thumbed through a small stack of messages from curious reporters, tossed them aside, and opened the discussion by providing all of the phone numbers from the cell phones taken from the dead driver at the accident scene as well as the deceased Mexicans from the shootout at Kincaid's trailer. Martinez had brought his laptop along and asked for a port to hook up. Miller pointed one out, and Martinez powered up, preparing to access the DEA computer database.

The search generated the names and addresses that were associated with the telephone numbers. Many of the numbers were in the Chicago area, while others were in El Paso, Texas, as well as the Mexican city across the border, Ciudad Juarez. Martinez forwarded the investigative leads to the DEA offices in both border cities to determine if the agents were familiar with any of the names or addresses.

Within minutes, he received a response from Willie Hood, a DEA agent in Chicago. Martinez had worked closely with Hood and trusted him implicitly. While both men had devoted their lives to stopping the drug trade in the nation, Hood had a personal interest, since he had grown up around it.

Willie's childhood was spent in Cabrini-Green, a predominately African-American neighborhood that is one of the poorest and toughest areas of Chicago's south side. Many of the boys he played hoops with ended up in rehab, prison, or the grave. Sleep never comes easy in much of Chicago's south side because of the ripple of gunfire and the wail of police sirens that pierce the desolate nights.

Willie's mother had ridden him hard, overprotective in every moment, fearful that her son would meet the fate of so many other sons on the block. But her love and guidance had paid off, and he never popped a pill, never smoked a joint, never shot up. He played football in the Public League high schools of Chicago, where games are no-holds-barred, and the talent level is among the best in the state. At five-foot-nine, Willie was usually one of the smallest players on the field, but always the grittiest.

He managed to earn a scholarship to nearby Chicago State University and graduated with a degree in criminal justice. Willie quickly landed a job with the DEA and was the hardest worker in the office, known for his relentless desire to clean up the streets of his boyhood. Now fifty-three, he was paying the price for the ridiculous hours, bad coffee, and stale ham and cheese sandwiches that had driven him for over three decades.

Though he controlled his high blood pressure with medicine, diabetes was claiming his body, and his diet was drastically altered so he could maximize every ounce of energy he could muster. His wife, who now taught in the same inner-city high school she had once escaped, and three college-age daughters who rarely saw him, felt his love every time they woke up in the comfort and safety of the family's condo on Chicago's west side.

Martinez felt his cell phone vibrate in his pocket, looked at the number, and saw that Willie was on the other side. "Mr. Hood!" he exclaimed, feigning formality. "That didn't take you long, did it?"

"Hell, it better not," laughed Hood. "Not like I don't have anything else to do. Can barely find my desk."

"Tell me about it," replied Martinez. "What do you have?"

"Those names you sent a few minutes ago," began Hood, "I ran them through our system to be sure, but I knew a lot of them anyway. A bunch of them are associates of the Gangster Disciples, and you know what that's all about." The Disciples were one of the meanest gangs on the south side, fueled by the drug trade that frequently turned violent.

"Just confirms what I was already thinking," mused Martinez. "We're connecting this to the Chicago drug trade. Not much doubt now."

"Well, I've got an informant in the Disciples," advised Hood. "It's a guy we've had for a while, and he usually knows what he's talking about. If you need any assistance, just give me a call, and I'll have him get on it."

"Thanks. Appreciated, as always," replied Martinez. "I'll be talking to you."

"Can't wait. Have a good one," Hood signed off cheerily.

Martinez had barely broken the connection when he received a call from Jesus Sanchez, an agent in the DEA office in El Paso. Sanchez was a nineteen-year veteran of the DEA, having grown up in a small town near El Paso, where his immigrant parents had scraped together a living as his father pumped gas while his mother waited tables. Like Hood, Sanchez had seen plenty of his friends fall to the drug trade and decided that if he ever made anything of himself, he was going to do something about it.

Law enforcement officials soon come to realize that they won't win every case and be able to nail every bad guy. Those inevitable failures, along with the grueling hours and the filth that he regularly saw on the drug-infested streets and slums, wore on Sanchez, and he sometimes suffered from migraines that racked his head and made it feel like his five-foot-eight, 160-pound body could take no more. But most days were good, and he had one of the highest arrest rates of any agent in the El Paso office.

Sanchez and Martinez were familiar with one another. Today's call was particularly welcome, as Sanchez provided information that several of the people identified in the phone records were associates of a cartel belonging to none other than Diego Garcia.

"Hmm," chuckled Martinez, remembering his association with Garcia from the failed terrorist plot. "Know that guy well. Too bad he's not still an informant for us. We contact him every so often, but he gives us practically nothing."

"Yes, yes," said Sanchez. "He basically owns the drug trade along the border here, as you know, my friend. Sits back in that huge mansion of his and just keeps running them across. Every time we think we've got him, he finds some other way. He's like a fox. He just keeps finding a way."

"More like a weasel," laughed Martinez. "I appreciate your help. Keep me posted."

"You know I will," said Sanchez. "Adios, amigo."

Martinez broke the connection and again dialed Willie Hood in Chicago. He filled him in about the details of the accident from November, the large amount of money that had been recovered, and the possibility of the second bag.

"Oh my God," exclaimed Hood. "The Disciples will be pissed over that. The idea that someone took a million dollars from them, God, I hate to think how they're reacting to that one. They'll be mad enough that the police got one bag, let alone what happened to the other. And they'd take it in stride compared to how that's going over with the cartel. A million dollars, they're gonna be pissed, big time."

"You're telling me," replied Martinez. "We don't know for sure if there is a second bag or not. But you and I both know that the cartel isn't going to go to this much trouble for just a little bit of money. Kincaid told us that the guys in the shootout kept screaming about a second bag, that there was more money. And—"

Hood finished the thought. "Why would he have just made that up?"

"Exactly," said Martinez. "So a second bag is a real possibility."

"Yep," Hood said as he shuffled through some papers on his overloaded desk and sipped from a paper cup of decaffeinated coffee. "I'm going to contact my informant. Hopefully, he can find out if any money was missing and where it was going. He may give us some more background on the dead driver."

"Appreciate it," responded Martinez. "You know what I need."

"Always do," laughed Hood. "I'll be talking to ya." He took another swig of decaf. "God, this coffee sucks."

Martinez laughed, hit "End" on his cell phone, and called Jesus Sanchez once again. As with Hood, Martinez briefed him on the details of the accident, the recovery of $1,263,000, and the possibility that a large amount of money was missing. Sanchez had much the same reaction as Hood and offered to contact his own informants in El Paso and Juarez.

"If that much money is missing from a shipment, someone is bound to be talking about it," remarked Sanchez between sips of his own coffee. "That's going to be a big deal to them. They aren't just going to blow it off and not tell anyone. They may well have a bunch of people on it, ready to go whenever they're told to."

"Thanks. Appreciate anything that you can do," replied Martinez before switching to Spanish, as he sometimes did with his Hispanic cohorts. "Gracias, senor,"

"Gracias," replied Sanchez, with a hint of a smile. "Buenos dias," he added before breaking the connection.

*****

Late that Monday morning, Martinez heard back from both Hood and Sanchez, who had received information from their informants. Based on the scuttlebutt from inside the Chicago gang, as well as the word on the street in Juarez, it was determined that over one million dollars was missing from the accident vehicle, and that there were, in fact, two bags in the trunk that night.

Martinez shared his findings with R.J. McIntire and Mike Miller. Both of them fell silent, recognizing the implications of the new information.

"Kincaid has to be a suspect," said McIntire, breaking the quiet. "He has to be. Who else would have seen what was inside that trunk?"

"Who all was on the scene that night?" pondered Miller. "There would have been Kincaid, the ambulance drivers, the tow truck driver, who else?"

McIntire pointed to the opposite side of the desk. "You've got the tow-in report over there? Let me see it." Miller tossed the sheet in McIntire's direction, and several seconds were spent in McIntire's review.

"Kincaid had to have found the money when he completed the tow-in report," said McIntire, pointing to the document for effect. "That has an inventory of the contents of the vehicle."

McIntire turned and stared at the wall, lost in thought. He drummed his fingers on the desk and then slapped at his right knee. "That would have been the last document Kincaid filled out at the accident scene. He wouldn't have done anything else. And look." He pointed to the sheet once more. "It just says the one bag."

Most cops never like to think that one of their own is crooked in any way. This was no different, and the idea that a cop would take over a million dollars added to the shock. McIntire and Miller stared at one another, and then each turned to look at Tony Martinez, who returned the stares.

"Damn..." McIntire's voice trailed off before he snapped back to the moment. "We need to interview the tow truck driver. What's his name"—he ran his index finger up and down the document. "Right here, Joe Murphy, up in Farmersville. Let's go up there tomorrow morning and see what he says."

Miller never responded, simply rising from this chair. Martinez, meanwhile, looked at both of his cohorts.

"If either of you need any more help from me, all you gotta do is call," he said. "Otherwise, I really need to get back to the office. I've got a ton of cases that need my attention."

"Sure thing," said McIntire. "We appreciate what you did for us today."

"Not at all. It's what I'm here for." Martinez shook hands with both McIntire and Miller and then walked outside to his car for the drive home, now treacherous from the heavy, blowing snow. R.J. and Miller then made arrangements to meet the next morning in Litchfield at 8:30 a.m. at the local Denny's restaurant before going to see Joe Murphy.

The drive from Litchfield to Farmersville is twenty miles, and despite the wintry conditions, McIntire drove as closely as possible to the speed limit, anxious to get there. Twenty-four minutes later, McIntire and Miller were turning off Exit 72 and onto the frontage road on the edge of Farmersville.

They found Murphy bent over at the waist, holding a flashlight while inserting motor mount on a midnight blue 1977 Ford Granada. He heard the men's footsteps on the concrete floor of the garage and raised up. "Hey, Mike," he said, looking at Miller as he removed his cap and slid his fingers through his hair. He had met Miller several times before and was familiar with him. "What brings you up here in this shitty weather?"

McIntire introduced and identified himself and displayed his credentials. "We'd like to interview you for a few minutes," said McIntire.

"Sure," said Murphy, pointing toward the other side of the building. "Let's go into my office."

The office was as grimy as ever, and Murphy's desk had a coating of dust that created a layer of grit on the splotches of grease across the surface. The white plastic of the chairs across from the desk were in contrast to the dark stains across the seats, and a dark layer of grime partially covered the back of one chair. McIntire swiftly took the cleaner of the chairs, leaving Miller with the dirtier one. Miller gingerly sat down but did not lean back, fearing he would leave a mark on his jacket.

To start, Murphy asked about Kincaid's condition, since he had read about the shooting in the Springfield newspaper. The interview followed and centered around Murphy's role at the accident scene in November.

Murphy recited every detail, adding that "nothing seemed any different that night. I've been in this business for over fifty years, and I've seen a lot of accidents like that. Guy's driving too fast, runs off the road, wraps it around a tree. Helluva way to go, and a sad one at that." He reached for a stained yellow travel mug and sipped the liquid that was inside before setting it back down.

"Was there anything that was unusual about that night?" inquired McIntire.

"Well, there was one thing, and it was a big one," laughed Murphy. "Kincaid found this duffel bag in the trunk that was full of money. He had me take a look at it. God, it was chock full of money. I've never seen that much money before in my life."

McIntire and Miller exchanged a slight glance before McIntire asked the question that mattered most. "How many bags of money were in the car?"

"One," Murphy answered quickly, looking directly at McIntire as he responded. "There was only one bag."

"Only one bag?"

"Yep. Kincaid had his flashlight, that big one like what state cops use, and it covered the entire floor of the trunk like it was noon. There wasn't anything else in the trunk. Just that bag."

McIntire raised an eyebrow. Miller noticed, since he turned his head to McIntire, expecting that reaction. "And what happened next?" said McIntire.

"Kincaid contacted the master sergeant. What's his name, Peal or something? A few minutes later, Peal gets there, and the bag with the money was placed in Peal's squad car."

"Hmm. And what next?"

"I signed the tow-in report with Kincaid, and he left with Peal. I finished hooking up the car and towed it here to my lot."

"So nothing else was left in the trunk after the bag of money was taken out?" Ever conscientious, McIntire wanted to confirm the details.

"Nope. Not a thing." Murphy continued to talk for a few minutes, and McIntire and Miller asked a few more basic questions. Eventually, they inquired if there was anything else that Murphy wanted to add.

"Well, yeah, there's one more thing," said Murphy. "A few weeks after the accident, these two Mexican guys came in here and introduced themselves as investigators for an insurance company. American Mutual, I think it was."

McIntire and Miller both looked at Murphy with surprise in their eyes. "What was that about?"

"It was the strangest thing. Been in this business so long and never had anything like that." Murphy grasped the stained yellow mug and took another sip. "Coffee's gone cold," he chuckled. "Like I said, these two Mexicans were in here, asking all sorts of questions."

"Like what?" McIntire busied himself to write again.

"Well, not the questions that you might think. They asked a few basic things about the accident, but all they really seemed to care about was the money. They kept asking if there was only one bag, had I seen only one bag, things like that."

"Uh-huh. Go on."

"I told them there was only one bag, just like I told you fellas. I couldn't figure out why they were so concerned about the money. It was like they didn't give a damn about anything else."

"Go on."

Murphy took off his cap, revealing the growing bald spot in his gray hair. He dropped the cap faceup on the desk. "Then they asked me the weirdest things. They asked me all about Kincaid, where he lived, what hours he worked, things like that."

"What did you say to them?"

"Well, by then, I was really starting to wonder if these guys were on the up-and-up. But I went ahead and told them about Kincaid, though I was—what's the word? Reluctant. I was reluctant to do it."

McIntire and Miller then knew how Kincaid's residence may have been located. McIntire pressed on. "And what happened next?"

"Then they went back to asking questions about the bag of money. I repeated myself, and the one guy, the big one, he had been outside inspecting the car. He had come back in by then and started walking toward me like he was going to kick my ass. He was this real big guy, big face, muscles out to here." Murphy imitated the size of the forearms. "Scary as hell."

"What happened next?"

"I knew for sure those guys were phonies, and I told them so. I was standing right here, behind the desk, and I got scared for a second. I didn't know if they were going to beat the hell out of me, shoot me, or what they were gonna to do. But they just looked at each other and walked out the door. They got into this gray SUV, a Cadillac Escalade, and drove off."

McIntire finished writing out his notes and then reached for his shoulder bag and pulled out a manila file folder with several photos. Two were photos of the dead men from the trailer. He handed those photos to Murphy across the desk. Murphy placed the photos side by side to analyze them at one time.

"Do you recognize these men? Were either of them the ones that came and talked to you like they were the insurance investigators?"

"That one was," said Murphy, pointing to the photo on the left, of Carlos Santiago. "That's the big guy I was talking about, the one who was scary as hell." He squinted to look closer at the photo of private eye Jose Hernandez. "I don't know who that guy is. Never seen him before in my life."

He handed the photos back to McIntire, who now had more questions to ask. "Did you ever talk to Kincaid after the accident, or after the two Mexicans came in here?"

"Yeah, I did." Murphy had been leaning forward to look at the photos and now relaxed, leaning back in his chair with his hands folded in his lap. "I saw him once. He was on a call for a disabled vehicle late one night, or early in the morning, I guess. A young lady had broken down three miles north of here on the interstate."

"Uh-huh."

Murphy held his hands upright and tapped his fingers together. "Well, I couldn't get her car fixed on the side of the road, so I towed her in. He was the officer working the scene, and he gave her a ride back here. He was hanging around as I was unhooking, and I mentioned to him about these two Mexicans that had come in here, asking all sorts of questions about the money."

He stopped tapping and paused. McIntire was anxious for more, though he couldn't let on, and simply said the words common to all DII agents, "What happened next?"

"I said I was suspicious of how the Mexicans had acted and that I didn't think they were with an insurance company, like they pretended to be. I also told Kincaid that they had asked where he lived, and what his shift was, because they said they would want to interview him, too."

"How did Kincaid react to all of this?"

"Kind of strange," said Murphy, shaking his head in wonder. "He acted like he didn't want to talk at first. But then he started acting antsy, nervous-like." Murphy shrugged slightly. "I didn't think much of it. I just thought he was running late or had someplace he had to be."

McIntire and Murphy raised their heads practically in unison and stared at one another. "Do you know the date that this happened? Your conversation with Kincaid, I mean."

"Yeah. It would have been the same date as that tow-in." Murphy began shuffling through a stack of invoices on the right side of his desk. "What was that woman's name? Fairly… Fairbaugh…Fairlane! That's it."

He kept shuffling until he found the invoice with her name on it. "Here it is," he said, glancing at the date. "It was January 12. Remember it like it was yesterday. She had a water pump that was leaking, and that car wasn't going anywhere."

"Could we have the copy of that report?" said McIntire, reaching across the desk.

"Sure." Murphy handed it over to him. He put his cap back on his head and looked at each man intently. "Is all of this regarding the shooting at Kincaid's place?"

"Yes, it is," said McIntire, almost spitting the words out. "We appreciate your time on this. Thanks for answering our questions." He shook hands with Murphy and handed him his card. "We may be back in touch."

"Anytime," replied Murphy. "Too bad about what happened to Kincaid. You just never know these days."

"Yeah," said Miller as he followed McIntire out the door.

CHAPTER 22

R.J. McIntire and Mike Miller now knew the pieces were coming together in their investigation. Just hours before, Miller expressed the opinion that Kincaid was likely not a suspect. Now, with the help of Tony Martinez and the words of Joe Murphy, it appeared that original hypothesis would not hold up.

The men were a couple of miles down Interstate 55 on the way back to Litchfield when McIntire broke the silence. "It looks like Kincaid may be good for the theft."

"Sure does," said Miller, shaking his head. "Too much is pointing his way for him not to be."

"We need to get a complete financial report on him," pondered McIntire, who was now forced to reduce speed in the inclement conditions. "We need to see if he has money, where it's going, and how he's spending it. Did he ever mention which bank he uses?"

"No," responded Miller. "At least, not to me. I had heard about his money troubles secondhand. It seemed like everyone knew that, because I heard it often enough. But Kincaid never talked about it. To hear him say it, you'd think he had plenty of money."

"Hmm." McIntire chuckled at the irony. "Well, we can get that information."

Miller hesitated and then turned to McIntire with his index finger pointed upward, as a thought had just occurred. "We know he spent a lot of time at Martin's Tavern. A lot of those bars will cash checks for customers. I wonder if Martin ever did that for him?"

"Worth a shot," said McIntire, hitting his wipers on high as snow blew onto the windshield, then cutting them back. "Let's go on down there. Maybe we could get lunch there first. I'm about to starve."

"Me too," laughed Miller. "But let me warn you. I've heard that Martin's is a lot better known for their booze than anything you eat there."

"Thanks. I really needed that," said McIntire, rolling his eyes. "Not like we haven't had crappy food before in this job."

"Yeah, tell me about it," said Miller. The snowfall was now easing, and flurries wafted across the pavement in front of them. By the time they reached the Mount Olive exit, twenty-nine miles from Farmersville and Murphy's garage, the sun was starting to glisten across the coat of white in the fields.

A little before one o'clock, they pulled into Martin's Tavern, where the parking lot was mostly empty. Though Martin called it the "lunch crowd," the place was never that busy at noontime, as there were plenty of better places to eat, even in a small town like Mount Olive. Business didn't really pick up until after five, when customers got off work and came to drown their sorrows until closing time.

The men got out of the car and stepped carefully around the snowdrifts that were starting to pile up on the gravel. Inside, they had their pick of places to sit, and they absentmindedly chose the first table they saw, a rough wood surface surrounded by four battered, non-matching chairs. Miller's chair had a bad leg, and rather than spend lunchtime rocking back and forth, he moved over to another seat.

Passing for napkins on the table were four threadbare washcloths, for Martin deemed it was cheaper to wash them than it was to buy paper napkins. A painfully thin, white-blonde waitress in her forties named Barbi, chomping her gum, dropped a couple of menus on the table in front of McIntire and Miller, along with a passing "hello."

Both McIntire and Miller were dedicated to healthy eating, but in a place like Martin's that was out of the question, since no salads were on the menu. So McIntire chose a grilled ham and cheese sandwich with fries and a glass of water, while Miller picked the shrimp basket and coffee.

As Barbi mindlessly scribbled their orders on her small green pad, McIntire asked if Russell Martin was around and if they could speak to him. "Yeah," Barbi barked as she chewed her wad of gum. "I'll get him."

A minute or two later, Martin appeared from a door behind the bar, dressed in a torn dark gray sweatshirt and baggy jeans pulled just below his considerable paunch. His hair was as scraggly as ever, and he walked with hunched shoulders. He glanced at a fading bouquet of flowers in a brown glass vase on the bartop, next to an 8x10 framed photo of Debbie Marks.

Martin set his palm down on the bar next to the photo, pursed his lips, and headed on to McIntire and Miller's table. "Sad around here these days," said Martin, using his thumb to point at Debbie's photo. "No one's in much of a mood anymore."

"We're sorry," said McIntire. "You remember us from the other night, and we told you we may want to ask you some more questions. Is this a good time for you?"

"Huh? Oh, ah, yeah," replied Martin with a sigh. "Don't have much else to do right now."

"Did James Kincaid ever cash a personal check at this place? Is that something you do here?"

"Not for everyone," said Martin. "I'll do it for my regulars, and my favorite customers. But you do it for everyone, you'll run into all sorts of trouble. Bad checks up the ass."

"I imagine," McIntire said with a slight laugh. "Did you cash checks for Kincaid?"

"Oh, sure, I did it all the time for him," said Martin, waving his hand as if to say it was no big deal. "He used to cash a check for $100 every Friday night. He said he needed some pocket money, and he got here after the banks were closed, and he needed to cash it somewhere. I'd cash his check, and he'd pay his bar tab for the night out of it."

"Do you know if he ever cashed checks anywhere else?"

"Shit, I don't know. I don't know what he does with his money."

McIntire was hastily taking notes on his pad, while Miller wrote in a stenographer's notebook. "When's the last time he cashed a check here?"

"Ah, it's been a little while now." Miller put his open right palm on the back of his head and exhaled, trying to think. "You know, it's been a few weeks now. That's strange." He removed his hand from his head and sat back in the chair. "He'd cashed a check every Friday for years, like clockwork. But dammit, you know, I can't remember the last time he did."

"Do you have any reason for the change?"

"No, not really. I never thought much about it," said Martin. "But you know, I heard something strange in here the other day about Kincaid. Someone from town, I can't remember the guy's name, said he knew the funeral director and was talking to him about the shooting at Kincaid's place. He said that Kincaid had called and insisted that he was gonna pay cash for Debbie's funeral."

McIntire and Miller turned their shoulders at ninety-degree angles and peered at each other with startled looks. Martin laughed in disbelief.

"Funeral director said that was really different, 'cause nobody ever pays for a funeral in cash," said Martin, who slouched in his chair, now suspecting that he should have picked up on something. "Course, I didn't know whether to believe that or not. You know how things get started."

"Uh-huh." McIntire kept writing away. He changed the train of thought. "Do you know if Kincaid rented his trailer or owned it?"

"Rented," said Martin firmly. "A guy named Walter Hamilton owns it. He's a retired electrical contractor and owns a bunch of property around here. Has rentals galore. He lives in the first house west of Kincaid, or the first one before you get to Kincaid's place. It's on the right side of Route 138."

At that moment, the officers' lunch order arrived at the table. McIntire glanced at his ham and cheese, which had been left on the grill for so long that it was dark on one side. His fries, meanwhile, were still white and clearly undercooked. Miller tepidly picked up a piece of shrimp from the small red basket in front of him, quietly marveling at the grease that coated it. He set it back down and grabbed a napkin to wipe his fingers and not stain his notebook.

"All right," said McIntire, returning to the task at hand. "Let's go back to the question with the checks. Do you know were Kincaid banks? What bank does he use?"

"Oh, geez. Let me think about that." Martin leaned forward and folded his arms on the table, in thought. "Damn, it's been so long—oh, wait! He banks at the Mount Olive State Bank. I remember it from the check. You know, the bank that has that 'MO' logo in fancy writing on it. I'd know it anywhere." He sat back with a hint of a smile, proud of himself for recalling it.

"Mount Olive State Bank," McIntire repeated the information as he wrote it down. "Did Kincaid ever give you a bad check?"

"Nope. Never bounced one to me," said Martin, guffawing at his own joke. He then turned serious. "Damn. I never really thought about it. But it is really different that Kincaid stopped cashing checks here. He always had."

"Did you ever see Kincaid with a large amount of cash?"

"Nah. He never had much on him," said Martin, leaning forward as if to tell a secret. "When he'd open his billfold, I'd glance over at it to see how much was in there. I do it all the time. I'm nosy like that." He laughed at his espionage. "He might have a hundred bucks on him. But never more than that."

"Okay. I think that's all we need," said McIntire. "Thanks for your cooperation. Like before, we may be back in touch with more questions."

"Sure, anything you guys need," said Martin, awkwardly pushing himself away from the table and rising to his feet, with sloppy posture. He looked over at the picture on the bartop. "Anything for Debbie."

McIntire and Miller nodded and then ate their lunch amid scowls and frowns. When done, they paid at the bar. Miller caught Martin sneaking a glance inside his billfold as he opened it to pay the tab. The men then walked outside, noticing that the snow had not started again, and the ground was no whiter than before.

They headed for the home of Walter Hamilton. On the way, Miller turned to McIntire. "I can see why Martin's isn't busier at lunchtime."

"No kidding," laughed McIntire ruefully. "I've got some Pepto in the back if you need it. God knows I'll need some myself later on."

*****

McIntire and Miller weren't given an address for the Hamilton home by Martin, but Miller Googled the name and found the correct street number. As they pulled off Route 138, they also spied a mailbox that said "Hamilton" on it, confirming they had the right location.

As they drove up to the house, an unassuming gray modular, they saw a man off to the side of the lot, picking up sticks and leaves amid the snow that now covered the grass. The man was clearly elderly and walked in a hunched stride.

"Hello over there!" the man shouted as the men approached. He looked up at the graying sky. "What can I do for you fellas?"

"We're looking for an individual named Walter Hamilton," said McIntire.

"You found him," said the man in a surprisingly cheery voice. "I'm Walter Hamilton."

McIntire and Miller introduced themselves and displayed their credentials, saying that they wished to ask some questions. As Hamilton approached, they had a better view of his wiry body, five-foot-eight and 145 pounds, as well as the trembling that appeared to be the onset of Parkinson's disease.

"Sure, I'll answer some questions. Just come inside," said Hamilton, walking past the men to the front door. "I was just trying to clean up outside before we get any more snow."

They walked inside, past a small end table decorated with several photos of the same woman, taken at different times of her life. "That's my wife," said Hamilton, shaking his head with a depressed smile. "That was Rosemary. She died seven years ago in August. Miss her to this day."

"I'm sorry," said Miller. "She looks lovely."

"Oh, she was that and more," said Hamilton, pulling off his tan work gloves and taking off his jacket. "Married fifty-two years." He chuckled. "Don't know how she did it, putting up with this old fool all the time."

"Do you live here alone?" asked McIntire, trying to make a little small talk.

"Yep. Since Rosemary passed, it's just me. We had two kids. My son lives in Arkansas, and my daughter's in Texas. They were home for Thanksgiving for a day or so." The mention caused his voice to rise in slight excitement.

"Good for you," said McIntire, who could always find something positive to say. The three sat down at Hamilton's kitchen table, and the officers politely declined an offer of coffee or tea. "We'd like to ask you a few questions about one of your renters, James Kincaid," said McIntire, pulling his yellow legal pad from his shoulder bag.

"Oh, yes, Kincaid. Horrible thing, just horrible," Hamilton said, shaking his head in disbelief and disgust. "Never had anything like that happen in one of my rentals. Oh, sure, you'll have an occasional domestic problem, some young guy beating his wife or girlfriend, or maybe a fire here and there. But never anything like this."

He looked over at his late wife's portrait. "I've got fourteen rentals, you know," he said. "I was able to take Rosemary to Europe and Hawaii with that money." He sighed. "Then I was able to pay for all her medical care before…"

"I'm sure," said McIntire. "But Kincaid rents the trailer from you, right?"

"Yep. He's the guy who pays me the rent. The lease is in his name."

"And how long has he lived there?"

"Oh, I'd say about two years. Actually, a little over two years."

McIntire, as usual, kept writing. "How much rent do you charge Kincaid? Was he ever late with a rent payment?"

"Well, he pays me $550 a month. He's also responsible for the utilities, you know, like electric, gas, water." Hamilton hesitated. "What was your other question?"

McIntire patiently repeated the question, seeing that his subject was in frail health, emotionally and physically. "Was Kincaid ever late with his rent?"

"Oh, a few times, but nothing that serious. I never had to threaten to kick him out," said Hamilton, stifling a chuckle. "His rent is due on the first of the month. There were a few times that he was a few days late, but he always paid. He never fell behind or anything."

"I see. And how did Kincaid pay the rent? Did he pay by check, cash, what?"

"He always paid by check. Actually, I rarely saw the guy. I'd just get the check in the mail. Guess he didn't have time to see me," laughed Hamilton ruefully. "That is, until a few months ago."

McIntire and Miller knew what may come next. "What do you mean?" inquired McIntire.

"Well, a few months ago, Kincaid came to me and asked if he could pay his rent with cash. He said that he'd rather do it that way. I told him no, that wouldn't do, because I wanted a paper trail to maintain proper records." He again laughed. "My accountant would slap me if I took cash like that. I mean, where would the records be?"

"Hmm." McIntire looked over at Miller. "I think that's all we need. We may be back in touch if we have more questions."

"Sure. No one ever comes by, so I'd have all the time you need," said Hamilton, again looking at his wife's picture. "Just stop in anytime."

McIntire and Miller offered their thanks and headed back for the car. The snow was picking up again, and they left fresh tracks across the walk and driveway. They climbed into the vehicle for the one-mile drive into Mount Olive and their next stop, Lawson's Funeral Home, which was scheduled to handle the funeral service of Debbie Marks.

The funeral home was a two-story, blond-brick structure with a large carport, designed to pick up families without fear of rain or snow. The officers entered the building and were struck by the dark red flowered carpeting and ornate flower arrangements scattered on every table and chest. Soft organ music droned in the background, and visitors could determine which services were scheduled for the day by a black-and-white signboard set near the entrance to the main parlor.

Just then, a thin, rangy man with salt-and-pepper hair and horn-rimmed glasses appeared from the parlor. "What may I do for you gentlemen?" he said in a sympathetic voice.

As usual, McIntire and Miller introduced themselves and showed their badges. "I'm Don Lawson," said the man. "I'm the director of this parlor. Won't you come in? Just follow me." He led them through several waiting rooms to a small office in the rear of the building. He sat on a grandiose maroon office chair, while McIntire and Miller each found seats in comfortable green cloth chairs that were more suited for a living room.

"Now, gentlemen," Lawson said in an easygoing voice. "You said you have some questions for me?"

"We heard that James Kincaid called you and asked if he could pay for Debbie Marks' funeral."

"Yes, he did." Lawson glanced at the calendar on his desktop to make sure he had the right date in mind. "It was late in the afternoon of the day before last. I was about to go into the service for the Vincent family when the phone rang."

Lawson sat back and tapped his fingers together lightly. "It was James Kincaid, calling from the hospital. Terrible thing that happened to him and Debbie, just terrible."

"Yes, we know," McIntire played along.

"Mr. Kincaid told me how badly he felt about Debbie's murder and that he blamed himself. He started crying, and I could barely hear what he was saying, poor man," said Lawson, shaking his head and clenching his lips in an empathetic way. "He was in a very emotional state, as I'm sure you can imagine."

"Of course. What else did he say?"

"He said that the least he could do was pay for all of the expenses for Debbie's funeral. I asked him if she had other family other than her mother, who I know lives in Mount Olive. He said yes, she had two kids and her mom, but that he felt like he should take care of it himself. I thought that was a wonderful gesture, based on what had happened. But then he said something that was really unusual."

"What?"

"He asked how much the service would cost, with the casket, vault, and everything. I told him $7,500. Then he asked me if he could pay for it in cash."

"Cash? That's what he said?" McIntire and Miller knew they had to confirm the rumor they heard from Martin, and they were on the verge.

"Yes, that's what he said." Lawson sat up to place his elbows on the desk and looked out the window. "I've been in the funeral business for thirty-six years. I could probably count on one hand the number of times that someone has paid me strictly in cash."

"Hmm. When is the service for Debbie Marks?"

"It's Thursday, the day after tomorrow. At 10 a.m."

McIntire wrote it down and folded the pages over his legal pad. "Thank you for your time, sir. We may be back in touch with more questions."

"I would be happy to help," replied Lawson. "Please stop in or call whenever you need anything."

"We will," said McIntire and Miller as they shook hands with the gentleman before heading back through the parlor to the front door. By now, it was nearing 4:30 p.m., and the snow was increasing once more against the foreboding gray sky.

Due to the late hour and the deteriorating weather, McIntire knew it was time to wrap things up. "Let's call it a day," he said to Miller. "We can meet at your office in the morning at eight thirty, and see if we can find more cash payments that Kincaid's made." Miller agreed, and the investigation took a break until early the next day.

*****

As eight thirty approached the next morning, McIntire and Miller arrived at the headquarters at practically the same time. Once inside, they proceeded to Miller's office and started talking.

"Sure seems Kincaid pays cash for a lot these days, doesn't it?" said Miller.

"Yes, it does," responded McIntire, setting his Styrofoam cup of coffee on the table. "I wonder how many of his other bills he's doing that with?"

"Wonder what he's doing with his alimony or child support," mused Miller. "That would take a big chunk of money, based on the fact he's been through two marriages."

McIntire nodded in thought. "Where are his ex-wives and kids at? Where do they live?"

"His first wife is in Raymond. He had two girls with her. Both are in college," replied Miller, trying to remember all the exes and kids. "His second wife, the truck-stop waitress, still lives in Litchfield, I think. Yeah, that's right, she does. I saw her a few months ago, when I had an investigation at the Busy Bee. Could never forget that coffee. It was just awful."

"So child support would be paid through Montgomery County then. The county clerk's office."

"That's right," said Miller, who knew what R.J. was about to say.

"Let's drive over there" were the words that Miller was expecting to hear, and he was ready as well. "Let's do it," he said jauntily. Like most good investigators, the excitement flowed through his veins, and he wanted as much information as soon as possible.

Because the blowing snow reduced their speed at times, the seven miles down Illinois Route 16 from Litchfield to Hillsboro took twenty-six minutes. Once there, the men pulled into the Hillsboro square, parked, and headed for the courthouse. They strode into the county clerk's office, where Miller identified himself.

There, they spoke directly to the clerk, Darren Turner, who checked the records on James Kincaid's monthly payments. Turner brought a thick manila file out to the countertop and opened it for both officers to see. "He's never missed a payment to the children with his first wife," said Turner. "He's been late several times to his kids for his second wife, but not enough to bring charges. He always caught up."

"How does he pay those every month?" asked McIntire.

Turner pointed to the log that indexed payments and payment methods. "Well, as you can see, he used to pay by check every month," said Turner deliberately. "But the last three months have been paid with cash."

McIntire and Miller just saw another red flag go up. "Uh-huh. Well, thanks. That's all we need for today." Miller then requested copies of Kincaid's payment records.

"Sure, anytime," said Turner, looking back out the window at the falling snow. "Take it easy out there."

The clock on the square read 10:31 a.m. as McIntire and Miller drove away. They headed back out Route 16 for the trek to District 18 headquarters, one mile on the other side of Litchfield. Both men were silent, watching the snowflakes hit the windshield, trying to mentally process all the information they had gained since clocking in this morning. They were a mile or so out of Hillsboro when Miller turned to McIntire.

"Why'd you transfer to DII?" he asked.

"What?" McIntire was lost in thought and was stunned by the question.

"I said, why did you transfer to Internal Investigations? Why'd you want to do stuff like this?"

McIntire sniffed in laughter. "Actually, it's what I always wanted to do. I'd always wanted to be a criminal investigator. But when I joined the state police, there weren't any openings in that division." He rubbed the back of his fingers on the driver's side window, which was frosting up. "Finally, an investigator's position opened up in DII, and I applied for it."

"What'd you do before you were in DII?"

"I was a sergeant in District 14, which is a rural area. But my wife and I both wanted to move to a metro area, and when an opening in DII came up, I applied for it. The opening was in Springfield, and that's kind of what we were looking for."

Miller smiled. "Well, Springfield is certainly a larger metro area."

"Maybe for you, Litchfield boy," teased McIntire, remembering Miller's hometown. Miller returned by cuffing McIntire on his right arm.

"Springfield's a lot smaller than what I'm used to in Chicago," McIntire continued. "But actually, it had a lot of what we were looking for. I talked it over with Darlene, and she liked the idea."

"So it worked out, huh?"

"Oh, yeah. We've been really happy with the move, particularly Darlene. She loves the shopping in Springfield. Spends every extra minute in a store somewhere."

"Kind of like my wife," said Miller. "I met my wife at Southern Illinois University in Carbondale, and she loves going to the malls in St. Louis. Seems like every few weeks, she's in a different mall. Good thing she's as cute as she is, and thank God for overtime pay, the way she spends it."

"Tell me about it," laughed McIntire. "Darlene and I, we really like where we're at. But I've got to tell you, this whole thing in DII has been an eye-opening experience. I had some idea of what I was getting into, but, God, there has been so much about this that has really surprised me."

Miller wiped the building frost from his side window with the cuff of his jacket. "What do you mean?"

McIntire had relaxed in his conversation with Miller to this point. Now, his brow furrowed and the lines wore in around his eyes. "You know, I've been in DII for nine years, going on ten. In that time, I've conducted Internal Affairs investigations for theft and perjury. I've had sexual assault cases that were just filthy, just horrible. I've even had homicides."

"Geez," said Miller. "I know it happens, even with cops. But when you go to the academy and think you're gonna spend your life doing this, you can't imagine that cops are out there, doing that crap."

"No, you can't. And it happens more often than you think," said McIntire. "But in truth, it's a small percentage. Over 98 percent of all police officers—whether they're in the state police, county, local, whatever—are dedicated, hardworking, honest officers. Most of them are the ones that do their jobs like they're supposed to and serve the public as best they can."

McIntire drummed the fingers of his left hand on the steering wheel in frustration. "But the other 2 percent are the ones we get to investigate. Those are the officers that shouldn't have been hired in the first place."

"The guys that drive us nuts, day in and day out," mused Miller.

"Yeah," said McIntire with a snort. "But really, I'm oversimplifying it. Sometimes there are people in the 98 percent category that make a mistake once in a while and have to be disciplined."

"Even the best ones can screw up," agreed Miller.

"They sure can. Even the best ones..." McIntire's voice trailed off as he saw an oncoming snowplow hugging the center line. He slowed and swerved as much as the pavement would allow, and then he proceeded. "There was this one case I worked a couple of years ago. This trooper had led the district in activity, and had this really high number of traffic citations and warnings.

"Because he did so much, the district command turned a blind eye, even though he blatantly violated the rules of conduct," continued McIntire, his voice quieting in anger. "I mean, it was so obvious, the stuff that he was doing. And after a while, the trooper is just out of control. So the district command calls us in to correct a problem that they had started."

Miller listened intently, eyes fixated, as McIntire went on. He slowed the car, as the stiff winds were causing snow to drift on the shoulders of the highway.

"There are several things you learn when you work in internal investigations," said McIntire, "and one is that if the supervisors did their jobs, the workload in DII would be a hell of a lot lighter."

His voice, normally stoic, took on a tinge of sarcasm. "It seems that everyone wants to be a supervisor for the money, or maybe the prestige," he cracked. "But very few of 'em actually want to supervise!"

Miller laughed out loud. "Drives me crazy. I can name guys in this district who do the same thing. We've actually discussed some of their names," he said. "I could tell you who they are, but I won't. You've probably figured it out anyway."

"Probably have," snickered McIntire. "I remember this one case that I worked in one of the northern districts. It's been a few years now, and I can't remember what the actual complaint was on what the trooper's actions were. But I'll never forget the interview I did with the trooper's supervisor, the sergeant."

McIntire chuckled and shook his head, still in disbelief. "I was interviewing the sergeant, and he was real brash, just had a hellacious attitude. He hates the trooper and tells me that he hopes we get the S.O.B. this time because the trooper had been doing this for years. I ask him for the paperwork regarding the trooper's conduct, and he goes, 'Well, I didn't write it down.'"

"I couldn't get over it. Here's this guy, ripping the trooper for something that's supposedly gone on for years, we've got a complaint about it, and he just sits there and tells me he didn't write it down. I drove four hours for that, and spent God knows how much time on it, and he tells me that. But that's typical of a lot of supervisors. And if it's not written down, it never happened."

Miller, who was a sergeant himself, felt a twinge of guilt, and hoped that McIntire wasn't sending a veiled criticism. "You've gotta take pride in the position. I told myself if I ever got this far, I was gonna make damn sure that I'd earned it."

McIntire sensed that Miller was uncomfortable with the comments and sought to smooth them over. "Oh, I know. I've seen your paperwork, and just in these few days, I've watched you enough to know that you do things the right way. If there were more guys like you, I'd be out of a job."

"Don't know if that's good or bad," laughed Miller, realizing that McIntire was not referring to him. "I guess I always thought that if someone below me was screwing around, then I looked bad, too."

"And that's how more people should look at it," said McIntire emphatically. "I get so frustrated that supervisors aren't held accountable for their subordinates' actions. I mean, how do you justify discipline for a trooper or someone when they do something wrong, and the supervisor never does anything to stop it, and he gets off with nothing?"

By now, the men had made their way to the outskirts of Litchfield, and McIntire slowed for the 45-mile-per-hour zone on the edge of town. "It's really been a learning experience for me in DII," reflected McIntire. "I know this would never happen, but I've always thought that all officers who get promotions should have to spend at least one year in DII. If they did, maybe they'd do their jobs different, and better. A lot of people don't think about what goes on with DII, and maybe they should."

"I wouldn't have minded," commented Miller. "I'm kind of fascinated by what you guys do. I know it's not easy, and I know that a helluva lot goes into it. But I would've liked to spend a year there."

"You'd have been good at it," complimented McIntire. "You know, the world's a tough place, and a lot of people try to screw you. Any cop who thinks otherwise doesn't deserve a badge. But I always think back to something my mom taught me. She always lived by the golden rule, treat others the way you want to be treated."

He smiled at the memory. "I know it sounds sappy. But I've always believed that, and I've tried to live my life that way. I've tried to do my job that way." He pushed his tongue forward in his mouth, as if to stifle a tear. "I've got a wife and two kids, and I never wanted to go home at night, look them in the eye, and have them think that I screwed people. I don't want to do that with anyone I work with. I like to sleep at night, you know."

Miller nodded his head, contemplating what had just been said. "I get the idea. My mom would kill me if she thought I wasn't doing something right or honest. She just didn't raise me that way. And you're right on the family thing. I see myself as a role model to them and the guys I'm around." He shrugged for emphasis. "People act like that's something special or you're being a suck-ass. But isn't that what I'm supposed to do?"

McIntire smiled admiringly. "We need more guys like you," he said as he maneuvered his way around the flow of rush hour that, in a small town like Litchfield, qualifies for high traffic volume. Midway through town, the red lights of a railroad crossing began to flash, and McIntire slowed to a stop, joining a line of traffic in wait of a slow-moving coal train. The windshield wipers kept brushing away snow that melted on impact with the glass.

"I always work cases like the one we're on with an open mind," McIntire continued. "It doesn't matter to me if the officer is guilty or not. It's not up to me to care, because no one really cares how R.J. McIntire feels about it." He continued in the third person, for effect. "What R.J. McIntire is supposed to do is conduct as thorough of an investigation as possible and get as many facts as possible. That's how the decision will be made."

As the coal cars rumbled by, Miller kept listening. "I want to make every effort to interview as many people as possible," commented McIntire. "It's my job to prove the officer guilty beyond any doubt, or innocent beyond any doubt." He turned to Miller. "Remember that lead sheet that you were asking me about? That's why I keep it. I don't want any potential witness to be overlooked."

He finished his train of thought, drew a deep breath from the impatience of waiting on the train, and turned back to Miller. "You know, you ought to apply for DII. I've seen what you do, and I like your attitude. You'd be a good investigator."

Miller was flattered. "Well, I've got to be honest, I'd like to do your job. Like I said a few miles back, I've always wanted to be a criminal investigator, but I like all investigations, period. It's just what I want to do, what gets me going."

"You've never told me. What'd you do before you were a detective?"

"I was on patrol for eight years. I've been in Narcotics for twelve."

"So you've been with the ISP for what, twenty years?" The train was reaching an end, and McIntire shifted back into drive.

"Yeah. Being a state cop was something I wanted to do since I was about twelve. Litchfield's my hometown, where I grew up. Did you see Magnolia Street, just past the hospital?"

"You mean that street that had that three-story brick Victorian with the green pitched roof on the corner?" McIntire's observation skills were always on display, at work or not.

"That's the street I grew up on. That house you're talking about was where the bank president lived. We lived three blocks back of that, down the street, north."

"What'd your family do?" inquired McIntire, listening with interest.

"My dad was a city cop here in Litchfield. Mom did all sorts of things for extra money. She babysat, did sewing, sold Avon, anything she could." The train having cleared the tracks, the vehicle began to roll once more. "I wasn't really that close to Dad, not like I was to Mom. Still am. Like I tell people, I'm a mama's boy and damn proud of it."

"But you ended up following in his footsteps," noted McIntire.

"Yeah, but not why you think," corrected Miller. "Dad really didn't care about being a cop. He'd always come home and gripe about the hours, the pay, his bosses, everything. To him, it was just a job. I was little, and even then I'd think, geez, if you're gonna be a cop, take it seriously. It's a big responsibility, no matter whether you're city, county, state, any level."

"Sounds like you wanted it at an early age," said McIntire, who was hitting every red light on the opposite edge of town.

"I guess so. I'd hang around the station when I got to be a teenager, talking to the guys down there. I'd watch them work, talk about their day, answer the phones, even do their paperwork. There were a bunch of pictures on the wall of former Litchfield officers, the past chiefs, even a couple of guys who died in the line of duty." Miller imitated the rectangular picture frames with his hands, and how the photos sat, side by side. "I'd stand there, just staring at those pictures and thinking how I wanted to be like that someday."

A sentimental tinge came over Miller's voice. "People think I wanted to take after my dad, but really, there was another guy who I wanted to be like. His name was Steve Drury, and he'd been on the Litchfield police for years and years. He was this outgoing guy, really knew how to talk to people, and everyone in town liked him.

"I'd be down at the station, and Mr. Drury"—he snickered—"I guess I still call him that. Anyway, he'd always talk to me, and sometimes when I'd see him on patrol, as I was delivering papers or riding my bike, he'd always pull up and talk a little bit. He took the job seriously and wanted to help his community. There was a lot to like about the guy."

McIntire turned his head slightly to hear what came next. "He died a few years back. By then, his wife had passed, his kids all lived away from here, and he was in a nursing home. I went by to see him one day, and he was bedridden, couldn't walk. I just wanted to tell him how much I respected him, and how he was kind of a role model for me." Miller's voice cracked slightly. "I'll never forget it. He squeezed my hand and told me that I was a helluva cop. I can't tell you what that meant to me."

The sentimentality in Miller's words then became terse, and he shifted his body uncomfortably. "I never really wanted to be like my dad. He wasn't a good cop and really was never that good to my mother. He just put in his time, and that was it."

He stared out the window, with lips clenched. "To this day with my wife or kids, or on the job, I'll think about what Dad would have done and then do it differently myself. I want to be better at home than he was, a better husband, better father, better man. And I want to be the best cop that I can be, because the position and the paycheck both call for it."

McIntire was struck by the intensity of his partner's words and the change in his demeanor. He thought, perhaps, a new topic was needed. "What'd you study in college?"

"I was in public administration, but I knew I wanted to attend the academy to be a state trooper. When I graduated from the academy, I was assigned to District 15 and then transferred back down here after two years. I worked patrol for eight years, but I've always wanted to be a criminal investigator, like you."

"Thanks. I guess that's flattering," said McIntire, cocking his head and laughing nervously. "And here you are now."

"Yeah. That was kind of a stroke of luck," replied Miller. "When I worked the road, I always had a high level of activity and was usually the high man for criminal arrest." A proud smile broke across his face. "Then the department decided to open an investigation office in the Litchfield district, and I applied. Which brings us to what we're doing now."

All of the lights finally turned green, and the vehicle made its way back to District 18 headquarters. McIntire and Miller picked their way through the blowing snow and through the front door, where they brushed snowflakes from their hair and jackets. Now drier than before, they walked into Miller's office, where another pile of messages, some from reporters, littered the desk.

The men discussed the Kincaid case and covered many of the pertinent details, including the security tape. "Wonder who installed that system for him," said McIntire.

"I know someone who might have," said Miller. "There's a guy named Bob England who lives near Standard City. He's a retired miner, kind of a crack electrician, and he's put in security systems for several cops I know. I wonder if he was Kincaid's guy."

"I'll call him," said Miller, reaching for an area-wide phone book. He located the number and dialed it. No one picked up, so Miller left a message asking England to contact him on his cell phone and possibly set up a meeting for tomorrow morning. The forecast until then called for dropping temperatures and increasing winds, and the backroads to Standard City, an out-of-the-way settlement, were sure to be treacherous.

CHAPTER 23

The next morning found seven inches of fresh snow on the ground, and the whipping winds created drifts large enough to cancel many schools in the area. Some offices and businesses also chose not to open. With the conditions in mind, R.J. McIntire planned to leave early for the forty-mile drive from his home in Chatham to District 18 headquarters in Litchfield. Before heading there, he shoveled the front drive, in case Darlene needed to get out.

Mike Miller's wife, Julie, had a scheduled day off from her job as a receptionist and planned to spend it in one of the malls in St. Louis. Peering out the window at the drifting snow, he talked her out of it, fearing that she would become stranded or be an accident victim. She whined about her husband's concerns before she grudgingly agreed, pacified by a couple minutes of cuddling on the couch before the kids got out of bed.

As fate would have it, Miller beat McIntire to headquarters by a matter of seconds, seeing him a few hundred feet behind in his rearview mirror as they pulled into the parking lot. Theirs were the only two cars visible on the highway in front of the headquarters as they both arrived at 8:45 that morning.

Some discussion about the Kincaid case, as well as some plans for the day, followed before Miller again called the residence of Bob England. This time, England answered and agreed to talk to McIntire and Miller, who left immediately.

The drive to Standard City from Litchfield was just over twenty miles, much of it over rural roads. Miller checked with local road authorities to determine conditions, though neither he nor McIntire had any intention of not getting there. They simply wanted the information and to see how long the drive would take.

The regular highways were partially covered by snow, causing numerous breaks in speed. The backroads were even worse, but the men persisted and finally were able to pull into the driveway of England's home, a yellow split-level ranch that, despite its fairly new age, was showing signs of disrepair. England chose to spend most of his time in the basement, tinkering with electronics and trying to overcome the loneliness that had set in after his wife, Betty, divorced him two years ago.

The officers pulled up to the house, plowing through snow that covered the way, another indication of England's disinterest in the property. Surrounding the house were three old pickup trucks, one up on concrete blocks, which England puttered around with from time to time. McIntire and Miller picked their way through the snow and knocked on the door, happy when Bob answered quickly and told them to come inside.

Bob sat at the table, looked over the officers' badges, and removed a cap given to him by a local seed company. Running his fingers through his hair, he sat back in his chair.

"Sorry I didn't get back to you last night," said England sheepishly.

"That's fine," said McIntire, ready to move on. "Did you install a home security system for a state police trooper named James Kincaid?"

"Sure did," said England. "I remember it well. It was early on a Friday morning, last month. He called me early in the morning and told me that he needed a system ASAP."

England stood up and stepped toward the counter, pouring himself a cup of coffee into a black mug that read in white block lettering "Miners Do It in the Hole" before he sat back down. "Sure too bad about what happened to Kincaid.

God, having some Mexicans try to get you like that. Probably some illegals who came here in the back of a van or something."

"Tell us about that call with Kincaid," said McIntire, ignoring the comment and writing away.

"Well, he calls, all hot and bothered, telling me that there's been a threat on his life, and he needed me to come over right away."

"How did you know Kincaid?"

"Oh, I'd met him a few times before. I knew he was a state trooper and where he lived, but not a lot else. We'd had coffee a few times, once or twice in Mount Olive and a couple of times at the Busy Bee, that place in Litchfield." He snickered. "I've seen him and his wife or girlfriend at McClintock's, here in Standard City, a few times and spoke to him."

"And what happened next with the phone call?"

"I tried to tell Kincaid that I was booked up and couldn't get there for a few days. But he kept after me and made some comment about a guy who wanted to put him in a pine box, or something like that. Finally, I gave in and said I'd move my appointments around and be there later that day."

"Okay. Do you have any documentation, like receipts, log books, something like that, to verify the exact day of installation?"

"Yeah, sure, give me a second." As England rose to leave the room, the Siamese in the corner popped up and ran after him. The sounds of shuffling and searching were then heard for a minute or two before England emerged, holding a half-full receipt pad, featuring yellow customer copies. The entire sheet was handwritten.

"Here's the job for Kincaid," said England, flipping through the pad and handing it to McIntire. The receipt listed the date, a brief description of the devices installed in and around the Kincaid trailer, a summary of hours worked, and how the bill was paid. In the middle of the receipt, England had written the words "Paid Cash" and drawn a circle around them.

McIntire studied the receipt and then held it up for Miller to inspect. "I see that Kincaid paid cash for the system," said McIntire.

"Yep. Don't get too many of those," said England. "When I was done, I remember asking Kincaid how he wanted to pay for it, and he asked how much the cost was. I told him $800, and he counted out eight $100 bills from his billfold."

Again, McIntire and Miller exchanged glances. "Can I have a copy of this receipt?" requested McIntire.

"Yeah. I don't need it." England reached for the pad from McIntire, tore off the specific receipt, and handed it over to McIntire, who noticed the date of the installation was January 12.

"Thank you for your time," said McIntire as he stood up. "We appreciate your help, and we may be back in touch if we have more questions."

"Yeah, sure. If I'm not here, I'm either on a job or out deer hunting," chuckled England. "But call whenever you need." McIntire and Miller offered their goodbyes and then headed for the front door.

*****

The sun was coming out as the officers turned back onto the road leading out of Standard City toward the highway. As a result, the road conditions were improving, and the wind was finally starting to subside.

As usual, McIntire and Miller used their time in the car to discuss the case. "God, how many things does Kincaid pay cash for?" said Miller. "It's like everything we've checked into, he's paid cash for it, at least for the last few months."

"And there's a red flag on every one," said McIntire. "From what you were hearing, he was just scraping by. And now he's got all this cash burning a hole in his pocket?"

"Especially when he was living like he was," commented Miller. "He's about the only twenty-year state trooper I ever heard of who was living in a rented trailer."

McIntire fell silent for a minute, lost in thought. "You know," he began deliberately, "I think we need to talk to the Montgomery County state's attorney. We've got to see Kincaid's financial records because that's going to tell us a lot. I wonder if we could get a grand jury subpoena for those records."

"I've worked with the state's attorney before," answered Miller. "Good guy. Really knows how to work with people and has been good with cops. A lot of people in his position don't understand us at all, but he really does."

"Let's get back to headquarters. I'll call from there to get an appointment to see him." McIntire instinctively pressed a little harder on the gas, wanting to get back to Litchfield sooner. Miller noticed his partner's eagerness and smiled to himself.

The interstate was now largely clear, and McIntire was able to drive the speed limit on the last nine miles of the trip. He parked and breezed across the parking lot, in the door, and down the hallway to Miller's office. Miller could barely keep up, walking two steps behind his fast-moving friend.

Once inside the office, McIntire never bothered to sit down. "What'd you say the name of the state's attorney was?" he inquired, reaching for the phone book.

"Brad Collins," said Miller. "I know the guy, so if you want, hand me the phone."

McIntire ignored the offer, flipping through the book to find the number and then dialing it himself. He spoke directly to Collins, who said he had to be in court later that morning but could meet at 1 p.m.

With several hours until the meeting, McIntire and Miller used the time to review the case, examining it from every angle and motive. They decided to eat lunch on the way to the courthouse in Hillsboro, though both were so focused that food became secondary. They offhandedly decided to eat at a Subway in Litchfield, where they ate so quickly that neither tasted their food particularly well, and were back in the car heading to Hillsboro. The roads having cleared in the midday sun, traffic was picking up, especially with teenagers already bored from a few hours home on their snow day.

The seven miles to Hillsboro went as normal, and the clock read nine minutes before 1 p.m. as McIntire and Miller strode into the office of the Montgomery County state's attorney and introduced themselves. The clerk greeted them, walked into Collins' office to advise him of his visitors, and told them to come on back.

As Miller said, Brad Collins had a reputation for working with law enforcement in his twelve years in the position. Part of that came from his upbringing, as his grandfather was a retired state policeman. His grandpa had helped Brad's mother raise him and, now at age 87, remained a large presence in Brad's life and a father figure, a position he had assumed before Brad turned five. That was when his real father had walked out, deciding that married life wasn't for him, but his new girlfriend was. He left the area for a new life in California, and Brad never saw him again.

The hurt from his absent father drove Brad, for he always felt he wanted to help other families that were experiencing the same thing. He attended Northwestern and graduated cum laude with his law degree, ran for state's attorney and won, and cracked down on deadbeat dads from day one. Thanks to Collins, Montgomery County became known for having the least patience of any county in the area for men who didn't pay their child support. His tough-on-crime, soft-on-women stance made him immensely popular at the polls, and he had been re-elected by overwhelming margins in each of the last two campaigns.

Brad never forgot where he came from, and a smile always accentuated his six-foot, 200-pound persona with thick brown hair and welcoming blue eyes. He had reason to smile in the upcoming election, as it appeared he would run unopposed for a fourth term.

The men exchanged pleasantries and, as usual, the officers displayed their credentials. Miller introduced R.J. McIntire to Collins as the lead investigator on the Kincaid shooting, and Collins nodded in approval.

"What can I do for you gentlemen?" said Collins as he slid out of his blue pinstriped suit coat and hung it on the back of his black office chair.

"You're aware of some of the particulars of the Kincaid shooting?" asked McIntire.

"Yeah, it's been in all the papers," said Collins. "Some of the state cops have told me about it, too. I presume that the information that's out there is accurate?"

"Pretty much," said McIntire. "Are you also aware of an automobile accident, a fatal, that happened in November, when over a million dollars was recovered?"

"Sure, I remember that," replied Collins. "I've heard about that one, too. Didn't Kincaid work that one?"

McIntire nodded, and it didn't take Collins long to make the connection. "Are you saying the two events tie in together?"

"Yes," said McIntire directly. "Based on the information, both Mike and I feel that Kincaid may have stolen a large amount of money from the accident vehicle that belonged to a drug cartel."

Brad Collins was in the loop on the state cops of District 18 and respected most of them. But he had never cared for Kincaid, remembering how the trooper had left his own family in Raymond for Sharon, the truck-stop waitress. Such choices brought back Collins' own pained childhood, and though he harbored resentment in this moment, his professionalism took over.

"What information do you have?" inquired Collins, his brow furrowing and his eyes piercing.

"It seemed that Kincaid had been living paycheck-to-paycheck before the accident. But since then, he has been paying a lot of his bills with cash." McIntire spoke slowly and extended an open palm to count off with his fingers. "We've learned that he paid for a home security system that cost $800 in eight $100 dollar bills. We were also over here yesterday and found out that he's been paying cash to the county clerk for child support."

Collins was fixated, taking in every word as McIntire continued. "Have you heard of this place called Martin's Tavern in Mount Olive?" he asked. Collins nodded his head in the affirmative, so McIntire continued. "Kincaid hung out there all the time, and his girlfriend tended bar there. The owner, a guy named Russell Martin, told us that Kincaid used to cash a check for $100 every Friday night. But he hasn't cashed any checks there since November, when the accident occurred."

As McIntire recited the facts, Collins began taking notes of his own. "What else do you have?" he inquired of McIntire.

"I've been in contact with the DEA, and they sent us Tony Martinez. I'm sure you know who he is."

"Sure do," replied Collins. "I've worked with him before. Really knows his stuff."

"Martinez contacted some of the other agents in DEA, and they called their informants. Apparently, the Chicago office has an informant who said that there were actually two bags of money in the trunk when the car left Chicago." McIntire's face clenched as he looked straight at Collins. "Kincaid only turned in one bag."

Collins kept writing, shaking his head in disgust. "Anything else?" he said through an increasing grimace.

"Well, there is one other thing, though we can't say for sure, since it hasn't happened yet. But Mike and I were concerned about it. We followed up on a rumor about the funeral for Kincaid's girlfriend and talked to the funeral director where her service is to be held. He said that Kincaid had insisted on paying for the funeral and asked what the charge would be. He then asked the director if he could pay in cash."

Across the desk, Collins' eyebrows raised in unison. He tapped his pencil on the desk and stared down, processing what he had just heard. After a few seconds, he lifted his eyes and looked at McIntire.

"I think there's plenty of evidence here to suggest that a grand jury subpoena is needed," said Collins bluntly. "Kincaid's financial records are relevant to this investigation." He pointed at McIntire. "We'll have you testify before the grand jury and get the subpoena."

"How soon can we do this?" asked McIntire.

"In the next few days or so. It won't take long to get this done." Collins clasped both hands behind his head and stared at the wall. "You never think you're going to have to do something like this when a cop may be involved. But you do what you have to do." He smiled ruefully. "Part of the job."

The officers rose and shook hands with Collins, thanking him for his cooperation and interest. The gravity of the situation was not lost on either of them, as they knew they were going after one of their own. But the evidence was piling up against James Kincaid, and a resolution was needed soon.

CHAPTER 24

The next day was Friday, February 12, and brought two occasions of note in Kincaid's life. The late morning brought his release from the hospital. The afternoon was the funeral of his girlfriend, Debbie Marks.

Simply getting from the hospital to home posed a challenge, as Kincaid was unable to drive himself yet and even if he could, his pickup and squad car were back at the trailer. As a result, he called District 18 headquarters, where his call was routed to Lieutenant Jim Mason. As usual, Mason was wired as ever, thanks to his third huge cup of coffee of the morning, and practically cut off Kincaid at the end of every sentence. Kincaid had made the call to request a ride home from the hospital. Mason agreed, telling him to call whenever he was released, and a car would be sent.

Kincaid then started watching the clock, because his remaining moments in the hospital could not end fast enough, and the last few days were among the most miserable of his life. He was plagued with guilt, knowing that Debbie's death was because of his choices, first to take the money, and then not giving it up during the confrontation in the trailer that night. He was also consumed with anxiety, knowing that the duffel bag of money remained in the rafters of the garage. The thought elicited a range of emotions, from fear that his theft would be found by investigators at the scene, to concern that his life on easy street was in those rafters unattended.

A couple of days before, Kincaid had lined up Service Master to clean his trailer, but he still dreaded going back to it, nauseated at the lingering blood stains that were sure to be found across the living room. Kincaid planned to move out of the trailer as soon as possible, away from the memories of the shootout, the thought of Debbie's murder, and her lifeless body on the floor.

Kincaid looked down at his left hand, still heavily bandaged from the loss of his little finger. His right shoulder was also tightly wrapped, still racked with pain so intense that he could barely lift his arm. While he grappled with the physical limitations, his mind was also clouded by a lack of alcohol and cigarettes, which he had not enjoyed in days. The withdrawal symptoms made him irritable with nurses and orderlies and left him fidgety as he rolled around in his bed, searching for some moments of comfort.

His bedside phone rang a few times, including calls from a couple of preening reporters and a one-minute conversation with Del Adams, the boisterous big man from the tavern, who informed Kincaid that he "looked forward to you being off your dead ass and back at the bar."

*****

Outside of the rare phone calls, the nurses, Miller, and McIntire were practically his only visitors, save for his mother and sister Mo, who stopped by on the first day to comfort and console him. His ailing mother, wheelchair bound and frail for her years, shook and sobbed uncontrollably at the sight of her son in heavy bandages, and Mo had to wheel her out of the room after just a few minutes.

There was also an unexpected surprise. Late in the afternoon of the third day, Kincaid's first wife, Judy, and daughters, Sally and Mary Ann, walked through the door. All three were impeccably dressed, Judy in a brown skirt outfit with knee-high boots and the girls in designer jeans and dark sweaters.

Kincaid's heart rate increased, not knowing where the conversation would go. He had not seen Judy face-to-face in eight months and had only spoken on the phone to the girls twice in that time. "Hi, Dad," said the girls, almost in unison. "How are you doing?"

"Better that you're here," said Kincaid, scooting his body to sit up in bed. His wisecracking then took over. "The old man's seen better days, huh?"

Sally shifted nervously on one foot, while Mary Ann glanced up at the ceiling. "Are you in a lot of pain?" asked Sally.

"Yeah. But nothing I can't handle," replied Kincaid. "I'll be fine." He looked over at their mother, who was staring out the window. "How are you, Judy?"

"Huh? Oh, fine," said Judy, momentarily distracted. "Everything's fine. The girls wanted to come by, so I thought I'd tag along."

"I'm glad you did," smiled Kincaid. "What are you hearing about all of this? I've had some reporters call here, and I'm guessing it's across the news."

"Oh, yeah, everyone's talking about it," blurted Sally. "Like, God, what haven't we seen it on?" She started counting off on her fingers. "It's been all over the Internet, the Springfield paper, the Chicago paper, CNN…"

"I get the idea," chuckled Kincaid, clasping his right shoulder with the remains of his left hand. "So I'm a celebrity. Trust me, I wasn't looking for it."

"I guess not," said Sally. "We've had some reporters call our house, too. Mom just hangs up on them."

"Thanks. Mom always knew what to do," said Kincaid admiringly. "I appreciate that."

"People are talking at college, too," said Mary Ann, a tinge of resentment in her voice. "God, we can't walk to class or hang out in the dorm without someone saying something about it."

"Sorry," said Kincaid, somewhat embarrassed. "That'll blow over in a few days. You know how people are."

Sally turned to Mary Ann, who was holding a small bag from the hospital gift shop. "We brought you something." Mary Ann thrust the bag at Kincaid, who opened it to find his favorite candy bar, a king-size Milky Way. "Oh, you shouldn't have," he said. "I'll eat that later on."

"Oh? Can't you have it?" Sally jumped to a conclusion, looked at Mary Ann, and said disapprovingly, "I told you we shouldn't have got that!"

"No, no, it's fine," reassured Kincaid. "I meant that they're about to bring supper in, and I'll eat my Milky Way after a while." His IV machine began to beep, and he slid slightly over in bed, to silence it.

"Oh." Sally looked over at Mary Ann, who was staring at a wall. An awkward pause fell over the room. "I guess we'd better go," said Judy. "You probably need your rest."

"Oh, no, stay as long as you want," said Kincaid, waving his hand. "It's so good that you all came."

"Yeah. Well, we don't want to keep you, do we?" said Judy, turning to the girls, neither of whom had removed their jackets. "Come on, girls. Let's let Daddy get his rest."

Mary Ann threw up her hand to wave goodbye and was the first one out of the room. Sally silently leaned over to give Kincaid a quick peck on the cheek and turned on her heel to head for the door. Judy stood at the foot of the bed, glanced at Kincaid, and placed her hand on the frame. She lingered for a moment, standing as tall and stately as ever.

"Take care, Jim," she said as she moved toward the door.

"Thanks. I'm really glad you came."

"Sure," said Judy as she disappeared into the hallway.

They had been gone for a few seconds when Kincaid settled back into bed, relaxing his body as he relished the fresh memory of the visit. The three minutes with his first family helped carry his spirits for hours.

A second surprise visit came from Sharon, who stopped by the next day with MacKenna and Alex. Sharon, freshly dyed white-blonde and dressed in skin-tight jeans with a black sweater that showed plenty of cleavage, seemed unusually interested in the pain levels that Kincaid had endured and asked several questions, including how much blood he had lost, if the pain kept him up at night, and whether he could go to the bathroom by himself. Sharon also inquired if Kincaid's injuries would affect his next child-support payment.

Neither of the children spoke to their father. Alex had brought two banged-up Hot Wheels cars into the room, which he shoved around on Kincaid's nightstand as MacKenna loudly told him to "stop it, dumb head." He then began to push a car hard up Kincaid's bandaged shoulder, causing a loud grunt and a harsh "Don't, dammit!" from his injured father.

Sharon made no move to correct the boy, but MacKenna slapped him hard on the top of the head, causing a cry of pain and quick tears. MacKenna then began to examine the IV machine, rattling it so hard that it beeped wildly, forcing a nurse to run in to reset it.

As she worked, Alex took a swig from Kincaid's water pitcher and carelessly set it too near the edge of the nightstand, spilling it onto the floor. MacKenna yelled, "Look what you've done, dumb head!" so loudly that the nurse curtly told her to "shush" before calling for an orderly to come in and mop up the mess.

This visit lasted only a few minutes before Sharon said, "Well, we'd better go. Dallas is waiting for us in the lobby."

"Who the hell is Dallas?" said Kincaid, still rubbing his shoulder from Alex's playmaking.

"Oh, he's my new guy. It didn't pan out with Tim," said Sharon as if Kincaid should know, which he didn't. She tugged at her snug jeans, which were in no danger of falling. "Dallas is a guy I met at work. He's thirty-four or thirty-six or something like that, and he drives a garbage truck for SaniStar. He stopped in for coffee all the time, and one thing led to another."

MacKenna interrupted. "You're on TV, Daddy. The men on the news say how you blasted those Mexicans' butts."

"Knock it off." Sharon half-heartedly swatted at MacKenna, but hit more air than the girl. She then turned back to Kincaid, who grimaced at MacKenna's insensitivity. "The kids sit glued to the TV, thinking you'll be on it."

"Obviously. Does Dallas live with you and the kids?"

"Yeah, since last week, or the week before. I asked him to move in. Tim had been gone for a month and a half or so, and I was ready."

"Hmm," uttered Kincaid, remembering how Sharon always moved fast. "Do the kids like him?"

"Oh, fine. They know I like him, too. Like they say, if you're happy, the kids will be happy."

That was enough for Kincaid. "Yeah, well, thanks for coming by."

Alex was passing the time by turning the water in the bathroom sink on and off. In response, MacKenna kept yelling, "Don't, you poophead."

Alex came running out of the bathroom with a washcloth in his mouth. Sharon told him to "take that out, dammit!" and tossed the cloth on Kincaid's table as she shooed the kids into the hallway. Minutes later, the nurse returned for Kincaid's scheduled blood pressure check, which, not surprisingly, registered the highest reading he'd had all day.

The most uncomfortable exchange of all, though, was a tearful phone call from Debbie's daughter, Shannon, who thanked him for offering to pay for her mother's funeral. Debbie had not left life insurance and had little in the way of an estate, so the burden of a burial was something else for Shannon to deal with. "Thanks so much, Jim," she said heartily. "I don't know what I would have done if you weren't so good about this."

Kincaid quietly replied, "That's all right," knowing his choices had caused her mother's death. Shannon spoke of the funeral and was uncertain if her brother, Dylan, would be able to attend because "he was having more problems." She worried that she may have to bring her baby to the service, since her husband said he might have another job interview.

"Is there anything I can do?" asked Shannon in an almost pleading tone. Her willingness to help riveted Kincaid with guilt, as she was blissfully unaware of his role in her mother's death.

His voice started to break, but he summoned enough strength to cover it. "Not really," he replied. "I talked to the landlord and had Service Master go in and clean up." He paused. "I just couldn't bring myself to walk back in that trailer and see all of that, you know. Even though I know it's been cleaned, I'm still dreading going back there. Too many memories."

"Yeah, I understand," said Shannon, her own voice breaking. "Could I at least bring you a fresh change of clothes?"

With everything swirling in his mind, Kincaid had not realized that he had no clean clothes in the room, save for his hospital gown. "That would be great," he said. "I don't know if you have a key or not, but if you don't, we've got one hidden on the property. Just go on the east side of the trailer, right along the outside wall, and look for a light gray rock. It's the only one there, since that's just bare ground otherwise. That rock is a fake and holds a key. Just pick it up, slide it open, and you'll see it."

"Okay," said Shannon. "I'll leave home right now and go straight there."

Since Shannon was still at home in St. Louis, it took over an hour for her to make the trip, first to White City, then on to Litchfield. She walked into his room and immediately burst into tears upon the sight of Kincaid. He extended a hand, and she took it as she set the clothes, in a pile and neatly folded, on the end of his bed.

He offered his gratitude, and she said, "I've got to go. I'll see you tomorrow at the funeral." Before she left, she quickly uttered that "Mom really thought you were something," words that pierced his sensibilities and sent tears down his face.

CHAPTER 25

The day nurse, Dorothy London, walked into Kincaid's room at 10:51 and informed him that he was about to be released. Kincaid reached for the phone and called Mason once again to let him know that he was ready for his ride.

The man for the job was Trooper Ben Carr, a seven-year veteran of the force who now worked the day shift on the south patrol. Carr was relatively popular at headquarters, with a solid activity record and the ability to get along with others. One guy he did not like, though, was James Kincaid, who had been arrogant and condescending when Carr was in his probationary period, always mocking his youthful looks and inexperience. Carr never forgot the poor treatment and avoided Kincaid whenever their paths crossed, which was rarely.

Naturally, Carr was less than thrilled when Jim Peal assigned him to drive Kincaid home, and, likewise, Kincaid was apprehensive when Carr strode in. Kincaid was sitting on the bed, dressed in the dark blue shirt and pants that Shannon had brought from the trailer.

Carr breezed through the door and offered no greetings. Kincaid buzzed the nurses' station and informed them that his ride had arrived. Shortly, a wheelchair was brought in, and Kincaid gingerly slid himself into it from the bed. "I'll get your bag," said Carr, pointing to the plastic sack that contained Kincaid's blood-stained clothing from the night of the shooting, as well as some of his hospital toiletries.

The nurse released her hand from the wheelchair handle and pointed to Carr, as if to tell him to take over. Carr grabbed the wheelchair and began pushing too fast for Kincaid's liking as he grunted softly with each bounce and rattle. When they approached the elevator, Carr swung the wheelchair around to back inside so wildly that Kincaid was nearly thrown from his seat.

The elevator ride was as silent as the drive back to the trailer, as Carr uttered one-word responses to Kincaid's half-hearted attempts at conversation. As they pulled into the driveway, Kincaid spied Debbie's red Celica, parked in the same spot as the night of the shooting, now covered with frost and light snow from days of winter weather.

"You can get in by yourself, right?" said Carr brusquely.

"Yeah," said Kincaid, knowing that no help was forthcoming and that his entrance would come with a great deal of pain. Carr reached across to shut the passenger door after Kincaid stepped out, and he was putting the squad car in reverse before Kincaid had even made it to the front step.

His shoulder jostled as he stepped up on the porch, and his heart ached as he glanced over at Debbie's beloved red gnome. As he entered the front door, his eyes immediately fixated on the living room, now painstakingly cleaned, with no traces of the blood that had splattered across the walls and floor on that nightmarish evening. The smell of the cleanser lingered, turning his stomach and making his head throb. Quickly, he turned away, for another task at hand.

For days, he had feared for his money in the rafters, and now he had to check. Though every step came with shooting pain, he stumbled toward the door to the garage, flipped on the light, and breathed a deep sigh of relief when he looked up and saw the tarpaulin covering the bag, untouched.

Though Kincaid was hardly in perfect shape before the shooting, climbing the ladder to the rafters hadn't been a problem. Now, struggling to regain his health, he knew the climb would be excruciating, but he had a funeral to pay for. Slowly, he walked to the side of the garage, reached for the ladder, and moaned in discomfort as he dragged it over to reach the rafters.

His shoulder ached and his left hand throbbed as he pulled the ladder apart to form the "A" needed to set it up. Now came the really hard part, as he knew that climbing upward would be practically unbearable. Slowly, painfully, he took each step, his moans growing louder as he went higher. After what seemed like forever, he was finally high enough to reach into the bag.

Kincaid was a right-hander, but his injured shoulder prevented its use, so he had to reach into the bag with his injured left hand, still heavily bandaged. He slid his hand into the bag, now wincing in pain as his body assumed an awkward position while trying to keep his balance.

He knew that he would not be able to do this again any time soon, so he tried to grab as much money as he could before his body could stand no more. Kincaid seized as much money as possible from the bag and then climbed downward, grunting in pain with every step.

As he reached the bottom rung, he stepped onto the floor and leaned against the ladder, panting for breath, face wrenched in agony. After several seconds, he collected himself sufficiently to fold up the ladder, set it in its place against the wall, and go back inside the trailer, where he carefully avoided the sight of the living room. As he passed by, he tossed the handful of money onto the kitchen table, never turning his head on his way to the bedroom.

He staggered down the hallway and pitched himself onto the bed, still unmade from its last use, now with a slightly musty smell from sitting unattended for several days. Though the thermostat was set on 66 degrees in the trailer, sweat beaded down his cheeks and neck and trickled into his bandages. Face down, he screamed into a pillow, muffling the sound of his frustration and despair.

*****

The release gave Kincaid respite, and he lay calmly on the bed, collecting himself for what came next. The funeral was just two hours away, and he had to get ready. Groaning in pain, he sat up on the bed, staring at the closet, thinking about what he should wear, and what he could pull on with the least discomfort.

Though he longed for a roomy sweater and baggy pants, he again recalled Debbie's horrific death and knew that a suit and tie was more in order. Wearily, he tugged off his shirt and underclothes and stood naked in front of the floor-length mirror, checking to see if his bandages were leaking. Finding no traces of blood, he shuffled over to the closet, and reached uncomfortably for a blue-checked Western-style shirt on a hanger in the back. He then leaned toward the only suit he owned, a navy blue, off-the-rack special from a Litchfield men's store that cost eighty-nine dollars, and laid it out on the bed.

Grunting and moaning, he managed to dress himself and button his shirt and coat one-handed. He had gained ten pounds since buying the suit a decade ago, and the jacket clung to his body, with the outline of his bandaged shoulder apparent at the top of a sleeve that did not fully reach his wrist. Pulling on his dark dress socks was torturous. Finally came his shoes, and he gladly reached for a pair of black slip-on loafers that required no tying.

With few friends and with Shannon consumed with the sorrowful activities of the day, Kincaid had few options for transport to the funeral, since he didn't know his buddies from the bar well enough to ask. So he decided to drive himself, and despite the cold air, he forewent an overcoat, since it would only add to his pain. Before he left, he counted out seventy-five $100 bills to pay for the funeral after it was over and stuffed them into a business-size envelope that he placed in his inside jacket pocket.

His body limited in mobility, the step on the running board into his battered pickup came with shoots of agony, as did the effort to slide into the seat. But he somehow managed, and unsure of his reflexes, he drove at a speed no greater than thirty-five miles an hour to the First Christian Church of Mount Olive, on the opposite side of town.

Upon arriving in front of the imposing, red-brick spired sanctuary, he was surprised to see the parking lot mostly full. The only available spots were in the back of the lot, and he reluctantly claimed one, knowing the walk would be unpleasant. He knocked on the front door and waited for an attendant to open it, hoping that he would not have to swing the bulky white-wood door with his sore shoulder and hand.

But the door did open, and standing inside was Don Lawson, the genteel funeral director, who greeted Kincaid with a soothing, "Please come in." He warmly took Kincaid's hand and expressed his sympathy.

"I'll have something for you later," whispered Kincaid.

"That's fine," said Lawson. "We'll talk afterward."

He took Kincaid by his tender right arm and led him toward the sanctuary, where Debbie's body lay in a closed casket, an appropriate choice in light of her disfiguring death. A large portrait of Debbie, framed in gold, sat on an easel next to the casket, surrounded by red and white carnations, her favorite flower.

Dozens of people milled about the room, mostly familiar faces from Martin's Tavern, where Debbie's upbeat personality won her the affections of many a customer, male and female. Some were lounging in the pews, while others were seated in white folding chairs nearer the casket. None of the mourners were fellow state troopers.

Like many funerals and visitations, the men stood on one side, talking about farming, football, and the local economy, while the women gathered elsewhere and gabbed the time away on local gossip and who was related to whom. A group of women sat near the casket, including Shelley Tipson, the retired, hard-drinking teacher who sobbed unashamedly at the loss of her bartender and friend.

Standing in the opposite corner was Larry Adams, the retired ironworker from the bar, dressed in his Sunday finest with his greasy hair combed straight back, hands in his pockets, clearly wishing he were somewhere else. His brother Del stood nearby, tie hanging loosely around his king-size neck and shirttail protruding from his prodigious gut, somehow finding a way to bellow in laughter amid the solemnity. Next to him was Ned Ullmann, finding every reason to complain about the funeral setup, from the time of the service to the "shitty organ music."

Sitting alone in a folding chair a few seats down from Shelley was Russell Martin. He stared at the casket, tears streaming down his face, mumbling about "my Debbie." His demeanor changed as Kincaid approached, and his quivering lips clenched as he glared down at the floor. For some unknown reason, Martin already blamed Kincaid for Debbie's death.

Kincaid put his hand on Martin's shoulder but the old man jerked away, not wanting the touch. Rebuffed and embarrassed, Kincaid spied Shannon standing near the casket, greeting mourners.

Shannon was holding up as best she could, offering her thanks in between bouts of tears to the many well-wishers who walked by. The day had been a trial from the outset, as the babysitter she had lined up called off sick at the last minute, and she frantically found a replacement while her husband, Dakota, impatiently waited in his tricked-out black Camaro.

As Shannon struggled to keep her composure in the receiving line, Dakota stood across the room, devoting his attention to Debbie's flirty eighteen-year-old blonde niece Tiffany and her friend Chelsie, who both seemed to be taking the loss well.

Kincaid approached Shannon, who threw her arms around him in a tearful embrace. "Thanks so much, Jim," she wailed. "I don't know how we could have done this without you."

"That's all right," replied Kincaid, shifting uncomfortably as Shannon lay against his aching shoulder. "Was your brother able to make it?"

"No-o-o," said Shannon through sobs. She whispered in Kincaid's ear. "You know, he had a relapse. He's in jail again."

"Sorry, I didn't know," said Kincaid awkwardly. He looked over at Dakota, who was acting out some of his old football moves for Tiffany and Chelsie. His eyes scanned back to Shannon, whose mascara was badly running. "Is there anything I can do for you?"

"Oh, Jim, you've done so much already," said Shannon. As she spoke, Debbie's second husband, who was Shannon's father and the paramour of the schoolgirl tramp from years before, passed by. Shannon quickly shook hands with the man with an offhanded utterance of "thanks" and turned back to Kincaid. Sensing he was unwelcome, the man briskly headed back for the door, shaking a couple more hands as he went.

Kincaid, in turn, sensed that someone was glaring at him, and he slowly swung his neck to see Martin's menacing stare. He turned his attention back to Shannon. "I better step away," he said.

"Oh, Jim, you're welcome to stand here with me," she urged. "Mom really liked you, and you were so important to her." Kincaid's guilt level continued to rise, even as he noticed that Shannon said Debbie "liked," not "loved," him.

"Thanks," he said. "But I better sit down. I don't know how much longer I can be on my feet."

He chose the closest chair to Shannon, and a few passing mourners, mainly regulars from the bar, stopped to offer their condolences to him as well. Del Adams finally made his way over to the casket, clasped Shannon in a bear hug that was too close and long for her liking, and slapped Kincaid hard on his good shoulder.

"She was a good ol' gal," said Del, adding, "Helluva bartender," as he walked away. In tow was Ned, who shook hands while looking down at the floor. "Bullshit way to die," he said and quickly moved on. Kincaid, though, could hardly look Del, Ned, or anyone else in the eye, knowing that his choices had brought him, and everyone else in the room, to this point.

Just then, Mr. Lawson asked everyone to take their seats and Reverend Lloyd Chalmers, a slightly built, bespectacled man with thinning gray hair, took the pulpit. Speaking into a microphone that unfortunately had some screeching feedback, he lauded Debbie's character, her work ethic, and her ability to make and keep friends. He turned to Shannon, now joined by Dakota, and professed his sympathy, assuring them that they were part of her legacy that would live on. As Reverend Chalmers addressed them, Dakota turned in his seat and made eye contact with Tiffany, several rows behind.

Reverend Chalmers next addressed Kincaid, calling him "the light of Debbie's life" and "the good man behind her very existence." Kincaid stared down his chest, while Martin, in turn, stared icy daggers at Kincaid.

A brief prayer followed before the service broke up. The pallbearers, all customers from Martin's, rose to carry the casket to the hearse for the trip to the church cemetery across town. Mr. Lawson calmly announced that Debbie's family and friends were invited to a celebration of her life at her place of employment later that afternoon.

As Kincaid pushed himself out of his chair with his good shoulder, Martin brushed by and nodded toward the casket. "You were supposed to take care of her, you bastard," he said in a cold whisper. "You know that celebration we're having? It doesn't include you." Martin turned to walk away, leaving Kincaid staring in silence.

The wind was picking up as the afternoon faded away, and the little funeral flags on the hoods of cars in the procession whipped fearfully on the drive to the cemetery. Reverend Chalmers delivered a brief prayer and the mourners dispersed.

Kincaid lingered for a moment over the open grave that would soon hold the vault and slowly turned back to his truck. As he began, he met Mr. Lawson, withdrew the envelope with the seventy-five $100 bills, and handed it over.

"I'll mail you a receipt," said Lawson in a soothing voice that masked his smile at receiving the cash. As Lawson strode away, Kincaid watched Shannon wearily walk alone to the Camaro as Dakota said his goodbyes to Tiffany and Chelsie.

His shoulder throbbing in the cold wind, Kincaid climbed into his Silverado, holding back the grunts of pain. From the driver's seat, he gazed back at the scene, and his choices again flashed through his mind.

Just as quickly, his mind switched back to the mental and physical exhaustion of the events of the day, and he could only think of getting home to bed, driving as fast as his taxed body would allow. Meanwhile, Debbie's other friends gathered at Martin's Tavern, laughing over memories and crying over drinks until late in the evening.

CHAPTER 26

Hours after Debbie's funeral, Kincaid lay awake in the cramped bedroom of his rented mobile home, staring at the ceiling. His physical wounds, suffered just days before, frequently sent pain piercing through his body, particularly his bandaged shoulder, which greatly restricted his movement.

He could barely turn over in bed without a riveting pain of discomfort, and even if he were able to settle on his other side, he had to be wary of his wrapped hand with the severed finger. As a result, he could only lay flat on his back, hoping that his exhaustion would force his eyes shut and into slumber.

But his physical woes were simple compared to his emotional anguish. For most of his adult life, he had made his own choices with no regard for the feelings of those around him. Though he had a career with a salary higher than most men and had steered himself to fewer responsibilities than many other troopers, he showed scant appreciation and never shied from complaint.

His marriage, to a woman that most men could only dream of, evaporated amid manly desires for another, and though he knew it was a mistake, he left his ex-wife and two lovely daughters in the dust. Then, as he tired of his new paramour, he moved on once again, flipping his hand at two more children whom he could have lived without. As his life shifted from a comfortable house to a trailer, cigarettes and alcohol remained a constant, and they consumed his body as much as the twinges below his belt whenever the latest good-looking woman passed by.

Then came Debbie, though he rarely said he loved her and when he did, it was usually to appease her or to ensure she would satisfy his desires in times of passion. But her income helped him out, and it had been nice to have a well-built woman in tight jeans flitting around, agreeing with him, laughing at his jokes, pouring more beer, listening to his gripes, putting out in bed.

Now, as the clock flashed 11:39 p.m., he had barely slept, his body rumpled in pain, his mind tormented with anxiety and guilt. As selfish as his choices may have been before, they had never cost anyone their life. Now Debbie was gone, the image of her bloodied face and crumpled corpse burned in his mind. It was his fault, his cross to bear, the result of his choices. As the minutes ticked agonizingly by, he withdrew his hands from below the sheet and covered his face, as if to hide his shame.

The clock would not speed up, and the darkness of the night seemed longer and longer. As the blame and self-doubt fell over him in a torrent, he still thought of the bag of money in the garage, up in the rafters, now difficult to reach as he had learned earlier that day.

Part of Kincaid now hated that bag, for he knew it was the cause of all this, the reason Debbie had died, the basis of his newfound self-loathing. But part of him saw the bag as his salvation, his way out, the start of a better life that would ease his misery, perhaps somewhere else, somewhere down the road, with retirement close, but still not close enough.

Finally, the clock reached 4:37 a.m. Kincaid decided he had enough and needed to escape the bed that had wrapped him in self-hatred. He threw the covers back and wearily put his feet on the floor, wincing at the pain that flew through his torso from his shoulder, the burning sensation that raced up his arm from the lost finger. Showering was out of the question, so Kincaid stumbled in the darkness to the bathroom, absentmindedly turned the hot water faucet in the sink, and slipped out of his pajama pants, preparing for a half-hearted stand-up bath.

As Kincaid washed, he gazed at himself in the mirror, his ruddy complexion, his ever-receding hairline, the paunch that dropped from below the bandages cloaking his shoulder. Just then, he heard a muffled thump from the hallway, and for an instant, he thought of the sound of Debbie's footsteps, flouncing toward him. But then he heard the swirl of the wind outside, and he knew that the sound was only that of the trailer shifting in the gusts.

His body washed as much as his patience would allow, Kincaid trudged toward the kitchen, reaching into the refrigerator with the hand connected to his tightened shoulder, since his other hand had its own bandage. He slid his arm inside and grasped a half-full plastic container of milk, glancing to make sure the date had not expired.

The date, stamped in black, was tomorrow. Reaching for a glass from the cabinet above the counter would be too much to ask, and now there was no one around to share with anyway. So Kincaid unscrewed the cap, lifted the bottle to his lips, and took a swig. Some of the milk missed his mouth and trickled down his chin and neck to the bandages, forcing him to grab a dishcloth and wipe himself amid groans of discomfort.

The clock now read 5:09 a.m., and even at this early hour, he had a call to make. At District 18 headquarters, he knew that Master Sergeant Jim Peal, his superior, would still be on the desk. Kincaid reached for the receiver on the wall with moderate discomfort, but his pain level rose as he punched in the numbers, as he was forced to rotate his shoulder with every entry. Peal picked up on the second ring.

His voice was direct, as usual. "Illinois State Police, Master Sergeant Peal speaking."

"Hey, this is James Kincaid. Gotta talk to you for a little bit." Kincaid's voice, usually brimming with bravado, was much weaker than normal.

"Oh, hi!" Peal was not known for compassion but tried to muster some here, and his voice softened slightly. "How you doin'? God, terrible thing that happened to you."

"Yeah." Kincaid's guilt over Debbie precluded his desire for sympathy. He referred back to his greeting. "You got a minute?"

"Sure, sure. Whatcha need?"

"I was released from the hospital yesterday morning. Had to go to my girlfriend's funeral yesterday afternoon…" Kincaid's voice trailed off before his regained his composure. "I still feel like shit, but better than I was, at any rate."

"I bet." Peal again was showing unusual empathy. "Yeah, you would feel that way, after what you've been through."

Kincaid ignored that comment. "I'm gonna be recuperating here at home. The doctor said there wasn't anything else they could do at the hospital, and he thought I could take care of myself." He winced at the thought, since the pain kept shooting through his upper body.

"Yeah. No place like home," said Peal, wincing at his use of a tired cliché, but he was struggling to find something to say in a situation like this. "How long are you going to be down?"

"I go back and see the doctor in two weeks. As soon as he releases me, I plan to come back to work." Kincaid hated the job, but he played along. "I mean, I want to come back. Really, I can't wait. Got a need to get things back to normal, you know."

"Mm-hmm." replied Peal. "Well, you know, things haven't exactly been normal around here either. You know, with all the reporters calling and people wanting information."

"Hmm." Kincaid again winced, this time at the thought of the trouble he had caused everyone. "Well, sorry about that. Trust me, I'd rather have not been through this and not had all those frickin' reporters all over me."

Peal realized his insensitivity. "Yeah, of course. Didn't mean it like that. It's just been crazy around here."

"Sure, I know. Don't worry about it. How's everything else there?"

"Well, I'll be glad when you get back to work. We've been so shorthanded around here." Peal uttered those words despite Kincaid's well-known record of low activity, and his penchant for disregarding authority.

Peal pushed a few papers around on his desk, causing a ruffle that Kincaid could hear on the other end. "That damn flu bug's about to knock this place on its ass. I got more guys out than I can count, and I got another one who's on long-term medical leave for back surgery. Then there's another guy whose wife's about to have a baby, and she's having all sorts of complications." He laughed sarcastically. "Course, that makes my life that much easier."

"Yeah, tell me about it." Kincaid never had sympathy for anyone before, and he wasn't about to start now. "Sounds like it's the same bullshit as normal there."

"Pffft." Peal blew through his lips and grimaced at Kincaid's comment, which he had heard all too often. "So when are you coming back?"

"Oh, God. Not for a while. Before I left yesterday, the doctor said it might take six weeks or more," replied Kincaid. "I mean, I hurt like you can't believe. I can't shift, sit up or down, move around, anything, and I got this one hand still bandaged. I look like a frickin' mummy with all this white tape. And I'm so tired all the time. I feel like I'm ninety years old or something."

Peal wondered if Kincaid was exaggerating as to what he could do but didn't push it. "Well, whenever you can. Your health's the most important thing."

Kincaid changed the subject. "One other thing. I know they're investigating the shooting. Mike Miller and this other guy, R.J. McIntire, interviewed me in the hospital." He paused, searching for words. "You heard anything about that?"

"No, not a thing. But I gotta tell you, in my opinion, it was justified. I mean, judging from what I know about it, I can't see how they're gonna rule any other way."

Peal could not hear the sigh of relief that Kincaid emitted on the other end, which sent another shot of discomfort through his shoulder. "Thanks," he replied, trying to sound offhanded. "I told them exactly what happened, but you never know how those things will go."

"Yeah." Peal was never one to spend much time on anyone, and the bits of emotion he had shown at the start of the conversation were now used up. "Well, take care of yourself. If there's anything you need."

"Thanks. See ya." Kincaid reached to hang up the receiver. The pain was replaced by relief over the first good piece of news he had received in days. The celebration was fleeting, however, as he turned his head back to the living room and the spot where Debbie had met her gruesome end just days before.

CHAPTER 27

Three days after Debbie Marks' funeral, R.J. McIntire had just pulled his unmarked squad car into the parking lot at District 18 headquarters in Litchfield when his cell phone in his shirt pocket rang. He answered to hear the voice of Brad Collins, the state's attorney, on the other end.

"We've got the subpoenas for Kincaid's bank records," said Collins. "It's ready to be served."

"Good deal," said McIntire. "I'll be right over."

The news gave McIntire an extra spring in his step, knowing that a major hurdle to the investigation had just been cleared. He briskly walked inside, tracked down Miller, and said that he was on the way to Hillsboro to Collins' office. From there, he would serve the subpoena personally at the Mount Olive State Bank.

"Do you need me to come along?" inquired Miller.

"Sure, let's go," said McIntire.

Twenty-five minutes later, McIntire and Miller were walking into Collins' office at the Montgomery County courthouse. "Didn't take you long, did it?"

chuckled Collins. He reached to the left side of his desk and grasped a sheaf of papers that composed the subpoena. "I think that's everything."

"Appreciate it," said McIntire. "We will deliver these to the bank today."

"I figured you would," smiled Collins. "If you need anything else, let me know."

McIntire and Miller said goodbye, eager to get to Mount Olive. They backtracked down Route 16 on the return to Litchfield, and, once there, turned onto Old Route 66 on the west side of town. Though his first instinct was to take I-55 from Litchfield to Mount Olive, Miller's local knowledge had taught McIntire a shortcut, and today, he didn't want to waste a minute.

The drive south flew by, and soon McIntire and Miller were approaching the Mount Olive State Bank, housed in a stand-alone, gray-stone building near the center of town. Unlike many other banks, it had rebuffed attempts at buy-outs and still operated from only one location. McIntire slowed into the lot, parked near the door, and the pair strode inside.

Once in the lobby, they approached a teller to find out who handled subpoenas for the bank. The teller was a brown-haired twenty-something named Marissa White, who clearly spent much of her salary on the jewelry she was wearing. McIntire and Miller displayed their credentials, and McIntire asked who they should speak to. Marissa seemed leery at the exchange, and then replied with no emotion apparent, "You need to see Theresa Rackpole."

McIntire asked where they may find her, which seemed to burden Marissa even further. With a hint of a frown on her heavily made-up face, she walked to the end of the counter, passed through a small, swinging half-door to step into the lobby, and escorted them to where they needed to be.

In an office with a large glass-front window that provided a full view of the lobby was Mrs. Rackpole, a medium-built woman in her early sixties, with neatly coiffed, short gray hair. McIntire and Miller each presented their ISP credentials and extended a hand in greeting. Rackpole introduced herself and asked both to have a seat in her office.

"So what can I do for the State Police today?" she said, being sure to make eye contact with both of her visitors.

"We have a subpoena for some banking records we need from you," replied McIntire, handing the documents to Rackpole. She examined the subpoenas closely, thought silently for a few moments, and then turned her eyes back to McIntire.

"This involves a lot of records," said Rackpole, pointing to the subpoena for effect. "Of course, we can get them for you, but it will take some time. I'd say at least week or so."

"Fine. We knew it would take a while," remarked McIntire as he handed Rackpole a business card. "Would you contact me as soon as the documents are ready?"

"Certainly," replied Rackpole in her usual businesslike manner. "I'll give you a call as soon as they come in."

With that, both officers rose from their chairs, thanked Rackpole, and headed for the parking lot for the drive back to Miller's office at District 18 headquarters. Once there, R.J. told Miller that he had to catch up on his reports, so he was going back to his Springfield office and would return to District 18 when the subpoenaed documents were ready.

Ten days later, McIntire received a telephone call from Rackpole, indicating that the bank records were ready for pickup. R.J. responded that he would pick them up the following day, thanked her and hung up, and then immediately telephoned Miller. When Miller answered, McIntire started talking without even a hello.

"I just heard back from the bank on the Kincaid subpoena," said McIntire with a tinge of excitement. "I'll meet you in your office, eight-thirty tomorrow morning, so we can go down there and pick them up."

"Good deal. See you then." Miller had barely finished speaking when McIntire broke the connection.

Both McIntire and Miller knew the subpoenas were crucial to the case, and they were anxious for the next morning to come to get their hands on the records. When McIntire strode into Miller's office the next day, both men were clearly in an upbeat mood and spent little time getting to McIntire's car for the drive to Mount Olive.

Once in the bank, they glanced around and asked Marissa where they could find Mrs. Rackpole. Marissa, who was checking her phone and seemed annoyed at the interruption, simply pointed to a small office adjacent to the lobby.

Rackpole had overheard the exchange and was getting up from her desk as McIntire and Miller approached the office. As they entered, she turned to a large box of materials sitting on the floor near the wall. The box was overflowing with photocopies, official documents, and assorted paperwork.

"I think that's everything you need," she said as she stood over the box, pointing at it. "James Kincaid opened an account here around seven years ago when he moved to White City. That includes records for that whole time, including checking and savings records, any receipts we had, any loans or mortgages he had, any other accounts that he held jointly with someone, all of that. It's basically everything we had on any account Kincaid ties to."

McIntire nodded in approval. "Looks like we've got some sorting to do," he said with the same hint of a smile. "Thank you, ma'am. You've been a tremendous help."

"Anytime," said Rackpole as she turned back to her desk. McIntire squatted down to lift the bulky box off the floor, rose, and walked toward the main door. Miller went ahead to hold the doors open.

"You need any help with that?" said Miller.

"If you've got a forklift, that would help," said McIntire in jest, between puffs of breath. "I should have pulled rank and had you carry it."

"Yeah, well, you're higher on the pay scale than I am," smirked Miller as he held the back seat door open.

McIntire dropped the box onto the seat, slid it toward the middle, and sighed. "And just think I busted my butt all those years to get promotions, and this is what I have to show for it."

Miller laughed out loud as he climbed in the front seat. McIntire got in beside him, winked, and threw the car into reverse.

*****

R.J. McIntire was a man of focus, a trait that was evident even to those who had just met him. Miller had known McIntire for a while now and was starting to know what to expect. As McIntire drove a little faster than normal up Interstate 55 to get back to Litchfield, Miller knew that he was anxious to get back to headquarters and into the records.

"I'll get the box this time," offered Miller as McIntire parked outside headquarters.

"How nice of you!" said McIntire. "Helping out the old man, huh?"

Miller snickered as he maneuvered the box to the door. This time, McIntire held the doors to the inside, and they walked down the hallway to the investigative office. There, a large conference table sat, big enough to hold the box and its bulging contents.

Both men sat down, divided up sheafs of documents, and began combing through the records. After a while, Miller got McIntire's attention. "Hey, take a look at this."

"What've you got?" said McIntire, setting down a folder of receipts and coming around the table to stand over Miller.

"Here," said Miller, pointing to a small stack of checking statements. "In the two years before the accident that Kincaid investigated until the month after, his bank account showed an average balance of around $350. I mean, give or take a little, and I'm doing this in my head. But his balance every month was somewhere around that."

"Not much there," said McIntire. "For a guy making eighty-two grand a year, not much left over."

"Not with all the alimony, child support, and everything else," agreed Miller. "But now look at this." He set out the most recent checking statements in the pile. "Here's the last one, from January. Take a look at that balance."

The figure showed $12,863.43. "Quite a jump there," said McIntire, nodding at the sight. He scanned the statement some more and found a string of deposits, one every two weeks, each for the same amount of money.

"Looks like his paycheck just sits in the bank," remarked McIntire, never lifting his eyes from the sheets in front of him. "Comes in every two weeks, and he doesn't do anything with it. Never withdraws it or anything. Just keeps building up."

"Seems he came into some cash somewhere along the way, doesn't it?" mused Miller, who pointed to an earlier statement. "It looks like he wrote checks every Friday for $100 a time. Let's see if those are the checks that Martin the bar owner was talking about."

"Right." McIntire came back around the table to the materials on his side and reached for a pile of canceled checks. Quickly, he located several examples of checks written to "Cash" that were endorsed with a business stamp reading "Martin's Tavern." He and Miller then compared the dates on the checks and the statements, and each indicated a match.

"All right. Now we've got those," said McIntire. "Did he keep writing those checks at Martin's?"

"Nope. The last one was in November. There aren't any listings for anything in that amount after that."

"So it's just like Martin said, that Kincaid had quit cashing checks several weeks ago," pondered McIntire, sitting back in his swivel chair. "When we talked to the county clerk, we found out that Kincaid was paying child support in cash. What have you got that verifies that?"

"Same thing," said Miller, holding up a statement. "There were checks for $800 every month up through November. Now there aren't any."

McIntire thumbed through the pile of canceled checks and found the last one for child support. It was dated November 15, twelve days before the accident.

"Damn, he did the same thing with the child support," exclaimed McIntire, tapping his fingers on the table in frustration. "The clerk never said that Kincaid was delinquent. I can call and check, but she said Kincaid was current on his support payments."

"Yeah," said Miller, looking McIntire directly in the eye. "Clearly, he's got money coming from somewhere."

"Obviously," said McIntire, who had a strong suspicion where the money was from. "Do you have the bank card records over there?"

Kincaid had two Visa cards backed by the Mount Olive State Bank, one of the perks of customer service. "I've got those," said Miller, who fell silent for a moment as he shuffled through the statements.

"It's the same thing, R.J. He paid them off in November," he said, breaking the pause. McIntire came back around the table. "He had a balance of around $800 on both of those cards as far back as I can see. Then comes November, and there is no balance. Look." He handed the statements to McIntire and pointed to one line on each. "He paid both of them off at the end of the month."

"And they haven't been used since," said McIntire, finishing the thought. He looked down at Miller, still sitting in his chair.

Miller shook his head, pursed his lips, and turned toward the wall. He never looked McIntire directly in the eye, but his words were clear. "That about cinches it, doesn't it?"

"Sure looks that way," uttered McIntire. "Kincaid's got more financial problems than any trooper I know. Then all of a sudden, he's throwing money around like water, got plenty of cash. Just happened to come in November, around the time of the accident." He drummed his fingers on the desk. "Damn."

McIntire was a highly trained investigator and was conditioned to remain unbiased. In his years in DII, he had examined the conduct of police officers, which had hardened him. Still, he despised the notion that a cop had gone astray, even though the evidence was clear. He moved his lips back and forth and glanced at Miller to see his reaction.

Miller, too, was grappling with a swirl of emotions as his eyes were transfixed on the wall. All his adult life, he had taken great pride in his work, and fleeting thoughts of the men who had influenced him, like his old mentor Steve Drury, flashed through his mind. Miller held himself to a high standard and expected the same of those around him. As his mind raced, he folded his arms and his glare intensified.

No more words were spoken because both knew what this meant. The evidence was mounting against James Kincaid, and Brad Collins was sure to proceed with charges. The split-second choice to steal the money was about to end a long career in law enforcement and land Kincaid in prison.

CHAPTER 28

The partial sunshine of late winter illuminated the horizon as R.J. McIntire rolled down a nearly empty Interstate 55, heading toward District 18 headquarters once again. This time, he was heading to a meeting with Mike Miller and Jason Webster, the crime scene technician, to review the findings of the investigation into the shooting at the Kincaid trailer.

McIntire's son had come home for a quick visit from Florida, and had claimed half of the garage alongside Darlene's black Chrysler minivan. As a result, McIntire's vehicle was left outside, and covered by frost the next morning. R.J. had spent a few minutes scraping the car off before leaving. Down the street, the automated sign at the bank branch flashed between the time, 7:01, and the temperature, 33 degrees.

As R.J. handled the ice on his windshield, Miller breezed through the kitchen of his Litchfield home as he prepared to drop off his thirteen-year-old daughter, Adrianna, at the middle school, saving a trip for wife Julie, who was sleeping in after struggling with a headache the evening before. Their sixteen-year-old son, Tyler, who had earned his driver's license just weeks before, stood at the front door as Mike strode by, waiting for a ride from a school buddy.

Julie's headache had arisen from an uncomfortable night, as Tyler had engaged Mike in a long, heated discussion about buying a car, to no avail. Meanwhile, Adrianna was having female problems, and burst into fits of crying throughout the evening over the changes and discomfort in her body.

Mike had managed to get some sleep after all of this, though Adrianna, like most young teens, had little to say to either parent on this day. She trailed behind Mike, clearly embarrassed that her father still had to drive her to school.

Tyler's eyes met Mike's as he passed by in the kitchen. "If I had my own car, I wouldn't have to wait like this," said the boy, needling his father.

"Get a three-point grade average and mow enough lawns this summer, and maybe you'll have one," replied Mike, never breaking stride. Adrianna sighed and rolled her eyes. Tyler swatted at her as she walked by.

Mike knew the drill as they approached the middle school: park two blocks away, so it would look like Adrianna had walked on her own. He slowed as she silently climbed out of the car and trudged down the sidewalk toward the school building, the swirling wind blowing her ponytail back and forth. Mike then drove back to his home, parked his personal vehicle in the drive, and climbed into his squad car for the trip to headquarters, pulling in just behind McIntire.

The two men swung the doors open on their respective vehicles almost in unison and exchanged a couple of pleasantries in the bitter cold air before Webster pulled into the parking lot, completing the drive from his Springfield home.

The normally stoic Jason had a hint of a smile on his face as he joined McIntire and Miller for the walk across the lot. They passed through the front door, waited on each other while pouring themselves coffee in white Styrofoam cups, and headed directly for the conference room.

Once inside, the men methodically emptied their briefcases, carefully arranging sheafs of documents on the gray metal table in front of them. Investigators are trained to keep their focus on what is in front of them, and this was a prime example. Here, Kincaid's innocence or guilt regarding the bag of money was not the issue. This discussion was about the shooting and whether or not it was justified. R.J. and Mike had been consumed for days on the paper trail that Kincaid was leaving with his sudden riches. Now, they set that aside and joined Webster in analyzing the shooting–and nothing more.

The three men silently reviewed the video ballistics tests, photos, lab reports, and other materials that lay before them. Each was aware of the findings of the reports, since they had remained in contact since that fateful night in the Kincaid trailer. In addition, all three had played some role in the investigation, including McIntire and Miller, who had interviewed Kincaid in his hospital bed. Now, they had the opportunity to carefully read each report and bounce ideas off one another.

As each man finished reading, Webster broke the silence. "I went back and looked at the surveillance tape after I got back to the office in Springfield," began Webster. "I watched it front to back three times. I've got to tell you, it looks like the shooting is justified. You look at where everyone was standing, and the body language and threats of the Mexicans, and that's really the only thing you could think at this point. But we'll know more when all of the evidence is evaluated and the ballistics tests on the bullets found at the scene are in."

Webster further stated that his office had a lip-reader named Holly Simpson who had also reviewed the tape. She had advised Webster that, due to the thick accent of the two Mexicans, she could not determine what they were saying. However, she did manage to determine that Debbie was saying something about stolen money.

"So, based on what I've got, I think Kincaid was justified," he repeated, turning his head first to look McIntire in the eye, then Miller. "I mean, I can't see it any other way. And Kincaid's testimony holds up. There isn't anything to disprove what he's saying."

"I agree," said McIntire. "I know you went over that trailer with a fine-tooth comb. You didn't miss anything."

Webster ignored the compliment and turned to face Miller. "What do you think?"

"I'm with you two," replied Miller, who opened his palm as if a sign of agreement "Everything lines up. That's really the only conclusion you could come to. But what about the lip-reader? I know she couldn't understand what the Mexicans were talking about, but she said she picked up Debbie saying something about stolen money."

"Yeah, that's something we have to consider," said McIntire. "I thought I'd seen everything, but this is kind of a strange one. It's something that doesn't happen to state troopers too often. I've been in DII for a while, and a trooper-involved shooting in his own home is rare."

"Yeah. It's pretty bad," nodded Webster. "Normally, I don't do investigations where the cop pulls the trigger in his own house."

"Right…" McIntire's voice trailed off as his attention went back to the paperwork spread on the table. "Okay. I'll compile all of the reports and submit them to my supervisors in DII. Once those are approved, Mike and I will meet with the state's attorney in Macoupin County and give him a copy. When everyone's reviewed and approved it, I'll set up a meeting with Kincaid to formally advise him of the findings."

With that, Webster shook hands with the others and headed to his car for the drive back to Springfield. McIntire and Miller spent a few minutes going over the other aspects of the Kincaid case before R.J. himself headed north to begin putting together the shooting reports. Now alone, Miller pulled out his cell phone, placed a quick call to check up on Julie and her headache, and faced the rest of the morning.

CHAPTER 29

After returning to his office in Springfield, McIntire spent most of March writing up the interviews and compiling the related reports of the shooting. When the case file was complete, McIntire then composed a synopsis that was provided to David Burge, the director of the Division of Internal Investigations, and Bob O'Brian, the superintendent of the State Police.

Both Burge and O'Brian had graduated from the State Police Academy twenty-nine years ago, and they had come up through the ranks together, remaining friends all the while. Burge scheduled a meeting with O'Brian so McIntire could brief him on the shooting incident.

The meeting was held in O'Brian's office, and McItnire provided a synopsis of the case. He also reviewed all the details with O'Brian, who had a string of pointed questions that McIntire answered in a satisfactory manner. McIntire also viewed the security tape from Kincaid's trailer with the superintendent.

After some discussion, O'Brian and Burge agreed that the shooting was justified. O'Brian added that he would brief the director of the State Police of the finding, and he instructed McIntire to schedule a meeting with the Macoupin County state's attorney for his review.

A separate briefing then followed, as McIntire discussed the other investigation on Kincaid with O'Brian. McIntire stated his belief that Kincaid may have taken a large amount of money from the automobile accident on November 27. Once that briefing was complete, O'Brian instructed Burge and McIntire to keep him advised of the ongoing investigation.

A few days later, McIntire was summoned to an impromptu meeting with his supervisors, who informed him that the director had read and approved his report on the Kincaid shooting. McIntire then called Vincent Moreth, the state's attorney for Macoupin County, to arrange a meeting and to provide him with a copy of the investigation. Moreth had been apprised of the Kincaid shooting and cleared some time on his calendar to meet the following afternoon.

His job as state's attorney was the latest stop in a career that had taken Moreth across the state of Illinois. He had spent ten years as an officer with the Chicago Police Department, and while working full-time, had received both a baccalaureate degree and a law degree. After leaving Chicago, Moreth joined the Illinois Attorney General's office in Springfield for six years and moved to Macoupin County.

He then operated his own law firm in Springfield for four years before running for state's attorney in Macoupin County. He won and became a true crime fighter, held in high regard by the police, his peers, and his constituents.

After the snow and howling winds of winter, spring was in all its glory as McIntire drove to Carlinville for the meeting with Moreth on this April day. The sun shone brightly above and temperatures rose into the mid-sixties, thanks to a southerly breeze. McIntire smiled ruefully as he gazed through the windshield on the drive south, wishing that he could have sneaked in a round of golf in the warming temperatures.

But the putter would have to wait, for the Kincaid case had plenty of arms, and all of them commanded attention. McIntire met Miller at a local restaurant and, after a quick cup of coffee, they drove the few blocks to the state's attorney's office. McIntire found a parking spot on the brick street that ran past the Macoupin County courthouse on its west side. He had been in the building several times, but never failed to gawk at the majesty of the imposing structure, topped by an enormous silver dome above a hulking yellow-limestone exterior.

Indeed, the courthouse of Macoupin County was a jewel of the area, the centerpiece of the town of Carlinville and visible in every direction for miles around. Completed in 1870, the courthouse was built amid corruption, as the county court apparently lined their pockets at the expense of the taxpayers, who wailed that they had no choice in the matter. It was decades before the building was finally paid off, and, by then, the members of the court had either spent their profits only to die in poverty or had fled the area, never to be heard from again.

McIntire had heard the stories from local history buffs, and the investigator in him wondered what had happened to the money 150 years before. But his focus quickly shifted back to Kincaid, and as he and Miller passed through the metal detector near the basement entrance of the courthouse, they saw Moreth's office down the hall and went straight there.

Moreth, a man in his early fifties of medium height and muscular build, greeted McItnire and Miller and asked them to sit down. Miller, who had worked with Moreth in the past, introduced McIntire, who engaged in some small talk with his new acquaintance before getting down to business.

McIntire presented Moreth with the entire file on the shooting investigation and showed him the security video from Kincaid's trailer. A lengthy discussion ensued as Moreth agreed that the shooting was an act of self-defense and therefore justified. He stated that he would send a letter to the ISP, along with a copy to McIntire, indicating that no charges would be filed due to the justification of the shooting.

Next came the meeting with Kincaid, which would be held in the office of the supervisor, Captain Kent Small. Predictably, Small had consulted with his superior in Springfield as he formulated his opinion, and he welcomed Kincaid with a hearty handshake as he stepped through the door. Kincaid put on a brave face and allowed Small to firmly grasp his right hand at the expense of the twinges of pain that shot through his still-injured shoulder.

The two men proved quite a contrast, as Small, who ran several half-marathons a year, looked several years younger than his age. His thick, sandy hair sat atop his tall, dignified physique that towered over the portly, balding Kincaid, who hardly looked younger than his fifty years.

McIntire and Miller sat down, and Small, in formal language, officially notified Kincaid that the shooting was deemed to be justified. Though he expected such a verdict, Kincaid exhaled a noticeable sigh of relief, for his twenty-plus years on the ISP had taught him to prepare for anything. He had also feared that a connection would be drawn to the shooting of the Mexicans and the missing money. With no mention of the money and his clearance in the shooting, Kincaid clenched his lips and nodded his head in silent victory.

Thinking the reaction was only to the shooting and unaware of Kincaid's theft of the money, Small understood, knowing that cops sweat out any investigation into shootings. He broke the ice with some small talk. "When do you think you can return to work?" he inquired.

"Not for a while yet," replied Kincaid, rubbing his injured shoulder for effect. He also held up his severed left hand to remind Small of the missing pinky. "My doctor said it will be at least four more weeks of therapy."

"Damn," said Small, shaking his head. "Well, I can understand. You're in no shape to be on patrol." He pointed to the mass of bandages that still wrapped parts of Kincaid's body. "It's been close to two and a half months since it happened. What is today, April 11? And look at you."

"Yeah. Look at me." Kincaid knew what Small meant, but his mind was a jumble of emotions. Part of him felt guilty for the gruesome death of Debbie and the multitude of lies he had told that brought him to this point. But he also liked to tweak people and make them feel sorry for him.

"Oh, I didn't mean it like that," said Small, recoiling. "You're just not ready to be back yet."

"Yeah, I understand," Kincaid said, waving with his obviously injured left hand, as if blowing off a comment that Small had never intended that way. Once again, Kincaid was the big man, if only in his own mind.

"Well, thanks for coming in," said Small, breaking off the meeting to avoid any more awkwardness. "I'll call the boss in Springfield to tell him when you think you can return, and to see what he thinks we should do while you're gone."

Kincaid smiled. "I appreciate it. I really want to get back here," he offered, knowing that he really didn't.

"Sure thing. Need anything, let us know," said Small half-heartedly as Kincaid pushed himself out of the chair with his good left shoulder and walked deliberately out. McIntire and Miller rose as Kincaid walked out the door, offered their goodbyes to Small, and made their own exit.

CHAPTER 30

As he loaded himself into his battered S-10, James Kincaid felt better than he had in a while. His shoulder throbbed less than before, and the pain in the stump of his missing left finger was numbing. He also reveled in the final decision that the shooting was justified and that Small mentioned no tie to the Mexicans and the bag of money that still sat in the rafters of the garage.

Though his body was crying for rest, his mind was on a high as he rolled back down Interstate 55 to White City and the trailer that now held so many foul memories. Another night in that place, he thought. Can't stand it…gotta get someplace new.

As he drove, his mind flashed to the bag of money that was still nearly full. What the hell am I still in that trailer for? Too many memories I don't need… In his mind, Kincaid replayed the moments of Debbie's death, when her hysterical screams were silenced by a deafening shot.

Though he had agonized over those moments for days, he now found a way to deal with them. Don't think, don't think… What's done is done… Nothing you can do about it now. He gazed out the side window at the tractor-trailers flying by in the northbound lanes, and he saw the sunshine peeking from amid growing rain clouds above. Get out of that frickin' trailer… You sure as hell have the money…Find yourself someplace better.

Still on a high from the meeting with Small, he was feeling better and better. You always wanted a cabin on a lake…someplace to go where nobody knew you…someplace where people would leave you the hell alone…no one riding your butt about being a cop, or how to get out of some damn stupid parking ticket. He thought back a few months, before the money and the shooting and the funeral, about an ad he had seen in the local paper.

There was this place on Lake Ka-Ho with this secluded drive, buried in the trees…couldn't hardly see the house from the road…had five rooms, a bath and a half, and a big-ass workshop in the garage. Kincaid remembered a story from scuttlebutt he heard one night at Martin's. Some guy with money had built that cabin for retirement, then dropped dead of a heart attack while chopping wood… One of the nicest places on the lake, and he was only in it for two months… Dumbass should have known better than swing an ax at his age.

Kincaid wasn't paying attention to how fast he was going, and when he thought to glance at his speedometer, he saw the orange needle ticking up toward sixty-seven. He hadn't driven this fast since before his shoulder was injured and thought he should slow down a bit. Still, he breezed along at fifty-nine, a slow speed compared to his racing mind.

Guy's kids just want to get out from under that place, don't give a shit about it…only asking $51,000 for it… God, for a place like that, that's close to stealing. Kincaid never saw the irony in that thought. Got this bag of money in the garage, still mine, nobody knows… If those assholes McIntire and Miller had something on me, I'd have known it by now…and Small never said anything…

Until Kincaid saw the Mexican intruder on his surveillance system, he had been riding a crest of adrenaline that he had never experienced in his life. That rush had evaporated into angst, fear, and guilt in the weeks since. Now, the rush was making its return. He pushed on the accelerator, and the transmission of the S-10 groaned as he picked up speed, shifting into the fast lane to shoot past a school bus rumbling down the right side.

Kincaid guided the truck back into his original lane and kept daydreaming. *Hell yeah…I got away with it…money's still mine, and I can do what I want until I retire…how long is that, anyway?*

His mind was a computer, ticking off how many days he had left. *Sometime next year…about 400, 410 days or so…then no more of that squad car, no more of Small's shit, no more of Peal riding my ass…pay off Sharon and those frickin' kids of hers…pay off college for my other girls, so they can go off and make big money and forget they ever knew me…and I'll be in my place on the lake, fishing whenever I want, sleeping till God knows when, money to burn… Hope the place is still available…gotta call and check on it.*

The White City exit was approaching, and Kincaid, lost in future plans, nearly missed it. Just as he nearly shot past, he saw the ramp and jerked the S-10 into a rightward veer so hard that the old truck whined and creaked. The force shifted him in his seat, and he grunted in pain.

He navigated the truck through the deserted streets of White City to the trailer, parking in the garage. Once again, he withdrew the A-frame ladder from its place along the wall, managed to climb it far enough to reach the bag, and grasped several bundles of bills.

Now drained from his morning and the emotions of the meeting with Small, he knew a nap was in order. But there was plenty of reason to celebrate later on, and he planned to take in the evening at Martin's to see some old friends and, hopefully, smooth things over with the owner after their awkward exchange at the funeral.

Kincaid planned to sleep the afternoon away before his big evening and headed for the bedroom, being careful not to look at the living room as he went. He sat on the bed, pulled out his cell phone, and dialed the number for McGee Realty, which had listed the cabin at Lake Ka-Ho. Not giving his name, he asked a few questions about the property, learning that a prospective buyer had pulled out just before closing and that it was still on the market.

The listing agent, Paul Bowman, was not in the moment, so Kincaid said he'd call back later and set up a time to look at the cabin. With that, Kincaid's mood improved even more, and he lay back, ready for the most blissful sleep he'd had in a while.

CHAPTER 31

The clock read 6:13 p.m. when Kincaid's eyes finally opened, and after a couple minutes, he emerged from his groggy awakening, rolled out of bed, and put his feet on the floor. An evening at Martin's awaited for the first time in months, and he was eager to escape the trailer and its torture chamber of memories.

Simply getting dressed was hellish, as not only did his aching shoulder cause discomfort, but also the thought of the surveillance monitor in the closet threw his mind back to the Mexicans who had infiltrated the trailer and later died there. Shaken by the memory, Kincaid reached in and turned off the security system. Equally galling was the sight of his red-and-white, button-down checked shirt that was a favorite of Debbie's, a garment that she had worn, with nothing else, before and after some of their most satisfying sexual encounters.

Though Kincaid had worn baggy sweatshirts, well-worn pants, and anything else that made him feel comfortable since coming home from the hospital, tonight would be different. He reached for a brick-colored polo shirt that he considered dress-up material, despite the fact it was now well-faded. Though he longed to wear his snug-fit jeans that showed off his backside, he had put on a few pounds in his recuperation since he was not allowed to smoke and was eating his addiction away. He chose a pair of dark blue work pants that he had bought from a local farm and home store.

As he struggled to button the shirt in front of the mirror, he took a moment to admire himself. Kincaid's opinion of himself was always higher than others saw him, and as he faced himself in the mirror, he liked what he saw. Damn, he thought. All the shit I've been through, and I still look pretty good. A lot of guys would have folded like a tent after what's happened to me, guys a lot younger than I am...

Kincaid swayed slightly back and forth, ignoring the twinges of pain as he continued his adoration, finding ways to ignore the growing paunch that hung above his belt, his thinning hair, and his increasing skin redness. Hell, I've still got it... Women would like what I've got, they always have... After all, Judy was gorgeous, Sharon had the best ass I ever saw, and Debbie had it in all the right places... Maybe I'll find someone else, after all...I'm not that old...I've still got some good years in me.

He had treated himself to a bottle of beer from the icebox a few days ago, and as the time passed, he allowed himself another, then a third. Gotta take the edge off, he thought. A man my age has got to relax, especially after what I've been through. Before leaving for Martin's, he grabbed a bottle out of the fridge and sat at the table, with his back to the living room, to savor it. Then he strode out the door to the garage.

The spring moon illuminated the countryside as Kincaid made the drive into Mount Olive and Martin's Tavern, his beloved hangout of recent times. The parking lot was half-empty, as usual, and he found a spot next to the door to save himself the walk. The S-10 creaked and groaned as he slowed to a park, and his rear brakes ground so loudly that another man turned his head and looked as he passed by.

Martin's looked much the same as the last time Kincaid was there, the night of the shooting. The floor was as dirty as always, and a few brightly colored plastic eggs, left over from Easter a few weeks before, sat in a glass dish on the bar, an attempt to brighten the place. The framed 8x10 of Debbie still sat at one end of the bar, as Martin didn't have the heart to take it down yet. Beside the photo was a glass jar, taped with a note asking for donations for Debbie's family. A few one-dollar bills and some change lined the bottom of the jar.

The jukebox blared Merle Haggard's classic "Mama Tried" as Kincaid stepped to the end of the bar opposite Debbie's shrine and ordered his favorite draft. The bartender, a tattooed twenty-something with flame-red hair named Cyndi, remembered Kincaid and asked how he was doing. His noncommittal reply satisfied her, and she went back to talking to another patron, an elderly man who had seen better days but had his billfold sitting on the bar, ready to tip.

On this night, Kincaid knew few of the other patrons. His usual buddies were nowhere to be found, as the loud, crass Del Adams had succumbed to his vices and suffered a massive heart attack in his shower a week before. He later died in the same hospital in Litchfield where Kincaid had recovered, with tubes sticking from every direction and brother Larry at his bedside. Their other friend, the perpetually annoyed school janitor Ned Ullmann, was working that night, or so Cyndi said.

Kincaid finished off his first draft and ordered another as Russell Martin entered the room from a doorway behind the bar. His eyes met Kincaid's, and a fearsome scowl spread across his face as he brushed past, not uttering a word. Cyndi noticed the exchange and looked quizzically at Kincaid, who simply stared down his draft on the bar, hoping she wouldn't ask why.

As the embarrassment subsided, Kincaid took a few more swigs and ordered a shot of whiskey on the side before a friendly face finally breezed through the door. Mary Bartello was a teller at the Mount Olive State Bank, where Kincaid had his accounts, and she sometimes engaged him in conversation over deposits and withdrawals.

*****

Their acquaintance carried over to Martin's, as Mary was a regular, seeking a place to blow off steam from another day of demanding bosses and rude customers. Judging from Mary's acid disposition, though, those customers may have needed a respite themselves. Three times divorced, she had a gravelly voice, the result of a two-pack-a-day habit that had drained the softness from her face and the meat from her sixty-year-old bones. She also had a penchant both for profanity and nosy questions. People often avoided her, or else endure a grilling on the state of their marriage, their finances, or their physical or mental health.

Mary walked into Martin's, lit up a Camel, and ordered her usual, a screwdriver. She whipped a comb from her oversized purse, dragged it through her bluish-black hair from her latest dye job, and spied Kincaid as she headed for a table in the corner.

"Evening, friend," she cooed sarcastically. "Been a while."

"Yep." Kincaid kind of liked Mary, making him one of the few. "How ya been?"

"Better than you." She pointed to his shoulder. "How're you getting along?"

"I've been better. But I keep going." Kincaid clutched his beer in his right hand and waved his severed left hand at Debbie's photo. "For her, you know."

That was the wrong answer, because it touched off an avalanche of questions from Mary about Kincaid's medical insurance, his next visit to the doctor, what he was living on in his recovery, his relationships with his kids, and the value of Debbie's estate. Kincaid answered each question with unusual patience, enhanced by the fact that he was now on his fourth beer and second shot.

Mary was putting them away herself, as she downed the first screwdriver, followed by a second and third and fourth. Finally, the conversation came back around to her, and she spent a couple of minutes grousing about the "shitheads" she waits on at the bank, including those "with so much money that they can't talk to the little people" and those "sumbitches I married" who didn't work hard enough to keep her happy.

As she ordered her fifth, her voice was starting to slur, and she nearly burned herself when a lit cigarette fell into her lap. She picked it up, dropped it into an empty glass to extinguish it, and pushed herself out of her chair, stumbling toward the bar for another round. Kincaid, whose shot glass was also empty, followed to stretch his legs.

Mary stood at the bar, impatiently waiting for Cyndi to acknowledge her, while Kincaid sidled up beside her. Cyndi was unable to hear Mary's commands of "Hey! Another one here!" as she was drowned out by the jukebox and the Allman Brothers' hit "Ramblin' Man."

Finally, Cyndi noticed Mary, poured her another screwdriver, then turned to fill Kincaid's glass. She then turned back to her elderly patron, who was pulling another tip from his billfold. Mary, emboldened by a few more sips, turned to Kincaid.

"You know, Jim, I'm not supposed to ask people about their banking business. And by God, you know how seriously I take my job." She extended a bony finger and tapped herself on the chest for effect. "So they could put my cute ass in a sling if they knew I was telling you this. But I thought you ought to know, in case there was some problem."

The alcohol was flowing through Kincaid's veins, making him more cavalier than usual. "Yeah? What I'd do, bounce another check?" he snickered.

"Hardly." She gulped hard off her screwdriver and went on. "About six or seven weeks ago, some guys from the state police were in the bank. They served a subpoena on us for your financial records. Wanted a shitload of information, all sorts of stuff. It took one girl days just to find it all, put it all together."

Her words were a sword, cutting away at Kincaid's soul. Immediately, he felt his heart race, pounding away like a torrent, about to leap from his chest. Beads of sweat appeared as if from nowhere on his forehead, and he could find no words in his throat, tightened as if the life was being squeezed from him.

His mind swirled like a hurricane, filled with thoughts of terror. Oh my God, he thought. They're on to me, they've figured it out. McIntire and Miller, putting the pieces together… Oh shit, oh God…they know what I've done…

CHAPTER 32

Kincaid's mind was a cesspool and his body was not far behind, still not fully recovered from his brutal wounds. His legs had no strength, his stance went soft, and he staggered, grasping the bar to hold himself up. "Jim! What the hell?" said Mary, who finally realized her friend needed help. She took a hold of his left arm and helped him, practically supporting his weight, to the nearest chair.

As she struggled to keep him standing, Kincaid's mind continued its flood of emotions. *Shit, they've figured it out… They know all about it, could be serving a warrant on me anytime… Could get home, hear a knock on the door, and it's all over…* Then he thought of what came next. *Hell, I don't have an alibi… got all this money all of a sudden and can't explain it… I'll go to trial, and they'll say my ass is guilty…haul me off to prison, rot in hell there…*

He was oblivious to Mary's efforts to pull out a chair and sit him down. *God, I'll be going to prison. I can't explain all that money. They may have it by now, know where it's at… What will I say, oh hell, I just came across this bag full of money in a ditch somewhere? No one's going to believe that… My ass is up the creek, I'm screwed…*

"Jim! What the hell's the matter with you? Jim? Can't you hear me?" Mary was virtually shouting at him, loud enough that a few other patrons heard and turned to see what was going on. Hearing Mary's cries, Russell Martin stepped from behind the bar, glanced over at Kincaid's struggles, and turned back to what he was doing. Finally, Kincaid was snapped from his stupor.

As always, he managed to play the part. "What? Oh, thanks." He put his hand on his forehead, which now throbbed from the pressure of the moment. "Wow. Don't know what came over me there. Geez..." He fumbled for something to say. "I guess I just did too much today. Caught up with me right there."

"Do you need an...an...amb...ambulance?" Coupled with the tenseness of the situation, Mary's liquor was taking hold, and she stammered the question.

"No, no. I'm fine," said Kincaid, knowing full well he wasn't. "I just got a little weak there, that's all. Really, it's to be expected. I'm still not a hundred percent, and I ran my ass off today. Should have known better."

Sensing no emergency, the patrons turned away and went back to their drinks and sob stories. Mary was also settling down, thanks to a few more swigs. "Do you need a ride home?" she asked, a dangerous proposition based on her alcohol intake.

"No, no, no," replied Kincaid, as if trying to convince himself. "Thanks anyway, and thanks for helping me out. I'm just gonna call it a night and head home. I've had enough for one day."

"All right, if you're sure," Mary said as he rose from his chair, still noticeably weak. She turned back to her glass, with a half-hearted wave goodbye. Kincaid walked toward the door, ignoring an icy stare from Russell Martin as he went.

The shock of Mary's words inflamed his body, and his face reddened as if singed in a fire. As he stepped back into cool evening outside, a chilling breeze hit him as a hard slap, causing his stomach to churn wildly. Unable to hold back, Kincaid hurried around the side of the building and vomited so hard his eyes felt like knives had been driven into them.

He dropped to the ground momentarily, trying to catch his breath. His mind, though, was unstoppable. God, it's all over, it's all over... All that work, all I went through... had it all figured out, how to get that money, spend it, so no one would know, survived being shot, lost Debbie, still came through it... Now it's all gone...

Kincaid pulled himself together enough to rise and make it back to his truck. The step on the running board seemed mountainous now, and he summoned his strength to pull himself into the seat. Fumbling in his pocket for the keys, he started the ignition, threw the Silverado into reverse so hard that gravel flew, and shifted into drive, foot already on the gas as the gear went down. There was a fleeting sense of relief as he broke free of the tavern where the news had hammered him, yet he that the nightmare had just begun and hoped he would wake up to escape it.

CHAPTER 33

The drive back to the trailer, normally a few minutes in length, seemed like an eternity. Oh God, Judy and the kids. What will happen to them…Judy, Sally, Mary Ann… Now their old man's going to jail… The looks on their faces when they find out… What will people say to them…your old man's a scumbag, a shithead, got what was coming to him… How will they live with that…and my mother, wasting away in the nursing home, thinking her son's the big shit… God, this could kill her…

Others came to his mind. Debbie's daughter, Shannon, thinks I'm the best, thanks me for all I do for her, tells me how much Debbie liked me, how I was the best man for her… Sure as hell won't think that now…she'll know I killed her mother, they all will… All for that money…that goddamned money…

His body and mind still battling the sound of Mary's words and the choices he had made, Kincaid was trembling so hard that he could barely steer the truck and nearly drifted off the shoulder before pulling back into his lane. As he fought the vehicle, images of the coming years raced through his tortured brain.

Hell, they won't go easy on me…cop takes evidence, that's official misconduct…guys in DII have a field day with that shit… Cops today are under the gun, everyone's watching what they do… No one's gonna believe me…no lawyer's gonna help me…they'll put me away for years…

And those badasses in prison, I've heard the stories…they don't take kindly to cops… They'd as soon rip my dick off as anything…beat my ass every frickin' day, break every bone I've got…use me as a girl, rape me, anything they want, those perverts…be lucky if I make it out alive…

Finally, he arrived at the trailer and screeched to a stop in front of the garage. The sound, though, was heard by no one, since no neighbors lived close enough to notice or care. Still in a stupor from the shock of Mary's words, Kincaid staggered out of the truck, fumbled with his keys to find the one that unlocked the front door, and pushed inside. He then headed directly for the door to the garage, terrified that the bag of money in the rafters had been discovered.

*****

For days, the climb up the ladder to reach the money was tortuous, causing pain from his multiple wounds. This time, however, his senses were dulled not only by the alcohol but also from his occupied mind. As he ascended the ladder, he was oblivious to the discomfort, his focus finally broken by the feeling of his hand unzipping the duffel bag and reaching inside, rifling through the crackling paper bills that were just where he had left them.

The tension then flowed out of Kincaid's body in that moment, and his body, now limp, pressed against the ladder as he exhaled a deep sigh of relief. As he recovered, he realized the pain that was still rippling his body, and he screamed an obscenity in response.

"Shit!" he yelled as he zipped the bag and shimmied down the ladder, his body now wrapped in the discomfort of the previous days. He reached the bottom rung, stepped onto the gray concrete floor, and his mind started up once again. What the hell should I do? he pondered. Can't leave the money up there…too obvious…shouldn't have put it there to begin with… Can't let those assholes from DII find it…they'll be here anytime now, just looking…

Throughout his life, Kincaid had a penchant for blaming someone else. Now, with his life in tatters and the walls closing in, he was no different. That asshole McIntire…thinks he's so frickin' much…sits in his office all day on a big-ass salary he makes from sticking it to people like me… Just think what he'd do if he finds this money…he'll ship my ass off to jail and smirk while doing it…son of a bitch gets off on screwing people like me…

Just like that dickhead Miller…walks around, thinks he's so damn much…perfect body, perfect home, perfect family, like he always lets us know…needs to wipe that goddamn smug look off his face… They'll both want to be the heroes, tell the world that they busted this cop who took a million dollars…both be living high on a big pension, and here I am…just tried to make ends meet, take care of everyone…I'm not hurting anybody… Why don't they just leave me alone, leave me the hell alone…

His mental tantrum now over and his childish frustration released, Kincaid returned to the pressing matters of the moment. Gotta get rid of the money… Can't let them find it… His neck swiveled around the garage, looking for something to help him. Finally, his eyes locked on a wooden-handled shovel sitting in the corner. Bury it, he thought. That's what I'll do…they'll never find it then, or at least, it will slow them down…

As he made the snap decision, his eyes also transfixed on a large, dark green Rubbermaid storage tub sitting along the wall, overflowing with tools. Right there…that's what I need. He strode to the tub and turned it over to dump out the tools, trying to overlook the pain that still rocked his body as he squatted and shifted beside the tub. He reached for the lid, which was propped up along the wall, and grabbed the shovel, carrying everything outside to a grassy area behind the garage.

Kincaid's eyesight was not what it used to be, and the pitch-dark night was broken only by the sliver of the moon and a bit of the reflection from a streetlight around the other side of the property. But he was loath to use a flashlight, fearful that he would attract attention, even though the trailer was isolated and partially concealed by trees.

Still, there was not a moment to waste. Kincaid quickly dug a hole deep enough to hold the big tub, ignoring the knifing pain that ripped his body with every shovelful of dirt. Once finished, he hurried back inside the garage and up the ladder, pulling the bag off the rafters.

His mind a hurricane of emotions, he hated the bag in that moment. Damn bag...cause of all my troubles... A million dollars sure as hell wasn't worth this, the shit I've gone through because of it... The recurring image of Debbie flashed through his head once again, and he quickly switched his brain to other thoughts.

As he stepped out the door, he peered in both directions before proceeding. In the darkness, he nearly missed a step but caught himself before he fell or dropped the bag. Grunting with another dagger of pain, he made his way to the backyard, slipped the bag into the tub, and placed the lid on it. The lid was not entirely snug, and he pressed on it until he heard the familiar snap that indicated it was locked in place.

Another fear flew through his skull that his new hiding place was not entirely waterproof. Son of a bitch...can't let dampness get into this...all we have is rain these days, can't let any damp get in...last thing I need is to lose all the money. Once again, he went inside the garage, scurried up the ladder, and pulled the tarp that had concealed the bag from the rafters.

Back outside, Kincaid wrapped the duffel bag in the tarp for some extra protection, placed the bag in the tub, set the tub in the hole, and covered it with dirt. Knowing that any excess dirt would call attention, he replaced every clump of the moist soil, tamping it down with the shovel. Then he dropped to his knees, reached for a handful of the dead leaves from last fall that littered the ground, and scattered them over the dirt. This he repeated several times, adding some handfuls of small sticks as well, until the yard debris completely covered the spot of his dig, obscuring it from the naked eye.

As he finished his work, Kincaid sat back on his knees and exhaled, trying to deal with the exhaustion that now consumed him. He pulled himself off the ground, stumbled back inside the garage, and put the shovel back in the corner, checking to make sure he had not left any fresh, muddy footprints on the concrete floor.

Seeing none, Kincaid stepped through the door into the kitchen, where the digital clock read 11:26. His inebriation from the evening of alcohol had evaporated amid the tension but was now setting back in, and his head was pounding. He reached inside the refrigerator, pulled out a Bud Light that he quickly twisted the cap from, and found a half-empty bottle of Jack Daniel's that he poured into a shot glass that had been sitting, still dirty, in the sink. Gotta take the edge off, he reasoned. Gotta clear my mind, think about what to do now.

He downed the whiskey and then started working on the beer. In between sips, a plan began to formulate. Gotta get out of here, get as far away as possible… But he also knew that an escape would never last, for the Illinois State Police have plenty of skilled investigators like McIntire and Miller and could track him down wherever he was.

That prospect offered little appeal, and he pondered the possibility. Hmm…I'd be living my life on the run…always looking over my shoulder… can't go anywhere without thinking I'll be arrested… Hell, my face may end up on a poster in the post office and all over the frickin' Internet. This will be a big news story, reporters will be all around here…they'll probably have a reward on my head, and some sumbitch who's sitting on his ass will see my face and turn me in…yeah, some shithead who thinks he can make a buck…

He then remembered that he, himself, had tried to make a buck, which was the reason he was in this mess. As usual, though, Kincaid found a way to rationalize. Yeah, well, I did a hell of a lot of good too…took damn good care of my wives and kids, busted my ass keeping the streets safe, did a hell of a lot right… So I made a mistake…shouldn't have to piss my life away over it…

As he downed swigs of Bud Light while his world crumbled around him, Kincaid found a solution and made another choice. This one would change his life–in the most literal sense possible.

CHAPTER 34

For weeks, James Kincaid's life had been in shambles, and the future held little better. The pressure had been building, and tonight was reaching the boiling point. Panic had set in, and chaos reigned. Now, Kincaid saw an out.

A new identity. God, that's it…become someone else, and cover my tracks…take on a new name, move somewhere, pick up where I left off… Grow my hair, dye it, grow a beard, something…move to California, Florida, somewhere the hell away from here…

But to assume a new identity, one other key event had to happen. I'll fake my own death. Get lost, make it look like I drowned, fell out of a boat or something…they won't have a body, but they won't have me either… They'll think it was an accident, and I'll make it look like one…

In that instant, the gravity of the decision crashed down upon Kincaid, and his mind was a battlefield of emotions. On one hand, he reveled in the thought of sticking it to McIntire and Miller, of moving on, of getting away with it. But he was also torn about leaving some important people behind. Before his next step, he stared off into space, knowing that he would never see Judy, Sally, or

Mary Ann again. There would also be no letters, cards, phone calls—he would be out of their lives forever.

He also thought of the heartache they would endure, thinking that he was dead, suffering through the funeral, the well-wishers, the memories. He then reflected on his mother, sitting in her wheelchair in the nursing home in her fragile state, thinking how his "death" would affect her and his sister, Mo. God, I've put them through so much already, he anguished. And now this…

Kincaid also thought that his life, for all practical purposes, would be no more. He would be leaving his time as a state cop behind, and though he relished the idea of never being in that squad car again, it had become a part of him, and he loved bragging about his work to anyone who would listen.

That would change, as he knew that he couldn't mention his past for fear that someone would figure him out. His beloved fishing boat, his favorite chair, his Silverado, his golf clubs, the pair of jeans that he thought he looked the hottest in, even the way he looked in the mirror–all gone. He had never lived anywhere but Illinois, and that, too, would change. For all of its annoyances, he could never come back home.

He finished his beer as he drummed his fingers on the table. For many men, the change would be too much to bear. James Kincaid, however, felt less emotional connections than most, except to himself. It's the only way, he decided. The only way out…And hell, I'll be doing all of them a favor. If I'm shipped to prison, they won't be able to hold their heads up…everyone will ridicule them. This way, hell, I'll be a hero. Everyone will feel sorry for them, and they'll remember the best of me. As usual, Kincaid thought of himself and his image. Hell, everyone will think I'm some kind of a god, even if I'm not around to enjoy it.

Kincaid smiled slightly, impressed with his latest choice, which would not only save himself but also cement a legacy. There was so much to think of now; a new name, a new place, a new way of life, not to mention wrapping up the old life he was leaving behind. Just then, a timely memory flashed through his mind.

Just over a year before, he had pulled over an errant pickup driver named James Wilson, who had run a stop sign off a country road off Illinois Route 48, Kincaid's usual beat. Wilson, a fifty-something resident of a little town in southwestern Arkansas, had made his mistake in the worst possible place, cutting Kincaid off and forcing him to slow down.

Never one to take anything off anyone, Kincaid activated his red lights and pulled the man over. A check for warrants turned up nothing, but Kincaid, his ego bruised by the insolence of someone cutting him off, was ready for a confrontation. Kincaid approached the battered Nissan Titan, saw Wilson sitting nervously behind the wheel, and proceeded to angrily lecture him about his driving. After this impromptu tongue-lashing, Kincaid wrote out a traffic citation, and after Wilson signed it, he was released.

Kincaid returned to his squad car and completed his necessary paperwork as he watched Wilson slowly drive away. As he did, he noticed that he had failed to return Wilson's driver's license to him. Kincaid thought about catching up with Wilson and returning his license but decided not to. Instead, he thought he would just mail it to Wilson, but he never got around to it.

Yeah, yeah. That's what I need... Kincaid tried to remember where he had put the license. Where the hell is it?... Kincaid, now tipsy once again, stumbled down the hallway to the bedroom and his dresser. The third drawer was a catchall, full of items that Kincaid or Debbie had tossed in there, ranging from coins to trinkets to tools. Kincaid yanked the drawer open, rifled his hand through, and felt something plastic and slick. He pushed aside some things on top of it to reveal the license.

He grasped it, held it up to his face, and studied it intently. The printing showed that James Wilson was a man of fifty-six with a height of five-foot-ten-inches–one more than Kincaid. His weight, 180, was 20 pounds lighter than Kincaid. While his forehead was balding, his hair in back was longish, enough to wear a ponytail. He also wore a beard, as his graying whiskers formed a goatee around his pursed lips. The date was still valid since Wilson had renewed the license just days before being pulled over by Kincaid.

Hell, I can make his work, thought Kincaid. Wilson's about my height, weight's nearly the same, and I can lose a few pounds. Been needing to anyway. He thought about the facial hair. And I can grow a beard. Always kind of wondered how I'd look with one. Kincaid snickered to himself, breaking the terseness of the night. And that hair...I've got plenty in back, I can grow more...and if I can't, then I'll buy me a bottle of Rogaine. God knows I've got the money...

Kincaid tapped the license with his right index finger and lifted his head, gazing into the mirror on the vanity. Several seconds were spent staring at his reflection, lost in thought, focused on the eyes reflecting in the glass. Kincaid stared into those eyes, looking inward at his own soul.

The face looking back at him represented a man in the last stages of his life. James Kincaid, the man about to lose it all as prison loomed, was about to die. James Wilson, the new man, the man with a million dollars and a fresh start, was about to be born.

CHAPTER 35

As Kincaid left the bedroom and walked back up the hallway to the kitchen, he settled on his plan of action, namely his impending death. He decided that he would fall out of his fishing boat, an apparent drowning. Then, while the search for James Kincaid set in, the new James Wilson would make his escape.

But there was still plenty of work to do. First on the list was to find another car since his S-10 would be a dead giveaway; if the investigators found that to be missing, an all-points bulletin would go out, and the vehicle would be tracked down in a matter of hours. Though he missed the newer Silverado he had sold years before, Kincaid still had an affinity for the older S-10 model, as it had carried him through the good times with Debbie and the bad times after her death. Giving it up, though, was a small price to pay. Anything, after all, was better than prison.

While many people would just go online to find a used car, Kincaid was not computer-savvy and rarely used the Internet. Other than browsing some porn, Kincaid was seldom online, and if some reason to search the Web was needed, he just stopped into the Mount Olive Public Library and signed in to use a computer.

While Debbie had a wireless plan on her phone, he had let it expire after her passing, so that was not an option. But he couldn't wait for the library to open; he needed a car, and fast. As he wondered what to do, he saw a copy of the Alton Telegraph lying on the edge of the table. It was a free sample thrown on April 8, three days before, by the local carrier who was hoping to pick up more subscriptions. With little else to do, Kincaid had looked through it, one of the rare times that he had ever read that paper, and thought that he might get around to subscribing at some point.

Now that paper was a gold mine of information. Kincaid reached for it and practically tore the pages as he sifted through, looking for the classified ads. The pages crackled and bent as he turned them until he found the automotive section. He weighed what he needed and what would serve him the best. Need something cheap. If I get something too flashy, that'll draw attention…just want something that's dependable and will blend in…

He thought of James Wilson and what the picture on the driver's license looked like. He also remembered the traffic stop, the battered pickup the man was driving. What would that sumbitch drive? he pondered as his eyes scanned the classifieds. Don't want to go to a dealer…that could draw attention and make more people wonder… Need a private sale, someone just wanting to get rid of a car…the kind of car that Wilson would drive…

Money was clearly no object, but that was not the issue. Kincaid considered several possibilities before settling on an ad for a 2006 Ford Focus. The car was listed as dark red with two doors and 110,000 miles. The words "runs well," "some new parts," and "dependable ride" were added. The price of $4,500 was given next to a phone number.

Kincaid, who knew most area codes from his years as a trooper, recognized the number as one in Hamburg, a sleepy settlement in Calhoun County, over an hour west, in between the Mississippi and Illinois rivers. He glanced over at the clock, which blared 12:59 a.m. in bright red, square numbers.

He knew it was hours before he could call about the car and that this night and its empty, lonely darkness would drag on and on. The severity of his latest choice began to fall upon him, and he buried his face in his hands, rubbing his temples to ease the crushing tension that surrounded his final hours as James Kincaid.

CHAPTER 36

Another restless night followed, and Kincaid spent some of it flat on his back, eyes wide open, staring up at the ceiling. The rest was spent nervously pacing up and down the hallway, dragging himself with every step, too jittery to relax.

The suspense was like a dagger, and by 8 a.m., Kincaid could stand it no more. He pulled out his cell phone and dialed the number to ask if the Focus was available.

A male voice, likely in his sixties, answered. "H-e-e-e-l-l-l-l-o," the voice said, stretching out the greeting.

Kincaid had never earned many compliments for good manners, and he wouldn't today either. "Yeah, I saw an ad in the Telegraph that you had a car for sale."

"Mm-hmm," replied the voice on the other end.

"You still got it available?"

"Sure do. Had a buyer fall through a couple of days ago." The voice saw fit to elaborate. "Some young guy, thought he could get the money together and didn't. I kept his earnest money, though."

That phrase tipped Kincaid that he was dealing with a no-nonsense seller. "Yeah, well, I'm interested. Could ya tell me a little more about that car?"

"Car's got original miles, I think. At least, I never turned the odometer back myself."

"Uh-huh." Kincaid was taking notes on a yellow legal pad. "Anything else?"

"The car actually belonged to my youngest daughter. She bought it used about seven years ago. But she ran off with her boyfriend and told me she didn't need it anymore." He chuckled. "Gonna go to someplace in Florida and thought her boyfriend was more important than the car."

"Hmm." Kincaid clearly did not care. "Car run OK?"

"Sure. It'll get you where you need to go. Runs all right on the highway, gets decent gas mileage. Accelerates pretty well, better than most Fords do. Shifts pretty hard into third gear, but the tranny should have enough life in it for a while."

"Yeah, guess so. It's dark red?"

"Mm-hmm. Got a few little dings in it." Another chuckle followed. "Daughter never was much of a driver. Her mother, God rest her soul, taught her how, you know."

The mention of a dead woman once again brought Debbie back to Kincaid's mind, and he brushed it off as soon as possible. "You still asking $4,500?"

"Yep. You interested?"

"Yeah. I wanna come over and look at it. Are you gonna be home this morning, say around eleven?"

"Should be. Gotta be at the doctor in Jerseyville at three thirty. Shoulder problem, you know. Aches like anything when it gets cold like this. Scheduled for surgery the day after tomorrow, so you just caught me," he chuckled. "But I should be home around at eleven. What's your name?"

"James Wilson." Kincaid blurted out his new name for the first time. "Yours?"

"Bobby Owens. I'm on River Street, which cuts off the main drag as you come in. Little white house, second on the right."

"All right, I'll be there at eleven, then. See ya."

Bobby broke the connection without a response. Kincaid hit "end" on his phone and finished scribbling on his legal pad before a thought of terror raced through his mind. *God, what if that guy had caller ID? He's got my cell number and my real name! Dammit! Why didn't I think of that?*

Kincaid calmed slightly when he realized that Bobby had not questioned his identification as James Wilson. *Maybe he doesn't have caller ID… Hell, maybe he didn't hear me, or doesn't care… Shit, gotta be more careful next time…*

He ended the thought as he stumbled up the hallway to the kitchen, heading for the door to the garage. Barring some unforeseen problem with the car, Kincaid had already made up his mind to buy it, and he needed cash to pay for it.

Most of his money was now buried out back, and he strode out to the spot, shovel again in hand. As he walked, his head turned back and forth, looking for anyone who may be watching. Since his backyard was secluded, few would have much of a view, except for the neighbor down the road who disapproved of Debbie and all the drinking. Fortunately, Kincaid noticed that neither the white Nissan Titan that the neighbor drove, nor the silver Volkswagen Passat that had belonged to his late wife, were in the driveway, meaning that no one was likely at home.

Once at the burial site, Kincaid squatted down, bearing the shoots of pain that still plagued him, and brushed away the dead leaves that covered the dig. He also set aside some of the sticks used for concealment. Methodically, he dug up the green Rubbermaid tub that held his fortune. The tub, already discolored from wear and neglect, looked even worse, as dirt stained every side of it. The sight of the soiled tub injected a new fear in Kincaid that his money was not wearing well underground. He lifted the lid, deliberately unwrapped the tarp, and, to his relief, found the duffel bag as he had left it, completely intact and dry.

The zipper was balky from the damp surroundings, but Kincaid massaged it open and reached inside for a handful of bills. Swiftly, he counted out eighty $100 bills, for a total of $8,000. Though he could hear the whirl of traffic on Interstate 55 a little ways off, no sounds of cars were heard to be driving down Kincaid's street, much to his relief. As he had the night before, he wrapped up the duffel bag in the tarp, set it into the tub and replaced the lid, and buried it once more, again covering the dirt with the leaves and sticks.

Kincaid then hurried back inside to prepare for the trip to Hamburg. His clothes were now dirty and rumpled from digging up his money, and from his years as a cop, he knew that anything out of the ordinary was sure to draw suspicion. Thus, changing into a fresh clothes was a must.

He opened his closet door and looked for something unassuming, selecting a light gray pullover sweatshirt with a pair of faded black shorts. The roomy comfort of the sweatshirt agreed with his injuries, as did the white sneakers with the Velcro straps in place of shoelaces. He slapped some cold water on his face in the bathroom, choosing not to shave so he would appear to have more facial hair, as James Wilson did. He stopped off in the kitchen, quickly downing a bottle of Bud Light that served as his breakfast. Kincaid then grabbed another bottle in case he needed some refreshment on the drive.

Normally, Kincaid would have taken his truck, but this trip posed different problems. He worried that Bobby Owens would see the vehicle Kincaid was driving and could identify it later on, after Kincaid had left to become James Wilson. So another mode of transportation was needed, and fast.

Since the night of the shooting, Debbie's Toyota had sat untouched in the driveway, another grim reminder of that horrific night. Kincaid had planned to get rid of the car when he had recuperated enough, just to make sure he never saw it again. Now, it served a purpose. Debbie had left an extra set of keys on a nail next to the refrigerator. Kincaid reached for the keys, drew a deep breath, and hoped that the car, now splattered from repeated snowfalls and mud from the past winter, would start after all this time.

Though the morning dawned partly cloudy, Kincaid pulled on a pair of dark glasses, and headed outside for the Celica. On this day, UV protection was certainly not needed, but he still felt better with the sunglasses on, providing at least a little cover.

He opened the door to the Celica and dropped inside, grunting as he went, since the car sat lower than his truck and required him to turn his aching body uncomfortably. The smell of Debbie's perfume still lingered inside, tinged by the persistent odor of cigarette smoke from her near-full ashtray. Racked by another bad memory, Kincaid steeled himself and turned the ignition. After several attempts, the engine turned over, and after the transmission had loosened following months of inactivity, he turned onto the street and headed for Hamburg.

CHAPTER 37

Much of the drive was down Illinois Route 16, a road familiar to Kincaid from his many years on patrol for District 18. As he rolled through towns like Gillespie, Shipman, and Jerseyville, his mind remained a whirlpool, knowing his old life was about to end and his new identity would take over. He chuckled to himself. Damn, these old roads…couldn't wait to get off them for how many years… Now, they don't look so bad… Guess that's what life on the run will do to you…

Terror still shot through his mind, the overriding fear of being caught, convicted, sent to prison. Gotta get out of here…get this Focus or something, get on the road…gotta do it now…no time to waste… The minutes were ticking away, and he knew that McIntire and Miller could be on him at any moment. And there was plenty else to think about.

On the night of the accident, the moment that the choice was made to take the money, Kincaid's life had flashed before his eyes. Now it did again. He thought of his childhood, playing Little League on the corner lot, his mother's brownies that he loved so much, playing football in high school, his prom, his graduation from the academy, all those nights in that loathsome squad car.

Images of Judy in her wedding dress, Sally and Mary Ann showing him the pictures they had colored and their favorite dolls, and Sharon in her sheer panties, lying on the bed with her legs apart, flew through his mind, followed by the neverending memories of Debbie's brains exploding onto the trailer wall. The fragrance of Debbie's perfume still was present in the Celica, and Kincaid cracked the driver's side window, trying to get rid of it. He stared out onto the sprawling farmland, rife with green shoots of freshly planted crops, trying to erase his mind.

The angst of his past, however, was now trumped by thoughts of his future. Despite the stress of the moment, he felt a rush of adrenaline and a surprising sense of freedom enveloped him. Just days before, his existence was drudgery, dreading the next morning, and the morning after. The crushing pressure of the last few hours had also overpowered him, knowing that his freedom, his life, was at stake. Now, an escape lay before him, and it was a beautiful, welcome thought.

Where will I go? he daydreamed. Florida, California, someplace warm…as far away from here as possible…sit on a beach all day, fish my ass off, grow my hair, live like a beach bum… Could do the same thing in Texas…always wanted to see South Padre…and if I need to get away, I'd be close to the border…could get into Mexico before anyone'd know it…

The lifestyle appealed to him, even in this, his darkest hour. Oh yeah…fish all day, sleep all night…all the beer I can drink…get one of those Tex-Mex girls, with a short skirt and a nice body. I got plenty of money and I still look good, I could turn any girl's head… Yeah, James Wilson, single man, I can do whatever I want…

Practical matters then broke in as he noticed his odometer hit seventy miles an hour. He eased off the pedal as he kept making plans. Gotta find a place to live…get an apartment, without a lawn to mow and leaves to rake…live quiet, not cause trouble, no one will know…nobody's gonna know me… If anyone asks where I'm from, just say "up north" or somewhere…tell them I got tired of working in dead-end jobs, had a bad divorce, needed someplace better, a fresh start… Hell, that's really not a lie…like anyone's gonna care anyway… I'm not going there to make new friends, and who the hell needs friends anyway…

Then his choice for a new home hit him in a flash. Texas…yeah, that's it. I'll find somewhere in Texas where no one knows me…I can get a place in some small town off the interstate, basic apartment, live quiet, keep to myself… No one's gonna notice…stay there for a while, then move on…keep moving on…

I can sleep all day, kick back, relax for a while… Everyone's been after my ass for so long, I don't know what it feels like to relax… Come and go as I need to…my time, my life, nothing like the shit I've put up with here for all these years…and if I need to, I'd be close to Mexico, like I thought…I could run across the border and they'd never find me…

As he turned it over in his mind, the choice became clear. The Lone Star State it was. But first, he needed a way to get there, namely the Focus in Hamburg. Time was running short, and he knew the alternative. If I can just get there, he thought. McIntire and Miller, they know what I've done…probably planning what they're gonna do to me right now… Hope I can make this work, get out of here in time…not much time left…not much time…have to get to Texas…just have to…

As he motored through the flatlands of Macoupin and Jersey counties on the way, the miles ticked off the odometer in agonizingly slow fashion. He crossed the Joe Page Bridge over the Illinois River in the village of Hardin and turned north. Calhoun County, sandwiched between two rivers, offered lush farmland that was prime for growing peaches, the area's cash crop.

Today was April 12, and many farmers were out in the field, driving their enormous John Deere tractors to work the land. A hundred and fifty years before, the rolling terrain reminded incoming European immigrants of their homeland, which led to the naming of the villages after those in the old country, including Hamburg, for the German city.

James Kincaid had never cared for history, and he wasn't about to take an interest today. All he wanted was for the drive to end and Hamburg to be in his sights. Finally, the clock on the dash blinked 10:55 as he saw the green population sign for Hamburg approaching. At that moment, Kincaid slowed to a stop on the highway, not seeing any other cars passing or following him. He glanced in the rearview mirror and used his fingers to readjust his hair to make it look more like the style of James Wilson on the confiscated driver's license. Kincaid also elected to keep wearing his sunglasses to disguise himself even further.

As he resumed his drive, he saw the population sign for Hamburg, telling motorists that XXX residents called the place home. The resident he cared about most, however, was the one selling the Ford Focus. Being such a small place, Hamburg had only a few streets, and it was easy to find River Street, just off the main drag as Bobby Owens had said.

Owens' place had clearly seen better days, a one-story abode with metal siding that was sagging in some areas, and with a roof that was missing more than a few shingles. A broken-down wire fence surrounded the property, which was littered with old tires and plastic milk jugs. Three vehicles sat in the driveway, including the Focus, which was the best of the lot. While there were more than the "few dings" that Owens had described, the tires looked fairly new, and the paint had more sheen than might have been expected.

Kincaid maneuvered Debbie's Celica into the end of the drive, slowing with the customary creak and groan. The noise did not go unnoticed to Owens, who was walking out the front door even before Kincaid had climbed out of the cab, sunglasses still on.

Just strolling across the yard was a chore for Owens, who walked as if his hip were stuck in place. The voice on the phone corresponded with his age, as he was on the back side of sixty, with a stubble beard, prodigious paunch, and a shaggy mound of dark gray hair underneath the NRA cap sitting on his unusually large head. The day was seasonally warm, with temperatures in the mid-seventies, and Owens was taking advantage, dressed only in a tank-style white undershirt and well-worn jeans. Following behind him was a small boy in a green Ninja Turtles T-shirt, around four years old, holding a bottle of orange soda and repeatedly shouting, "Grampa! Grampa!", trying to get the old man's attention, to no avail.

"You James Wilson?" offered Owens, with little sense of welcome.

"Yep." Inside, Kincaid heaved a sigh of relief, as apparently Owens did not have caller ID after all. He shifted around from one foot to the other, gazing at the Focus. "Just lookin' it over." Kincaid made his voice take on a slight Southern accent, in keeping with the home state of his new alter ego, Arkansas.

Quizzically, Owens noticed the bandage on Kincaid's hand and how he still held his shoulder stiffly. "What happened to you?" he inquired, pointing at the injuries.

"Oh, car accident," replied Kincaid, thinking as fast as ever. "That's why I'm here. The last car I had is in the junkyard, and gotta get me somethin' else." Ever brash, Kincaid waved his finger at Debbie's beloved Celica. "That car ain't worth a shit anyway."

Owens chuckled and raised an eyebrow, flashing a little sympathy. "I kinda know what you got, son. I ripped out my shoulder the other day when I was moving furniture for my daughter." He rubbed the shoulder with his opposite hand and then rotated the shoulder with his arm extended. "Hurts like hell. That's why I got the doctor's appointment today. Going in for surgery the day after tomorrow."

"Huh," sniffed Kincaid, who could not relate because no one ever had a worse injury, worked harder, or suffered more than James Kincaid, at least in his own mind. Owens returned to the matter at hand, pointing at the car with a sly smile on his face.

"Well, you'll find a good one here. That Focus is well worth the money, son."

"Looks like it." Kincaid walked around the car, kicking the tires in the way that buyers do when they really know nothing else about cars. He opened and closed the doors a couple of times, continuing his fake inspection as the child made his way over, finding himself underfoot.

"Who're you, boy?" Kincaid asked glaringly.

"That's Schuyler," said Owens. "He's my grandson. I look after him now." His lips clenched in a show of bitterness as a breeze blew across the bangs on his forehead. "Yeah, my grandbaby. Remember how I said my daughter thought her boyfriend was more important than the car? Guess she thought the same thing about Schuyler."

"Hmm." Kincaid couldn't have cared less. "Well, you mind if I drive this?"

"Nope." Owens reached in his right front jeans pocket for the keys and handed them over. "Take as long as you need. Besides, I know you ain't going anywhere." He pointed at the Celica. "You've got your car parked right there, and that one's just as good as the Focus."

Owens was no doubt a savvy character, knowing if Kincaid made off with the Focus, the Celica was his. Kincaid, in turn, knew that if Owens had kept earnest money from the last guy, he'd also lay claim to the Celica.

"Don't worry," chuckled Kincaid. "I'll be back in a bit." He climbed into the Focus, allowing for his limited mobility with the persistent injuries, and turned the ignition. After a couple of rumbles, the engine turned over, and Kincaid shifted into reverse. As he backed out, he noticed as Owens brushed past the Celica, peering through the window for a peek at the interior as Schuyler lagged behind, still trying to get his attention.

Kincaid knew little of the backroads of Calhoun County, so he decided to stay on the center-lined two lanes. He also knew that he needed to determine highway performance, since that was how he would drive the Focus on most of his escape. As he drove along, he paid close attention to acceleration and maneuverability.

Once or twice, he slowed to a stop in the middle of the road, then pressed hard on the gas to see how quickly the Focus could accelerate in case he was being pursued. He also pondered how well the color of the car would blend into the dark of night, and if there were any distinguishing marks about the car that would be easily noticed. Though the car had some imperfections on the body, the paint job was still intact, and there was not a lot of rust below the doors. The car also ran fairly quiet, another sign that few passersby would notice it.

Owens had been truthful in how well the car accelerated, as well as the hard shift into third gear. What he hadn't said is that the shocks needed work, since the car bounced and rippled at every bump in the road. He had also neglected to mention that the heater had to be turned to full max to spit out much hot air, or that power steering seemed to be wearing out. Still, Kincaid decided the car fit his needs, especially since it was so unassuming and would attract the least attention.

After a half hour or so, Kincaid was rolling down the street in front of Owens' battered residence. Prior to pulling in, he stopped a block away and counted out half of the money in his pocket, forty $100 bills, since he feared attracting Owens' attention by showing him all the money he was carrying.

Once more, Owens heard the sound of the car grinding up the drive and stepped outside before Kincaid had shifted into park. Schuyler was in tow, holding a small toy fire truck that he ran up and down the side of the house and the fence post. "Well, whaddya think?" Owens asked.

Kincaid always viewed himself as an expert negotiator, and even in this moment, he thought he could pull one over on the old man. "Well, I'm interested, yeah," he said, trying to sound nonchalant. "But I gotta tell you, I don't think I can pay $4,500 for it. I noticed some problems with this baby that are gonna need fixin' here pretty soon."

"Yeah? Like what?"

"Oh hell, there are several," Kincaid said, big-wheeling it as ever in his newfound Southern drawl. "Gotta put some shocks on it, gotta work on the heater, tires are wearin'. I'd need to spend several hundred on this thing pretty quick. I mean, if I was takin' it to my mechanic and told him I paid $4,500 for it, he'd have my ass."

Owens had no way of knowing that Kincaid was going to be halfway across the country in this car as soon as possible and had no intention of taking it to his mechanic. He was also annoyed at how Kincaid was freely cutting down his car.

"Well, I don't agree with any of that," he snapped. "That car's been a good one for me and my daughter, and we never had any problems with it. None that I couldn't fix anyway." He then started back toward the door, waving his hand at Kincaid. "If you don't want the thing, hell, I'll find someone else."

In that instant, Kincaid knew he had overstepped, since he needed a car fast and didn't have time to go elsewhere. The thought of McIntire and Miller at his door also terrified him, and he had to move fast. "Hey, I didn't mean I didn't want the car," he said, stepping toward Owens. "I just meant that I'm not gonna pay $4,500 for it."

Owens hesitated at the front step and then turned back around, squinting at Kincaid. "Well, how much did you want to pay for it?" he asked sarcastically.

Kincaid assumed his usual role of the big man, chest puffed out as usual. "Well, I couldn't go over $4,000 for it. I'd like to have the car, and help ya out. But that's as high as I could go."

"Help me out? Yeah," snorted Owens at Kincaid's condescension. But Owens actually did need the help, since the bill collectors were always calling, and now there was another mouth to feed with Schuyler. He also worried if his insurance would pay for the work on his shoulder, since the agent was arguing that the impending surgery was elective and therefore unnecessary. He doffed his NRA cap and scratched his head, putting on his own act as Schuyler wandered toward the side of the yard. "Well, I guess I could let it go at that price. I'd be giving you a hell of a deal on it, though."

"Yeah, yeah." Kincaid waved his hand as if dismissing Owens and then uttered the magic words. "I can pay you cash for it, right now, if you're agreein' to this."

The sound of quick cash made Owens perk up, and his voice took on a slight charge. This time, there would be no earnest money, no waiting around for a final decision. "Cash now, you said? Well, if that's how you want it, then yeah, I'll take it."

"Fine." Kincaid was a better actor than Owens and didn't let his relief show. Step one in his plan of escape, getting the Focus, was nearly complete. "Can I get some kind of receipt for this?"

"Sure, come inside." Owens yelled for Schuyler to "get in here" and held the door for Kincaid, who left his sunglasses on, despite the outdated fluorescent lights on the ceiling of every room in the house. He had to step over an assortment of Schuyler's toys, as well as a scruffy, agitated black Scottish Terrier named Butch, on the way to kitchen table, cluttered with newspapers and mail. Owens pointed for Kincaid to sit across from him and tried to engage in a little small talk.

"So, you from around here?"

The blood flowed quickly through Kincaid's veins in alarm because he knew he couldn't let on. To Owens he was James Wilson and had to act accordingly.

"Nope," he said, shaking his head and pursuing his lips in disagreement. The fake Southern drawl was again coming in handy. "Originally from Arkansas. Just stayin' here for a bit until I get to where I'm going." Kincaid was ticked off at the question but kept his anger to himself. Shut your mouth, old man…you're just wasting time here…

"Huh. What do you do for a living?"

Kincaid had no idea what Wilson did for a living, so another lie was needed. He waved his hand nonchalantly for effect. "Oh hell, I've done a little of everythin.'"

"Oh, yeah? Like what?"

Owens wouldn't leave it alone, so Kincaid kept spinning tales. "Oh, a whole lotta things. Worked construction for a while, worked on farms, that kind of thing. Lately, I've been runnin' a gas station for a buddy of mine. He's about to open a new one back home, so I'm probably headin' there." As he spoke, Kincaid's mind raged in silence. *Who the hell does he think he is, playing "twenty questions" like this? He's never going to see me again…if he doesn't shut his damn mouth here quickly, I'm gonna shut it for him…*

The response finally satisfied Owens, who reached to the edge of the table for a spiral notebook, tore out a page, and scribbled the words, "Received, $4,000 from James Wilson for Ford Focus. Paid in full." He then signed the sheet, adding the date. "Will that work?"

Kincaid nodded and pulled out his wad of cash from his sweatshirt pocket. He counted out forty $100 bills as Owens watched, slightly wide-eyed at the sight of that much money. "Got a favor to ask of ya," said Kincaid, still looking through darkened lenses.

Owens, suddenly richer, was happy to act. He slapped his hand on the table, as if at attention. "Sure. Whaddya need?"

Kincaid ran his fingers from both hands through his hair, brushing it back in James Wilson's style. "I wanna pick up the car tomorrow, and I gotta get a ride back here, 'cause I don't know if that damn Celica's even gonna make it all the way back here or not. Thought it might give out on me just getting here today."

One lie followed another, and Kincaid pressed on. "There's a place I saw as I was comin' in called the Duck Shoot, that bar that sits out a little ways, right on the river, with the really big parkin' lot. Could you leave the car there for me?"

Owens's brow furrowed, struck by the oddity of the request. He repeated Kincaid's words to make sure he was on the same page. "You want me to leave the car in the lot at the Duck Shoot?"

"Yeah. That way, I won't have to come all the way into town, and it'll just be sitting there for me."

"Okaaaaaaay…" Owens was still surprised but didn't press it further. "You want me to lock the keys in it?"

"Yessir, I do. You got an extra set to it, right?"

"Mm-hmm." Owens pushed himself away from the table, reached in the top drawer of the countertop, and fumbled around before displaying a black rubber keychain with two keys on it. "Here," he said, handing them to Kincaid. "Looks like you want this thing in a hurry."

Hell, yes, I want it in a hurry, thought Kincaid. I wouldn't be asking if I didn't... If this old fool would just shut up, I could be out of here quicker... he's not the one whose life's on the line, I am... He played it cool, however. "Yeah, I just want to get this thing done. I gotta get somethin' better to drive."

Owens then remembered something else. "Let me get the title for you." He walked out to the living room, kicking aside a toy tractor-trailer of Schuyler's on the way, to a grimy chest of drawers next to the television. He pulled open the middle drawer and withdrew a red discount-store folder, sifting through it until he found the title to the Focus. Owens then returned to the kitchen, studying the title as he went. Owens sat down at the table, signed the title, and handed it to Kincaid.

"Very good." Kincaid liked to sound important. "What about the plates?"

"What about them?"

"They're about to expire. Sticker on the rear plate says it expires the end of next month." As a trooper, Kincaid was used to checking license plates, and loved to tweak drivers on their registrations.

"Oh." Owens hadn't thought of that. "Well, just keep them until you get new ones. Doesn't matter to me."

"Okay." Kincaid rose from the table, not offering to shake Owens' hand. "Just leave the car for me down at the Duck Shoot."

"Sure," replied Owens. "I can get my nephew to tail me down there and give me a ride back." He extended his hand to Kincaid. "Nice doin' business with ya, Mr. Wilson."

Kincaid nodded and gave him the obligatory shake. Though Schuyler waved and said "bye," Kincaid ignored the well-wishes as he headed for the door and Debbie's Celica for the trip home.

CHAPTER 38

As James Kincaid maneuvered the hour-plus drive back to White City, his mind was again a whirl of what to do next. A new life lay ahead, and everything that went with it.

On the trip over, he had worked up some ideas of life as James Wilson. Now, he refined and finalized those ideas. Okay, what am I gonna tell people when I get to wherever I end up in Texas. I'm James Wilson, from wherever the hell the town is on the driver's license…tell them I was born in Little Rock, or Pine Bluff, or somewhere like that…tell them I'm just in town for a while, passing through… They won't ask many questions…at least, they better not…who the hell would care about little ol' me anyway? I won't be bothering anyone…I won't even be around people that much, don't give a shit about making friends…I'll be keeping to myself anyway, and I sure as hell won't be there long…

He thought of the pitfalls he would face as a new man and, as usual, had all the answers. I better not do anything that requires any background checks… I don't know if this James Wilson asshole is alive or dead…if he's alive, I don't want him to find out, and start asking questions...better watch out for anything that I'd need a credit check for... Shit, that takes out living in a nice apartment...bastard landlords always want to run a credit check on you to see if you're worthy... Oh hell, I'll just pay a year in advance...cash up front, they won't ask questions...everyone's out for a buck these days...it's all people care about...

As he stared ahead through the windshield, Kincaid kept thinking and dreaming. When I get there, I'll get rid of that shitty Focus and get me something nice sometime...yeah, a brand new truck, that new Dodge Ram I've always been wanting...I can pay cash for it from a dealer out there, won't need a loan application...won't even need a savings account...I can just hide the money at my place, or buy a safe, or something...won't ever have to step foot in a bank...all those sumbitch bankers do is ask questions, like they're so damn much...screw them, they ain't getting a piece of my million...

Kincaid mentally reeled off other aspects of life, opening accounts for water and power, getting a new cell phone, buying furniture, food, groceries. Since he was flush with cash, he saw little concern for any of that, and he had suitable ID if he needed it. A lot of that stuff doesn't go on any financial checks. Wilson will never know, assuming he's still alive...and if he isn't, he won't know or care anyway, poor bastard...

Though he was naturally cavalier about his choices, the gravity of the moment also ripped through his body, churning his stomach and throbbing in his head. God, this is it, he thought. If I can just get out of here in time... The terror of being apprehended consumed him in a instant, knowing that was inevitable if he stayed around long enough. God, they could be waiting for me now...they could be sitting in the driveway, just waiting until I pull up... If that happens, no way could I get away from them...this old car can't drive fast enough...I'd be a sitting duck...

Pride was never in short supply with James Kincaid, and the ramifications of an arrest flew through his brain. Shit, it'd be in all the papers and on television...pictures of me in cuffs, being led to the squad car and courthouse and back...they'd find me guilty in a heartbeat...they've got me dead to rights...if they've subpoenaed my bank, they already suspect something...nothing I can do…they'll check every place I do business with, find I paid cash, wonder where the hell I got that much money all of a sudden…

I can see the headlines, "State Cop Steals Drug Money Off Dead Man." Frickin' liberals who hate cops anyway, they'll have a field day…CNN would run that story 24/7…everyone in the country will know my name, the shithead cop who stole the money…everyone laughing at me…Judy and Sally and Mary Ann and my mother and sister, what would they think…I couldn't even look them in the face…all I've done to them anyway, their lives have been hell because of me…this would be that much worse… Then it's off to prison to be some guy's bitch…God, I'll never make it out alive…won't last a day in there…

Though a draft was blowing inside the cracked windows of the Celica, beads of sweat began breaking out on Kincaid's forehead, and droplets of moisture inside his sweatshirt made him even more uncomfortable. He fought the urge to floor it, to push on the pedal hard enough to make the miles go faster, to arrive back at the trailer and end the suspense of whether the authorities were waiting there for him. But he knew that being pulled over would create additional risk, so he kept the odometer over the speed limit, but just enough not to run the chance of a ticket.

He glanced at the clock on the dash, knowing the minutes were ticking off. His blood pressure, normally high, surged even more, and his head pounded from the strain. His shoulder, which had felt somewhat better the last couple of days, throbbed, and his bandaged hand hurt so badly that he almost wished he could cut it off entirely to alleviate the pain. Inside, his stomach was a torrent, writhing so that he was forced to pull over to vomit on the side of the road.

Finally, he saw the outskirts of White City, and the anxiety heightened with each passing second until he turned down the side road to the trailer. His torture then evaporated, at least momentarily, when he saw no cars in the driveway and nothing sitting on the street. Oh God, oh God, he thought as he exhaled deeper than he ever had. They aren't here…still got some time left… still have a chance…

Kincaid wanted to leave the Celica in the exact same spot as before, so no one would realize he had driven it. Fortunately for him, there was a slight bare spot where it had been parked, since the vehicle had blocked the snows from the past winter from falling to the ground and prevented the sunlight from bleaching the ground below. Deliberately, he maneuvered the car into the same place as before, though he worried that the spring mud might reveal fresh tire tracks.

As he exited the car, he again looked up and down the neighborhood, only to find, once again, that the couple down the street was still not at home. Kincaid then hurried inside the trailer, headed straight for the refrigerator, and pulled out a bottle of Michelob Ultra, which he quickly downed as he dropped into a ladder-back chair at the table. Having taken the edge off, he reached for another to relax a little more before finishing off with a shot of Jack Daniel's, poured into a red Solo cup.

Though he was fortified with alcohol, sleep did not come easy for Kincaid that night, as he tossed and turned until the early morning hours, fearing a knock on the door from McIntire or Miller. Finally, a few hours sleep came to him before the alarm clock went off at 7:30 a.m.

Now, it was time to finalize his escape plan. After showering, he dressed in mundane clothing, already hoping to not attract attention. He never bothered to shave, since James Wilson had a beard, and James Kincaid now needed to grow one, too. But there was plenty of time to kill, since he would not shove off from Rip Rap until that evening, and he worried that McIntire and Miller had plenty of time to come knocking with an arrest warrant at any minute.

So Kincaid planned to go shopping. He pulled on his jacket, passed into the garage into his S-10, and headed for St. Charles, Mo., a suburb of St. Louis over an hour away, where a Bass Pro Shop was located. Kincaid loved browsing in outdoor megastores like Bass Pro Shop; they were one of the few retails stores he ever cared to spend time in.

But this trip was not just for relaxation. Kincaid knew that, after he "disappeared," authorities would investigate his credit card purchases. With that in mind, he intended to buy some new fishing equipment, a seemingly logical purchase for someone planning a fishing trip. *It will make them think I just wanted to go fishing*, he reasoned. *That will throw them off my trail. After all, how could it look like I was faking my own death, if I was buying stuff to fish with? After I'm gone, it will just look like an accident, a terrible accident...*

Kincaid pulled out of his driveway around 9 a.m. and drove southward on Interstate 55, stopping off first at a Bob Evans restaurant in Troy, Ill., a half-hour away from White City. He loved the chicken and steaks at Bob Evans, and since today was going to be a tough one, he wanted to treat himself. Just as he was planning at the Bass Pro Shop, he figured that it would look normal if there was a credit-card charge from one of his favorite restaurants. Last meal as James Kincaid, he laughed to himself as he ordered a big platter. *If I'm gonna die later today, this son of a bitch might as well go out in style... Wonder if James Wilson likes eating at places like this? Oh, well, he will when I become James Wilson myself...*

After a leisurely brunch, Kincaid then continued down I-55 to Interstate 70, which carried him westward through St. Louis and toward St. Charles. Though a monumental choice lay ahead that evening, he relished the idea of spending a few hours in the Bass Pro Shop. *Never had any time for myself in here,* he mused. *Judy never cared about it, and those frickin' kids of Sharon's wouldn't let me have any peace whenever I tried to stop here... Debbie never had the time, and I was always working my ass off, so I didn't, either... Well, now, I'm gonna take the time. Got all afternoon to piss away in here.*

Rather than go on an expensive spree, Kincaid wanted this shopping trip to look as normal as possible. So he resisted the urge to buy a lot of equipment, choosing only to buy a few items, keeping his purchase total under $75. *Hell, this is nice stuff,* he thought. *I can use this wherever I end up. After all I've been through, I'm gonna need plenty of time to relax, and I'll fish whenever I damn well feel like it.*

As mid-afternoon approached, Kincaid thought he needed to head back to White City, and he retraced his route on the interstates, arriving home around 3:30 p.m. Before pulling into his driveway, he drove up and down the road by the trailer, checking to see if any surveillance or police cars were in place. Seeing none, he drove into the driveway and parked the S-10 behind the trailer.

*****

Now satisfied and thinking his mind was clearer, the next step in his escape awaited. He had planned to "fall" into a river while fishing, and the stage had to be set. Kincaid hustled back out the door to his truck, which he slipped into reverse and backed around the garage to the rear of the property. There, his beloved twenty-foot bass boat was parked on its two-wheel trailer, as it had sat since the fishing season had ended last fall.

The boat was one of the few things that Kincaid, who was perpetually unsatisfied with life, ever formed an attachment to. Some of his best times with Debbie were spent in that boat, for she was a woman who could bait a hook, much to his admiration. He smiled slightly at another memory of their time in the boat when Debbie, who never shied from spontaneity, slid toward him on one chilly morning on the lake, unzipped his trousers to expose his manhood, and gave him something to remember. But the happiness of the memory was fleeting, as the guilt over her death returned, as did the terror that his time was nearly up.

Backing up was a strain for Kincaid, since he had to turn his body and throw his bad shoulder over the seat to look behind. Amid grunts of "ugh" and "oh," he finagled the truck close enough to the hitch to hook on. He left the truck and the boat behind the garage in another effort not to attract attention. Though no one was around, he kept his sunglasses on, partly for concealment, to control at least that much of his now-crumbling life that was perilously spiraling out of control.

Now that the boat was hooked, he walked around to the garage door to fetch his fishing equipment. Since he was an avid fisherman, Kincaid had plenty to choose from, between several rods and reels and a couple of tackle boxes, not to mention nets, rubber boots, and the like. He determined to take it all, which took two full armloads to carry it around to the back and into the boat.

The sunshine that provided the unseasonable warmth of the day pounded on his sweatshirt, again building an uncomfortable moisture on his body. But he kept the sweatshirt on, thinking that the dull color blended in better with his dilapidated surroundings, again building his false sense of incognito. With the fishing equipment loaded in the bass boat, Kincaid then entered the garage once more to get his trusty shovel.

He stood over the dirt patch once again, for what would be the final time. Glancing around to ensure that no one was watching, Kincaid hurriedly spaded up the soil, still damp from the spring rains, until the top of the tub holding the duffel bag appeared. Kincaid leaned over, yanked the tub from below with his now-usual painful discomfort, and set it on level ground.

Opening the lid, he unwrapped the tarp to find the bag, which he placed in the passenger seat of the truck. He then locked the truck, strode back to the hole, and dropped the tarp inside the soil-stained tub. Kincaid knew that the tub, with its fresh dirt smudges, would raise eyebrows, so he carried it to the bed of the truck and tossed it in, thinking he would discard it somewhere later on. Next, he seized the shovel and filled in the hole, again to cover his tracks as much as possible. He completed the task by covering the fresh dirt with leaves and sticks for additional concealment, as before. Finally, Kincaid tossed the muddy shovel into the tub in the back of the Silverado.

Kincaid knew he could take only a handful of possessions because anyone entering the trailer after his "death" would wonder why all of his personal papers and clothing had been taken on a simple fishing trip. Besides, he had plenty of money to buy new threads on his journey of escape, and he wouldn't need any of his papers since he was about to be reborn as James Wilson.

So he chose to leave with only the clothes on his back, with a couple fresh pairs of socks and underwear that he carried in a brown paper bag. For good measure, he tossed an extra pair of shoes in as well.

He then went to the refrigerator, grabbed the bottle of Jack Daniel's and four cans of Bud, leaving plenty of alcohol behind despite his urge to take it all. He dropped the booze into a rumpled paper bag of its own.

As he finished with the liquor, he rummaged in his pocket to find his trusty pistol, which he had carried practically every waking moment since learning that the Mexicans had been poking around the trailer, weeks before. In a jerking motion that sent pain ripping through his shoulder, he clutched the gun as if it were his last possession. Anyone tries anything, this son of a bitch is gonna be ready, he thought. Someone gets his hands on my money, I'll blow lead up their ass. And if push comes to shove, I'm not going down without a fight. Emboldened, he rammed the gun back into his pants pocket, appreciating the cold steel as it lay against his thigh.

His moment of machismo now fleeting, there was one other thing he wanted to remember. He walked down the hallway to the bedroom, opened the top drawer, and withdrew two wallet-sized photos–one of Judy, the other of

Sally and Mary Ann. Kincaid gazed down at the pictures in his hand, knowing that this would be as close as he would ever be to his old family again. The severity of the moment, and of his choices, swept over him like a hurricane, and he grew weak in the knees, unsure if he could stand anymore. But he knew what his newest choice had to be. He opened his billfold, placed the photos into the plastic sheeting inside, and walked up the hallway for the final time. As he clutched the paper bags with the clothing and the liquor, he glanced over at the living room wall, that damnable spot that was forever burned in his memory.

He turned away, closed the front door and locked it, and walked around to his truck and the boat trailer. As he rolled around the yard and down the driveway, James Wilson felt no regrets about leaving the trailer and James Kincaid's horror of memories behind.

CHAPTER 39

The last few hours as James Kincaid passed uneventfully for the man behind the wheel of the S-10, the bass boat in tow, as the truck traversed Illinois Route 16 back to the Joe Page Bridge for the turn north to Hamburg. It was Thursday, April 14, which would be the last day of his life–or so the world would think.

Kincaid's mind, however, was anything but quiet. The current of the Illinois River below the bridge was nothing compared to the flow of adrenaline in his veins, knowing that he was this close to pulling off his plan, and time was running out.

The fear of capture pulsated through him, as he knew from his years on the force that arrests can happen in the blink of an eye. The Illinois State Police prides itself on getting criminals off the streets as quickly as possible, and investigations are geared toward that end. The subpoena at the bank in Mount Olive was just the beginning, and Kincaid knew it. Armed with that information, McIntire and Miller could go back to the grand jury, and warrants were soon to be issued.

As he had on the drive to Hamburg the previous day, Kincaid also knew that any infraction could cause additional problems. He checked his speed regularly, made sure he hit his turn signal whenever needed, and always slowed to a stop whenever the octagonal red sign was in view.

He was also careful not to attract attention when he disposed of the dirty tub in the bed of the truck. Halfway between Shipman and Jerseyville, on the drive the day before, Kincaid had noticed an illegal dumping site, where someone had tossed a variety of garbage in a muddy ditch just off a side road, a few hundred feet from the highway. With the sun sliding behind some dark clouds on this early evening, Kincaid seized the opportunity to toss the tub unnoticed.

He turned off the highway onto the side road, glanced around to make sure no one was watching, and stepped out of the cab of the truck, leaving the ignition running with the gear in park. In one swift motion, he reached for the tub with the tarp and shovel still rammed inside, turned his body, and tossed it into the ditch with the rest of the refuse, where it blended in nicely with the mud-splattered objects strewn around.

Then it was back on the road to Hamburg, arriving as the time on the dash flashed 7:03. As he rolled by, he looked over at the parking lot of the Duck Shoot, perched at the side of the road with its view of the Mississippi River, and saw the Ford Focus parked on the far end of the lot, one of several cars sitting around that early evening. Bobby Owens had held up his end of the bargain, as he had deposited the Focus in the lot as promised.

Hours before, Bobby had enlisted his nephew to follow him down to the Duck Shoot, to give him a ride back after leaving the Focus. The nephew also ended up taking Schuyler home for, as Bobby told the little boy, "Grandpa's going under the knife in a couple of days and needs some time to rest to think about it," drawing tears and a tantrum from the toddler.

At this moment, there were only a handful of other cars scattered about the Duck Shoot, a sign of a slow night. The bar owner may have fretted over the lack of business, but it was exactly what Kincaid wanted to see, knowing there would be less chance of being spotted.

That is, of course, whenever Kincaid decided to claim the car. For now, though, it would have to wait. His choice was all going according to plan, and the next step awaited. He never stopped at the Duck Shoot, choosing instead to roll on through the main drag of town, passing on another five miles to the north, to a place called Rip Rap Landing.

Rip Rap Landing was part of the Calhoun County Conservation Area and a favorite spot for fishing in the area. Sandwiched between Illinois Route 96 and the Mississippi River, Rip Rap ran north to south, and attracted its share of sportsmen in the summer and fall. This, however, was the offseason, and few people were around, particularly after sundown.

Kincaid had been to Rip Rap several times over the years and was aware of the layout and the access roads. There were only two boat launches dotting the river bank. He chose the second one on the south, which had a narrow rock lane secluded by trees.

The clock on the dash flashed 7:14, and the sun was getting ready to set behind the clouds. Rip Rap was now shrouded in darkness, which was what Kincaid wanted to see. He flipped his headlights off as he navigated the narrow lane, driving a half-mile off the highway. Once, he felt his right wheels slide off the rock and into the muck off to the side, but he quickly turned the wheel to pull back into the lane, jolting his still-sore shoulder.

The end of the lane was marked by a small parking area where fishermen could leave their vehicles and boat trailers. Kincaid turned the truck around, trailer dragging behind, to back into the launch and set the boat in the water. He nervously looked back toward Route 96 to see a couple of vehicles whiz by in the darkness, discernible only by their lights. Once they were past, he caught his breath and completed the task of backing the trailer into the water.

Before he backed down the launch entirely, he shifted the transmission into park and reached to the passenger seat, where the duffel bag with the money and the two paper bags, one with his clothing and the other with the booze, rested. Kincaid snatched all three and climbed out of the truck to head back to the trailer. With the utmost care, he gingerly set each of the bags in the bottom of the boat before returning to the cab to cover the last few yards of the launch.

As the boat touched the water, he tied it up and repeated the process, getting out of the truck to finish setting the craft into the Mississippi before returning to pull up the launch and park. Ever sly, Kincaid pulled his pickup, trailer creaking behind, toward the side of the small parking area, deliberately stopping at a point where it would be difficult for a tow truck to hook on the rig to drag it away. They're not getting this thing easy, he snickered in his mind. Sons of bitches want to come pull this out after I'm gone, I ain't gonna make it easy on them…

As he switched off the ignition, Kincaid pulled the key out and dropped it in his shirt pocket, again to make it that much harder for recovery teams to clear the truck away later on. He also knew that leaving the key in the ignition might raise questions after his "disappearance."

Smug as always, he scurried down the launch on foot to his boat, fearful that the vessel might somehow float away unattended, along with the money. As he dropped one foot into the boat, he breathed a slight sigh of relief, knowing that the money was in his sight once again.

As he shoved off, Kincaid glanced back at the S-10, barely visible in the darkness up in the parking area. Glad to be rid of that son of a bitch, he mused to himself. Guy like me needs something better than that… Damn near threw my shoulder out every time I had to turn it, the steering was so bad, and like to froze my ass off with that shitty heater… But then the image of Debbie, sitting in the passenger seat, legs crossed underneath her hot pants, pushed its way into his mind, and he turned away.

Just getting to the boat was a big step, one closer to his escape and his new existence as James Wilson. But Wilson would have to wait a little while longer to be reborn, because James Kincaid chose to relax rather than quickly killing his old persona. Kincaid hit the starter on the boat motor and headed downriver.

CHAPTER 40

One of the few things that James Kincaid enjoyed in life was fishing and in need of something to calm his nerves, now was the perfect opportunity. Because of his injuries and the horrific events with Debbie, he had not fished in months and had actually missed it. When he was fishing, Kincaid was normally alone, with no present or ex-wives, kids from various families, or superiors to harass him, and he tried to throw a line in the water whenever he could.

His fishing gear lay in the boat, and there was just enough moonlight for him to see to bait a hook. The night air had cooled considerably from the warmth of the day, and, with a light mist falling, he pulled his collar up around him to protect against the elements. Though his shoulder throbbed in the dampness and his left hand was a hindrance, Kincaid managed to drop a line in the Mississippi to see if he had any takers.

Every so often, his bobber twitched, and he jerked on the line, sometimes to find nothing. A few times, he pulled in a bluegill or a small carp, one of which swallowed the hook, forcing him to repair the line. Kincaid threw each of the fish back, knowing that he could not take them along in his flight as Wilson.

Kincaid spent the next couple hours in the boat, surrounded by the stillness of the night, catching an occasional fish and tossing it back, anxiously turning his head every time he thought he heard a noise on the bank. Once, he heard a loud rustle and he whipped around in the boat, only to see a deer bounding through the dense treeline.

He continually checked his Timex watch, holding it close to his face to read it in the dim moonlight. Finally, he read it once more, to see the large hand on the eleven and the small hand nearly on the twelve.

That was time enough for the final step. The current had carried Kincaid downriver toward Hamburg, and from the water, he could see the neon sign of the Duck Shoot in the distance, flashing in orange for motorists going by. In the receding moonlight, Kincaid could see that he was about a quarter of a mile from the tavern. He motored his boat to the bank, close enough that he could step out on the shore without getting his feet wet.

Though the bank was only seconds away, it seemed like hours to Kincaid's pain-racked body. Before getting out, he reached for a coil of rope lying under a seat. Still fearful of being spotted, he waited for a tractor-trailer to rumble by on Route 96, just over the treeline, before stepping out. Now on shore, he then tied the boat to an imposing oak tree that leaned perilously over the water, about to topple in when the next flood eroded the riverbank.

Fortunately for Kincaid, he had tied up near an unimproved, partially rocked driveway that led toward the highway. Reaching back into the boat, he clutched the duffel bag and the paper bags and headed up the bank. The drive let out a little to the north of the Duck Shoot parking lot, and he deliberately strode toward the end, wary of anyone that may be coming or going inside. But the parking lot had cleared out, as he had hoped, and there were only two vehicles sitting around, none near the Ford Focus that was waiting for him.

He was about to step on the pavement when the side door to the Duck Shoot swung open, revealing a thirty-something couple who obviously had too much inside. The man, bearded and dressed in a black Harley-Davidson jacket, was holding up a dyed-black woman, who chose not to wear a coat in the cold weather in order to show off her low-cut white tank top and skin-tight jeans. As both staggered to one of the vehicles outside, he helped with her balance by keeping his right hand firmly squeezing her backside as both giggled like schoolchildren.

Startled, Kincaid quickly crouched behind a brown garbage dumpster in the rear, watching as the inebriated couple climbed into a battered Ford F-150 that would soon be weaving all over Route 96. Being a hard drinker himself, Kincaid saw little concern for DUIs, even though as a state trooper he was supposed to feel otherwise, and on this night, all he wanted was for the couple to get out of there. After some effort, the F-150 backed out of its parking spot, turned to the highway, and sped off, sure to threaten the lives of some innocent passersby.

As the truck was nearly out of sight and with no other vehicles in view, Kincaid stood up from behind the dumpster, looked around once again, and strode briskly toward the Focus. Reaching for the key from the pocket of his dark pants, he unlocked the door and placed the duffel bag of money in the back seat along with his other possessions. Quickly, he settled into the car, again looking back toward the door to the Duck Shoot to make sure no one else was coming out.

This damn thing better start, thought Kincaid. That'd be all I'd need, for this son of a bitch to give out, or for that dumbass Bobby Owens to have done something to it. But the engine turned over, and he knew he was nearing his goal. Inside, he could hear the strains of the jukebox starting up, volume turned to the max, belting out "All My Rowdy Friends" by Hank Williams Jr., which he knew would drown out any sound the car made. He moved through the parking lot to the unimproved driveway that led to his boat, leaving his lights off to not draw attention.

As before, navigating the path with no headlights was treacherous, but Kincaid safely made it to the end where his boat lay in the water. He climbed out of the car, walked down to the river bank, and got into the boat, never sitting down as he leaned back to start the motor. Next, Kincaid stepped back out of the boat, untied it from the tree, and turned the boat around so he could reach the motor. He then put the motor into gear and pushed the boat out into the current, watching it fade away into the darkness.

Turning to the tree, he then untied the other end of the rope and tossed it in a pile on the back seat floor of the Focus, not worrying about the wet mud that had caked on it. As the boat motored aimlessly away, Kincaid climbed back into the car, knowing he would have to back it up the driveway to get back to the pavement.

The task was tougher than motoring down the driveway forward, but in a few seconds, Kincaid was back on solid ground. The scattered pebbles left no obvious tire marks, and Kincaid knew he was now home free.

Carefully watching to make sure he wasn't pulling out in front of someone, Kincaid maneuvered the Focus onto Route 96 and headed south. As he drove away, a sense of relief blew over him like a hurricane, the release of tension from the last days evaporating from his body. It would be hours before anyone found the boat. His choice was now made, and he was leaving his old life, burdened by responsibility and tortured by memories, behind.

He mourned little for James Kincaid, who had just died in a boating accident in the muddy Mississippi. Instead, he welcomed James Wilson, and as the neon sign of the Duck Shoot faded in his rearview mirror, he felt in every sense like a new man.

CHAPTER 41

The clouds that had wrapped the moon the night before gave way to bright sunshine at dawn the next morning, and that was just how Ronnie Ford liked it. Having retired last fall from his job in a St. Louis auto plant, he now had time on his hands as well.

Sixty-six years old with a shock of gray hair that overshadowed his hook nose, Ford had been sitting in his johnboat fishing in the Mississippi since arriving from his home in Meppen, at the south end of Calhoun County, an hour ago. The fish were biting fairly well on this glorious spring morning, and Ford had little time to enjoy the surroundings, illuminated by the blinding sunlight that bounced off the river and enhanced the ripples in the water.

Finally, the fish slacked off, and Ford leaned back to stretch his arms and shoulders. As he did, he looked toward the Winfield Dam, an imposing concrete water control structure just to the south that came with a set of locks, to compensate for the drops in river levels. Against the light gray concrete, he spied an unmanned fishing boat, riding the ripples and blowing in the breeze, unimpeded against the current.

A longtime fisherman who had spent more hours on the river than most men, Ford knew something was amiss. He reached for the motor and puttered downriver toward the boat, expecting that someone may be lying in the bottom, unconscious or stricken.

Ford slowly approached the boat and called out to see if anyone answered. Hearing nothing, he motored even closer, until he could see that the boat was empty. Only some fishing gear, a couple flotation devices, and a few empty beer cans were found in the boat.

Glancing at the registration number on the boat, Ford reached inside his shirt pocket for his cell phone and dialed the number of Carl Davis, the local game warden. Davis was well known to the sportsmen of the area, a veteran of twenty-two years on the job, and his fairness and decisive nature had earned the respect of all. Fishermen all laughed about the squint that Davis always seemed to have in his eye whenever someone asked a question, or how his head seemed to tilt to the right at was being said. But he never failed to deliver the correct response, and fishermen and hunters appreciated that he understood their needs and desires, like he was one of them.

Within a half hour, Ford heard the whirring of a motorboat, driven by Davis as he came to investigate the scene. As Davis approached, Ford could see that he had his game face on, and his furrowed brow nearly reached the khaki-colored cap that partially hid his sandy-red hair.

While Davis squinted and tilted, Ford explained what he had found before Davis himself surveyed the boat, also focusing on the registration number. Davis whipped out his cell phone and called headquarters to search the registration database and find the owner of the boat.

As he waited, he sat in his boat, drumming his fingers and gazing from one side of the river to the next, while the girl on the other end searched the computer. Moments later, he heard the response. The boat belonged to a James Kincaid of White City, Illinois.

"Say it again?" said Davis, shock apparent. As a law enforcement officer himself, he recognized the name James Kincaid as a state trooper. He had met Kincaid a couple of times before, when Kincaid came over to fish at Rip Rap and elsewhere, and remembered that he was stationed at District 18. The girl repeated the name, verifying it.

"All right, thanks," replied Davis offhandedly as he hung up. He turned back to Ford. "Boat belongs to a guy named James Kincaid, and I know him. He's a state trooper from this little town over in Macoupin County." Ford nodded as Davis pressed on. "You seen anything else around here today that looks unusual?"

"Nope, not a thing. Nobody's been out here yet. You're the first person I've seen all morning. But as far as anything in the water or on the shore, no, nothing."

"Hmm," said Davis as he looked around, lost in thought. "Well, I'm gonna call this in to the state police. He's with District 18, and they're gonna want to know about it."

With that, Davis scrolled down in his phone until he found the number of District 18 headquarters. His call was shuffled to Captain Kent Small, whose eyes widened when he heard that James Kincaid's boat had been found, unattended, floating in the Mississippi River.

CHAPTER 42

As the shock wore off Small's body, Mike Miller was sitting in his office down the hall, intently analyzing the reports generated in the Kincaid case. R.J. McIntire had been called to a meeting in Springfield that morning, and Miller expected him later that afternoon. Miller took a brief break from his work to call his wife and was heading to the coffee maker for another cup when Small cornered him in the hallway.

"Hey," said Small, pointing Miller toward his office. "Got something for you."

Startled, Miller followed Small into the office, where the news was dropped on him like an anvil. Miller stammered for a moment, his speech jumbled between the shock of the moment and the questions racing through his head. Small, though, had few answers, only the bits of information relayed to him by the game warden, Carl Davis.

Small, as expected, said that he had to talk it over with his supervisor in Springfield. Miller, meanwhile, had his own call to place to the capital city. He stumbled back to his office and dialed McIntire's cell phone, hoping to catch him on a break.

As it was, McIntire's meeting had ended early, and he was available. "Morning, Mike," he said cheerily, reading Miller's name and number off his caller ID.

"Got some news for you, and you aren't gonna believe it," responded Miller, who proceeded to tell McIntire the story.

Like Miller, McIntire fumbled for the words to say before the investigator in him took over. "All right," he said firmly. "Anyone been sent to check out Kincaid's trailer?"

"I presume so. Small was here, and he was supposed to talk to his supervisor."

"Figures," said McIntire, remembering Small's penchant for putting off decisions. "Well, see if someone gets over there now. Something about this seems a little too coincidental."

Those were the exact words that Miller was thinking, but he played along. "You think this might be a ruse?"

"With this case, nothing would surprise me," replied McIntire bluntly. "I've got a couple of things I've gotta do here, and I'll get there later this morning. Keep me posted until then."

After conferring with his Springfield boss, Small sent a trooper out to Kincaid's trailer. The man assigned to the task was John Smith, the same young officer who was the first on the scene on the night of the shooting. Smith was working the day shift today, and was less than thrilled when he received the dispatch from John Edwards, the ubiquitous "voice of District 18," telling him to go to the trailer.

Despite their intensive training, state troopers are also human beings and have emotions like everyone else. The night of the shooting was a bitter memory for Smith, as most troopers have experiences that haunt them and would rather forget. The thought of going back to the trailer made his stomach churn, but he had a job to do. He received the call when he was two miles north of the Mount Olive exit on Interstate 55, in the northbound lanes, so he turned around in the restricted median area to get southbound and was at the trailer in around four minutes.

The sunlight from the clear April sky bounced off the metal trailer as Smith climbed out of his squad car, walked to the front door, and pounded, then pounded some more. He received no response. Noting how quiet the residence seemed, he walked around outside, noticing that no lights were on, and nothing like appliances or heaters seemed to be running inside. He also saw that Kincaid's truck and boat were nowhere to be found.

Smith dutifully returned to his car and radioed headquarters with this information. Small received the dispatch from Edwards and had just informed Miller when the phone rang in his office. Small walked back and picked up the receiver to hear the voice of Eddie Jensen, a Calhoun County deputy.

Jensen had been on his usual patrol along Route 96 north of Hamburg when he received a call from Carl Davis, the game warden, advising him of Kincaid's empty boat. The news tipped Jensen to look for abandoned vehicles or anything else that seemed unusual in the area. As a result, he drove to Rip Rap Landing to see if anything was out of the ordinary.

Eventually, he made his way to the parking area where Kincaid had left his truck, hitched to the boat trailer. Scanning the plates, he radioed back to his own dispatch in Hardin for a license check. The response was that the truck and trailer were registered in James Kincaid's name.

Small called down the hall for Miller to "get in here" and then repeated the information. His head still spinning from the news of the boat, Miller walked back down the hall and dialed McIntire once more.

"I've got more for you," said Miller. "We got another report from a deputy in Calhoun County. He says he found a truck and boat trailer registered to Kincaid, parked at Rip Rap Landing." Miller was somewhat familiar with Rip Rap but was unsure if McIntire was. "You know anything about that place?"

"Yeah, I've driven by there," replied McIntire, who went silent for a couple of seconds, then broke the pause. "Convenient, isn't it?" he cracked sarcastically.

Miller was thinking the same thing. Their suspicions, though, only added to the task in front of them, as an open investigation was in process, and the sudden apparent death of James Kincaid added another angle. Miller hung up the phone and anxiously awaited the arrival of McIntire later that afternoon, when they would continue their analysis.

CHAPTER 43

As Miller sat at his desk, waiting for McIntire and pondering the latest twist in the Kincaid case, the man at the center of the investigation was hundreds of miles away. After pushing his boat into the river, Kincaid drove nonstop in his banged-up Ford Focus, aiming to get as far away from the site of his death as possible.

As the moonlight hung over western Illinois and the dew built on the rooftops and grasslands, Kincaid maneuvered the Focus from one two-lane highway to another until he reached the Great River Road, a popular four-lane tourist throughway along the Mississippi River, which took him into Alton.

He was about six miles from Alton when, in his rearview, he saw the sight he dreaded most. An Illinois State Police car was traveling at a high rate of speed to catch up with him, and though the trooper wasn't flashing his red lights, he sat for several seconds following Kincaid.

In an instant, terror swept over Kincaid like a cloak, and he suddenly became uncomfortably warm in the coolness of the night. Oh shit, Oh God, thought Kincaid. They're on to me. They know I faked it, and they're tracking me down...

He squirmed in his seat as the seconds passed and the trooper still remained behind him. Oh, shit, he's asking for wants and warrants, thought Kincaid, referring to standard police procedure before a traffic stop. That's what the delay is...he's gonna pull me over, and I better know what the frick I'm talking about. Kincaid summoned several deep breaths to settle his flying nerves and his soaring heart rate. Just pretend to be James Wilson, like you did with that old shithead Bobby Owens... you got the driver's license, you got the look...just play along if you have to.

Kincaid glanced at his speedometer and saw it read 54 miles per hour. Instinctively, he dropped his speed a couple of miles an hour, to 51. That was enough for the trooper behind him to lose patience, and he swerved into the left lane to pass Kincaid, never turning his head as he went. Now free of alarm, Kincaid gasped for air as his stomach churned and the blood drained from his pounding head. By the time he had collected himself, the lights of Alton were upon him. Once downtown, he turned right onto the Clark Bridge to cross the river on his way to St. Louis.

The midnight darkness helped conceal his flight, and he carefully kept the speedometer under 55, fearful of being pulled over and still unnerved from the false alarm on the way into Alton. Though he longed to floor the pedal, he knew better, and besides, he realized the aging Focus could stand little hard driving. As he motored through the north suburbs of St. Louis on his way to Interstate 270, he spied a flashing sign at a bank branch, alternating between the temperature, 37 degrees, and the time, 12:43 a.m.

Kincaid pulled his jacket up around his neck, reached for another Marlboro from the pack in his shirt pocket, and fumbled for his lighter as he kept driving, knowing that I-270 would take him to Interstate 44, his escape route out of Missouri. The traffic in the dead of night was sparse, and save for an occasional police car that made him edgy, there was little in his way. Within minutes, the exit ramp to I-270 approached, and he shifted to the right to join the bare flow of traffic.

I-270 is a bypass around the west side of St. Louis, normally clogged with commuters during the daylight hours. Tonight, however, there were few drivers on the highway, and none who cared who the scruffy, stubble-bearded man in the Focus was as he rolled by. As he rolled around St. Louis, he looked to his left and, in the distance he saw a sign, illuminated by floodlights in the blackness, that signified the wholesale florist where Shannon, Debbie's devoted daughter, worked as a receptionist. Kincaid winced as he turned away, though he noticed that the guilt was not quite as strong, as imposing, as before.

When he saw the sign for I-44, Kincaid breathed another sigh of relief, knowing that another hurdle had been crossed in his flight. Oklahoma would come next, and that was six hours down I-44. Just a few miles into this leg, however, was the sign for Six Flags, the sprawling amusement theme park where Kincaid and Judy had often taken the girls when they were little.

The traffic flow was practically nonexistent as Kincaid traveled down the lonely highway, remembering one time in particular at Six Flags that had always been a favorite memory. On that pristine summer day, the girls were both as cute as ever, five-year-old Sally in a pink top and matching shorts and three-year-old Mary Ann, still unsure while walking, in a little lavender flowered dress. Judy was as lovely as ever, wearing a black tank top and white shorts that accentuated her long legs and soft curves.

The girls never quit smiling that entire day, and Kincaid noticed as man after man turned his head to take a second glance at Judy, the prettiest girl in the park. One guy even muttered "lucky son of a bitch" to Kincaid as he trudged by with his pudgy, preening wife, hair thrown up on her head, trying to corral three rowdy boys who refused to listen to direction.

The memory seemed like the millionth one that had polluted Kincaid's mind since he had signed off on the divorce so many years before. But just like the image of Shannon a few minutes before, this latest flashback seemed further away, dulled by time and space, dimmer in his mind.

*****

The negative thoughts were also tempered by a heaving release of stress that flowed from his body as the miles from Rip Rap now added up. Damn, he thought. It's really happening…I'm really pulling this off. A sly smile turned his lips slightly upward as he stared straight ahead, watching the broken white lane lines fly by as one. Can't believe it was this easy…hell, no one even noticed…all I got is open road in front of me…

His body was now wrapped in relaxation, the tension gone from his shoulders, the pressure relieved from his worn temples. For weeks, the slightest movement had racked his torso with pain from his gunshot wounds. Now, alone on the road in the dark of the Missouri night, his discomfort was minimal, his shoulder feeling better than it had in weeks.

For hours, his mind was a vacuum, directed only on the road in front of him and the escape that seemed to get easier with each passing mile. Now, his mind flashed back to the bloodshed of the trailer that night when Debbie was blown away, images that he never seemed to shake. He then thought of Judy and the girls, wondering how they would react to the news of his "death," or if they would even care. But the past was just that, the past. James Kincaid was gone, but James Wilson had plenty of living to do.

Or so it seemed. As he cleared the overpass at Exit 230 on I-44, the sight of flashing lights atop a police car racing down the on-ramp filled his rearview mirror, and struck his heart with horror. "Dammit! He's coming for me!" screamed Kincaid out loud, and he began to push down on the accelerator, only to catch himself. His chest pounded like a hammer, his heart rose in his throat, and he pounded the steering wheel with both hands in frustration, thinking he had reached the end.

As he agonized in the Focus, however, the police car swung to the outer lane and sped by, not noticing or caring that Kincaid was having a meltdown just a few feet away. The flashing reds dimmed in the distance as the car sped away, leaving Kincaid to once again settle his mind and his now-aching head.

Kincaid kept driving until he reached Rolla, when his tired body could take no more of the Focus and his nerves could tolerate no more episodes like the last one. His bladder, weakened by his high blood pressure, also needed to be emptied, and fast. He sought the worst-looking convenience store he could find, a gray-block building that flashed a neon sign reading "Stop In Mart."

The restrooms were on the outside, and Kincaid could see that the men's room door was standing ajar. His shoulder now free of pain, he reached into the rear seat, grabbed one of the lukewarm beers from the sack in back, and headed for the dingy, damp john to relieve himself. Inside, he gulped down the beer in private, thinking it best not to have an open container in the Focus for any passing cop to see.

His rest break done, he felt some hunger pangs, so he took a chance. Kincaid strode inside the store, nodded at the dumpy, greasy-haired, middle-aged guy working the counter who clearly didn't give a damn, and spied a cooler containing Saran-wrapped sandwiches whose freshness was long gone. Kincaid grabbed a couple and took a six-pack off a floor display for good measure. He paid the man up front, got his change, and was back in the Focus in moments.

The remainder of the trip through Missouri was uneventful, though he was wary of picking up the Will Rogers Turnpike, a toll road that opens at the Oklahoma border. With the sun now working its way up in the sky, Kincaid also knew that the daylight offered a better chance for him to be spotted. As a result, he wiggled his way around several of the two-lane highways in northeast Oklahoma until he reached U.S. 69, for the trip south.

By now, crushing fear was giving way to supreme confidence. Kincaid was far away from the trailer in White City, his "death" at Rip Rap, and the horrors of the last few weeks. His manhood, lost amid debilitating wounds, pounding guilt, and a myriad of lies, was now ebbing back to him, and he never felt better, stronger, more full of life.

CHAPTER 44

For most of the long winter, R.J. McIntire had dreamed of warmer weather. A golf nut, he loved to be on the lanes whenever the opportunity allowed, which these days was rare due to his hectic work schedule and demanding family life. Today was one of those perfect days for golf. As he steered his vehicle through the current and maneuvered through passing tractor-trailers and commuters in their minivans and sedans, though, he was too distracted to notice.

He was in the midst of the seemingly daily trip down Interstate 55 just before the noon hour, heading to yet another meeting with Mike Miller on the Kincaid case, which remained open and active. While McIntire yearned for the golf course, Miller needed his work day as a distraction. His wife, Julie, was down because she had gained five more pounds on her chubby frame and decided to skip breakfast amid a tear or two. His son, Tyler, was sick in bed, the latest victim of a strep throat outbreak that was sweeping the high school. His daughter, Adrianna, sat in a living room chair, lips pursed, pouting for no other reason than she was a teenager and that is what they do.

The sudden demise of Kincaid had induced a rescue effort, led by Lieutenant Jim Mason of District 18, who organized a search and rescue team to scour the Mississippi River and the surrounding banks from Rip Rap Landing to the Winfield Dam, to look for Kincaid. McIntire and Miller became part of the rescue effort, leading to longer drives and work days that stretched even further into the evening.

State police are prepared for practically any scenario, and even in a prairie state like Illinois, water searches are on the list. An Illinois State Police dive team was dispatched to the Rip Rap area, and they combed beneath the water for several days, searching for any signs of Kincaid's body. Meanwhile, man and K-9 teams walked up and down the banks, looking for any personal effects or indications that Kincaid had pulled himself out of the water and was on land, either dead or alive.

For several days, the silence of the searches was interrupted by the whirring of an ISP helicopter above, flying along the Mississippi in pursuit of any clues to Kincaid or his whereabouts. The helicopter was then replaced by a drone, which quietly flew above the river, armed with video cameras that were monitored by ISP personnel on the ground.

Fisherman Ronnie Ford, game warden Carl Davis, and several residents of the surrounding shorelines were interviewed by the ISP, to no avail. There had been one man in the area who could have helped them, though the ISP did not know it, and neither did he. Bobby Owens, the old man who had sold his Ford Focus to a guy named James Wilson, was barely paying attention to the search and had none of the particulars.

As Kincaid/Wilson was heading south in his old Focus, Owens was lying in a hospital room in Alton, struggling to recover from complications arising from his shoulder surgery. His blood pressure plummeted during the operation, and his heart, weakened by years of neglect, fell into cardiac arrest. As a result, what should have been an overnight stay in the hospital stretched into three weeks.

The television news media covered the story while Owens was in a coma after surgery, and after he had awakened a couple days later, the reporters had moved on, no longer showing Kincaid's photo or covering the story at all.

Owens never bothered with newspapers, since he was only semiliterate and could barely read them.

All he knew was that some state cop had drowned in the river, unaware that same cop had bought his Focus under an assumed name. So while Owens languished in the hospital, the ISP search and rescue team labored in muddy water and overgrown shores, trying to find one of their own.

*****

The search teams were unable to locate a body, and after several days, the efforts were called off. To Jim Peal, Kent Small, and many others, the outcome seemed clear.

"He fell out of the boat," said Small, hanging up the phone after another conversation with his superior in Springfield. "I mean, what else could have happened? They found his boat empty and floating alone, and his truck and trailer were sitting right there in the parking lot where he had left them."

"Right. I can't see it any other way," said Peal, standing in front of Small's desk. To his left was Lieutenant Mason, Small's immediate subordinate, who clutched his usual large Styrofoam cup of coffee and was as fidgety as ever. With racing speech, Mason nearly cut off Peal in agreement. "Yeah, yeah, yeah. That's all it could have been. Looks like an accident all the way."

"God, I wish we had some witnesses on this," lamented Small. "Someone, somewhere, that could have seen Kincaid doing something, like pulling in, or getting into the boat, or sitting out there in the river. But really, I don't think it'd make a difference. That had to be an accident, pure and simple."

The trio then began theorizing the events of the night, more to shoot the breeze than for anything official. Small offered that Kincaid may have been standing up reaching for something and merely fell out of the boat. Peal thought, perhaps, that Kincaid had hit a log or something else in the river. Both recalled the worst-kept secret of District 18 and speculated that Kincaid was drunk and may have been too intoxicated to stand up in the boat.

Mason kept gulping coffee and ripping off other possibilities, like Kincaid may have suffered a massive heart attack and fell over the side or was reeling in such a large fish that he lost his balance. "After all," added Mason, "I heard about a guy that caught a 180-pound carp in that river a while back. That could really take a man down if you weren't ready for it."

Nearly everyone else at headquarters agreed it was an accident, though none paid attention to Mason's carp theory. Sitting down the hall in the conference room, however, were a pair of doubters.

"Something about this just seems contrived," said R.J. McIntire, with his usual directness. He tossed a file folder on the table in front of him and looked Mike Miller squarely in the eye to determine his reaction.

Miller himself was a skilled investigator and knew to consider all possibilities. He thought the same as McIntire; perhaps Kincaid had staged the whole thing.

"Yeah," agreed Miller. "Do you think he was on to us?"

"Don't know, don't know." replied McIntire, his voice trailing off in thought. "Maybe someone tipped him off. I know it sure as hell wasn't Brad Collins, the state's attorney in Hillsboro. That guy's as solid as anyone I know. I can't imagine that Kincaid would have talked to anyone else in that office either. I mean, if you stole all that money, you sure aren't gonna talk to anyone who could nail you for it."

"I doubt anyone here said anything," mused Miller. "I mean, he had no friends here. I can't see anyone in this place liking him well enough to say something. If anything, the guys here would have kept their mouths shut, hoping to get rid of him."

McIntire chuckled. "That's for sure. Not a likable guy, to say the least."

"What about his bank in Mount Olive?" inquired Miller, extending his palms as he questioned. "How well does he know people there?"

"Maybe well enough." McIntire grabbed a pencil from the table and started flipping it around in a nervous release. "Those little banks, you never know what they'll do. Everyone knows everyone, and half of 'em never seem to understand that little idea of confidentiality."

"Could be," said Miller, running his left hand through his hair once, then again. "But it's all too easy, or at least, it seems like it. Everything points to Kincaid stealing the money, and we're getting closer and closer. Then, all of a sudden, he just happens to fall out of a boat and there's no body, no trace of him. Nothing."

"I've seen worse. I've investigated worse," said McIntire. "I think we have to look at this from all sides. He could be dead or alive, but no matter what, we've still got a case to solve. Until a body floats in at some point, we've got to treat it from every angle."

Miller nodded in agreement. "So what's next?"

"Well, I don't know how much help Peal, Small, and the rest are going to be here. But I know my boss is gonna think the same things we are," said McIntire. "He'll be on our side. And I think we need to go back and talk to Collins. We also need to get inside Kincaid's residence and see what we can find."

That meant a search warrant, which Miller fully expected McIntire to think of. "Yeah, that's what has to be next. If you're gonna call Collins, let me know. I want to go along."

McIntire, likewise, expected nothing less from Miller. "All right. Let me do it right now." He picked up the receiver and dialed the number of Brad Collins, the first step in continuing the investigation into James Kincaid, now perhaps posthumously.

CHAPTER 45

As he sipped his morning coffee while halfheartedly listening to the television, James Kincaid heard the weatherman mention the forecast high for the St. Louis region–an unseasonably cool day with the chance of heavy thunderstorms and flood warnings.

He stood up, walked to the window, and pulled back the curtains to be bathed in sunlight, its yellow splendor set against a crystal blue, cloudless sky. Looking down the street, he saw the temperature flash in red on the electronic sign of a used-car dealer–a perfect 74 degrees at 8:19 in the morning.

Still basking in the rays of the sun pounding through the glass, Kincaid snickered to himself. He had been in Brownsville, Texas, for four weeks now, and the mercury was yet to drop below 86 degrees for a high temperature. As he swallowed his coffee, he gloated thinking about the folks back in his former home of Illinois. Serves those shitheads right, he chortled to himself. Everything they put me through, they deserve to drown their asses in the rain…

Such was life in Brownsville, a city of 175,000 that was one of the southernmost points in the continental United States, just across the Rio Grande from Mexico and only a few miles west of the gulf. It was also the new home of James Wilson, a transplant from Arkansas who had landed in town after the accidental death of his alter ego, James Kincaid, back in Illinois, a mishap which preceded a long drive through Missouri and Oklahoma, then all the way through Texas to the Rio Grande.

The first few hours of the journey had been nerve-racking, but the latter half was calm, and Kincaid– er, Wilson–had enjoyed the ride. As the miles racked up and the hours passed from Illinois, he was bolder and brasher, cocky as ever, knowing that his grand plan was coming to pass.

His choice of Brownsville was for its proximity to the Mexican border, knowing that he could slip across if the walls started closing in. The city was also full of transients, a mixture of Tex-Mex unmatched by few other locales in the U.S. There, it would not seem unusual for a middle-aged guy with scraggly hair and a growing beard in a roughed-up Ford to set up housekeeping for a while.

He pulled into Brownsville in a pouring rainstorm, exhausted from his grueling two-day excursion in the Focus, which had barely made it that far. Unused to constant highway driving, the old car's acceleration grew weaker on the trip, and its transmission grinded and squealed as if on its last legs. But it had just enough left to pull its owner into the Nite-Rite Inn, where he spent his first night in town in a single room that cost a mere thirty-two dollars.

Though the mattress was lumpy and the sheets were littered with long, dark hairs, Kincaid slept like a baby, better than he had in weeks. He rose the next morning, showered in the lukewarm water, and left with a string of things to do in his adopted new city.

At the top of the list was an apartment search. After driving around for an hour or so, he passed by a long, red-brick, single-story structure that had once served as a motel but now offered boarding rooms that housed sixteen permanents. A shabby, decaying sign out front called attention to the place, The Texican, aptly named for the combination of whites and Mexicans that inhabited the place.

Rooms at the Texican were small and were now all singles. A folding table with two ladderback chairs, a scratched-up dresser, and a television stand served as furniture, and though the place had seen better days, it seemed quiet and clean, at least to a point. Kincaid also knew that management was unlikely to ask for a credit card, which could have been dicey under his new name of Wilson.

The manager was a Mexican lady named Inez, a portly woman of sixty-six with shaggy dark hair tied up in a bun, who spoke broken English. Her dialect was little problem, for she didn't say much, and what she did say was blunt and rude. She asked Kincaid a couple of questions, mainly if he was a drug user or an ex-con, and when he answered no, she was more amenable. She also liked the fact that he was willing to pay two months up front, in cash. Inez seized the money and handed him the key to room number nine, which he moved into by noon.

And there Kincaid would stay for most of the time thereafter. The television offered sixty-one channels, fewer than he had back in White City but enough to keep him occupied, and the stained white telephone on the nightstand by the bed never rang. The dresser was big enough to keep his money, still in the same duffel bag that he had pulled from the wreck that fateful night, and on the rare times he left the room, he made sure the bag was locked in the trunk of the Focus.

The best part, though, was the solitude, as Kincaid was able to sleep whenever he wanted, a welcome respite from the last few harrowing months that had ravaged both his body and mind. Now, many mornings did not start until eight thirty or later, or whenever he decided to roll out and face the ever-present sunshine.

He did, however, welcome one visitor on a regular basis. On the day that he had rented the room from Inez, he was about to leave the office when her niece, Marla, stumbled into the room. Clearly, the night before had been long and hard, typical for this forty-one-year-old with flaming red hair who stood five ten and fought to maintain the body of a twenty-one-year-old.

She certainly dressed to impress. A snow-white tube top showed off both her bare, tattooed shoulders and navel piercing, while a pair of jet-black hot pants barely covered her lower half. Her skin emitted a cast of dark tan, partly from the nude sunbathing that had earned her two misdemeanors, and also from the years of drink. Upon entering the room, her first act was to reach on the counter for a half-empty bottle of vodka, which she swigged as Inez barked her disapproval. Marla glanced at Kincaid and batted her eyes as he said his goodbyes and left.

Later that day, Marla, still intoxicated, stopped by room number nine, "to see if you needed anything or could use some company." Kincaid extended his hand, showing her inside, and she plopped down on the bed, crossing her legs as her hot pants rode up, showing nothing underneath. A few minutes of slurred conversation ensued before she jumped up, said, "I'll be back, cowboy," and left.

Two days later, she made good on her promise, showing up in a tight black dress so short that both of her buttocks showed beneath the hemline. She knocked on the door with a bottle of vodka in one hand and a can of Bud in the other, and it didn't take long for her to wiggle out of the dress. Moments later, she pushed Kincaid back onto the bed, causing his shoulder to throb from the impact. But the discomfort was offset by her wandering lips, which had few inhibitions amid her drunken stupor.

It was Kincaid's first time with a woman since Debbie, and as Marla became more amorous, he wondered how it would be, if he could perform at all. But his manhood had grown with every passing mile since Illinois, and he was ready for pleasure. He lay back and let Marla have her way, and as her lips slid down to his most sensitive areas, he knew the time was right and that he was entitled.

So began a fling that continued whenever Marla was not sitting on a barstool somewhere or sleeping off a hangover the next day. Whatever she did in between, and who she did it with, was anyone's guess, and she wasn't talking. But Kincaid hardly cared, since the more she drank, the more accommodating she was in the bed, shower, or wherever her libido took over.

Marla asked few questions, only wondering what he did for a living, to which he simply replied, "I'm on disability." While she never pressed him for details, she was more than willing to share her own. She had come to Brownsville from Houston, where she was a dancer in a men's club, the place where she had met her third husband, an overweight, seventy-seven-year-old oilman who owned five Cadillacs, three Ford F-150s, and a pair of Hummers.

The union lasted eight days before a six-figure divorce settlement was negotiated by his kids and his legal team. She blew through the money in short order ("Easy come, easy go," she giggled) and now slept on a cot in Inez's quarters. Though she was a heavy smoker, she always had to mooch a cigarette off Kincaid–at least the regular kind. Marla never left home without one of her "other" cigarettes, hand-rolled with a different kind of tobacco with a sweeter smell, which always left her eyes glassy.

Thanks to her chronic inebriation, Kincaid also learned more of her sexual history than he cared to know. She told him she had slept with "a lot of people, sixty-five or sixty-seven, or something like that. All but six of 'em were men." Twice, she had ended up in trouble, but "I had abortions both times. Don't need a kid, you know. Finally just had my tubes tied and said, 'screw it.'" Disease was not a problem because "I don't sleep with just anyone." She was tight-lipped, though, on another issue. Once in the afterglow, when Kincaid asked if he was good at it, she simply smiled and said nothing.

That rousing endorsement aside, there were no strings, and her visits to room number nine a few times a week were erotic diversions in an otherwise uneventful existence. And Kincaid liked it that way.

Geez, everything's so quiet, he thought. Damn, it's great...all the bullshit I put up with back home, and none of it here...come and go as I want, sleep whenever I feel like it...don't have kids crying at me, ex-wives with their hands out...don't have to work or worry anymore...no one coming after my ass, like those Mexicans did... My time is mine, like it always should have been. I deserved a helluva lot more than I had back home.

He also reveled in his escape. Just think, McIntire and Miller are back there, and I got away. They can't do nothing...probably sitting back at headquarters, crying like babies that they can't screw me...that's all that guys like them do anyway-come after hard-working guys like me, just trying to take care of things...well, who's the big shit now? I got me a million dollars and don't have to do a damn thing for it...they can work until their butts are in the ground, and they still won't be as rich as me. Peal and Small and all those other assholes can keep pushing the papers, and they won't be living like me either.

Seldom did he leave the apartment, though there were a few occasions. Shortly after arriving, he went down to the nearest Wal-Mart to treat himself to a shopping spree for new clothes, boots, and some DVDs. His blood pressure medicine and Viagra prescriptions needed to be refilled at some point, so he found a doctor in a low-rent district of town who didn't ask many questions of James Wilson, a new patient formerly of Arkansas. Armed with the scribbled prescription sheets, he went back to the Wal-Mart, picked up his new drugs at the pharmacy with Wilson's ID, and was on his way.

A few times, he stopped by the local bars, including a visit one afternoon with Marla, who seemed to know every guy in the room a little too well. One even hit on her while she was sitting with Kincaid, who cringed when she didn't blow off the man entirely. But by the time they were back at room number nine, she had already slipped out of her hot pants in the front seat of the Focus, strolling inside panty-free as if no one could see her in light of day.

He also drove the few miles to the seashore to see the gulf, which he had always wanted to do. The white seagulls circled aimlessly above, and the waves gently crashed to shore as Kincaid kicked off his boots and walked barefoot in the sand for a few hundred yards, up and down the beach. The sky was blue and the sun was shining, as it always seemed to do these days. As he relished the warm breeze and the panoramic view, he thought to himself, *This is life.*

CHAPTER 46

McIntire and Miller's visit to the office of Brad Collins, the state's attorney of Montgomery County, Illinois, was brief and to the point. Collins had never trusted Kincaid either, and listened intently as McIntire and Miller explained their doubts. Collins quickly shared those concerns, setting the tone for the entire meeting.

Any successful investigation requires mutual trust and respect among the participants, and in this case, there was plenty to go around. Collins recognized McIntire and Miller as the best investigators in the area, and if they had even an inkling that Kincaid had staged his own death, they must have good reason. In turn, McIntire and Miller both knew that Collins was the ultimate professional, always wanting to do the right thing regardless of the upcoming election.

Collins authorized a search warrant for Kincaid's trailer with little persuasion, shook hands, and wished them luck. The warrant was issued that same day, and McIntire and Miller wasted no time in hitting Interstate 55 for the ten-mile journey from headquarters to the now-vacant trailer in White City.

Once inside, they found the residence largely untouched, as if nothing was amiss. Kincaid's clothes, service weapon and other firearms, and other personal items were all present, and nothing appeared to be missing.

"It looks like he left with just the clothes on his back," said McIntire.

"Yep," said Miller. "I can't find anything out of the ordinary. Looks like he just walked out the door as normal." He paused with a chuckle. "Or wanted to make it look that way."

"Yeah," replied McIntire as he strode to the thermometer on the wall. "It's 73 degrees in here. He even left the air furnace on."

Miller did not respond, instead turning his attention to the kitchen table, where lay the copy of the Alton Telegraph that Kincaid had used to locate the ad for the Ford Focus. Instinctively, he opened the paper and glanced at every page, hoping to find some type of markings, scribblings, or other clues as to Kincaid, his last actions, or his whereabouts. But Kincaid had not marked up the paper in any way, so McIntire and Miller had nothing to go on.

McIntire opened the door to the refrigerator and found several selections of food and booze scattered across its shelves. Turning around, he opened the cabinets to find other foodstuffs. "He left food behind," mused McIntire, "and he didn't take all his booze."

"Wonder how long he'll last without that," cracked Miller, who had located Kincaid's checkbook, showing generally the same balance as the subpoenaed records had revealed. It also seemed that no checks were missing, based on their numbers on the pad as compared to the attached register. They also examined the security system, which had been turned off.

"Kind of odd," said Miller. With that, he began walking to the garage, with McIntire stepping behind. Like the trailer, nothing there seemed out of the ordinary, with no signs that the occupant was not planning to return. Having completed their observations of the garage, the men walked outside, not seeing anything until McIntire spotted a pile of brush around back.

"Hey. What's that?" he inquired to no one in particular as he headed for the pile. Barely visible underneath was freshly dug dirt, still damp the same spot where Kincaid had buried his bag of money.

"What do you think that is?" asked Miller, perplexed.

"I don't know..." McIntire's voice trailed off. "Looks like he was digging around for something or burying something."

"Wonder what that was," said Miller, looking around for any signs of gardens, flower beds, construction, or anything else that might inspire someone to dig around. Finding none, he leaned over and pushed his foot down on the dirt. "Still soft," he noted. "That's fresh, just dug around."

McIntire looked around, hoping to find some clue. But nothing obvious was to be found there or anywhere else on the property. The men were on site for around ninety minutes as they completed their notes, took an array of photos, and returned to headquarters.

*****

McIntire and Miller continued their investigation for several more weeks as summer stretched into fall, working with their usual conciseness, leaving no angle untouched. They continued interviews, analyzed evidence, and reviewed financial records down to the last detail. They had been suspicious for some time, and their minds were not changed after the work was finally completed. Both were convinced that James Kincaid had taken the money from the accident scene.

Armed with the findings from the investigation, R.J. appeared before the grand jury of Montgomery County and received a true bill. The arrest warrant for Kincaid was then issued for official misconduct, theft over, false reports, and tax evasion. Once that was received, R.J. entered the information in the National Crime Information Center (NCIC), which provided a photo of Kincaid and the arrest information to every law enforcement agency in the United States.

With that, James Kincaid, a twenty-six-year state trooper, became a wanted man. Any simple encounter with a police agency, including basic traffic stops, subjected him to arrest and extradition. Most, however, thought the process was unneeded. To them, it was apparent that Kincaid had lost his life in a boat accident on the Mississippi River.

While Peal, Small, and the rest considered the matter a done deal, six months passed without a body being pulled from the river. McIntire and Miller had expected no such body to be found, but they were discouraged by the fact that no reports of Kincaid sightings were ever received. Moreover, there were no reports of anyone, including his children, ex-wives, and surviving family, hearing from him. Whatever the outcome, as the months rolled on it seemed less and less likely that any trace of James Kincaid would ever be found.

CHAPTER 47

Though James Kincaid had relished his month in Brownsville, sleeping late in the morning while receiving manly pleasure from Marla in the afternoon and evening, he thought that his time in Texas should come to an end.

Kincaid had always loved classic country music, thinking that the lyrics of singers like George Jones and Merle Haggard spoke to him, since many of their songs were about hard-working, long-suffering guys who fell victim to heartbreak from selfish women. The radio in the Focus was spotty at best, with as much static as music. But one clear day, the reception was strong enough for him to pick up Mel Tillis's hit "Send Me Down to Tucson." Unsure of where his next destination would be, he was inspired by the song. Tucson, it would be.

Like Brownsville, Tucson offered plenty of advantages. As a city of over 520,000, it would certainly be easy to blend in and attract no attention. It was also just a hundred miles from the Mexican border, in case another escape was needed. Though the heat could be brutal as summer approached, it seemed a natural fit for a man on the run like James Kincaid, or for a man just passing through like Kincaid's alter ego, James Wilson.

But there was plenty to do before leaving south Texas. First was a new set of wheels, since the Focus was on its last legs and was unlikely to last the 1,100-mile drive to Tucson. Kincaid was loath to do anything that required an identity check or documentation, so he shied away from car dealers, who might ask too many questions.

One day, as he was coming back from Wal-Mart, he drove by a forlorn, split-level ranch home with a red-and-white auction sign, to sell off the remainder of some poor soul's estate, planted in the front yard. Parked in that yard was a late-model, brown Dodge Ram, which looked like formidable transportation for a long trek across the American Southwest.

The auction was scheduled for the coming Saturday, and Kincaid, flush with cash, knew that he could outbid any competitors. His position was strengthened by a drenching rain on the morning of the auction, which kept many bidders away.

The Ram was a 2013 model with 68,000 miles on it, and only one other guy showed any interest. After a little jockeying back and forth, it was clear that the man did not have deep pockets, leaving Kincaid to walk away with the truck for a mere $6,000. He paid cash up front, taken from the duffel bag earlier that day, and signed the minimum of paperwork to assume the title and take the keys. Everything completed, he drove the Ram back to room number nine, leaving his Focus parked along the street in front of the auction to pick up later.

The man in the apartment next door, a down-and-out sort named Pablo who always seemed to have a wrinkled paper bag pressed to his mouth, was only too happy to ride along with Kincaid later that day to drive the Focus back, offering his services "for just a ten-dollar bill, my friend." By now, the Focus, which could barely make it a few blocks, was worth almost nothing, and Kincaid just wanted to get rid of it.

He thought about just giving it to Marla, who never seemed to have a car of her own. Pablo, though, had other ideas. Seeing that Kincaid now had an extra vehicle, Pablo, preening as ever, said he "would gladly pay you $100 for it." Though Kincaid had thousands of $100 bills in the duffel bag, he saw no problem with having one more. He agreed to Pablo's offer and signed over the vehicle.

The duffel bag and his few other belongings were already locked in the Ram when he walked down to Inez's quarters to tell her he was leaving. Though he was paid up and had two weeks left, she never suggested a refund. Marla was sprawled out on a brown leather couch, icebag to her head and dressed only in a clingy white T-shirt with nothing visible underneath, as Kincaid dealt with Inez. He asked if he could see Marla in room number nine, which he had left unlocked.

She groaned, pulled herself off the couch, and walked back to Kincaid's apartment where he told her, in just a few words, that he was moving on. Marla shrugged and muttered, "Well, it was fun while it lasted," before saying, "Hell, I've give ya one for the road." She pulled off her T-shirt, dropped to her knees until his pleasure was complete, stood up to redress, and stumbled out the door.

CHAPTER 48

Kincaid zipped his pants, shut the door and climbed into the Ram, and drove north out of Brownsville on Route 77 to Interstate 37, and then to Interstate 10, headed for southern Arizona. As he had done in his flight from Rip Rap, he made few stops, only pulling into an occasional truck stop or convenience store for a bite to eat or to fill up. The lonely Texas prairie offered little to distract the mind, and he had plenty of time to think, but now he felt little of the guilt that had consumed him for weeks. As he kept the Ram just under the speed limit, he only thought ahead.

Geez, this is living, he thought. Got my whole life in front of me, no one to answer to, no responsibility. Emboldened, now he cared little if a police car passed him, or settled into his lane. No one suspects anything. If they had, they'd have been on to me by now…hell, it's been over a month. I'm home free.

Thoughts of Debbie, frequent just weeks before, were seldom in his mind, and Sharon and the brats from his second marriage were a distant memory. Though he had never managed to put Judy and his first kids in the past, they were rare visitors to his thoughts now as well, though never fully erased.

The massive land area of Texas makes for tortuously long drives, as eleven hours is required just to get from Brownsville to El Paso. After driving until nearly midnight, that is where Kincaid chose to stay over, not knowing El Paso was familiar territory to Miguel Perez and Carlos Santiago, the Mexicans that had shot Kincaid and murdered Debbie. The compound of their boss, powerful drug lord Diego Garcia, was mere miles away, across the Rio Grande.

Kincaid never knew where his attackers hailed from, so he was blissfully unaware as he pulled into the Chamizal Motor Lodge to spend the night. The Chamizal had been a favorite haunt of Santiago, particularly when he needed a place to take a hooker, and as fate would have it, his little brother, Rami, was being entertained by his own paid girlfriend in a room just a few doors down.

As his latest glassy-eyed bimbo did her work, Rami had no idea that the man who gunned down his brother in Illinois was just a few yards away. Had he known, James Kincaid's journey would have likely ended then and there. Rami had idolized Carlos and longed to be like him, despite the fact that, at five-foot-eight and 145 pounds, he was dwarfed by his big brother. He also never had Carlos's style or panache, as Rami always thought his sibling looked so cool in his cowboy attire. Though Carlos was never the smartest guy in the room, he was a scholar compared to Rami, a fixture in every learning-disability class before dropping out in the ninth grade.

Despite his lack of intellect, Carlos had been useful to Diego Garcia, the drug lord who was worshipped by all the underworld types along the border. However, Rami, scrawny and slow-witted, was of little value to Garcia, who blew him off whenever he came around professing his loyalty and looking for work. As a result, Rami made a menial living as a runner in the lower-end drug market, unlike his well-paid late brother.

Ever since his brother's violent death up north in Illinois, Rami had sworn vengeance on Carlos's killer, vowing to uphold the family name. Since Rami knew that any move on Kincaid had to be approved by Garcia, he begged the cartel leader to let him avenge Carlos's loss. But Garcia dismissed Rami every time, brusquely replying, "That is not good for our business" and "When and if I need you, I will tell you so."

On a small table in his two-room apartment in a battered boarding house, Rami maintained a shrine, an 8x10 framed photo of Carlos decorated with a wooden cross and prayer beads. Every Sunday, just before turning in for the night, Rami would look at the photo, cross himself, and whisper, "Someday, my brother. Someday."

*****

The graveyard-shift desk clerk at the Chamizal, a chunky Tex-Mex millennial named Enrique, had never bothered to ask questions of Rami, who haphazardly filled out the check-in card while the wide-eyed, scantily-dressed girl with him stared off into space. A few hours later, Enrique also neglected to take the ID of James Wilson, the fifty-something man from Arkansas who only needed a smoking room with one bed at a cost of forty-one dollars for what remained of the night. Kincaid never left the room, ordering dinner from Taco Chacos, a place down the street with a billboard that trumpeted "We Deliver."

By ten the next morning, Kincaid was on his way again, with a tank full of gas and a sound night's sleep under his belt. He left Texas and into New Mexico, staying near the border on Interstate 10 as he traversed southwestern New Mexico on the way to Arizona. Lunch was at a Burger King near the Arizona border, though he changed his order to carryout when he saw three cops sitting near a window, trying to relax for a few minutes after their meal. Otherwise, the trip passed uneventfully until he reached Tucson.

His first night in town was spent in the Desert View Inn, where the clerk asked for an ID, glanced at it, and handed it back to his new customer, Wilson, with no questions asked. Kincaid spent the evening lounging in Room 196, watching the pay-per-view adult selections on TV while drinking Coors and munching on a double pepperoni pizza delivered from Ronaldo's, six blocks away.

Kincaid slept until ten thirty the next day and had to scramble to make the 11 a.m. checkout time. Still, that was early enough to look for an apartment, and after checking at three different places, he hit on his fourth try, a four-unit pre-fab managed by a Mr. Thurston, a transplanted eighty-something retiree who struggled to get around on his bad right hip. Mr. Thurston, who used a walker and never gave his first name, was not interested in "things like credit checks and references and all that jazz" and just demanded money up front.

Like in Brownsville, James Wilson paid for two months in advance, a total of $1,000 in cash, and became Mr. Thurston's newest tenant.

The apartment was a step up from the old motel in Brownsville, with three furnished rooms and a kitchenette and bath, a fairly attractive option for a single man from Arkansas who was on his way somewhere but didn't know where yet. The place was on a quiet side street, blocks away from most business, save for Howie's, a mundane, white-clapboard diner on the next street, a relic that remained from the old days when grocery stores, eateries, and bars were just around the corner. That looked like a good choice for breakfast the next day, and Kincaid fell into his new bed, falling asleep just after his head hit the pillow, free of the ghosts that had plagued him for weeks before his "death" at Rip Rap.

*****

That is, until he walked into Howie's for the first time. As he breezed through the door, he became transfixed on a young waitress, and his life flashed before his eyes. Standing five-foot-eight with dark, partially curled hair, caramel skin, charcoal-black eyes, and long, slender legs, the waitress bore a striking resemblance to a younger Judy.

Kincaid froze in his stride, staring at the waitress as she moved from table to table, smiling at the customers, making small talk, turning her body to slide past people as they walked by. Her build was similar, her moves were alike, and her hair was nearly the same style as Judy's. For a moment, Kincaid was transported back twenty-five years, to the days before his marriage and the months after, when Judy looked much the same as this girl who was balancing round trays of water glasses, trying to keep from spilling, answering the demands of impatient diners in the booths and on the stools.

Within seconds, though, the differences in the young waitress and Judy became obvious. Her name was Imelda, the product of an American mother and a Mexican father, who had left just after her birth twenty-six years before, never to be heard from again. She was dressed in denim cutoffs and a white T-shirt with a big red heart on the front, which went with the hot-pink, sequined handbag that she never left home without. It was normal attire for someone of her immaturity, a young girl in a woman's body.

A few years before, Imelda had enrolled at the University of Arizona, hoping to become a singer like those that filled her MP3 player, and whom she idolized as perfect people, better than everyone else, role models for all. But she was ill-equipped to handle the courseload as she racked up one F after another and left after just one semester, disappointed that college was not more like high school. After bouncing around, she finally landed in this job at Howie's, where she naively ignored the countless stares she received from the male customers.

Imelda hoped someday to marry, dreaming of life like the princesses in England or the pop stars she adored, and had gone through a string of boyfriends, to no avail. Many times, she had set her heart on older men, for though she did not realize it, she was drawn to father figures, trying to fill the void of the real daddy who had left her behind.

Still, as she spoke in current slang peppered with repeated uses of "like" and "oh my God," her physical appearance was remarkably like the first wife of the man who found a seat at a cramped booth with a black-checked, vinyl tablecloth near the door. Imelda greeted Kincaid, brought him his coffee with the morning special of ham and eggs, and moved on, gullible to the fact that his eyes never left her every move.

Thus began a morning ritual for Kincaid, who stopped in every day for the next two weeks to sit at Imelda's station, mindlessly ordering whatever the special was, paying more attention to how tiny her skirt was, the color of her short shorts, and the way her tight tops wrapped around her ample cleavage. Kincaid had always derided what he called "dumbass women," but managed to overlook Imelda's naïve manner, for while she was nowhere near as smart or sophisticated as Judy, she certainly looked the part.

After a few days, he tried to engage her in conversation and Imelda, lonely for friendly chatter and drawn to men of that age, was happy to respond. In no time, he became her favorite customer, doting on him as others complained of her service, and walking by his booth as often as she could. Soon, he learned what time her shift ended and planned his day around it. Imelda responded in kind, sitting at his booth for a while after she had clocked out, prattling on about her mother, her favorite hair and clothing styles, her top movie stars, her dreams.

As the days passed in the scorching-hot Arizona summer, alone with a new life and his duffel bag of money, trying to stay a step ahead of the law, James Kincaid was experiencing emotions that he had felt only one other time in his life. Though it should have been clear that Imelda was like Judy in appearance only, that seemed sufficient to Kincaid, who had let the past go from his mind over the last few weeks, only to have it creep back in.

He remembered the exhilaration of his youthful manhood when Judy was his, the days playful and the nights romantic, before life went off the rails and he had thrown it all away. He struggled with himself, knowing he should leave Imelda aside, forget the feeling, avoid her shift at Howie's altogether. But as Imelda flounced to his table, giggling at his every joke, hanging on his every word, Kincaid was smitten, with feelings of tenderness only Judy had inspired in him.

CHAPTER 49

The conversations in the booth after Imelda's shift gave way to carefree talks on the park bench across from Howie's, sometimes after walks with her arm locked in his as the scorching Arizona summer sun hung above. She freely put her head on his shoulder, snuggling into him on the bench, oblivious to the stares of passersby who wondered why a good-looking young girl in a Scooby-Doo T-shirt was hanging all over a rumpled, middle-aged guy with a high forehead, scruffy beard, and protruding paunch.

Kincaid was not immune to the stares, though, as he stood naked in front of his mirror after his morning shower, maintaining his usual rose-colored view of himself. His gut carried an extra twelve pounds, the product of his ability to eat whatever he wanted, with no doctor to tell him otherwise. He was forced to suspend his two-pack-a-day habit while in the hospital after the shooting, but now he was going through closer to three packs. His salt-and-pepper beard was rough and his hair was long in back, emulating the style of James Wilson, but with less and less in front. Still, as his reflection shot back to him in the glass, he swayed to admire himself, thinking he looked good in light of everything he had been through and had been done to him.

Imelda certainly never criticized his lagging build and receding hairline, and she decided that he needed someone to cook for him. Several times, she brought groceries to cook at his apartment, usually hamburgers and chips, since she could afford little else. She liked to eat her meals while sitting, cross-legged Indian style, on a footlocker positioned next the sofa, which housed Kincaid's bag of money. She laughed that "sometime, we can go on a real date," to which Kincaid simply replied, "Yeah, sometime."

His other replies were equally vague, particularly when she pressed him for details of his life. Kincaid explained that he had headed west looking for a fresh start, which was not entirely a lie. His ex-wife back in Arkansas, he said, never understood him and had run off with a truck driver, which, where Sharon was concerned, was also partially true. It had resulted in a bad divorce, an accurate statement in Kincaid's real life twice over. For an occupation, he replied "in a factory," where he had suffered an accident, leaving the missing pinky and still-stiff shoulder. That ordeal, he said, had left him on disability, which, unlike the rest, was a flat-out lie. Imelda swallowed every tale with sympathetic tears in her eyes, hugging him because she thought he needed one, just like Judy sometimes used to do, way back when.

Lying came natural to James Kincaid, as he was accustomed to stretching the truth, with plenty of practice in the last few years. But fibbing to Imelda seemed wrong, and deep down, he resented himself for it. She was naïve to a fault, never wanting to hurt anyone, even worrying if she whacked a housefly too hard with the swatter. But as she cleaned his apartment–something else, she said, he needed from her–he resisted the urge to slip off her shorts and have her, and after the innocence of their flirtations, he was often bursting out of his Wrangler jeans.

He had jumped into bed with Sharon and Debbie and Marla, but it was different with Imelda, the way it had been with Judy. Imelda certainly wanted to move faster, but her boyfriend, "tired from his problems and wanting to take it slow," had only allowed himself several passionate kisses.

He thought of staying on in Tucson, ending his flight right there, spending the rest of his days in this new city that increasingly appealed to him. Though their relationship was hardly two weeks old and they barely knew each other, Imelda, always the dreamer, was signing her texts and e-mails to him with "Love" and chattering about moving in together. A part of him liked the idea of waking up next to her as well.

    A couple of times, he had slowed his late-model Ram to take a second look at apartment buildings with vacancy signs out front, but the consideration was brief. If he were living with Imelda, he was unsure if he would be able to hide his duffel bag, still chock full of money, sufficiently so she would not find it.

CHAPTER 50

On the evening of the seventeenth day of their flirtation, Imelda showed up at Kincaid's apartment unannounced, as usual. Her girlish mind consumed with her crush and her womanly body wanting, she dressed for effect, in a tight white tank top and candy-pink shorts that flattered her voluptuous curves and shapely legs. She breezed through the door, sat down next to Kincaid on the couch, and breathlessly kissed his lips without so much as a "hello."

He had restrained himself since that first day he had seen her in the diner, but now his willpower was fleeting. He jerked with a rise from the couch, grasped her hands, and led her to the bedroom, where he pushed back a strap from her tank top and set his lips on her butterscotch shoulders. As Imelda's mind and body were at odds, so were his. Though his damaged, middle-aged body was inflamed for the naïve young girl in his arms, his mind was flashing back, twenty-five years before, when he felt the same pangs of emotion for Judy in the newness of their marriage.

As he ran his hands up Imelda's sides to remove her tank top and then down again to her shorts, as he tugged her flowered panties off and unhooked her lacy, black strapless brassiere, he was slipping off Judy's white negligee, caressing every part of her, kissing her shoulders, her milky-soft skin, her beautiful full breasts.

As he fell onto the bed, Imelda in his arms and a ghost in his heart, he remembered what it had been like with the woman of his dreams in the glory and optimism of his youth. His thoughts were tempered by the unusual passiveness of Imelda, her young, naked body pressed against his below, letting him dictate the encounter as a virgin might have, though he knew there had been others before him. He realized that she was living the moment, lost in her fatherly dreams, her feelings directed solely at him as he played out a years-long fantasy, trying to satisfy the long-suppressed feelings of what once had been.

The climax was electric, leaving his worn-out body gasping for breath and his mind blissful with tenderness that was unfamiliar to him. As he rolled over to lay on his back, Imelda continued moaning softly beside him before settling into a kitten-like purr, completely satisfied, dreamily cuddling against the new man that finally fulfilled her schoolgirl dreams. She lay her head on his chest and wrapped her arms more tightly around him, finally uttering a few words as the chemistry still simmered.

"The way you were with me," she cooed. "I've never had a man touch me like that. You must really love me."

The last few words drove through Kincaid like a dagger, and the innocence of the previous days shattered like glass. In the warmth of the afterglow, he realized what he had done, the mistake of the last two weeks, the fantasy and longing that had made it happen. Judy was gone, back in the bungalow in Raymond, still a parent to their two daughters while in the arms of another man, out of touch since Jim Kincaid had died and James Wilson was reborn. In her place was a woman-child, lovestruck and gullible, thinking he cared, believing he had made love only to her, their shared passion the start of a life together.

Now, as Imelda curled into him, lovingly running her fingers up and down his chest, Kincaid felt as trapped as he had in the bungalow in Raymond, a dungeon he was chained to. He longed to jump out of bed and run to his truck, driving as fast as his feet could push the pedal. But the evening was still young, and as it became clear that Imelda planned to stay the night, he feigned weariness, saying that "maybe he had pushed a little too much," and "why don't we just get a little sleep?"

Starstruck at his touch and her body still reeling from the explosion of her climax, Imelda was willing to do practically anything he suggested, and she snuggled into him, dozing off in peaceful slumber. Kincaid's eyes, though, stayed wide open as the clock ticked past twelve, then one, then two, counting down the minutes, hoping to escape once again.

Imelda had to open the next morning at Howie's, and as she awoke at 4:11, she knew she had to be on her way. Kincaid now pretended to be asleep as she showered and redressed in her tank top and pink shorts, not even twitching as she leaned down to warmly kiss his cheek goodbye. She grabbed a piece of scrap paper and scribbled out a note that she left on the pillow beside him, reading "See ya tonight, big guy!" and signed off with "Love," including plenty of Xs, Os, and hearts.

Moments later, Kincaid opened an eye as she tried to start her car outside. The vehicle, a white 1991 Honda hatchback with the strength to barely reach forty-five, rumbled once, then twice before finally turning over, and she backed out of her parking spot, careful not to scrape Kincaid's pricey pickup as she went. Inside, Kincaid breathed a sigh of relief as he heard her drive away and quickly rolled out of bed, as if time were running short.

He ran to the bathroom for a quick shower and then pulled on clothes as if late for a bus. Kincaid had only a few possessions scattered around the three rooms of the apartment, and after ticking off in his mind which were the most important, he jammed them into any box or plastic bag he could find. The duffel bag with the money took precedence over any other item and was carefully toted outside to the Dodge Ram and locked inside. Then he returned to gather the rest, stuffing them haphazardly in the passenger seat.

His final duty was to knock on Mr. Thurston's door, though it was still only 5:29 in the morning. After a lengthy delay, the old man opened the door as he leaned on his walker, glaring at Kincaid as he snapped, "What the hell is it?" Kincaid told him he was leaving and handed him the keys.

"Oh, for God's sake." Thurston had little patience for any such drivel, though he had seen it all before and was used to tenants coming and going on a moment's notice. "You're paid ahead, so I guess I owe you some money," he added, dragging out the sentence to show his reluctance to refund.

"Don't worry about it," replied Kincaid, shifting from one foot to the other. "Just keep it."

"What the hell do you mean, 'don't worry about it?'" Thurston's eyes flared in anger and disgust. "You damned fool! Wake me up at God-knows-what-hour to tell me you're leaving, and you walk away from a month's rent! Dumb son of a bitch!" His eyes then turned accusing. "You get arrested and on the run or something?"

Kincaid played it cool, though the last words were like a knife. "No, no, nothing like that," he replied, words racing from his mouth. "Just got a call and there's an emergency. Gotta go."

"Hmm." Thurston couldn't have cared less. "Well, don't think you're gonna come back here some day and get your money. Once you're outta here, it's gone. I ain't giving it back."

With that, Thurston slammed the door. It had barely closed when Kincaid had already turned around, heading for the Ram and the interstate that would carry him out of Tucson. Hours later, as Imelda was sobbing to her mother about her latest lost love, Kincaid was hundreds of miles away, crossing the Arizona desert with his mind spinning from the outcome of his latest choice.

CHAPTER 51

Throughout his thirty-one years of marriage, Illinois State Police Master Sergeant Ron Wilton had tried and tried again to talk his wife, Ruth, into a trip to Las Vegas. Six months ago, he had made a deal with her; he'd go with her to Door County, Wisconsin, her destination of choice, this summer if they would take the Vegas trip the next winter. Ruth agreed, and as she dragged him through every boutique in Door County, he dreamed of next year, when Vegas was the place.

It was a bucket-list excursion for Wilton, who had spent the last two decades with the ISP, mainly on patrol on the highways of central Illinois. Sixteen of those years were spent in District 18, where he made a ton of friends with his gregarious personality and attention to detail. His big-hearted ways belied his appearance, as he carried 210 pounds of muscle on his six-foot frame, the product of dedicated exercise in his home gym and eating right in the kitchen. His shaved head added to a look that intimidated some, particularly the law-breakers that he busted and the speeders that he ticketed. But everyone knew that Wilton was a solid guy, dependable, the kind that made the ISP proud.

Four years ago, Wilton had requested a transfer to District 13, in extreme southern Illinois, so Ruth could be near her ailing mother in Murphysboro. He hated to leave District 18, but Ruth feared for her mother and he knew it was best, so he swallowed his feelings and made the switch. While the rolling, tree-covered hills and lakes of southern Illinois appealed to his fixation on hunting and fishing, the curving roadways were tougher to drive, and he missed the ease of the straightaways through the cornfields of central Illinois.

Now, as he dressed in Room 972 of Caesars Palace Hotel, he was unusually calm and relaxed, the result of the decompression of the last two days, when he had left the stress of his job a thousand miles away on the flight that carried him away from St. Louis to Las Vegas. Ruth, always an early riser even on vacation, was already up and dressed, her slight frame clothed in a new black-and-white dress and her short, auburn hair covered by a stylish, wide-brimmed, beige hat, apparel that she had bought specifically for the trip.

It was the third week of December, and Wilton had planned the vacation to coincide with the holiday. He hated cold weather and had always thought it would be fun to wake up on Christmas morning to see palm trees outside. The Wiltons were booked on a ten-day excursion, so they would spend this Yuletide in the Nevada desert and not return home until December 28, just how Ron wanted it.

Today was Monday, December 19, and there were plenty of gaudy Christmas decorations scattered on the streets of Las Vegas. But the holiday was six days away, and there was plenty of time to think about it later. First on the agenda on this sun-splashed morning was breakfast in the hotel dining room, which was nearly empty at this hour of the morning, for the gamblers that filled the casino at night were still in bed.

Ruth wanted to do a little shopping before taking in the slot machines, so after a hearty breakfast of steak and eggs, Ron drove her to one boutique, then another and one more, waiting patiently in their rented white Chrysler Sebring. In a couple of instances, he strolled the streets nearby for some exercise and people-watching while enjoying the bright desert sunshine.

His wife's desire for "a little shopping" took all morning, and by the time she was done, it was lunchtime. The noon hour found Ron and Ruth back in the Caesars dining room, which again had plenty of empty seats, as the gamblers were busy elsewhere. They both ordered the surf-and-turf platter, which he devoured and she left half of. Finally, with lunch complete and the afternoon in front of them, Ron steered Ruth toward the casino, where he had longed to be all morning.

Ron was not a heavy gambler, having only been in a casino or two in his life, but nothing like Caesars. He was taken aback by the size, the spectacle, the décor, the number of tables where gambling fans could try their desire. The people in the casino were from all walks of life, black and white, fat and thin, attractive and not, and most did not seem to care that their hard-earned dollars were going to line the pockets of the billionaire casino owners.

The Wiltons strode around the room deliberately, Ron taking it all in as Ruth seemed somewhat bored. The police officer in him was trained to study all scenarios, even in leisure, and he seemed to relish the opportunity to observe his surroundings, including the customers scattered across the room. Even at this hour of the day, business was good in the casino, and dozens of small-time vacation gamblers were trying their luck.

Ron also noticed some hard-core professional gamblers, ones that see the casinos as a workplace, and their attitudes were obvious to anyone. One man, however, seemed to pique Ron's interest at first glance. At a blackjack table sat a middle-aged man, bearded with long hair tied back in a ponytail, who seemed familiar to him.

That struck Ron as unusual, since he did not know anyone in Vegas. He took a second look, observing the man's physical build, somewhat stocky and overweight with a ruddy complexion. Damn, he thought, I should know that guy…looks so familiar…where have I seen him before?

In tune with his police training, Ron kept observing, looking for any detail. Standing yards away, he watched as the man played a hand, then another, tossing his cards if folding and scooping up chips while winning. His posture, his movements, and the sullen look on his face then became clear to Ron. The man was James Kincaid.

Ron had known Kincaid from their days in District 18, though, like most, the two were not close. Ron preferred to spend his evenings at home with Ruth, and disdained Kincaid's well-known habits of drinking and womanizing. Not surprisingly, he was offended by Kincaid's bravado despite his low activity rating, which grated on Wilton, a cop who played it by the book. He was also aware of Kincaid's "death" at Rip Rap and how a body had never been found.

"Hey," he said to Ruth, tugging at her sleeve. "I think that's James Kincaid."

Ruth had never met Kincaid but, like her husband, was aware of his disappearance, which had made for some interesting dinner-table chatter. She looked as her husband pointed. "You mean that bummy-looking guy sitting there?"

"Yeah. That's got to be him. I worked with the guy for sixteen years. I ought to know."

Ruth was still skeptical. "Come on, Ron, you mean that guy? I thought you told me Kincaid had drowned in the river."

"Yeah, but they never found a body. And remember what I told you? The guys at District 18 were investigating him for official misconduct, theft, and other charges. They thought he stole a lot of money." Wilton tried to convince his wife, who simply looked back at him in disbelief.

"You're telling me that a guy you thought was dead is really alive? That guy?" inquired Ruth, still incredulous. "He looks like he just came in off the street! I know you always said Kincaid was a jackass, but did he look that bad?"

Ron chuckled slightly but was still insistent. "No, but that's gotta be the same guy. He's got that beard and long hair, but it's him. I'd bet anything on it."

Ruth smiled at the reference to betting, surrounded by people doing it all around them. She also sensed the policeman in her husband was taking over, even on vacation, and that he would not let the situation slide. "What are you going to do about it?"

She knew the answer. "I'm gonna stay here for a bit. You go on, and I'll catch up with you."

With that, Ruth shook her head and strolled off, settling in at a slot machine, where she spent her self-allotted fifty dollars, winning nothing back. Her husband, meanwhile, stood in the distance, partially concealed by a pillar, eyes transfixed on the man at the blackjack table.

He spent the next ten minutes or so in surveillance, increasingly convinced the player was Kincaid, and he knew what to do next. He pulled his phone from his pocket and dialed the number of his old headquarters, District 18.

Wilton's call was routed to Mike Miller, who was sitting at his desk nursing a Styrofoam cup of coffee and analyzing files. "Mike? Ron Wilton. Remember me?" said the voice in the receiver.

Miller was startled at the call, not expecting to hear from Ron, and not having seen him since his transfer. "Ron? Hell yeah, I remember you! Been a while!"

Wilton and Miller had always been on good terms and took a moment to exchange some pleasantries. "Yeah, it has. God, I miss you guys."

"Miss you too, Ron," Miller leaned back in his chair, relaxing at the sound of his old buddy's voice. "Whatcha been up to?"

"Oh, you know. Job down there's going all right," said Wilton, a reference to District 13, three hours away from Litchfield. "But that's not why I called. I got something you aren't gonna believe."

Miller was nonchalant. "Yeah? Lay it on me."

"I'm calling you from Las Vegas. My wife and I are out here on vacation, and I'm standing in the casino at Caesars Palace. I'm looking right at this guy at a blackjack table, and I think it's James Kincaid."

Miller's eyes grew wide as saucers, in shock. "Say that again?"

Wilton calmly but emphatically repeated his words, glancing over at the blackjack table every few seconds as he spoke. "I think it's Kincaid. I mean, it has to be. The guy looks the same, acts the same, same size and build, everything. He's got a beard and long hair that he wears in a ponytail, which I know he didn't have. I know Kincaid supposedly drowned in that boating accident. But Mike, I gotta tell you, I really think it's him."

Miller recalled Wilton's ability on the job and always trusted his judgment. If he was standing in Vegas saying that he saw James Kincaid, he was probably on to something. "Ron, are you sure about this?"

"Yeah," Wilton replied with increased insistence. "I'm positive. It has to be him."

"Damn…" Miller's voice trailed as the shock wore off. He then snapped back to attention. "Ron, look for something for me. Did you hear about a shooting at Kincaid's trailer about ten months ago?"

"Heard about it? Oh, hell yeah. It was all we were talking about down there for a while. I mean, God, that was on the news for days."

"All right." Miller knew a way to prove the man at the table was Kincaid. "Did you hear anything about the details of the shooting? Like where Kincaid was shot?"

Wilton tapped his fingers together and looked off into space, trying to remember. "No, not much. I knew he was hit twice, but the papers and the TV never said much on where."

Trying to maintain his composure, as he had been trained to do, Miller deliberately explained the specifics. "He was hit in his shoulder, and the little finger on his left hand was blown off. If the guy at the blackjack table is missing that finger, we may have something. Can you see anything from where you're at?"

"No, no," said Wilton, disappointment evident. "I'm standing twenty-five, thirty feet away from the guy, behind a concrete pillar. I can't see anything that close. And I know if I get any closer, he'll recognize me."

"Who else is there with you? Is Ruth there?"

"Yeah, and she never met Kincaid!" Wilton's despair turned to excitement. "She's around here somewhere. I'll get her and have her walk by to see if she sees anything."

"Okay," replied Miller. "Call me back as soon as you know something."

Wilton hung up and slipped away, careful not to let Kincaid see him as he left the casino. Ruth had given up on the slots and exited the casino as well, finding something of interest in the hotel gift shop. After searching the halls for a couple of minutes, Ron caught up with her, pulled her out into the hallway, and explained what was going on.

"So you want me to just walk by the table and see if the guy is missing his left pinky?" asked Ruth rather bluntly.

"Yep. That's all you need to do. If you can pick up on anything else, great. But the point is to see if he is missing his left little finger." Wilton emphasized the last few words, to ensure Ruth understood.

CHAPTER 52

The Wiltons returned to the casino as if nothing was unusual. Ron resumed his vantage point behind the pillar as Ruth, with the brim of her hat pulled down just above her eyes like she was incognito, sashayed over to the blackjack table where Kincaid was seated. She strolled around the sides of the table a couple of times, acting as if she was just passing by and watching, all the while glancing over at Kincaid's left hand.

On her first try, Ruth saw that he had no little finger on his left hand. Kincaid, consumed with the game, barely noticed her, even as the dealer said, "You playing, ma'am?" She shook her head and lingered for another few seconds, getting the best view of Kincaid's left hand as possible.

She then wandered on, or so it seemed, on her way back to Ron. He motioned to her to meet him outside the casino to discuss what had happened.

He didn't have to ask first. "Ron, that guy doesn't have a left pinky," exclaimed Ruth, pushing her hat higher on her forehead. "That was clear as day. It couldn't have been more obvious."

Ron nodded and clenched his lips, knowing his suspicions were confirmed. "All right. I need to call this in." Ruth winced, knowing their vacation was just interrupted, but Ron compensated. "Tell you what. I'm gonna be here for a while. Why don't you take the rental and check out that mall we saw as we came in from the airport?"

That was all Ruth needed to hear. "Sounds good. How long are you going to be?"

He shook his head and shrugged. "Could be a few minutes, could be a few hours. You never can tell."

"Yeah. Should have known the answer to that one, being married to you all these years." She leaned up to peck him on the cheek, turned, and headed for the parking lot.

Ruth was mere yards away when Wilton had reached Miller back at District 18 headquarters. "Mike? Ron. I just had Ruth walk by the guy at the blackjack table, and she saw it. He didn't have a left little finger. She was certain about it."

For the first time in months, Miller had a break in the Kincaid case. "All right. I need you to keep Kincaid under surveillance." Miller realized what he was asking, since Wilton was giving up vacation time for official business. "Can you stay on him until I get back to you?"

Wilton knew that Miller now had several steps to take, and it could be a while. "Sure," he said, and he gave Miller his cell phone number. "I'll stay here as long as you need me."

"Thanks." Miller expected no less of an answer from a textbook cop like Wilton. "I'll be back in touch as soon as I know something."

*****

Wilton remained in the casino, trying to remain as anonymous as possible, keeping his eye on Kincaid all the while. Kincaid, meanwhile, was oblivious to the situation, focused on his blackjack hands and completely unaware that he was being watched.

As Wilton settled in, Miller called R.J. McIntire at his Springfield office to inform him of the latest, startling developments. He also supplied Wilton's cell number to McIntire.

"Didn't see this one coming, did we?" laughed McIntire, in a release of relief and frustration in the case over the last few months. "I think we've got probable cause to take this person into custody to question him. When I hang up with you, I'm calling the U.S. Marshal here in Springfield to see if they can have their people in the Las Vegas office meet with Wilton."

"Sounds good," said Miller, cracking a smile. "Keep me posted."

"Sure will. Thanks, Mike, good work." With that, McIntire dialed Wilton's cell number, to speak directly with the man who was breaking the case open.

As usual, R.J. was to the point. "Ron Wilton? This is R.J. McIntire with Internal Investigations."

Wilton had never met McIntire, though he had certainly heard of him. He had also expected that Miller would contact DII. "Yeah, good to hear from you, what do you need from me?"

"First, I need confirmation of your location. You're still at Caesars Palace, in the casino?"

"Yeah, I've never left. I'm standing in about the same location as I was when I called Mike Miller."

"All right," replied McIntire. "Can you still see the man you think is Kincaid?"

"Sure can," said Wilton, turning his eyes back in Kincaid's direction. "He's sitting in the exact same spot. Hasn't moved since I first called."

"And you've still got him under surveillance?"

Wilton nodded instinctively, as if McIntire could see him. "Yeah. I stayed here where I was. He hasn't been out of my view since." Before McIntire could ask, Wilton said the words he wanted to hear. "And I'll stay here as long as I have to."

"Thanks," said McIntire. "I'm gonna call the marshal's office here in Springfield, to see if they can effect the arrest with their people in Las Vegas. Just stay where you're at until they get there."

"Will do," said Wilton, dedicated to the job in front of him. McIntire's call went to Rick Hubbard in the marshal's office in Springfield, whom McIntire had worked with before.

A man of medium height and stout build, Hubbard was a wisecracker, which helped him keep his sanity in his high-pressure job that he had held for nine years, but when the moment called for it, he was all business. The marshal's position was a dream job, one he had held from his days in college in Wisconsin fifteen years before, and one that had made his mother, a dispatcher at the city police office back home, very proud.

Hubbard had followed the Kincaid case since the disappearance at Rip Rap and listened intently as McIntire advised him of the morning's developments. He also passed along Wilton's cell number. Hubbard, in turn, informed McIntire that he would contact Rita Dykes, his counterpart in the marshal's office in Las Vegas.

*****

Dykes had overcome plenty of obstacles in her fifty-five years on earth, including the fact that she was a woman in a male-dominated environment. Her feverish work ethic, coupled with her high level of competence, had earned her the respect of all, though few really knew her, an introverted, distant sort with short gray, curly hair who threw herself into her work at the expense of a personal or social life. Her job was all she knew, which was good for her since she did it so well. Hubbard and everyone else in the marshals' offices around the nation were quite aware of her acumen in the heart of Sin City.

As Dykes sat in her cramped office, piled high with folders and files, she had little time to notice the taupe-colored walls that had recently been redone, or the new mahogany desk she had finally received after years of toil at her old, broken-down model. When the call came in from Hubbard, she was ready as always, and after a few minutes of discussion, she hung up and called Wilton.

Wilton, eyes still transfixed on Kincaid even as casino security began to wonder why he was standing behind a pillar and not playing the tables, confirmed his location inside Caesars, as well as that of Kincaid. Armed with this information, Dykes and her team of three subordinates piled into her black Buick Enclave and headed straight for Caesars.

As the Dykes team was en route, Kincaid suddenly stood up from his blackjack table, stretched his arms and shoulders to remove the kinks from prolonged sitting, and lazily strolled out toward the lobby. Wilton followed, staying a careful distance behind, fearful that Kincaid was leaving the property, and would get away. But Wilton breathed a little sigh of relief to himself when he saw Kincaid settle into the lobby at one of the slot machines and begin feeding it tokens.

With their game faces on, Dykes' team breezed into the casino, where they were spotted by Wilton, now standing in an out-of-the-way spot in the lobby. He nodded his head as if telling them to come to him, and the four marshals, trying to blend in as much as possible, made their way over.

Dykes and her team showed their identification, and Wilton displayed his. "He's right over there," said Wilton, pointing to the scruffy, long-haired man feeding one of the slots. "He moved out here from the blackjack table about five minutes ago."

The marshals gathered some more information from Wilton and discussed their next moves. Walking briskly and authoritatively, the marshals then approached the man at the slot machine, identified themselves, and asked for his name.

"James Wilson..." Kincaid's concentration on the slots was broken by the question. As he returned to the moment and realized he was being quizzed by law enforcement, uneasiness swept over him. He reached for his wallet in his right back pocket and withdrew his Arkansas driver's license. "What is this all about?" he asked, trying to stay cool.

With that, Ron Wilton, who had remained behind in his corner of the lobby, came striding along. He looked Kincaid squarely in the eye. "Hi, Jim, remember me?"

Kincaid certainly remembered who Wilton was. For months, he had been able to relax, live his own life, leave District 18 and the ex-wives and Debbie and all the bad choices behind. Now, terror wrapped around his body as it had on the night that Mary Bartello, the prickly bank teller, had told him he was under investigation. But he had steeled himself for this moment, knowing that someone might ask questions someday, and he was prepared.

"No." he replied calmly to Wilton's question. He assumed the slight Southern drawl that Wilson might have had. "I don't. You must have me confused with someone else, buddy."

"You sure about that?" said Dykes, not wanting to waste any more time.

"Yeah," Kincaid was not going down without a fight, and more lies. "Look, I don't know what y'all are talkin' about." He pointed at Wilton, a tinge of anger evident. "I ain't never seen you before, and I don't know what the hell's goin' on here."

The fight, though, was not to be. Kincaid repeated himself, trying to stay afloat, hoping that the five threatening faces in front of him would somehow believe him, and just move on. But he knew that Wilton remembered him and that the walls were closing in fast.

Nervously, he began to stammer, pleading that he didn't know Wilton and didn't know what was going on. His voice became loud and shrill, waving his hands in desperation as he felt his heart rate skyrocket and his breath become shorter.

After a couple of tries, though, he realized his efforts were in vain. James Wilson, the long-haired man from Arkansas who had come west for a fresh start, was dying on the spot. James Kincaid, the cop on the run with a duffel bag of a million dollars, was reborn, and his time was up. As he felt the icy steel of the handcuffs around his wrists and heard the click that locked them into place, his mind was a cyclone, spinning with images of the choices that had brought him to this point.

CHAPTER 53

Not long before, James Wilson was living the life of luxury, throwing money at the blackjack table, surrounded by the opulence of Caesars Palace. Now, James Kincaid was staring at the sedate colors of the mundane block walls of Rita Dykes' office at the marshal's headquarters.

Throughout his forty-nine years of life, Kincaid had been defined by his bluster, always speaking up, forcing his opinion on listeners whether they wanted it or not. Now, as the body warmth of his wrists began to thaw the cold steel of the cuffs that encased them, he was silent and stoic.

After some basic questions, he was escorted down the hall to a no-frills conference room, not unlike the one back at District 18 headquarters. The irony was not lost on Kincaid. Just over a year before, he had sat in that same conference room near Litchfield, bragging to a cub reporter about his "honesty" regarding the traffic accident, where he had found the money in the trunk. He was a hero then. Now, today was the first day of a lifelong disgrace.

Dykes and her team went through the drill, but Kincaid was beaten, and he knew it. There was no reason to put up any resistance, for it only prolonged the inevitable. He finally admitted to being James Kincaid and provided Dykes with the address of his apartment in Las Vegas. He also signed a waiver, allowing her team to search the premises.

Out in the hallway, Wilton dialed the number of R.J. McIntire. "We got him," said Wilton, without so much as a hello. "He was the one. I'm at the marshal's office right now. They're in there questioning him."

"All right," said McIntire, clenching his fist as if in victory, knowing his months-long quest to track down Kincaid had finally ended. "Thanks, Ron. You did a tremendous job on this, and I can't thank you enough."

"Don't mention it," said Wilton, waving his hand as if McIntire could see. "Just doin' what I'm paid to do. Even on vacation," he cracked.

McIntire laughed back and hung up to call Mike Miller. He, too, was overwhelmed by the moment and felt a wave of satisfaction wash over his mind and body, the culmination of all the long hours, tension headaches, lost family time, and bad coffee that had gone into the Kincaid case. McIntire then called his supervisor in Springfield to advise him of the particulars of the arrest.

Like most officers in his position, Wilton was caught up in the events of the day and hung around the marshal's office to hear of any developments, including the results of the search of Kincaid's apartment. Knowing that had left his wife hanging, he dialed Ruth's cell number and told her that he "would be here for a while." Ruth, used to the killer hours of a state cop, laughed it off and said she'd just do some more shopping until Ron was through.

*****

Several hours later, word on the search was received at the marshal's office. The team had recovered over $1 million from Kincaid's apartment, a three-room studio flat in a high-end part of town. The room was dominated by an array of electronics, including a mammoth big-screen television and stereo system, as well a king-sized bed, overflowing with down pillows and draped in blood-red sheets that would have made any style expert wince.

Underneath the bed was the money, still in the same duffel bag that had been lifted from the trunk of the Camaro months before. Rather than count by hand, the team had taken the money to a Las Vegas bank and used the cash counter there to expedite the process. The money count from the bank was $1,103,040, and the bag was placed in evidence at the marshal's office.

Extradition from Nevada was a certainty as the state of Illinois was the site of jurisdiction, and Kincaid, still showing the white flag of surrender, again waived his rights. With the issue of extradition settled, McIntire and Miller could quickly fly to Las Vegas to bring Kincaid back, which was not only protocol but also a final touch for the men who had given so much of their lives to bring Kincaid to justice. A Learjet belonging to the state of Illinois was provided for transport, and McIntire and Miller quickly made arrangements to fly out two days later, on December 21.

Any celebration, however, was muted. Miller had plenty on his plate for the rest of the workday, as the Kincaid case was not the only file that sat on his desk, and dozens of newer, fresher cases had arisen in the months since. McIntire, meanwhile, had a schedule full of meetings that required his attention, leaving him little time to revel in any satisfaction of ending the Kincaid saga.

When Miller finally arrived home, his moody daughter, angry again at the world for whatever reason, scarcely spoke as he walked in the door. In the kitchen, Julie was flustered from a telephone quarrel with her sister, and her emotions ran higher as Miller announced he was flying to Vegas in the morning, hardly sharing his enthusiasm at closing the case with Christmas less than a week away. Needing a way to soothe Julie as well as a respite for himself, he offered to pick up their son at basketball practice and offered to get a bucket of chicken for dinner on the way back.

Normally, R.J. McIntire had the longer drive of the two, as he routinely made the forty-mile drive from his Chatham home to District 18 headquarters. This time, though, Miller had the longer run, going from Litchfield to the Springfield airport.

The next morning was brilliant in its sunshine, creating a glistening reflection off the festive Christmas decorations that lined the front yards and telephone poles. But the temperature read 16 degrees as Miller made the drive up from Litchfield, fully expecting McIntire to beat him to the airport, which he did. They shook hands, exchanged a couple of offhanded pleasantries at their relief and satisfaction, and boarded the Learjet.

While not as luxurious as a corporate jet, the plane offered comfortable surroundings, and the men settled into their seats, plugged in their laptops, and reviewed the facts of the Kincaid case as the Learjet soared silently, first over the plains, then the mountains, before crossing the deserts of Nevada on the way to McCarran International Airport, on the south side of Las Vegas.

*****

Rita Dykes had sent a car for them at McCarran, which transported them to her office. There, Kincaid sat waiting in handcuffs, having just been brought up from the Clark County Jail, where he had spent a sleepless night. Though he sat slouched over in a ladderback chair, disgraced and humiliated, the shock of the previous day had worn off, and he still had a little arrogance left in him. He straightened up as his eyes met McIntire and Miller's.

"Wondered when you two'd get here. What took you so long?" scoffed Kincaid, holding his hands up to display the cuffs. "Nice moment for ya, huh?"

McIntire and Miller, trained not to respond to the trash talk of criminals, remained silent. They handled all the necessary paperwork with Dykes, who summoned for the bag of money to be carried in from the evidence room. Ron Wilton, who had been contacted by McIntire, waited outside, hoping to have a moment with his old friends who had become intertwined in a freak occurrence on his vacation.

After finishing up the paperwork for Kincaid's release and the release of the money, McIntire and Miller greeted Wilton out in the hallway, taking a minute or two to catch up and thank him for his part in apprehending Kincaid. Then it was time to leave. McIntire and Miller escorted Kincaid, still in cuffs, to the waiting car for the trip to the airport and the flight back to Illinois.

For months, Kincaid had directed his enmity at others in law enforcement, somehow blaming them for his woes. Now, as the Learjet raced above the plains on the trip back to Springfield, he threw a few more verbal jabs for his captors, which McIntire and Miller ignored.

Four hours later, the Learjet was taxiing down the runway in Springfield. Once off the plane, Kincaid was transported to McIntire's vehicle and placed in the back seat with Miller. They then hauled Kincaid to his next stop, the Montgomery County Jail in Hillsboro.

Months earlier, Kincaid had been toasted by reporters for his honesty, and pitied for his wounds in the shooting at the trailer. Now, some of those same reporters shoved microphones in his face as he was escorted to the jail, with questions like "Do you have anything to say for yourself?" and "Why did you do it?" Kincaid said nothing in reply, turning his face to the ground to avoid looking into the cameras.

Back in Hillsboro that evening, he tried to ignore the strains of the television as the ten o'clock news with an anchor dramatically reporting that "a wayward area cop who thought he could steal a million dollars and caused a woman's death is now behind bars."

It was the final indignity in a day full of them for James Kincaid, who glanced at the crescent moon that hung above his cell on this chilly December evening. He turned around to see the imposing, vertical dark gray bars that provided one wall of the cell that encased him. He lay on his cot, stared at the white-block ceiling illuminated in the dim light, and dreaded what would come next.

CHAPTER 54

While Kincaid remained stoic in his cell, his beloved bag of money, the focus of an endless string of foul choices, ended up in District 18 headquarters.

The media continued to have a field day with the case, as the national morning news shows all reported on the sensational story of the Illinois state cop who stole a million dollars, got his girlfriend killed, and then ripped off someone else's identity so he could run off to Vegas. On the couch at Fox News, the anchors acted in disbelief as they discussed how this "crackpot lawman" had "embarrassed all the great first responders of this country." Over at CNN and MSNBC, the anchors and self-styled social experts told of "yet another cop gone wrong in America."

Kincaid, though, paid little heed to the reports, as he had other things lined up. The morning after Christmas was his initial court appearance, as he was to be arraigned in a Hillsboro courtroom on official misconduct, theft over, and filing false police reports.

In that courtroom, he would face Brad Collins, the Montgomery County state's attorney, who had worked with McIntire and Miller throughout the case.

His stance on crime and support of law enforcement had just resulted in his fourth straight election victory in November.

Collins had scant use for rogue cops like Kincaid, who could also count on little support from Gerald Gregg, the judge assigned to the case. Gregg, a balding, bespectacled, fifty-something man whose erect posture accentuated his thin build, likewise had campaigned on fairness and justice, and he had made good on that promise in his eight years on the bench. He spoke little, and when he did open his mouth, it was usually direct.

The hearing was set for 11 a.m., and it was a short walk from the courthouse to the jail. Two Montgomery County sheriff's deputies accompanied Kincaid, now dressed in an orange jumpsuit with "Montgomery County Jail" in black lettering on the back. Kincaid did not know the younger of the two deputies, but he was familiar with the older one, a portly, sandy-haired sixty-two-year-old named Forrest Harmon. Their paths had crossed over the years while on patrol, and Kincaid always found a way to be condescending to Harmon, never believing that county cops were his equal.

Today, however, the tables were turned. Minutes before, Harmon strode into Kincaid's jail cell, held up the handcuffs as if to taunt Kincaid, and flashed a hint of a smile across his jowls. "Been a while, hasn't it, Jim?" he said, clearly relishing the moment. Kincaid offered no reply, simply sticking out his wrists to await the click of the cuffs.

A few reporters with their cameramen, dotted the few hundred yards along the sidewalk from the jail to the courtroom, and Kincaid remained silent as they shouted questions. A passing car also honked derisively at Kincaid during the short, yet agonizing, stroll.

Inside the courtroom, Kincaid was reminded of the ongoing media circus when he spied a sketch artist, hired by the news crews to provide a visual reference to the proceedings. The courtroom had been closed to onlookers, which suited Kincaid just fine. Judge Gregg entered the courtroom, shoulders stretching to the sky underneath his black robe, and quickly moved to the matter at hand. McIntire and Miller were in attendance, watching every moment.

Kincaid was told to stand as he was advised of the charges. Judge Gregg asked Kincaid of his plea, and the reply was "not guilty." Bond was then set at $250,000. Facing the judge with his hands cuffed in front of him, he only nodded and said "yes sir" to Gregg's gruff questions and directives. Now without his precious bag of money and with his accounts frozen, Kincaid had no means to hire legal representation, so the Montgomery County public defender, Thomas Franklin, was appointed for counsel.

In a brief conversation with Franklin, Kincaid decided that a guilty plea was the only option. The evidence against him was mountainous, Debbie lay dead in her grave as a result of those misdeeds, and there were plenty of witnesses who could be lined up to testify against Kincaid's character. A court fight simply delayed the inevitable, and Kincaid, defeated and disgraced, simply wanted to get the matter over with. In his next appearance before Judge Gregg on January 25, he changed his plea to guilty.

The proceeding was done in minutes, and Kincaid was escorted back to the jail with the two deputies on either side. As they walked, they passed a St. Louis TV newswoman, dressed in tight jeans and designer knee boots below her blue North Face jacket, doing a live report on "the bad-boy cop who thought he was above the law and left people dead in his wake."

*****

The sentencing date was set for Thursday, February 16, and Kincaid's home until then would be his county jail cell. On bright days, a few rays of sunshine penetrated his window and reflected on the opposite wall, while on the worst of the gray days, the rain pounded on the roof and sounded a little like the gunfire that had reverberated in the trailer on the night that Debbie died. As he whiled away the hours, rain or shine, day or night, he wondered what would happen next: how long the sentence would be, what his future prison and its level of security would be, and how the other inmates would react to him.

He also pondered if anyone would come to visit, though his feelings on that subject were decidedly mixed. Part of him longed to see Judy, still missing the idyllic life he had thrown away so many years before, dreaming that he could somehow return to it, though knowing it was hopeless. But he also knew the crushing shame if she were to see him through the bars, dressed in his jumpsuit, disgrace heaped on him from his string of choices.

He felt the reverse for Sharon, as he thought she would come to visit solely to laugh at him. That image in his mind was usually followed by a fantasy of reaching his hands through the bars, trying to strangle her in disgust. Debbie's remaining family, particularly sweet Shannon, the loyal daughter who blindly trusted her mother's judgment in the boyfriend that helped get her killed, was not likely to stop by any time soon, much to Kincaid's relief. But he mostly dreaded a visit from his mother, wheelchair-bound in her retirement home, knowing there would be no way to face her without breaking down.

As it was, Kincaid needn't have worried, for none of those people bothered to come. The only contact he had was an emotional letter from Imelda, his girlish ex-lover in Arizona, who had seen the national news reports and took the opportunity to rip him in writing for his selfishness and her broken heart. The note, on bubblegum-pink paper topped with the image of a teddy bear, was written in her usual overdone cursive, complete with circles over every "i" and closing with the biting words "I hope you rot in hell."

The remainder of human interaction came in the form of informal banter with the county prison guards, who showed far less inclination to talk to Kincaid than vice versa. The boredom was punctuated by a longing for sex, as Kincaid had spent years ensuring he would get some whenever he wanted it. The only female he had any access to, however, was the custodian, a chunky, tired-looking sort named Bobbi, who had cleaned for the county for over half of the fifty-seven years since her birth in the tiny nearby village of Donnellson.

Her scraggly dyed-blond hair, rubbery skin, and bulging forearms had seldom attracted men, though Kincaid seemed interested as he flirted with her from behind bars while she swept the hallway. Her lonely mind was tempted, fantasizing about a red-hot, illicit romance with one of the inmates she was supposed to avoid, finally being in the arms of a loving man. But she eventually decided her pension was more important, to Kincaid's frustration.

Kincaid also met periodically with the public defender, Franklin, who was willing to devote only the bare minimum to the case. Franklin, a thirty-three-year-old with slicked-back dark hair, styled goatee, and bigger dreams than being a small-town public defender, frequently took calls on his cell phone during meetings with Kincaid, sometimes from headhunters helping him look for lucrative jobs with big private firms. Since Kincaid decided to plead guilty, there really wasn't much to do anyway, and Franklin planned on playing one of the few cards available to him, trying to sell the judge on Kincaid's many years of public service in asking for leniency.

After twenty-three days of a dragging calendar, the sentencing date finally arrived, though this time fewer reporters were on hand, having moved on to more pressing news, like traffic snarls and the latest shootings. As Kincaid was steered by two deputies, including the smirking Forrest Harmon, back to the courtroom, the winter sun shone brightly above, blinding him and making him long for the dark sunglasses that he loved to wear with his trooper's uniform.

The proceeding was over in a matter of hours as McIntire and Miller again looked on. Brad Collins, as expected, presented an intricate case against Kincaid, with plenty of detail on the choices that began with the money in the trunk of the Camaro and had spread into a spider web of lies and deceit. His actions, argued Collins, had taken Debbie's life and violated the public trust a state policeman was duty bound to uphold. Collins bolstered his case with a string of exhibits, including Kincaid's bank records, his police reports relating to the bag of money, and the accounts of his life on the run in Las Vegas under an assumed name.

Franklin fulfilled his obligation by stressing Kincaid's many years on the ISP and that he had no prior police record. He added that Kincaid was remorseful for his actions and wished to apologize to everyone involved in the matter. As Franklin's words echoed in the nearly empty courtroom, Kincaid nodded in agreement, hoping Judge Gregg would notice and sympathize.

He didn't. Gregg went strictly by the book. After a brief admonishment of "shaming your fellow law enforcement officers" and "undermining the trust the public must have in its police force," he proceeded to sentence Kincaid along set guidelines, ignoring the minimum that Franklin had half heartedly begged for.

For the charges of official misconduct, theft over, and false police reports, James Kincaid was sentenced to eight years in prison, to begin immediately. After his release, he was also ordered to spend five years on parole. The crack of Judge Gregg's gavel rung in Kincaid's ears as he was swiftly led out of the courtroom and past the gauntlet of television cameras on the return to the county jail.

That night on the 10 p.m. news, Shannon Marks, tears smearing her mascara, turned to the camera and shrieked, "My mother is dead, and all he gets is eight years?" In the same segment, Brad Collins tersely noted the sentencing guidelines, adding, "People like James Kincaid can't be allowed to run roughshod over the public good. We have a duty to bring them to justice." As the segment ended, viewers had their last glimpse of Kincaid, in his orange jumpsuit and silver handcuffs with his head bowed in shame, being led silently away by men in the same profession he had disgraced with his choices.

CHAPTER 55

A drizzling rain added to the humidity of this August morning as James Kincaid pulled on a light blue T-shirt, the usual cool dress for this time of year. Though it was his first day as a free man, he found little reason to celebrate.

Just yesterday, he was an inmate at the Rend Lake Correctional Facility near Ina in southern Illinois, completing the sentence handed down by Judge Gregg at the behest of Brad Collins in a spartan Hillsboro courtroom. Thanks to good behavior and the prison overcrowding issue, Kincaid was released after serving forty-two months of his eight-year sentence.

He kept mostly to himself during his incarceration, choosing not to antagonize the cliques and gangs that dominated the prison yards. With plenty of time to spare and no desire to connect with other inmates, Kincaid devoured every book and newspaper he could find, becoming a regular in the prison library and forcing interest in any subject he hadn't already read.

He also worked on his fitness, spending some time in the prison gym, and managed to shed a few pounds from his protruding gut while taking some points off his blood pressure. He also began shaving his head in prison, ridding himself of the beard he had grown in his months as James Wilson and the longish strands that he tried to grow beyond the receding hairline of James Kincaid.

The solitude of prison helped Kincaid ease his addiction for alcohol, but he still loved the smokes and reached for a cigarette whenever possible. His bottomless pit of lust had to go on hold, though, as women were scarce at the Rend Lake facility, and for once, Kincaid didn't seem to care. Though he was propositioned a couple of times by gay inmates, he naturally declined, choosing to retain his masculine sexuality, one of the few things he could hold on to these days.

Years before, he had scoffed whenever Johnny Cash's hit "Folsom Prison Blues" came on the radio, particularly the line "If they freed me from this prison / If that railroad train were mine." Never one to shy from sarcasm, Kincaid always managed to make a crack at that "dumbass prisoner, thinking he could ride that train when he knows damn well he can't."

Now, the song took on some irony as Kincaid was just a short distance from Rend Lake, the massive man-made reservoir that gave the prison its name. Rend Lake is a sportsman's paradise that draws tourists from across the region, known for its great fishing on the glistening blue water and prime hunting on its tree-lined shores. Remembering the hours spent in his bass boat, one of the few pastimes he truly enjoyed, Kincaid longed to be on the gentle waves of the lake, free of the bars and barbed wire, casting his hook in the water until something yanked it from below.

He had ample time to think about the lake or read the latest book he found in the library. None of his family or friends called or came to visit, save for his sister, Maureen or "Mo," who was still the rebel of the family. Standing five-foot seven with a pixie cut that was normally preferred by vain younger women, Mo had just turned fifty the previous year, though she hardly looked her age, thanks to dark brown hair dye and the heaps of Avon moisturizers she bought from her next-door neighbor.

Kincaid and Mo had drifted apart over the years and actually saw little of each other as Kincaid blew through marriages and moved from trailer to trailer. But as the rest of his family washed their hands of Kincaid and tried to move on, Mo, as usual, chose the different path.

About six weeks into his sentence, Mo paid a surprise visit to Kincaid, creating an awkward conversation across the glass pane that separated prisoners from their guests. On the closed-circuit telephone, they exchanged a few words, such as "How've you been?" and "Are they treating you all right in this place?" before Mo decided it was time to go, needing three-plus hours for the drive back home.

She made the drive to the prison a couple more times over the next few months, including one visit just after Kincaid learned of his impending release. Having lost everything, he had nowhere to go after he walked out, and she knew it. Hearing her voice through the phone across the glass pane, he was surprised to hear her say, "You know, Jim, if you need a place to stay, I've got room."

Mo's kids were both in high school now, and her dreams of the empty nest could not come fast enough. The rest of the Kincaid family made no move to help their wayward relative, remembering his sarcasm and arrogance, as well as the scandal that remained fresh in their minds. Mo, however, liked to tweak people, a trait she shared with Jim, and seemed to revel in the disdain of her ailing mother and siblings.

As Kincaid rose on his first morning under Mo's roof, he listened to the strains of the radio from the kitchen and the Aaron Tippin country hit "Kiss This," one of her favorites. While his relief from his release was like a tsunami, he also knew his future had plenty of potholes. He was on a work-release program and needed a job, but for an ex-con in his mid-fifties, the options were few. He also had piles of debt, as his domestic support obligations to Judy and Sharon continued, since such judgments normally stick with a defendant for life.

Browsing the classifieds of the Springfield paper, he found few opportunities for someone in his situation. He had spent time in prison pondering his future as well, and one possibility was obtaining a commercial driver's license, or CDL. With that, he could become a truck driver, though the irony was not lost, even on him. Truckers and law enforcement have a natural rivalry, and Kincaid had always hated the attitudes of most guys in the big rigs, who always try to stay one step ahead of the law and often think the rules of the road are for someone else.

Now, he was thinking of going over to the other side. Using Mo's computer, he looked up the requirements for a CDL and, the next day, discussed the possibility with his parole officer and work-release program supervisor. Kincaid filed the application with the Lincoln Land Community College truck driver training program in Springfield, borrowed the money for the required fees from Mo, and submitted to the necessary medical checks. His blood pressure, now lower, was not as much of a problem, which also helped the process along.

After the six-week training, Kincaid took the skills test, which he passed with relative ease, and the written test, which was a little more difficult, since he had been bored with the study guide. Applicants have to correctly answer 80 percent of the questions, which Kincaid did, with no room to spare. As a result, James Kincaid, the disgraced cop trying to rebuild his life, became the proud owner of a CDL.

Next came the job search, and he began asking around, seeing if any of the local trucking companies needed a driver. Since he didn't have transportation of his own, Kincaid drove one of Mo's two cars. Her primary car was a white Dodge Stratus, but she also had a yellow Volkswagen Golf with a huge scratch along the passenger side, a missing taillight lens, and a rear window held in place with blue duct tape. Reflecting his sister's carefree attitude, the car was adorned with a vanity plate that read "BABY MO." Kincaid felt silly driving the Golf, but no other wheels were available, and he needed something to get around in as he hit many of the trucking firms in the area.

But the stigma of a felony, coupled with Kincaid's past arrogance, made the process difficult. Most times, Kincaid would walk into a dispatch office, ask if the company was hiring, and hear the supervisor reply offhandedly, "Yeah, we're looking for someone." The next words, however, usually ended the process. When Kincaid gave his name, the tone changed entirely, as a couple of blow-off questions were followed with the supervisors saying, "We'll call you," which they never did.

After a week or so, Kincaid was still hopeful, though dejected. Mo, worn out from a tough day at her job as a teacher's aide, didn't feel like cooking that particular evening and asked if Kincaid wanted to go out.

"Hell yeah," he said, with one condition based on his financial state. "But it's gotta be your treat."

Mo snickered. "Oh, all right. At least you can clean this place for me tomorrow." Kincaid snickered, pulled himself off the burnt-orange couch that also doubled as his bed, and reached for his jacket. They took Mo's Dodge Stratus, which Kincaid offered to drive.

He didn't ask where Mo wanted to go because he knew already. She was a regular at McClintock's Saloon and Steak House just outside Standard City, which had become a hotspot for the locals in its years of existence. Located in a renovated building that formerly housed a seed company, McClintock's featured country entertainment, homestyle food, and friendly service to its hard-working customers, who came from across the county and beyond.

While Mo was at McClintock's as often as her checkbook would allow, Kincaid hadn't been there in a long while. He was a bit edgy at the thought of walking through the door, as people tended to stare and turn away from him, awkward reminders of his checkered past. He also remembered that Debbie had liked the plac and they had dined there often, sometimes having a tough time finding their way back to White City in their resulting inebriation. He and Judy had also dined there from time to time.

Kincaid didn't plan on drinking that way on this evening, as he had been forced to kick the habit while behind bars at Rend Lake. Rather, he had a hankering for a steak and told the waitress as such as he ordered one, along with fries and a small salad, a half-hearted effort to keep down his waistline. Mo ordered the shrimp dinner and turned to Kincaid and asked, "You're driving home, right?" When he answered in the affirmative, she ordered a pitcher of beer.

Kincaid had one glass out of the pitcher, while Mo took care of the rest. Sullen when they walked in the door, Mo loosened up as she drained the pitcher, and she wisecracked through the rest of the meal. Most of the other diners in the room stared at them, shaking their heads as Mo grew louder and louder, whispering their amazement at Kincaid's early release from a relatively short sentence.

One man, however, did not join in. Larry "Mousie" Steward was the owner of the place and had known Kincaid for years, due to his patronage of McClintock's. Steward was one of the rare people that had remained on friendly terms with Kincaid throughout the winding road that had brought him to this point. Their paths had first crossed during Kincaid's earlier days as a trooper, and Steward never failed to tell Kincaid "how good-looking that wife of yours," Judy, was. He also never seemed to judge when that marriage evaporated in favor of Sharon, the waitress, who had also flirted with Larry over coffee at the Busy Bee.

As the years passed and Larry opened McClintock's, he always welcomed Kincaid and his latest flame, Debbie, whenever they drove up from White City for dinner and drinks. Larry had even tried to lure Debbie away from Russell Martin, promising her a higher wage and better tips if she ever wanted to give McClintock's a try.

A couple of times, Larry had asked Mo about her brother, which she had relayed to Kincaid. So when Kincaid looked up from his seat along the wall and saw Larry start to pick his way through the tables in the middle of the room, heading toward him, he felt no apprehension.

Larry was in his usual attire on this night, bib overalls and a blue-and-white checkered cotton shirt that hung from his six-foot frame. His gray hair clung around his gold-rimmed glasses, which revealed his bifocals. He pulled out a chair from the next table, turned it backwards and sat down, resting his arms on the top of the ladderback. Peering over his bifocal line, he offered a cordial greeting to Kincaid.

"How are ya, Jim?" he said, extending his open palm. "Been a while, hasn't it?"

"Sure has. Damn nice to be here," said Kincaid, stating the obvious as he stuck out his hand to clasp Steward's. He looked around the room. "I've missed it here. Where I've been, the food wasn't worth a shit compared to this place."

Steward chuckled. "Yeah, I bet. When'd you get out?"

"About two months ago. Been staying with Mo," said Kincaid, mindlessly pointing at her. "She told me I could sleep on her couch, never telling me the springs were shot or that it smelled like someone died on it."

"Go to hell, Jim," said Mo in mock protest, her speech slurring. "I don't give the assholes the good stuff. Whenever I have a real man over, he gets to sleep in my bed and can lay wherever he wants. On top of me or underneath." She cackled with laughter so loudly that patrons at neighboring tables turned their heads, and then she poured herself another glass.

Steward snickered at the exchange, then turned his attention back to Kincaid. "So how're you doin'? Are you workin', or what?"

"Trying to," said Kincaid, between mouthfuls of steak. "I just completed my training for a CDL a few days ago, and I've been looking around, seeing if anyone needs a driver." He sighed. "But you know, with my background. Once they hear who I am and where I have been, they turn tail and tell me to kiss their ass."

"Yeah, yeah," replied Steward, shaking his head in sympathy. "Must be tough."

"Sure is." Kincaid's reply was muffled, amid bites of the fries. "You know of anyone who'd take a chance on me? You know a helluva lot more people than I do, and there's gotta be someone who needs a driver, whether he's a felon or not."

Steward nodded his head in thought. "Actually, there is a guy. His name is Jim Brown. Most people call him Chubby Brown, and he's got a trucking firm over in Carlinville. I talked to him the other night he was in here. He started telling me that he was shorthanded and had more loads than he knew what to do with. He might be looking for someone."

Kincaid nodded in pleasure. "Sounds good. Do you have the guy's cell number on you so I could call him later on?"

"I'll do you one better," said Steward, waving his hand. "I'll call him right now." He reached in the front right pocket of his bibs and pulled out his smartphone, hitting Brown's number on speed dial.

Steward was slightly hard of hearing and had the receiver volume turned on high. As a result, Kincaid could hear most of the conversation himself, sitting a couple of feet away.

The voice on the other end sounded older and gravelly, but direct. "Larry, how are ya? Whatcha need?"

"Well, remember we were talking in here the other night, and you mentioned you might need a driver? I may have one for you."

"Oh, yeah?" said Brown offhandedly. "Who?"

"Jim Kincaid. He's sitting right here with me now."

"Oh." Kincaid could hear a decided pause on the other end and figured his reputation had preceded him, once again. Just then, Brown started talking again. "Well, has he ever drove a truck?"

"No, but he just got his CDL and wants to find work. Seems to be doing all right, as far as I can tell."

"Well…" Brown's voice trailed off, causing Kincaid to again think his chances were over. "I could sure use a guy. I got loads I've put on hold…just got work up the ass."

Steward seized the opportunity. "Tell you what. How about if I have Jim back here tomorrow night, say around six o'clock? You could come out here and meet him and talk it over."

"Sure," cracked Brown. "And that way, you'll get my business, too."

"Oh shit," laughed Steward. "Fine. Tell you what. The first drink is on me."

"Hell, I'm there," roared Brown. "Six tomorrow night then. Just have Kincaid in the place when I get there." He then signed off with "Later."

Steward chuckled and hung up. He shrugged slightly at Kincaid, as if to say "told you." Kincaid thanked Steward for his efforts, one of the few people that had tried to help since his release, other than the now-tipsy Mo. He finished his dinner as Mo finished the pitcher, and he helped her to the Stratus for the drive home.

CHAPTER 56

As Kincaid was helping Mo up the front walk in her inebriated state late that evening, Diego Garcia sat in the grand parlor of his secluded compound near Ciudad Juarez, staring at the walls, lost in reflection as the soft strains of Mexican folk music murmured across the room. His wife, Rosa, had retired to her suite as usual, leaving him alone with his thoughts, as she had since the death of Juan Rodrequs years before.

Garcia slept little, normally going to bed late and rising early. As the head of the most powerful cartel on the border, he expected everyone else to adhere to his schedule. Though most do not like receiving telephone calls past 10:00, Garcia was still awake and active, so he figured everyone else should be, too. The clock read 12:09 when he dialed the number of his top distributor in Chicago, Tyrone Williams.

That name struck fear in the hearts of most men on the streets of south Chicago, and that was just how Williams liked it. Thanks to his affiliation with Garcia, Williams had raked in tens of millions in the drug trade, and his mansion not only had the finest furniture and electronics that money could buy, but also five luxury cars, ranging from Cadillacs to Hummers, were parked in his garage. With his power and money, Williams could have his pick of any whore he wanted, and on this night, he had two, Farrah and Jacqui, who jabbed their forearms with needles containing the heroin they craved and then peeled off their clothes to please Tyrone as he desired.

He had just ordered Farrah to kiss his neck and pointed Jacqui to lower parts of his body as the phone on his marble-top vanity rang. Neglecting to read the caller ID, Williams, interrupted in the midst of his manly pleasure, snapped, "Hold on a sec, bitches," to his visitors, who both fell back on the king-sized poster bed, their veins flowing from their latest fix. Williams' temper was raging, and he yelled into the receiver, "What the hell do ya want?"

Garcia was not used to being spoken to with such insolence and rudeness. "Excuse me, senor?" he said incredulously, the anger apparent in his voice.

"Oh, Diego, my man!" Williams knew he had riled his top supplier and sought to smooth it over. "So sorry, man, so sorry. Thought you was someone else. I was just getting ready for bed, you know, and I thought it was one of my guys."

"Hmm," sniffed Garcia. "Well, I am not 'one of your guys,' as you put it."

"No, no, no," replied Williams nervously. "I mean, you're my main man. You know me, we been together for years. I'd do anything for ya."

"Well, I've got something for you," said Garcia in a patronizing tone. "You remember the man who stole the million dollars from us? The state policeman, James Kincaid?"

"Remember? Hell, I never forgot the son of a bitch," Williams clenched a fist, his anger still evident from the incident over five years before. "I always said I'd put that mother's ass in the ground for what he did to you. Not a day goes by I don't think about how he screwed us."

Williams was laying it on thick, and Garcia knew it. But he chose to remain in the moment. "I never forgot Kincaid either," he replied coolly. "I was wondering, what ever happened to him? Is he still in prison, or what became of him?"

"Shit, I don't know," said Williams. "I know they sent his ass to some prison in southern Illinois. Hope one of my boys was there and made a girl out of him."

Garcia ignored the coarseness of that comment. "I want you to find out what happened to Kincaid. Let me know if he is still in prison, or when he's getting out. Or, if he's already been released, then tell me what he's doing right now."

"Hell yeah," replied Williams. "Just say the word, and I'll cut his ass up like nothin' you ever saw. I got the guys here to do it, and I'll have it done for ya just like that," he said, snapping his fingers for effect.

"No, that is not what I want," said Garcia tersely, imposing his will over Williams. "I only want the information. Nothing more."

"All right, all right, no problem." Williams backed down, knowing he had overstepped. "I'll get my guys on it and get whatcha need."

"Very well. And do it soon" Garcia hung up without a goodbye and then rose from his overstuffed, genuine leather easy chair to stroll about his parlor, pondering his next move.

CHAPTER 57

Kincaid correctly suspected that Jim Brown was not one to wait. Rather than run the risk of showing up late, he arrived at McClintock's at 5:45 the next evening in the yellow Golf and ordered a hamburger and fries for himself, having borrowed twenty dollars from Mo so he could pick up his own tab. With such an important meeting, Kincaid chose not to order alcohol, instead settling for a Sprite.

At 6:03, a man in his early seventies pushed through the door and into the dining room. He walked rather erectly for a man his age, though the fading hairline and silver-gray hair gave one an idea of his days on earth. Dressed in a dark blue shirt and bib overalls and wearing a dark brown hat, he looked like a man who owned trucks, so Kincaid had an idea that Chubby Brown had arrived. His suspicions were confirmed when Steward strode across the room, shook hands with the man, and pointed toward Kincaid's table.

The man cracked a quick joke with Steward, roared with laughter, and headed for Kincaid. "Jim Brown," he said bluntly, extending his hand. Kincaid grasped the hand and Brown sat down. Brown immediately motioned the waitress over, told her that he did not need a menu, and ordered a sirloin, a loaded baked potato, and a bottle of Coors to wash it down.

Kincaid was anxious about discussing his recent past, but Brown did not seem particularly interested. Instead, a lengthy conversation ensued on Kincaid's work habits, his knowledge of the trucking industry, his willingness to handle long hauls, and his ability to do what he was told. Needing a job and with nothing to tie him down, Kincaid was willing to take practically anything that Brown offered.

"You know, I do a lot of business with ADM in Decatur," Brown said, referring to a city of 75,000 some seventy miles northeast. Decatur was the home of Archer Daniels Midland, or ADM, one of the top food producers in the nation, and the headquarters of one of the biggest trucking operations in the Midwest.

"They've contracted with me for years now, and they know I can get the job done. They don't get any shit from me," continued Brown, immodestly. "I ain't like the other guys who own trucks. I'm a businessman first, pure and simple, and I get it done. I've been in this business for over fifty years and worked my ass off the whole damn time. I run twelve trucks now and got so much work that none of them are sitting empty. That's why I get a brand-new Cadillac every two years," he said, pointing to the parking lot as he continued.

"I got a need for a guy to run Houston. The last guy I had on that run took another job and left me high and dry, and the truck is just sitting." Brown removed his hat and ran his hands over his bald head and exhaled deeply in frustration. "So I've been goin' around in circles and need to hire someone damn quick.

"What you'd do is run up to Decatur with the tractor and trailer," he explained. "There, you'd pick up cooking oil at ADM and haul it down to their Houston plant. Then you'd drive across town to this other place I do business with.

"Once you're there, you will load the trailer with bananas," continued Brown, "and bring it back to St. Louis. You'd drop off the load there, and dead head back here."

"What is it to Houston from here in miles, around 800 or 850 or something?" inquired Kincaid.

"Yeah, around 700. Can't remember the exact number," replied Brown. "The round trip pays $1,050 plus expenses and takes three days or so."

"Fine by me," said Kincaid jocularly, hiding his anxiety as he referred to his felonious past. "You know my history, right?"

"Oh, hell, I know all about it," said Brown, waving his hand as if to dismiss the thought. "Doesn't bother me. I've had plenty of run-ins with the law myself. Got out of most of them, but they stick it to you, no matter how they come out. I ain't gonna judge you, or any other man, because of their past. Like I've told people, I don't care what type of man works for me. I only care about what type of driver he is."

Kincaid tried hard to stifle a sigh of relief. "So, are you offering me this job?"

"Yep. I'll hire you on a temporary basis. You'll get the $1,050, some benefits, things like that. After a while, if it's working out, I'll put you on full time. If it comes to that, you'll make more money, and the longer you stay, I'll keep bumping up your pay. You'll also get full benefits, like retirement, health insurance, all the good stuff."

The offer sounded great to Kincaid, but he had some details to take care of. "Well, I'll have to check with my parole officer about leaving the state," he said. "But I don't think that will be a problem. So, I'm in."

"I'll go with you the first trip or so to show you the ropes. But after that you're on your own," said Brown as he slapped his open palm on the table, reflecting his satisfaction. "All right. I need you to start on Monday. I've been putting off ADM as long as I can while I've been shorthanded, and I got to get that first load to Houston yesterday."

"Monday's all right." Kincaid played it cool in his usual style, knowing that he needed the paychecks to start, and fast. He also had to make sure he could connect with his parole officer by then. "What time do you want me to leave?"

"Get to the shop around five in the morning. I'll be there and walk you through the truck I'm putting you in." Brown then reached into his shirt pocket and withdrew a business card with the address of his trucking business, which he handed to Kincaid.

"No problem," said Kincaid, gesturing toward Brown's sirloin, which had just arrived at the table. "That one's on me." He was bluffing, knowing that the twenty-dollar bill in his pocket would not cover both his meal and Brown's.

"Oh, hell no," said Brown through a mouthful. "I ain't gonna take your money. Besides, I know what you drive," he said, again pointing toward the parking lot. "That yellow Volkswagen out there, with your sister's name on the plate. If you're driving that piece of shit, I know you ain't got nothing."

Kincaid hesitated for a moment and then opened up with the heartiest laugh that he had uttered in a while. Brown smirked back, and the two men finished their meals with some occasional small talk.

CHAPTER 58

Tyrone Williams knew that Garcia would not wait long on his demand. The next morning, he dialed the number of Brian Smart, his longtime attorney.

Or, former attorney. Smart had been kept on a string by Williams because of his insatiable heroin addiction, which finally caught up to him late one night when he heard a pounding on the door of his luxury condo. Within seconds, several DEA agents came bursting through, tipped off by a disgruntled former client with an axe to grind.

Thousands of dollars in illegal drugs were scattered about the condo, courtesy of Williams, who paid his retainer both in cash and controlled substance. Smart knew he could never rat on his top supplier, so he refused to answer any questions relating to Williams and declined any plea deal from the government. As a result, he was sentenced to three years in prison and was disbarred from the practice of law.

After serving nineteen months, he was released and, on his first day of freedom, resumed his addiction. Though he was no longer a lawyer, Williams had plenty of use for him as a legal advisor and gopher to any of his whims. As

Smart's addiction descended into hell, he relied on Williams more and more, and now he lived in a basement room of Williams' mansion, holed up and high for most of his waking hours when he was not needed for something.

Rather than walk downstairs, Williams just picked up the phone. Knowing the power he had over Smart, he no longer bothered with any semblance of civility. "Hey, bitch," were the words on the other end when Smart picked up the receiver. "Got something for ya."

Williams relayed the request from Garcia, telling Smart to "get your ass on it." Smart muttered something in the affirmative and moved right over to his computer, sensing that withdrawal symptoms were about to begin. He typed away on his keyboard, made a couple of calls, and learned that Kincaid had been released from Rend Lake Correctional Facility just a few weeks before. He also collected information on Kincaid's whereabouts, in his sister's home in Standard City.

Armed with these facts, he dialed upstairs to Williams, who scribbled the information down and signed off with, "All right, bitch. Got some product here for ya, so get your ass up here and get it." After Smart picked up his stash and left, Williams reached for the phone to call Diego Garcia.

Garcia never spoke as Williams provided each bit of information, simply saying "Thank you, senor" as he hung up. He thought for a moment, drumming his fingers together the whole time, planning what he wanted next.

CHAPTER 59

For over twenty years, James Kincaid had felt trapped in his squad car, hating the monotony and solitude of patrol as a state trooper, night after night up and down the highway. Now, in his new job as a truck driver, he kind of liked it.

In those days, Kincaid's work was in a state-of-the-art police car, equipped with the latest computer technology and enough electronics to leave any gadget guru breathless. Now, his office was a green 2008 Mack double-axle cabover with a sleeper and white cursive on each door, telling the world the truck belonged to DL Brown Trucking in Carlinville, Illinois.

The Mack was the oldest truck in Brown's fleet, and though no one else wanted to drive it, Kincaid had no problem with it. As he looked out its windshield at the broken center lines on the highway and the telephone poles that seemed to blend together as he raced by, he saw his next paycheck, and a fresh start.

In the darkness of the early hours of every Monday morning, Kincaid would make his way to Brown's terminal in Carlinville and climb into the Mack. He and Brown would then motor the seventy miles to the ADM plant in

Decatur, sometimes stopping for coffee and a bite to eat at Gert's, a hole-in-the-wall diner on the outskirts of Taylorville, a town of 8,000 just past the midway point between Carlinville and Decatur.

They usually arrived at ADM before 7 a.m. and exchanged some paperwork and a few words with Al Timberlake, one of the chief dispatchers at ADM, who steered Kincaid toward the docks. The silver reefer trailer held 8,000 gallons of cooking oil designated for the Houston plant. Kincaid quickly learned how to hook up a tractor-trailer, and a few minutes later, they were heading back down the two lanes to Interstate 55 for the drive southward.

As they did the loop from Decatur to Houston to St. Louis and back, Kincaid was faced with plenty of memories, and few of them were good. The drive from Carlinville to Decatur took him on Interstate 55, and he could look over to the frontage road of the southbound lanes and see the site where the Camaro had crashed on that fateful night in November years before, carrying the bags of money that sparked a string of poor choices.

The ride into Decatur and back to I-55 covered Illinois Route 48, part of which was the patrol route of Kincaid in his state trooper days. On that section was Raymond, his former home, where Judy still lived. On a couple of occasions, he looked out the side window of the Mack and saw Judy, driving her new black Buick Regal, sometimes with her new husband, Roger Daniels, the handsome vice president of a local bank. Judy had never wanted to leave the bungalow that Kincaid hated, and Roger understood, choosing to move in with her to set up a new household. In those moments that Judy and Roger were rolling by, Kincaid had to look away, lest he see the smile on Judy's face that always seemed to be a part of her new life.

The route to Texas took him through Missouri and Arkansas, and the latter state posed some discomfort. James Wilson, whose identity Kincaid had lifted in his flight, was from Arkansas, and Kincaid sometimes worried that he might run into the man himself. When he was captured, Kincaid expected that he would face additional charges for using Wilson's identity, but nothing ever happened, and Kincaid certainly had no stomach for more trouble. But he tried to limit his stops in the state of Arkansas, making sure he fueled up before he hit the state line and had eaten before he crossed over, leaving only a few stops to stretch his legs or grab some fresh air.

There were plenty of other times that Kincaid became bogged down in his mountain of baggage. Being in the cab alone gave him plenty of time to think, and he was still haunted by Debbie's death, the estrangement with his kids, the shame of his arrest and imprisonment. He well remembered the dark nights he stole the money from the Camaro and faked his death at Rip Rap, knowing those were two of many choices that had brought him here, sitting in the cab of the Mack, trying to make enough money to support himself and the wives and children he had left behind. Most of the time, however, Kincaid managed to suppress the memories, choosing to focus on the task at hand and the earnings that would be direct-deposited into his bank account four times a month.

It has often been said that prison can change a man, and three-and-a-half years behind bars certainly had an effect on Kincaid. Before, he was full of machismo, braggadocio, his ego so large it could hardly fit in his squad car. He loved shooting the breeze with anyone who would listen, talking about how tough his job was, how hard he worked, and how much money he made. Now, he stuck mostly to himself, sitting alone in the truck stops and diners, saying "Hey," "How are ya?" and little else to anyone who walked by. His voice, once the loudest in the room, was much quieter, and his personality, once angry and sullen, was stoic and sheepish.

His appearance was also different. He continued to shave his head bald and had continued losing weight, now carrying nearly twenty pounds less on his stocky frame than before. He dressed somewhat differently, foregoing the Western shirts of younger days for T-shirts and jeans. His ruddy complexion lightened as he stayed off the booze, and many people now did not recognize him. More than once, he ran into people he used to know, and they walked by as if he were a stranger, their stares blank and their thoughts lost in space, clearly not knowing they were passing the formerly arrogant cop who had stolen a ton of money, got his girlfriend killed, and faked his death, among his other long list of misdeeds.

Mobile homes were unpleasant memories for him, and though he never liked the house in Raymond, he looked for one this time. Apartments were not an option, as he longed for solitude and did not care for neighbors just a few feet away. A friend of Brown had a five-room fixer-upper on the east edge of Gillespie, twelve miles from the terminal in Carlinville, that he was offering contract-for-deed. Brown put in a good word for Kincaid and he moved in right away, saying farewell to Mo's couch as he put his few belongings in the bed of his new wheels, a brown 1999 Toyota Tundra with four mismatched tires and a missing tailgate, which he had seen for sale on the side of the road on his way back from Houston one day.

On the days he was not on the road, Kincaid either spent the time sleeping, watching television, or renovating his new place, if he was lucky enough to find some secondhand materials that he could afford. Neighbors rarely saw much of Kincaid, and some did not even know he was there. That was just the way Kincaid liked it. The last few years had taken an emotional toll, and he just wanted to be left alone.

Kincaid laughed to himself that if he had taken his years as a state cop as seriously as he did with trucking, his life would have been different as well. With little else in his life, his job became his purpose, and he did whatever Brown asked of him. He usually made runs from Decatur to Houston twice a week, racking up the miles that led to money. As the months passed, Brown hired him full-time, as promised, and increased his salary.

Though his bank account still had plenty of outflow, thanks to his domestic-support obligations, Kincaid was doing as well as could be expected, if not more so. He had become a responsible citizen once again, and a good employee, at least to hear Brown tell it. During the lonely nights in his cell, Kincaid had wondered if his life would be worth anything once he got out, and judging from his prior track record, there was plenty of reason for doubt. But now his world seemed all right as his mid-fifties approached, and Kincaid felt a satisfaction that he had made some good choices for a change.

As he pieced his life back together, he never noticed the older-model, black Hyundai that was sometimes in his rearview mirror. A small-built, shaggy-haired Mexican slouched in the front seat, not wanting to attract any attention, and even a former state trooper like Kincaid never took note. Without money and wishing to be anonymous, the Mexican spent his nights in the Hyundai, which he parked in a lonely back alley across town in Gillespie. For over a week this continued as the young Mexican stayed out of sight, just as Diego Garcia had instructed him.

CHAPTER 60

Kincaid had just dropped off the Mack in Carlinville and was heading to his Tundra for the drive home to Gillespie when Brown stepped out of the temporary trailer that had become his permanent dispatch office. It was late October, and a cool, damp breeze blew across the lot, forcing Brown to turn up his collar against the elements. As he did, he bellowed out to Kincaid, "Hey, Jim, I'm heading to McClintock's, hungrier than a son of a bitch. You wanna come along?"

"Sure," said Kincaid, who hadn't eaten since mid-morning. I'll follow you."

The two men tooled down the road, an odd pairing of vehicles as Brown drove his newest smoke-gray Cadillac, which he had just bought last week. Following behind was Kincaid, trying to keep up in his Tundra with its sluggish, well-worn acceleration and sun-faded exterior.

They reached McClintock's and were greeted by Steward with a hearty handshake and a couple of friendly wisecracks. Brown and Kincaid found a table by the window, where they usually sat, and waited for service. The waitress, a broad-shouldered woman in her forties named Connie, had worked for Steward for years and was familiar to both Kincaid and Brown.

In the past, Kincaid regularly flirted with women, but now, he rarely took the opportunity. Rather, he sat and smiled quietly as Brown played up to Connie, saying he'd "take a side order of her smile," and "if she cooked as good as she looked, well, he just might marry her." Connie played along, knowing that Brown was her best tipper, and wrote down his usual order of a sirloin, baked potato, and a Coors. Kincaid ordered the catfish and fries and was about to choose the Sprite when Brown chided him.

"Oh hell, Jim, you need something stronger than that," he said, turning to Connie. "Make that two Coors."

Kincaid rarely drank these days, but a beer sounded good, and he didn't want to argue with his boss. Brown scribbled some figures on a napkin as Kincaid sat back and relaxed, letting the tension out of his body after hundreds of miles in the cab.

Brown kept writing, lost in thought, as Kincaid stared at the walls, waiting for their food to hit the table. When Connie finally brought it over, Brown dropped his pen, said, "Thanks, hon," and dug in. Kincaid joined him, cutting through the breading on his catfish with a steak knife from his place setting.

"Damn good food here," said Brown after a few mouthfuls. "Sure am glad that Larry opened this place."

Kincaid nodded in agreement as he shook some catsup out on his plate for his fries. The two men spent several minutes in silence, too engrossed in their food to mutter any bits of conversation. Finally, Brown sat back, took a long swig of his Coors to wash down his dinner, and fixed his eyes on Kincaid.

"How's everything been workin' out for ya?" inquired Brown in his usual direct manner.

"Good, good," replied Kincaid, somewhat taken aback by the vague question. "I mean, the job's going well. Got no complaints."

"Is your parole officer satisfied?" inquired Brown.

"Yes, he is," replied Kincaid. "Got no problems there."

"Glad to hear it." Brown cut deeper into his baked potato, digging out the insides. "I always try to take care of my guys."

"You sure do," said Kincaid, who began to realize exactly what Brown had been asking. "Yeah, this job is just what I needed right now."

"Good. Anything else you need from me, just give me a holler." As he spoke, Connie stopped by the table to ask if the men needed anything. Brown replied, "Nothing, hon, doin' just fine," giving her a wink as she passed on.

Kincaid stuffed a couple of fries in his mouth and then put both of his elbows on the table and looked wistfully to one side. "You know, I'm really doing better right now than I ever thought I'd be. All that time I was sitting in prison, I had no idea what my life was gonna be like. Hell, I had no idea if I'd ever find a job, or what."

Brown nodded as he kept eating, and Kincaid kept talking. He put his fork and knife down and slumped his shoulders. "I knew that after everything that had happened, that my name was mud around here. I had kind of expected that, but it really didn't sink in until I started looking for jobs right after I got out.

"I drove that damn yellow Volkswagen of Mo's from place to place, every trucking outfit I could think of. And almost every time, I'd introduce myself or they'd see my name on the application, and it would be all over. I'd hear the same thing, 'Can't use you right now,' or 'We'll get back to you,' or some blow-off like that. One place even told me, 'We aren't hiring right now,' even though I walked in holding a copy of that day's newspaper with their ad that said they were hiring immediately."

"Doesn't surprise me," said Brown, reaching again for his Coors. "I've been in this business long enough to know when someone's blowing smoke up your ass. I've heard all that shit before."

"Yeah, no kidding." Kincaid took a sip off his own bottle of beer and looked straight at Brown across the table. His face softened, and his voice dropped in tone as his emotions began to flow. "You know, I really appreciate the fact that you gave me a chance. A lot of people wouldn't hire someone who's been in prison like I was. I owe you a hell of a lot, because this has really turned my life around."

"Aw, hell, don't mention it," replied Brown, waving his hand in dismissal. "Just glad I could help. And you've done a good job for me, which is all I wanted to begin with."

"Thanks. This has really helped get my life back in order." Kincaid leaned back in his seat, folded his arms, and looked aside once again. "And God knows I needed some of that. I've made a boatload of poor choices, one right after the other. When you're screwing up like that, you don't always think of what you're doing. But after a while, it catches up to you, and it's all you think about. Having this job helps keep my mind off it, because if I didn't, I'd probably go nuts."

"My daddy always said, 'A good day's work keeps you honest,'" chuckled Brown. "It sure as hell never hurt anybody."

Kincaid smiled and kept reminiscing. "When I look back on it, God, it's just been one thing after another, and I've only got myself to blame. I mean, look at my first wife. Did I ever tell you about her?"

"Not really." Brown's eyes were momentarily distracted by Connie, standing at the next table. "I knew you'd been married a couple of times but never paid much attention otherwise."

"Yeah, well, you're one of the few," laughed Kincaid. "My first wife was named Judy, great gal. She was tall, thin, dark-haired, just had it all in the right places, but that wasn't the only thing about her. She was smart, carried herself well, nice to talk to, just everything you could want in a girl.

"We were high school sweethearts, just did everything together. We'd go to football games, the prom, anything you could think of. God knows how many times we made out in the parking lot. Still can't believe we didn't get caught for that at least once."

As he spoke, Connie stopped by to clear away their dinner dishes. It was now after the dinner hour, and the crowd was starting to thin out.

Kincaid smiled at Connie as she slid his plate away and returned to his story. "Anyway, we kept going out after high school and got married several years later. We had two great kids, both girls, and they looked just like Judy, thank God." He patted what remained of his paunch, which was shrinking as he now took better care of himself. "Sure wouldn't have wanted them to look like me."

"Oh, hell no," cracked Brown sarcastically. "Wouldn't want that, now would we?"

"Nope." Kincaid ran his fingers across his bald head, trying to break the strain of looking back. "We ended up moving to Raymond, where Judy had this house she just loved. Kept the place great, just a spotless housekeeper, had great taste, place was really fixed up cute. But as we got older, we grew apart, and really, that's my fault. I never was one for the family life and was never a guy who liked being at home all the time. So I just got more and more bored and pushed a lot of stuff off on Judy."

He continued, sighing every little bit at the bitter memory. "We'd been married about twenty years or so, and I have this big-ass mid-life crisis, because I'm in my forties at the time. I was so goddamned full of myself, thinking I deserved better, that I needed more. So I get to know this blonde waitress over at the Busy Bee named Sharon, and she's really just a piece of trash, the kind that goes from man to man."

"Sharon? Yeah, I know who you're talking about," remarked Brown. "I talked to her a couple of times when I was in there. Always had her boobs stuck out when she poured my coffee. Did the same thing with everyone in the place, which is why I guess the place was so busy all the time. The coffee sure wasn't worth a shit."

"Yeah, that's the one." Kincaid shook his head. "Of course, I'm too dumb and horny to see that, and we end up in bed together. Before I know it, I'm over at her place all the time, whenever I get a chance, because I want her so much." Kincaid slapped the table in a release of frustration. "I knew it was wrong from the start, because I knew what I had at home in Judy. She's the kind of woman that doesn't come along every day. But I just let that affair consume me, and I was thinking about it all the time, every minute I was in the squad car. Couldn't wait to get over to Sharon's place and just get naked with her."

Brown was somewhat surprised at Kincaid's graphic description and remained silent, just listening. "Anyway, Judy found out and wanted to go to marriage counseling. Can you believe that? Here I was, running around on her, and she still wants to save our marriage. If that doesn't tell you how great Judy was, nothing will." Kincaid grabbed his Coors, finished it off, and put it down so hard that it clinked on the table. "But I was too damn stupid to go along with it. I just had to have Sharon and asked for a divorce."

For most of his life, James Kincaid had blamed everyone but himself, constantly grousing about how hard his job was, how no one cared about him, how everyone just had their hand out. Now, contrition had taken over, and emotions like that can change a man. It was certainly changing Kincaid as he bent Brown's ear in a now-empty restaurant.

"I end up marrying Sharon, and we have two kids together. But all the while, I knew it was a mistake, and it had been a mistake since the first time I walked in that damn Busy Bee." He stared down at the table, regret washing over him like a tidal wave. "But the biggest mistake of all was the day I signed the papers to divorce Judy. Knew it was wrong from the minute I agreed to it, and knew it was wrong when I was sitting in the lawyer's office, but I did it anyway. I thought I'd gone too far and there was no turning back."

"Time makes a man think about his choices, doesn't it?" said Brown.

"Sure does. God, does it ever." Kincaid uttered a rueful chuckle. "Anyway, the marriage to Sharon was a disaster from the outset, and I end up divorcing her, too, because by the time it's over, I can't even stand to look at her. I end up paying $800 a month in child support, which is something else I screwed up, because Judy had got the best of my first divorce settlement, which she should have."

Connie stopped at the table once again, and Kincaid ordered another Coors before she could even open her mouth. Brown asked for another as well, grinning at her as Kincaid's eyes looked elsewhere. She brought the bottles over, and Kincaid unscrewed his top, needing a gulp before he went on to even worse memories.

"I end up moving to White City, and by now, I've pretty much pissed it all away," mused Kincaid. "And I'm drinking so heavy that I barely notice, because I'm always feeling sorry for myself. I don't have much else to do, so I go in this particular tavern all the time, and I meet this bartender, named Debbie. She was a lot like me, loved to drink and chain-smoke, and liked doing the things I liked. She'd watch the Cardinals, go fishing with me, all that stuff. Pretty soon, we moved in together, and it seemed like everything was going all right."

As he finished his sentence, Kincaid's stream of memories was flooded by the bloody image of Debbie's lifeless body tumbling to the ground. He went silent for a few seconds, unable to speak, knowing that his worst choice of all had caused that memory that he would never shake.

"It's my fault that she died," said Kincaid, his voice barely above a whisper. "I know that. If I hadn't done what I did, she'd still be here today." He stared down at the table, hoping to ease his shame, if only for an instant. "I live with that guilt every day. Most times, I can't sleep through the night without having horrible nightmares. I just hear her voice, see her face..." His voice trailed off. "And watch her dying."

A tear slid down Kincaid's weathered cheek, and he wiped it away with his left hand, the one with the missing pinky. "It's been my own private hell," he said. "My retribution."

Brown wrinkled up his face in sympathy, sensing how hard the moment was for Kincaid, but knowing he needed to talk about it. Kincaid collected himself, his range of emotions from his tormented mind on full display. His face hardened, the self-anger bursting through as he spoke in a slow, cool monotone.

"I took that bag of money because I thought I deserved it," he blurted out, choosing not to go into detail about the night he took the money, since everyone else knew about it by now and he figured Brown did, too. "I'd been a trooper for over twenty-five years and had nothing to show for it. Judy had half my pension and a big alimony check, the girls I had with her were getting tuition money from me, Sharon had the child support, and I had nothing.

"I was driving up and down the road every night in that goddamn squad car and didn't even have a ten-dollar bill in my pocket most of the time. The bills were piling up, and I watched the other guys I worked with driving new cars and living in nice homes, while I was scraping to pay trailer rent."

By now, it was nearing closing time, and Connie and the other workers were starting to put chairs up on tables. Kincaid heard them and knew he needed to end his train of memories soon. "I looked at that bag, and in that split second, I saw it as an opportunity," he continued. "I really thought I could pull it off." He realized the irony of his words and remembered his years of experience in law enforcement. "But then again, what crook doesn't?"

"Yeah, been there," sighed Brown. "Always think you're invincible, that nothing bad could ever happen."

"Hmm," snickered Kincaid, knowing the feeling. "Well, I had plenty of time to think about it in prison. You're sitting behind bars for three and a half years, all you can do is think. None of my kids or friends came to visit me and really, who can blame them? I've messed up so much, made so many mistakes, hurt so many people. I've got to live with that, and God, sometimes it's all I can do to keep going."

He looked over at Brown and made direct eye contact, never blinking. "Really, all I've got now is the job you gave me. It's the reason I get up in the morning and why I can make it through the day. I can't thank you enough for it."

"Don't mention it," said Brown as he slid away from the table. "We've all made mistakes in our lives. Lord knows I have." He shook his head at the thought. "If we can show we've learned from them, then anyone deserves a chance to start over."

He dropped two bills, a twenty and a ten, on the table to pay for dinner and leave Connie a healthy tip. He then slapped his hand onto Kincaid's right shoulder, which still bore the scar from the night of the shooting.

"I'm glad to have you on board," said Brown. "You've done everything I've asked you to. And I've got something else to ask you now."

Kincaid cocked his head quizzically, wondering what that comment meant. "I need you to make another run for me tomorrow," said Brown. "Remember Kenny, the guy I've got in the white Peterbilt? His wife went into labor today, and he's out for a while. So I need someone to make his run to Houston…" Brown's voice trailed off, making it clear what he wanted.

Hours before, Kincaid had returned from a run of his own, and was worn out. But the extra pay sounded good, and he didn't want to anger his new boss. "Sure, no problem. You want me to leave at five, as usual?"

"Yep. You do this for me, and I'll remember you when the eagle flies." Brown's offer of a little more money sweetened the deal.

"All right." Kincaid extended his hand to Brown, who shook it heartily and then dropped the keys to the Peterbilt in Kincaid's open palm. "See ya tomorrow."

"Later." Brown was turning away when he heard Kincaid's voice once more. "Hey, Jim."

"Yeah?" replied Brown, gravel in his voice as ever.

"Thanks for listening." Kincaid waved slightly in appreciation as he walked back to his Tundra and the drive back to Gillespie, for a few hours sleep before leaving once again.

CHAPTER 61

The stars hung like diamonds in the black morning sky of late autumn as Kincaid steered his Tundra in to Jim Brown's truck lot, heading for his last-minute run to Houston. The sunrise was over an hour away, and none of the other drivers had arrived yet. Brown was not there, either, as his office was still dark.

The temperatures had dipped to 36 degrees the night before, and a light, cool wind rustled the dry leaves that seemed to blow everywhere, even on the gray rocks of the dispatch lot. The leaves crinkled further as Kincaid stepped over them in his Red Wing boots and toward the Peterbilt, passing by several other rigs as he walked.

In his mind, Kincaid was already spending the money he was about to earn from this surprise trip to Texas. All of his domestic-support obligations had been covered with the money from his last run, and his earnings from this one would pay for some of the things he had been wanting, like building materials to fix up his house, tires for his Tundra, and a couple of pairs of new jeans.

Damn, he thought. Can't remember the last time I had any extra money. As always, he remembered the misery of his past, but this time, it was tempered with a tinge of optimism. Good to have a job like this…wouldn't be doing this well without it…things are finally looking up, and God knows that was the only direction I could go in…

Lost in thought, his concentration was broken by the sound of footsteps coming from around the driver's side of the truck. Kincaid heard the sounds in the darkness and broke his stride in front of the grill of the truck. In an instant, his eyes were met by those of a young Mexican man, slight in build and hair blown in the breeze, details that were barely visible in the shadows cast by the pole lights that partially illuminated the lot.

Before Kincaid could say anything, the Mexican brandished a gun, pointed straight at him. "You killed my brother and stole our money," screamed Rami Santiago, anger pulsating in his words as he pulled the trigger.

A single bullet ripped through the center of Kincaid's forehead, opening a torrent of blood that poured down his face. Kincaid's body crumpled to the ground, the life draining from him as he fell. He only had a few seconds to remember, for the final time, the choices he had made.

EPILOGUE

The murder of James Kincaid has never been solved. The only evidence recovered from the murder scene was a 9-mm cartridge case located next to the body and a 9-mm bullet removed from the victim's head.

The Illinois State Police laboratory determined the bullet was fired from a Smith & Wesson semi-automatic pistol. The cartridge was also compared with similar cartridges that had been recovered from other murder scenes. After analysis, it was determined the cartridge from the Kincaid case was a match for two homicides in Chicago.

Perhaps someday, more information will come forward or the killer will be arrested in possession of the weapon. Until then, the murder investigation of James Kincaid will remain open.

*****

In his office in Springfield, R.J. McIntire was dreading this afternoon. It was his final day on the job after twenty-nine years with the Illinois State Police, the last ten as director of the Division of Internal Investigations.

He had been promoted to director months after cracking the original case on James Kincaid, the shooting in White City and the theft of the duffel bag of money. With the promotion, he moved down the hall to a larger office and enjoyed a bigger payday wired into his bank account twice a month. But he also felt the satisfaction of all the top ISP officials, that they are the best in their profession and have earned it with intelligence, integrity, and skill.

McIntire knew that retirement time was nearing, and a part of him welcomed it. No position in the ISP is easy, and he was sick of the long hours and never-ending demands that go with investigations, which are often gritty and unpleasant. Now with three grandchildren, he longed to spend more time at home with Darlene, travel a little and visit the kids, play some golf, hang out with his old buddies from the force in a non-work setting. Still, leaving DII after so many years was difficult, and he wondered how he would pass the time each day without the people around him and a stack of investigations piled on his desk.

He hurried to finish packing his proudest belongings, sighing as he placed some of them in cardboard boxes to be hauled to his car. Meanwhile, the unavoidable retirement party was waiting down the hall. There, he would be forced to make small talk, accept the usual "Congratulations" and "We'll miss you" from coworkers, and joke around during one of the most bittersweet moments of his life.

As his final hours in his office ticked by, there was a knock on the door from one of his top assistants. "Hey, R.J.," said Mike Miller, who had worked at his friend's side ever since the promotion to director, earning a lieutenant's stripes himself.

Miller certainly understood McIntire's decision to leave, but he hated the thought of not having his friend to work with and talk to. He watched for a few seconds as McIntire stared blankly at the walls, clutching frames that held some of the many awards he had earned. Knowing the moment was hard on McIntire, he tried to crack a joke.

"Come on, R.J.," he chuckled. "It's just retirement. It's not like you're going to your own funeral or something."

"Hmm," sniffed McIntire in mock protest as he boxed the last of his framed certificates. "You want to sit down for a minute?"

"Sure." Miller stepped over to one of the two chairs across from McIntire's desk and took a seat. "But you know they're waiting for you down the hall. Probably cutting the cake as we speak."

"Let them." McIntire walked around the oversized mahogany desk and plopped down in his cushy, black swivel office chair. "They're probably happy to be getting rid of me anyway."

"I doubt that." Miller knew how he felt, too. "I know I'm not."

"Thanks." McIntire appreciated the words. He sighed again, heaving his shoulders. "Been through a lot, haven't we?"

"Oh, God," laughed Miller, shaking his head. "Wonder how many investigations we were on together?"

"Too many. And if I'd had more guys like you, I damn sure wouldn't be leaving." McIntire looked at each of the four walls, reflecting on the past. "Talking about those investigations, any of them stick out in your mind?"

"Geez." Miller exhaled deeply, lost in the memories of some of them. "Quite a few of them stand out, really. But you know, there's one I never forgot."

McIntire knew which one. "Kincaid," he said.

"Yep. The first one we were on together." Miller smiled at the thought of meeting his friend.

"That one always stayed with me," said McIntire as he reached for a bottle of water and took a sip. He screwed the cap back on. "You know, I did a helluva lot of cases in DII and dealt with some horrible things. I investigated sexual assaults that were just sickening, made your skin crawl. I had things like battery, theft, embezzlement, you name it."

McIntire looked up at the ceiling as his career flashed before him, and he tapped his fingers together. "Remember that day in the Kincaid case, when we were driving back from Hillsboro to District 18 headquarters? It was snowing like mad, and we were shooting the breeze about why we got into this business. I remember, just clear as a bell, telling you how shocking it was to me that cops could do the stuff that DII investigates. Well, all these years later, I can tell you this—it still shocks me."

Miller snickered. "You don't have to tell me. I've been here for a while myself, remember?"

"Yeah. I guess I'm saying that I've seen it all, and some of it has really been tough. But that Kincaid case was one I never let go of. I still think about it every so often."

"I do, too," Miller said with a nod. "And not just because it was my first case with you. It was just such a strange one. I mean, a cop who steals a million dollars in evidence, gets his girlfriend killed over it, and fakes his own death with an assumed name. There was so much to it, so many angles, so much to process. It just went on and on and on."

McIntire nodded in agreement, rolling his eyes for effect as he picked up a silver ink pen and examined it before putting it in his shirt pocket. He leaned back in his chair, taking another look around his office as he steeled himself for the awkward retirement celebration down the hall.

"Kincaid was one in a million," he said. "Thank God."

About the Author

C. ED TRAYLOR retired from the Illinois State Police with the rank of captain after 29 years of service. During that time, he served as patrolman, investigator, investigator supervisor, Bureau Chief and staff officer. He subsequently served as police chief of a small central Illinois town before returning to the ISP with an assignment as investigator on the Federal Health Care Fraud Task Force. He is currently retired and lives with his wife Pat, in rural Waggoner, Illinois. The couple have two adult daughters.

Also by C. Ed Traylor

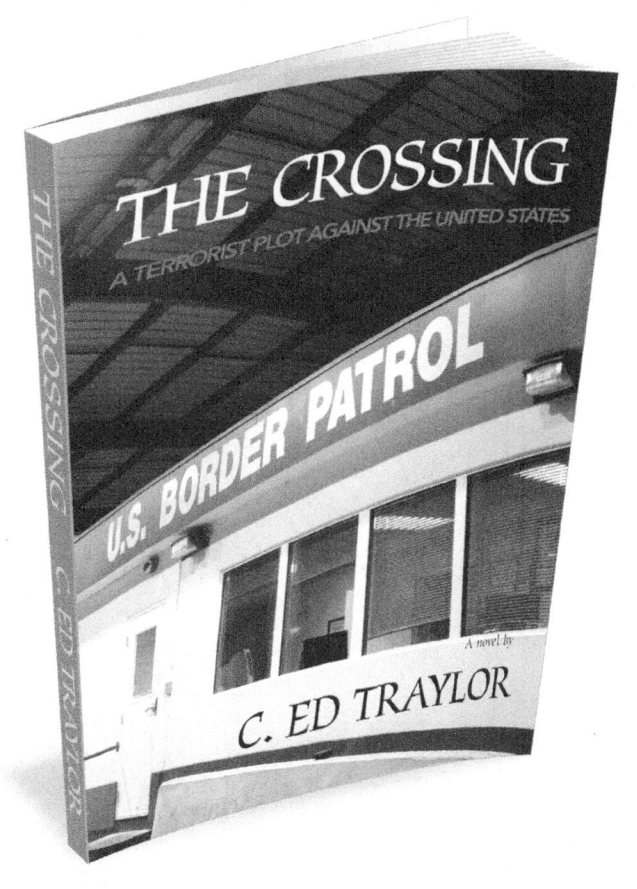

The Crossing focuses on Racheed UL-Bashar, a Pakistani whose grandfather and sister are killed in an American drone strike in Pakistan. Driven by revenge against the United States, the obsessive Racheed develops a minutely detailed plot, a synchronized attack that will hit three American Cities on the anniversary of September 11. He obtains contact information of Juan Rodrequs, a violent, ruthless drug cartel leader in Jauarez, Mexico, who agrees—for a price—to move terrorists across the border and supply all materials needed for the attacks.

Available at Amazon.com and everywhere books are sold.

Made in the USA
Monee, IL
06 February 2021